NOT MY PRINCE CHARMING

HAILEY SHORE

My Three Favorite Things

My Mom
My shell garden
My Dad/Pappas' Diner (they go hand in hand)

Lola, Age 9

E verything changed the summer I turned nine, and the Dumonts bought the public beach.

When I was a kid, Mom would take me to the ocean every Saturday morning before her shift at Pappas' Diner—the diner that's been in my dad's family for generations. We'd go at low tide because Mom dug quahogs for chowder, and I liked to pick up shells.

The best place to do both those things was the spit at the very end of the Calico Cove public beach. It went public beach, rocky spit, then wild scrub land where all these birds had their nests, and every spring, tons of people came with binoculars to watch those birds.

My ninth summer, on the other side of the rocks, in the scrub, a sign had been put up.

Private Property.

"How can someone own the beach?" I asked my mom, squinting at her through the sunlight. "It's the beach."

Mom, wearing her old denim shirt with the hole in the elbow and holding a red bucket full of clams, sighed.

"When you're as rich as the Dumonts, you can do whatever you want."

"What are they gonna do with it?" Where would the birds go?

"Build a house as ugly as their hotel, I imagine."

The Dumonts owned the big fancy hotel south of town.

Mom led a whole protest and got a petition signed by hundreds of people to save the birds' nesting grounds, but it didn't work.

That fall a mansion went up where the birds used to live.

THE NEXT SUMMER

"NO ONE IS EVER THERE!" Mom cried.

The diner was quiet; it was that time between lunch rush and afternoon snack. I was using a little funnel to fill the salt shakers. It was not going well. I was too interested in what Mom was saying to pay attention to how straight the funnel was, and salt was getting everywhere. I brushed it onto the floor to be swept up later.

"I heard you the first time," Dad said. "The first

dozen times." He grabbed Mom by the shoulders and got her to stop wiping down the already spic-and-span counter. "They are summer people. They do what they want."

"They destroyed that land, built that ugly house and now they don't even show up."

"You sound like you're taking it personally," Dad said with a smile.

"I am!" she cried. "It's our beach. It's Calico Cove property."

Dad hugged Mom. Pulled her into his big chest then pinched her bum until she started laughing. I went back to the salt shakers, no longer worried about the Dumonts.

If Mom was laughing, everything was fine.

THE NEXT SATURDAY MORNING, we stood in the soft silty sand of low tide, Mom with her bucket of clams, me with my bucket of shells and watched the Dumont house.

"People are there," I said, holding Mom's sandy hand.

"So it would seem."

"There are kids!" I said, catching sight of a boy and girl running out onto the fancy stone patio. The patio had statues and giant flower urns. It looked like a picture of a palace I'd seen in a book.

"Hmmm," was all Mom said. A big wind blew off the ocean, and the scarf Mom used to tie back her messy black curls finally gave up its fight and flew into the air like a green and blue parachute.

It flew over the rocks and onto the pristine sand of the Dumonts' home.

"Crap," Mom sighed. "That was my favorite."

I dropped Mom's hand, put down the bucket and took off after the scarf.

"Lola!" Mom shouted. "Don't—"

But she was too late, I was over the rocks and onto the Dumont property. The scarf fell to the sand, then tiny breezes would send it spinning again. I raced to catch it, jumping when it seemed in reach.

"I got it!" a boy said, and he leapt up and snagged it. We both laughed, out of breath.

"Thanks," I said, taking it out of his hand. He had blond hair that was cut really short. I'd had to get my hair cut that short once when I had lice in kindergarten.

I did NOT ask him if he had lice.

"I'm Lola," I said, instead. "Lola Pappas."

"What kind of name is Lola?" he asked.

"A friendly and unique one." That was my mom's line whenever people gave her grief for naming her only child after a show girl from a song. "What's yours?"

"Jackson," he said, but didn't tell me his last name, like I should already know.

"Jackson!" A woman with blond hair, wearing a dress and pearls, who didn't look like she should be within ten feet of a beach, came running out onto the sand. "What are you doing?"

"Just helping Lola."

"Young lady," the woman said. Man, she had a mean face. A *mean* face. "This is private property. You belong over there." She pointed over towards where my mom was now climbing onto the rocks to come and get me. She made *over there* sound bad and for a second it made me *feel* bad. Like her sand was better than my public beach sand which made her better than me.

Embarrassed, scarf in hand, I took off, back to my mom and our side of the beach.

THE NEXT WEEKEND Mom and I were at the beach, and the Dumonts were still around. There was a woman cleaning dishes off a table on that stone patio. I looked for the boy but didn't see him. I wanted to tell him his sand wasn't better than ours. His mom, or whoever she was, was just wrong.

"Come on, honey," Mom said. "Ignore them. Look for your shells."

There'd been a storm the night before so the mark for high tide was way up the beach. And storms meant good shells. Star fish and sometimes, if you were lucky...

Sand dollars!

There was one, fully intact, which was rare after a storm.

But it lay just on the other side of the private property sign.

I took the risk and ran for it.

"What are you doing?"

Crap.

It was the boy again. Jackson. Coming down the path that led from that huge patio to the beach. He had on a ball cap and khaki shorts that looked like they might itch.

"I'm Lola," I said with a shy wave. "We met—"

"I remember. What are you doing?"

"I'm looking for shells. That's my mom, over there. She's looking for clams."

"This is my beach," he said, crossing his arms over his bony chest. Both the T-shirt and shorts he wore looked too big for him.

"You can't own a beach," I told him. "It's a beach."

"My dad bought it."

"Fine," I said and rolled my eyes. "I'll get off your beach, if I can just get that shell."

He looked where I was pointing, the pristine sand dollar, at his feet. "Why do you want this shell?"

"I have a shell garden," I explained. "It's where I keep all my best shells."

He picked up the shell I'd pointed to and walked it over to me.

"I've never heard of a shell garden," he grumbled.

"It's a thing."

"How old are you?" he asked.

"Ten. How old are you?"

"Twelve."

That settled, we ran out of things to talk about.

"So, you just come out here and collect shells?" he asked, like it didn't make any sense. I held out my bucket, and he looked inside.

"What's this?" he asked, lifting out a fat twisty shell.

"A periwinkle."

He put it down, gently, like he knew they could break. "What's this one?"

"Icelandic Scallop. It's one of my favorites."

"It's really red. Did it come from Iceland?"

I shrugged. Who knew the ways of shells and oceans?

"Do you come here all the time?" he asked.

"Only on Saturday mornings. I have to work other days."

"Work?" he said the word like it was gross. "Where do you work?"

"My family owns Pappas' Diner." Home of the best lobster roll in Maine and Larry the Lobster. The Lobster my grandpa caught, had stuffed, and hung on the wall of our diner right by the cash register. "You should come by sometime."

"Jackson!" the mean woman came out onto the patio and called out for him. Jackson took off running without another word.

But the next Saturday he was waiting for me, right by his private property sign.

"Hi," I said.

"Hi," he said, and he held out a shell. "What's this?"

"Oh, that's a quahog shell," I told him.

"You want it?" he asked. "For your garden."

"No. They're really common." He looked a little disappointed. "But thanks."

"Do you ever look for shells out on those rocks?" he asked, pointing to the rocky spit that started halfway down the beach and jutted out into the water between his land and what was left of the public beach. "There's probably tidal pools."

"No way," I said. "Don't even think about climbing on those rocks."

"Why not?"

"There are rules about Calico Cove you have to know if you want to be a local."

"I'm not a local."

"An honorary local then."

"Fine. What are the rules?"

"One, don't feed the feral cats, but I break that one a lot. Two, if you pet Larry the Lobster at my dad's diner, it brings you good luck. Totally true. Three, no swimming off the Pointe. There's a bad riptide there. People have drowned and died."

He looked at the water like he didn't believe me. Then his stomach made the sound of a wild animal.

"Whoa!" I laughed. "Are you hungry?"

"Yeah, I'm..." He was blushing as bright red as the Icelandic Scallop Shell. "I haven't eaten in a while."

I unzipped one of the pockets of my pink sweatshirt and pulled out a bag of goldfish crackers. We served them at the diner with the chili. Dad thought it was clever. "You need a snack," I said and handed him the bag.

He ate them, in, like, zero seconds flat.

So, I unzipped my other pocket and pulled out a tiny bit squished and very cold grilled cheese sandwich. Which was how I liked my grilled cheese. Cold, not squished.

"You have a lot of snacks," he said as he took the sandwich from me.

"Mom calls me the snack queen."

"This would be better hot."

"You'd be better hot," I shot back, which was a joke with me and Georgie who worked in the kitchen with Dad. Whenever I complained about something—*this is too salty. This doesn't taste right. You look funny with fake eyelashes*—he shot it right back. *You're too salty. You don't taste right. You look funny with fake eyelashes.*

It was one of Pappas' Diner's inside jokes, but Jackson laughed like he got it.

"Why are you so hungry?" I asked.

Jackson ate the last bit of sandwich, his lips shiny from the butter. "My dad was mad at me," he said.

Well, I had a million more questions, but the way he held himself so still, like one of the feral cats in town who was scared of being kicked but really wanted to be petted, I kept my questions to myself.

"Let's look for shells," I said. And, somehow, I knew that we needed to keep to the sand that was out of view from the Dumont house.

THAT NIGHT MOM turned off my light and hit the little switch on the twinkle lights she'd hung around my closet. Like she usually did, she sat on the edge of my bed and stroked my hair back from my face. I closed my eyes and breathed in the smell of her, hand lotion and French fries.

Mom smell.

"What were three of your favorite things about today?" Mom asked. She asked me this every night.

"Mmmm," I said. "I found a horseshoe crab at the beach. Madame Za told me I was going to grow up to be a princess." Mom laughed. Madame Za told fortunes down at the town square to tourists, and she came into the diner every Saturday for a tuna melt. Mom said Madame Za's fortunes were just little lies she told people, but I liked the idea of being a princess. "And Jackson."

"Honey," she said, and my eyes flew open. She was using a weird voice. "About Jackson."

"Yeah."

"I don't know if it's a good idea being friends with him."

"Why not?" But I knew her answer before she said it.

"Summer people."

Mom liked the tourists because they liked us. They came into the restaurant and wrote glowing Yelp reviews and came back every year like distant, but beloved, cousins. And she loved the locals because we were Calico Cove through and through. But the summer people who owned fancy houses on the shore and only visited a few weeks a year and only ever ate at the Dumont Hotel south of town...she didn't like them. They acted like all the locals were servants, which...well, lots of them were.

I nodded, because I understood. Sure, I was only ten, but

it didn't take long to catch onto the way things worked when you lived in Calico Cove.

"He was really hungry," I said.

"Jackson?"

"Yeah. He said he was hungry because his dad was mad at him."

Mom sucked in a breath and let it out slowly. "Crap," she muttered.

THE NEXT SATURDAY I jumped out of the car and waved to Jackson, who was standing at the private property sign. He waved back.

"Here." Mom pulled a to-go container from the diner out of the backseat. Inside were two hot grilled cheese sandwiches and some fries. She also handed me a Tupperware of watermelon.

"Mom!"

"Just...if he's hungry, let him have it."

So, I trudged with my bucket and all the food over to the sign out of sight of the Dumont House.

"Hey," he said and held out a shell. "What's this?"

"Oh!" I said, genuinely excited. "That's a whelkie. A good one."

"You want it?" he asked. "For your garden?"

"I'd love it." He put the shell in my bucket, and I handed him the food.

"What's this?" he asked.

"Lunch. If you're hungry." He was. He ate everything. I sat with him, and we talked about shells and the feral cats and school. "What are your three favorite subjects?" I asked.

"Science, Math and Art," he said. "Yours?"

"Recess, Gym and English."

"My mom is gone today," he said, when he was done eating. "She went back to Boston to see my dad."

"Why is your dad in Boston?"

"He's too busy to waste his time out here," Jackson said, and I sucked in a breath.

Waste his time? Here? In Calico Cove. Impossible.

"What are you going to do?"

"I don't know." He squinted against the sun and looked at me. "What are you going to do?"

"You want to come to town with us? We can ride bikes and go to the park. The ice cream store opens—"

He was nodding before I even finished. "Let me go tell Dani," he said and raced off.

Right. I had to go tell my mom, who was probably not going to like this.

Weirdly, she wasn't mad. "Of course," she said.

Jackson came back to the beach with a backpack and his bike. Dani, a housekeeper, and Mom talked for a second and then it was happening. Jackson was coming to hang out with me in town.

"What about your sister?" Mom asked, looking at Jackson where he sat in the backseat. His bike was shoved in the trunk.

"Vanessa has to do schoolwork."

"School!" I cried. It was July!

Jackson shrugged, and I caught Mom's look and kept my mouth shut on the injustice of school in July.

That's how I became friends with Jackson Dumont. When his parents were gone, he rode his bike to the diner or got dropped off by one of his family's employees, and we rode our bikes all over town. Or played with some of my other friends at the VFW park. We went swimming at the beach. We played a million rounds of slap jack and Uno. Ate fries and watermelon by the pound in the big middle booth when it was quiet at the diner.

We picked blueberries, jumped off rocks, tried to learn how to surf. Failed at learning to surf.

We laid in the shade in the white-hot heat of summer in Maine and scratched our bug bites and made plans for the next summer. To enlarge the shell garden. To climb Hanolan's Pointe. To take tents into the National Park and spend the night.

Vanessa came with us a few times. She was right between us in age, but she complained a lot about the heat and the bugs and blisters. So mostly, three or four times a week, it was just me and Jackson and the endless summer days.

No one tells you, when you're a kid, how important your friends will be. How you meet someone who isn't family and you have this chemistry. Like love, but different. Or maybe the same. I didn't understand it at all at the time. But I looked at Jackson Dumont and I *knew* him. And he knew me. With him was the only place I wanted to be.

"WHAT ARE three of your favorite things?" I asked Jackson.

We were at the cove where the surfers took their boards into the water. It was the last of the nine coves that I'd shown him, and we were lying on the big rocks, the sun hot but the breeze was cool.

"Oh, my God," he said. "I've answered this question a million times."

It was true. He had. But my thirst to know Jackson was bottomless. "Okay, three least favorite things?" I asked him.

We'd already covered favorite colors, TV shows, sandwiches, Patriot players, singers and authors. We hadn't done least favorite things yet.

"Okay," he said and folded his hands across his stomach. He'd gotten bigger this summer. Less skinny. Mom fed him constantly. "Mushrooms on pizza. Parties my parents throw and..." He paused, and I rolled my head to look at him. Only to find him looking at me. "Leaving."

"Leaving where?" But I knew. It was almost the middle of August. This summer couldn't last forever. "Leaving when?"

"Next week."

"Yeah," I said, looking up at the sun until the tears dried up. "I hate that, too."

2
_____

My Three Favorite Things About Jackson Dumont

When he laughs
How he taught me to pedal my bike standing up with no hands
When I got scared at the fireworks and he held my hand until I
calmed down

Lola, Age 10

The next Saturday was Labor Day weekend. Jackson wasn't at the private property sign and the Dumont mansion was full of people closing the house up for winter.

It was over. Just like that, the best summer ever was over.

"Come on, honey," Mom said, when I just stood there staring at the house, willing Jackson to come running out. "He's probably busy."

He wouldn't be too busy to say goodbye. I knew Jackson. I was one of his favorite things. Just like he was one of mine.

Mom pulled me down the beach, and I found another horseshoe crab. This one was still alive so I ran it down to the ocean to set it free.

When I turned Mom was very still, shading her eyes against the sun looking over at the rocks. Since I did whatever my mom did, I looked over, too.

That's when I saw him.

Jackson. Only he was out on the boulders I'd told him he couldn't climb. I'd told him it was dangerous. I'd told him bad stuff could happen if he fell in the water there.

As an avid rule follower, I got that feeling in my stomach, that *oh no, things are not right* kind of feeling, and Mom must have gotten the same feeling.

"Hey, Lola," she yelled, setting down her bucket of sandy, thick-shelled clams. "I'll be right back. Stay put, okay?"

Then she was picking her way across the rocks until she got to Jackson, her long black curls getting blown all over the place by the wind. I couldn't hear what they were saying, but I saw her lips moving, then Jackson turned to face her.

One look at his face and Mom put her hand to her mouth before reaching for him. Jackson shook his head and stepped back, nearly tripping on one of the rocks.

That *oh no, things aren't right* feeling went haywire, and I was suddenly sick to my stomach.

"Jackson!"

It was Mrs. Dumont coming out of the French doors, running across the stone patio and down the path that led to the sand. She wore big black sunglasses.

"Come in, Jackson. Now!"

I looked back over at my mom. Thankfully, they were off

the boulders, back on the sandy beach. She was talking to Jackson, but he wasn't listening. He walked by her and when she reached out to put a hand on his shoulder, he slapped it away. Then he shoved her. Jackson *shoved* my mom.

"Jackson," I whispered.

That was mean. What he did to my mom was mean. He shouldn't have done that. He shouldn't have been on the rocks at all. I told him...he was supposed to be an honorary local.

"Hey!" I shouted to him.

Only when he turned his head to look at me, it was like he wasn't the same person anymore. Like someone else was staring at me instead of my friend. Someone who thought I was total garbage. My cheeks went hot, and I looked out at the water, suddenly embarrassed I'd said anything.

Mom followed Jackson up to his mother, and there was some kind of argument. I could only hear the sound of Mom's angry voice over the wind, not what she was saying.

Finally, Mom came back, huffing a little from the argument or trekking across the beach. I wasn't sure. She stroked my hair and pulled me up against her soft tummy. I wrapped my arms around her and breathed her in, salt air and French fries.

"Was he okay?" I asked her.

She didn't answer me.

~

AT THE DINER THAT NIGHT, I did what I always did on Saturdays—dusted Larry, folded napkins and refilled the salt shakers.

I also broke rule number one and fed the feral cats out back then got yelled at for it.

Mom used to say it was a shame I had to spend every Saturday night at the diner, but Dad always said it was nice. I was with Dad on that one.

Where else would I want to be?

I had just screwed the top on the last salt shaker, when the bell rang over the door.

There was Mrs. Dumont. Just standing there with this look on her face like the place smelled bad. Which it didn't. It smelled like French fries and pancake syrup, which, I could only guess, if everyone voted on the best smells in the world, would show up in the top three AT LEAST.

Mrs. Dumont wore the glasses she'd been wearing on the beach that day, which was weird because the sun was already going down. I looked behind her, thinking maybe Jackson had come to say goodbye after all, only I could tell she was alone.

"You can sit anywhere," Dad said, carefully. "But the kitchen's closed."

"I didn't come to eat," Mrs. Dumont said, like the idea was funny.

I tucked into my favorite booth, the big round circular one that had a bench seat that went almost all the way around and could hold up to eight people or, like, ten kids.

Mrs. Dumont sat at one of the two-tops as far from the windows as she could be.

"I'd like to see Michelle, please."

I was supposed to be rolling silverware into napkins next, but now, I was just staring at this woman wondering what she was doing here.

Pappas' was a diner for the people who lived here and for tourists. The rich summer people ate at the fancy steak restaurant in the Dumont Hotel. One time Mom and Dad went to the steakhouse, and when I asked how it was, Mom said, "Meh."

Still, the Dumont Steakhouse was the special occasion place in town, and Pappas' was the everyday place in town, and I liked it that way.

Mom came out of the back, and if she was surprised to see Mrs. Dumont, she didn't show it. She looked mad. She marched right up to that lady and said something I couldn't hear. I scooted to the far end of the booth, trying to get closer.

"For you, Mrs. Pappas'." Mrs. Dumont took a check out of her purse and slid it across the table.

"For what?" Mom asked, not even looking at the check. Mrs. Dumont probably didn't know this, but that was my mom's angry voice.

"For understanding that it's…a family matter."

"I don't know," Mom said. "It looked like a Family Services matter to me."

"You know who my husband is, correct? What might happen to a family like yours, to a business like yours, if you chose to inconvenience him in some way?"

Mom's mouth dropped right open.

"You come here, to my diner, and threaten me?" She whistled. "The balls on you, lady."

Mrs. Dumont just pursed her lips and put her hands over her purse. Mom finally looked down at the check and her foot was tapping. Dad always called that Mom's thinking foot. Whenever she was really working something out, that foot got busy.

"You know what I understand? You people aren't worth shit," Mom said, and I jumped at the language. "Get out of my diner and don't come back. But so help me, I see another bruise on that kid…I'm reporting you."

Mrs. Dumont's face was like a storm cloud, all dark and angry, and I wanted to get my mom and pull her away from whatever that woman was going to say. But Mrs. Dumont just got up and walked right past me like I wasn't there.

Mom tore up that check and threw it away, and I wonder, to this day, how many zeros were on it.

MOM AND DAD sent me outside while they cleaned up, but I knew they were arguing about that check. I was looking down at my shell garden, a two-foot square area in front of the diner my mom and I had cleared of weeds. My dad had marked it off with white painted rocks and had made a little sign that said Lola's Shell Garden.

There were all the shells I'd collected for summer.

Angel Wings and Kitten Paws and shiny blue Mussels. Eastern White Slipper shells and fully intact whelks. Including the one Jackson had given me. And the sand dollar he'd picked up the first day we talked.

I'd decided to reorganize the whole thing, and I was halfway through all the pearly white oyster shells when Jackson rode up on a bike and screeched to a stop right beside me. He wore his ball cap pulled down low over his eyes. So low I could barely see his face.

"Hey," I said. He must have ridden from his house, which was a seriously long way.

I felt weird. Nervous. I didn't know if he was coming to say goodbye or sorry for being mean to my mom or what. I only knew that this was probably our last day together and everything felt totally ruined.

"You better tell your mom not to do it," he said.

"Do what?"

"She knows," he snarled. "She's only going to make it worse."

My mom did not make ANYTHING worse. My mom was the best.

"I don't know what you're talking about, but you're kind of being a jerk-face right now."

Jerk-face was the meanest thing I could say about anyone. It didn't feel good to say it, though. Not to him. Even if it was true. He rolled forward into the last of the evening's sunlight, and I saw his face. The black eye. The split lip.

"Jackson," I breathed. My stomach sucked right into my throat. "What happened?" I jumped to my feet and reached for him, but he rolled away.

"Whatever. Just tell your mom what I said."

He looked like he was going to ride off then without saying goodbye.

Summer Jackson. My summer Jackson.

"You can't leave like this!" I said.

"Like what?"

"Like we're fighting. You're hurt, Jackson. Someone hurt you, and we're friends."

His upper lip curled, then, into a sneer. "*You* are not my friend."

"That's not true," I whispered.

"Every minute with you was a waste of time."

As if he had to prove it to me, he rode his bike over the rocks into the middle of my shell garden and just started breaking all of them, crunching them under the wheels of his tires.

"Jackson! No! Those are my shells!" I cried.

I finally pushed him hard enough, he tipped over on his bike, but he put his foot down smashing the silver dollar shell.

"Why did you do that?" I shouted at him. I didn't even realize I was crying until I tasted tears on my lips.

"Because these shells are stupid. Just like this diner. This whole town. Especially you."

He pedaled off as fast as he could go. Like he couldn't wait to leave.

3

———————

My Three Least Favorite Things About Jackson Dumont

His stupid face with its stupid dimples
His mean friends
The way he ruined everything. Especially summer

Lola, Age 13

The Dumonts didn't come back again for two years. The house sat empty, and the birds nested in the fancy urns and the cupped hands of the statues.

For a while, I was able to forget about Jackson Dumont.

But every reprieve comes to an end.

We had no warning. One day the house at the end of the beach was dark and quiet, and the next day it was full of people, and Jackson was there on the patio with some other boys his age. Jackson's hair was long and darker then it had been, and he wore a white necklace and a backwards baseball cap.

His arm was in a sling.

I got one look at him and wanted to run, but Mom just stood there, watching him. And when he didn't come down from the patio to come say hi, Mom stepped across the boundary onto Dumont sand.

"Mom," I groaned, dying inside. "What are you doing?"

Jackson grinned like my mother had made his day, and even though I wanted to get away as fast as I could, I stood shoulder to shoulder with her. The Pappas' women in cutoffs and rain boots, holding our ground.

"You lost?" Jackson asked, his lip curled in a special kind of disdain. I couldn't even look at him. That kid on the rock telling me his least favorite thing was leaving...he was long gone.

"Good to see you again, Jackson," Mom said and the smile on her face was real. I clenched my hands into fists. "You're here for the summer?"

"We're here until we get so bored, we can't stand it. I give it two days," he said. His friends, scenting drama, came down the steps, too, and it felt like we were being surrounded by predators. "You know you're trespassing," Jackson said.

His eyes met mine and my stomach twisted. Had I imagined that summer? Had he been pretending? Had I been wrong?

"Still collecting shells?" he asked. His tone said, *like a baby?*

"What happened to your arm?" I asked. My tone said, *was it your dad?*

I didn't know for sure. He never really talked about his dad that summer. But in the two years Jackson had been gone, I'd pieced together a little bit of what must have happened and the dad who got so mad at his son he didn't let him eat, must have decided that wasn't enough of a punishment.

Our eyes met and I knew I was right. I *saw* I was right. And I saw that he *hated* it.

"Get the fuck off my beach," he said and turned around. His friends laughed and followed.

"You better do what he says," one of the friends said over his shoulder. "The Dumonts are litigious as fuck."

I didn't even know what that meant.

That summer we started getting spammed with bad reviews on-line. We had to start asking people to leave good reviews if they enjoyed their food—which Mom hated.

"It feels like begging," she said, her head in her hand. She was scrolling through her phone, looking at the one-star reviews. "Listen to this one," she cried. "My three least favorite things about Pappas' Diner."

"What?" I asked. "It really says that?"

"It sure does. 'Number one; the filthy bathroom. Number two; the cold grilled cheese. Number three; the stuffed animal on the wall.' Who hates Larry?" Mom asked, genuinely baffled. She wasn't wrong. Larry was a legend for a reason.

That night I rode my bike out to the public beach. Uphill. I arrived dripping sweat, my long blond curly hair sticking to my probably beet-red face. I walked right up onto the Dumonts' precious sand along the path but stopped just short of the patio and waited for one of the jerk-faces to see me.

Vanessa came out first. She was all long legs and arms and a neck like a swan. She was only fourteen, but she was already beautiful.

"Lola?" Vanessa said, with a kind of confused smile. "What are you doing here?"

"I need to talk to your brother."

"Oh." Vanessa's eyes went wide. "That's probably not a great—"

"I'm here," Jackson said, stepping out onto the patio. He wore deck shoes without socks, which only seemed like it would be sweaty and smelly, but whatever.

"What do you want?" he demanded.

"Jackson," Vanessa breathed. "Be nice."

"I'm always nice. Aren't I, Lola?" Jackson asked. Except when he smiled at me, he was an absolute stranger. Not the kid I knew. The one who went blueberry picking with me and was scared of bears and held my hand when we jumped off the cliff into the water at Hideaway Beach.

"I'm asking you to stop leaving the reviews," I said.

"What reviews?" he asked. His lip was curled in a way that told me he knew exactly what I was talking about.

"You're hurting us. You're hurting our business," I said, so real and vulnerable I surprised myself. There was nothing I wouldn't do for the diner and my parents. "And we never did anything to hurt you."

He looked at me for a long time. So long I thought maybe he'd stop pretending, stop being this stranger. He'd smile the smile I remembered and call me by name, and we'd go get mint chocolate chip cones down at Scoops.

Please, I thought, *please come back to me, Jackson.*

"I don't know what you're talking about. Just go," he said and turned away, taking his sister with him.

Vanessa looked over her shoulder and mouthed, "I'm sorry," at me.

But the next day the reviews stopped.

THE NEXT SUMMER

JACKSON GOT a driver's license and Pappas' Diner became his destination of choice. He brought in his friends, and they were loud and rude. They ordered things that weren't on the menu, and everything had to be special. Then they didn't even eat it. They took selfies with Larry, but they were mean selfies. Mocking selfies.

Jackson would sit there with his arms spread wide across the back of the booth like he was the king of everything.

One Friday night in the middle of July, I came out of the kitchen to find Jackson Dumont taking up the largest booth in the restaurant. With two other guys and three girls who were all looking at their phones. Making kissing faces and taking pictures. The people he came in with were completely interchangeable. The girls had over-glossed lips, and the boys couldn't grow facial hair.

I groaned and just swallowed my bile and rage and went over.

He blinked his aqua blue eyes at me, flashed that stupid dimple, and I wanted to tell him he wasn't cute. The boy I'd known that summer—totally cute.

I was fourteen. I knew cute. He was gross now.

"There's a sign that says wait to be seated," I replied, jerking my thumb behind me. It was hard work pretending he meant nothing to me. I didn't know how to do that. Yet.

Of course no one ever waited to be seated. It was sort of an unspoken rule in town, but he was taking up the biggest table like a...like a...yeah, I was still going with jerk-face.

"Well," one of the girls said, rolling her eyes around the room. "The place is practically empty."

"Because we close in a few minutes," I said.

"Is that any way to treat customers?" he asked me.

"What would you like?" I asked, biting the words.

"Grilled cheese," he said. "Six of them."

"Oh, do you have provolone?" one of the boys asked. "I like mine with provolone."

"And I want mine without butter."

"Me, too."

"Do you have lactose-free cheese?" a girl asked.

"No," I said.

"I'll have mine with a burger," the other boy said.

"You mean a cheeseburger?"

"No. A burger in a grilled cheese."

"You know," I said, something in me snapping after weeks of this with these people. "We're out."

"You're out of bread and cheese. What kind of fucking diner is this?" Jackson asked.

I winced. He called Pappas', this place I loved, a *fucking diner*. I wanted to kick him in the shins. I wanted to smash pie in his face.

I wanted him to be the boy I knew. The boy who was once my friend.

"Totally out."

"We'll have french fries then. Looks like you're not out of those," he said.

He pointed to the booth across the restaurant where the Petits, Jolie and Verity, were having a late-night snack with their dad.

Jolie and Verity were locals. We went to the same school. Verity was a grade above me, and Jolie was two years below.

I didn't look over there because I didn't want them to see

how rude Jackson was being. Mr. Petit might have tried to step in. Besides, I had no choice. We were a diner that served food, after all.

"Fine."

"Do you have curly fries?" one of the girls asked.

"Can you make them baked, not fried?" the other girl asked.

I didn't bother to answer. I walked away. My mom was wiping down the counter that didn't need to be cleaned so she could watch the whole thing.

"Be nice to him, Lola," she said.

My jaw nearly dropped. "Be nice to him? He's rude, dismissive. He's a total...jerk-face."

"I'll wait on him," she said. "You don't have to."

"Why can't we just kick him out?" I asked her. "He doesn't even tip well! They make a mess and ask for stuff we don't have. They're the worst."

She looked over at where Jackson was sitting in the center of the booth. His arms stretched out on either side of him, looking like he belonged there. In the center of the restaurant.

"I feel bad for him."

"You're kidding."

"He's an unhappy kid from an unhappy house. You need to be empathetic, Lola. That's an important quality to have. To try to understand what people might be going through that causes them to act out."

Ugh. Fine. I would be empathetic. Only, I was doing it against my will.

∼

THE NEXT SUMMER

· · ·

"PERFECT," I muttered, staring down at the flat tire on my bike. I was stuck on the side of the road.

My parents had given me a day off from the diner. Actually, it was more like an order than a request. I think they were getting worried I was spending too much time there. Like they didn't want the diner to be my whole life.

But it *was* our whole life and I was okay with that.

I'd decided to head to the surfers' beach and try again to get on top of a wave. I'd been trying every summer since Jackson and I first gave it a shot. And every summer it was a total fail. Either I wasn't coordinated enough, or surfing was really, really hard.

I was riding my bike back into town. Surfboard under one arm, the other on my handlebar. I was working so hard keeping my balance I didn't realize the tire blew out until it became impossible to pedal. I dragged my bike to the loose gravel on the side of the road.

I didn't have a phone to call my dad. Mom was holding the line on my own phone until I was sixteen next year, but this was going to be a strong argument for why I needed one now. For the most part, Calico Cove was small enough that you could bike/walk anywhere. But standing here on the side of Harbor Road, with a flat tire, a surfboard and the sun starting to set, I was out of options.

I heard the car coming up behind me and realized that the driver was pulling over to the side of the road.

Please let this be someone I know and not a tourist coming into town.

There was no way I would get a ride from a stranger, but maybe, if they had a phone, they could call the diner and send someone to get me.

"Problem with your bike?"

It was like getting splashed with icy cold water. My worst nightmare.

Just my luck.

"Not your problem, Jackson," I said as he hopped out of his Jeep. I was, I guess, grateful he was alone and not surrounded by his posse of asshole friends.

He looked down at the flat tire. Saw the surfboard.

Put two and two together and knew which beach I'd been out to today.

"You..." he started, then stopped. Then, like he couldn't help himself, he asked, "You catch a wave?"

I folded my arms over my chest, trying not to remember how much fun we'd had that day at the surfers' beach.

"No, I can't get up on the board fast enough. I fall every time."

Why was I telling him this? He was like...or had become...my mortal enemy.

"You got to pop it. Like this," he said.

He took my surfboard, and I started to protest. Certain he was going to do something nasty like toss it in the middle of the road and wait for someone to drive over it.

Instead, he laid it out on the side of the road. Then he got on his knees and showed me how to lean forward and use my hands to help pop up until his feet were flat on the board.

He looked up at me, and there was something there, in his face. Something that reminded me of the friend I used to have. A rush of longing and loss overwhelmed me.

What had happened between us? Why had it all gone so wrong?

I mean, I knew that things weren't good for him at home.

Didn't that mean he needed more friends? More people outside of his family who would support him?

"Anyway, I got a surfing coach. That's what he showed me." He got off the board and handed it back to me.

"Thanks," I said.

"I'll give you a ride into town," he said.

I huffed. "Thanks, but no."

He shoved his hands into his shorts and nodded, his hair falling down over his eyes. No backwards baseball cap to keep it out of his face today.

"Look, Lola, I get it. Just...I'll give you a ride and drop you off."

"Why? Why are you being even remotely nice right now?"

"Fine. I'll give you a ride into town, and when I drop you off, I'll say something really mean. How about that?"

I rolled my eyes.

"I'm not leaving you on the side of the road, Lola. So we either wait here until someone you know comes along, which means more time in my company, or you let me drop you off."

It was a no-brainer.

"I choose less time with you. I'll take the ride."

He put both the board and the bike in the back of the Jeep, lifting each of them like they weighed nothing. I hopped into the passenger seat but didn't say a word as we drove into town.

Didn't ask about his family or his friends. Didn't ask him when he'd gotten a surfing coach.

Just sat on my hands and said nothing. He didn't talk, either, but I knew he looked over at me. Not once, but a second time, too. I could feel it. His eyes on me.

There was this crazy tension between us, like he wanted to say something, but ultimately decided against it.

In the end, he dropped me off at the diner, and he didn't say anything mean.

He didn't say anything at all.

THIS PART IS hard for me to talk about. So I'll just say it;

My last year of high school, my mom died.

It was February, and she was driving back from Boston. The car slid on some ice then flipped down an embankment.

They told us she didn't suffer.

Pappas' closed for a month. Then another. My grades had always been good, so my teachers were kind, and they let me take tests from home and papers were turned in very late, if at all.

Mr. Franklin, the school's guidance counselor, had been trying to get me to think about a business school program at Colby College, but now he dropped off pamphlets for Kennbec Valley Community College instead.

I didn't care about any of it. College had been Mom's dream, and, without her here to dream it for me, I pushed those pamphlets aside. Four-year college. Community college. I didn't want any of it.

I graduated. Dad took pictures of me in my gown and cap at graduation. Both of us trying very hard to be happy for the other person. Except, the person who would be the happiest, the person who made us happy, who carried our happiness around in her pockets like little stones or scraps of paper, was gone.

Then it was June, and the tourists started coming up the coast.

Looking back at it, we should have been closed longer because Dad and I were a total mess, but my dad didn't know what to do with himself if he wasn't working.

So we opened up and the town...the town showed up for us in such a beautiful way. The restaurant was packed all day, every day. Someone filled my shell garden with new shells. Because, of course, I hadn't let Jackson's destruction ruin my happiness. If anything, I'd kept the shell garden going probably longer then I would have just to spite him.

Roy Barnes gave us weeks of free lobster for our lobster rolls. Madame Za started handing out coupons for a free Pappas' milkshake at the end of every psychic reading she did down at the pier.

It was profound, really.

Previous to that awful moment in my life, Calico Cove was just the place where I lived. I'd planned to do what my mother wanted for me. Leave, go to college, see what the world had to offer.

After mom died, it became my *home*. The people of Calico Cove were my family.

Calico Cove, Pappas' Diner—this was my world. It was all I wanted.

Dad hired a new waitress, Tiffani with an i, who'd moved to town following a bad divorce. She had two girls, twins, my age. They also got summer jobs at the diner, which was helpful, until it was revealed they cared a lot more about their shared TikTok account (@twinsforlife1) than actually waiting tables.

"Just think," Tiffani with an i, said. "They could attract more customers through their social media."

I looked at her to see if she was joking, but I was soon to learn when it came to Zoe and Chloe, Tiffani did not joke.

Spring turned to summer, and the place was different without Mom, but I found myself being louder. Bigger. Taking up more space to fill the hole she left behind.

I put on a smile for all our customers. For my dad. If sometimes I had to go into the supply room, and scream into a bag of napkins, well, that's just how it was.

Then *he* showed up.

4

Top Three Things I Miss About My Mom

Mom smell
The way she called me honey. *No one calls me honey anymore*
Saturday mornings at the beach

Lola, Age 18

It was a bright day, a perfect day. The restaurant was busy, the blue sky full of puffy white clouds and sea gulls.

The bell above the door rang, and Jackson walked into the restaurant alone.

He'd turned twenty over the winter, and when he walked through the door, it was obvious he'd had a growth spurt because he was much taller, but he was also really thin.

Scrawny was the word I would use, and I would use it with relish. He looked *scrawny.*

Except that smug grin, the one I always wanted to smack off his face, was suspiciously missing this time. He wore jeans and a grey shirt that made him look kind of...normal.

His hair was longer than it had ever been, and it curled around his ears like the inside of a mollusk shell.

Gross. He was gross.

I was suddenly delighted he was there. He was the one person I didn't have to smile at. Or convince I was doing just fine. In fact, here was someone upon whom I could take out all these feelings that were tearing me apart.

He would say one mean thing to me, and I could just lose it.

He sat in his usual spot—the big booth, even though it was just him today. Once again, without even waiting to be seated.

The nerve.

I took my time getting over to him. Filling water glasses and coffee cups along the way.

"My dear!" Madame Za, grabbed my hand as I refilled her coffee cup. "How are you? Really?"

"I'm fine," I said, smiling as bright as I could.

We were all right in that we were showing up every day. Breaking the rules by feeding the cats. Feeding the people. One foot in front of the other, wondering how we were going to find our happiness when it was buried in my mother's pockets.

I reached for some small talk. "We haven't seen you in a while. Where have you been?"

"I was visiting my sister in Boston," Madame Za said.

"The ghost again?" I asked.

"The ghost, yes!"

Madame Za had a sister in Boston who, according to

Madame Za, lived in a haunted house, and every once in a while, she went down to try and kick the ghost out.

"What a pest he is. My poor sister. But I think we got rid of him for good this time."

The thing about Madame Za, she was an absolute sham. Her fortunes barely made sense, much less came true. She was an eccentric, but she was our eccentric.

"I hope so, Madame Za. For your sister's sake."

"Oh." Madame closed her eyes, pressed her hand, with a ring on every finger, up to her forehead. Her accent started to lean away from Maine, towards, France, maybe? Eastern Europe? She told her fortunes in a voice that sounded a little bit like the Count on Sesame Street. It was very hard work not to smile. "Something very exciting is going to happen to you this summer."

"You say that every year, Madame Za."

She opened one eye under an elaborately arched eyebrow. "And am I wrong?"

Yes. Usually.

"Of course not," I said.

"I'm seeing it so clearly," she said, her eye closing again. "A mysterious stranger. Tall. Very handsome. With fair hair."

I hooted and then tried to school my face into serious lines. "For me?" I asked. "I think you're picking up the wrong future. Maybe you're talking about the twins."

We glanced over to where they stood behind the counter.

"Are they...?"

"Yes," Madame Za said. "I believe they are."

They were trying to braid the ends of their hair together.

Madame Za laughed, and the psychic act dropped for the moment. "Your mother," she said, her accent pure Maine once again, "would not tolerate those two."

It was nice, but sometimes I wished people wouldn't come in and talk about my mom. Or ask me how I was doing with those sad, serious eyes. Sometimes, I wished we could skip this part and go right into whatever was next.

I promised Madame Za that I would look out for tall blond handsome strangers and made my way around the diner.

Finally, when I'd served everyone else in the place, I turned to Jackson.

We didn't have uniforms, only T-shirts that said Pappas' across the back. I wore a pair of cut-off shorts and running shoes. My hair, curly like Mom's but blonde like Dad's used to be, piled up high on my head.

"What do you want?" I asked, my order pad and pen out.

"Long time no see, Lola." Even his voice was different. Low and rough. It sent a hot shiver through me, and I crossed my arms over my chest, hiding my suddenly hard nipples.

"Not long enough if you ask me."

He let the insult slide right on by. Instead, he just looked at me. His eyes not leaving my face.

I hadn't noticed before how they were the same color as the ocean just inside the breakers. An aqua blue. Pretty, really. His eyelashes...well, that was unfair. Those thick long eyelashes.

"You've changed," he said, and I bristled. "You grew up."

"Yeah. It happens."

I was not going to comment on how tall he'd gotten.

"I'm just saying." He looked me up and down, and my skin nearly blistered off my body. It was like when Mom died, she'd said, *you're going to need these,* and gifted me her boobs and her butt practically overnight. Suddenly, just wearing cut-offs and a T-shirt was a whole thing. I was self-conscious but trying to own it at the same time, which was exhausting. "You look good."

Ugh. So did not care what he thought.

"What do you want, Jackson?"

"I heard about your mom," he said. Explosions went off in my head.

I sucked in a breath and met his turquoise eyes.

"Don't talk about my mom."

His jaw tightened. "Look, I just wanted—"

I leaned down, right into his face, so close I could see his perfect skin and smell the woodsy smell of him, and I screamed.

"WHAT THE FUCK DO YOU WANT?"

Well. It was a whole scene.

Dad came rushing out from the back. Madame Za was there ringing some little cymbal thing, clearing the bad energy. Tiffani came over to try and smooth things with Jackson, but he just looked at me. Right in my eyes.

Like he knew me. Like he had the right.

He'd been my friend once. I needed a friend now. He could have helped me. He could have comforted me. Instead, he ruined everything.

I hated it. I hated him.

"Fuck you," I spat at him. Actually, spat at him, like, so bad he had to wipe it off his face. I would be mortified about that later.

"Go," Dad said, pushing me away. Zoe and Chloe pulled me into the small office beside the kitchen. I sat on Dad's squeaky rolly chair, feeling the buzzing aftereffects of adrenaline. I curled my hands into fists and let them out and wished with my whole heart that I could go out there and punch him.

That, and only that, would make me feel good.

The twins stared at me, popping their gum. Their blond hair in perfect shiny sheets down their backs, despite being told a million times a day that they needed to wear it in ponytails when they were waiting tables.

They were impossible to tell apart in their blonde sameness.

"Wow," one of them said.

"Yeah," the other said.

"Do you know who that is?" the first one said.

"Of course," I said.

"Jackson Dumont."

"Like, of the Dumont Dumonts."

"I know who he is," I sighed. These girls were like... vampires or something. Draining me of the will to fight.

"Well, then you should know you shouldn't yell at him like that."

"For sure." The other one said. They popped their gun in unison, and I swear to God, my soul left my body.

"Hey!" Georgie, who worked the kitchen with Dad, clapped his hands when he came into the office and the twins scattered like birds. Georgie watched them go then shook his head. He wore a white apron splashed with grease and a red bandana tied over his bald head. He wore hoop earrings, tasteful gold glitter eyeshadow, and his eyebrows were absolute perfection.

Georgie claimed he was descended from one of the French-Canadian pirates who landed on Calico Cove's sandy shores hundreds of years ago, and as a child, I'd believed him.

I still did. Because a girl had to believe in something. And Georgie had never let me down.

He sighed. "Those girls are about as interesting as..."

"Glue?" I offered.

"Dish soap?"

"Filling out forms at the doctor's office?"

"Standing in line at the DMV?"

"Yeah." I laughed. "That one."

Georgie was like me, Calico Cove through and through. He'd been my mom's very best friend. He went down to Boston every-once-in-a-while to, as he said, "get my freak on." I wasn't sure what that was, but it usually resulted in Mom going there to bail him out of jail.

"He loves a good protest," Mom had always said about him. "Can't pass up a chance to put on a gold thong and yell at a cop in riot gear." Mom said it was because he was an out and proud gay man in a world that wanted him to be smaller and quieter. Dad always laughed and said it was because he couldn't resist trouble.

"You all right?" he asked, leaning against the desk.

"I screamed at Jackson."

"I heard that," Georgie said.

"I hate him."

"He does have a very punchable face," Georgie said.

"I miss my mom," I whispered.

"Oh, Lola," he breathed and pulled me up into a big hug. "I do, too."

"How are we supposed to do all of this without her?"

"We figure it out, honey. One day at a time. But you can't scream in the faces of customers. As much as I might really enjoy what you just did, it's not good for business. Your father—"

"I know," I whispered.

My father was barely holding on. We all knew it. We all saw it, except maybe the DMV twins. Tiffani with an i, saw it. She watched my dad so carefully it made me a little nervous.

"Should I go out there and apologize?"

"He's gone," Georgie said.

As much as I wished that might be true, I knew it wasn't. Jackson was a reoccurring rash and he would be back.

THE NEXT DAY I arrived early to open the diner up for the lobstermen. They liked to fill their stomach with strong coffee, eggs, bacon and toast before heading out onto the water.

It was four in the morning. Which you think would be awful, but I actually liked this shift. The quiet of it. I liked to watch how night became day, how the change was so slow and sly, then suddenly, BANG, there was the sun dazzling the whole world.

The diner was quiet as I turned on the lights. I hadn't slept much last night thinking about Jackson. Hating him. Remembering a time I didn't hate him.

I was going to have to apologize to him. I knew that. I just was dreading it.

In the supply room, I stopped for some dry cat food. My babies, all four of them, but mostly Big Mama, would be waiting for me. It was breakfast for them, too.

I opened the back door, armed with a bowl full of food, then stopped when I heard Big Momma hissing at someone.

Big Mama didn't like strangers.

"Tell her to back off," Jackson said, looking at the over-sized calico cat like he might actually be afraid of it.

I set the bowl of dry food down on the other side of the door away from Jackson, and Big Mama quickly lost interest in him.

I folded my arms over my chest and tried really hard to stop my chin from wobbling.

"What are you doing here so early?"

"Couldn't sleep. Sometimes I like to go for a run."

He was wearing running sneakers and basketball shorts. He also wore a black T-shirt that was soaked through. Like he'd been running for a long time.

"I'm supposed to apologize," I said. Although it didn't sound like much of an apology.

"No, you don't. Not to me."

We stood there in awkward silence for what felt like hours but was probably only minutes. I pushed the pebbles on the ground back and forth with the tip of my sneaker.

Then, with no warning, I started crying. For real.

"Oh, my God," I moaned, in pain with grief and embarrassment. Sick with everything I felt but didn't want to. "Leave," I said.

But he didn't. He didn't leave, and that made me cry more.

"Jackson, please." Sobbing like I hadn't...ever. Not at the funeral, not while I packed up her stuff. The uncontrollable grief rolled through me. I wrapped my arms around my stomach and turned for the door, for the privacy this asshole wasn't going to give me, but he stopped me. His hand on my arm.

I sucked in a breath, and in the second I was too stunned to move, he put his arms around me, and he held me. Tight. The way I needed to be held. I tried to push him away, tried to get distance. I couldn't *do* this. I couldn't *feel* this.

"Lola," his voice was a low dark murmur that wrecked me.

I pushed my tear-soaked face into his sweat-drenched T-shirt and I clung to him, like the storm might pull me away and he was all I had. I gave him everything. Snot. Tears. All of my grief. All of my rage. I gave him all of it, and let him carry it for a bit.

Just a while.

Finally, I stopped, and as soon as I did, I pushed him away. He was, after all, my nemesis. And I couldn't imagine how he would use this to embarrass me later.

Thankfully, he didn't say anything. Just nodded his head then ran away, disappearing into the dawn.

Big Mama howled at me, and I wiped my face.

"We're just going to pretend that never happened," I told the cat.

5

One Month Later

Lola

By July, we'd fallen into a rhythm without Mom. It felt a little like a drunk, one-legged man trying to dance the polka kind of rhythm, but we were making it.

At least I *thought* we were making it. Dad started coming in the office, looking at the old computer with his head in his hands, and it occurred to me that Mom had taken care of all the bills, and maybe he was struggling with that.

"Dad," I said, one morning, coming into the office and shutting the door behind me. There was a kind of vinegary tang in the air from the hot sauce debacle we had a few years ago. Dad had tried to make his own, but it fermented in the jars and exploded like gunshots one Sunday morning. Mr. Duggan, who was eating his sausage and eggs, had an actual heart attack. He was all right, but he never came in for sausage and eggs anymore. "What's wrong?"

"Nothing, Lola" he said, giving me a tired but fake smile. My father was big. He had wide shoulders and a belly and hands so large he used to carry me around in just one of them until I was, like, eight.

I remembered being little and watching my parents in the living room in our pink house just down the road behind the elementary school. They would put on old records, and Dad would twirl Mom, lift her up, toss her around like she was made of feathers, and she would laugh and laugh. He'd pull her in close and kiss her, his big hands on her cheeks.

I'd gotten out of there before I saw something that would scar me for life. But you want to know what love looks like? It looks like that. Kitchen dancing and kisses.

Dad wasn't looking so big these days. His hair was getting thinner, and his eyes didn't come close to sparkling.

"Dad," I said, the diner starting to come alive on the other side of the office door.

Georgie had the radio on in the kitchen and the dishwasher was hissing. It had been making alarming sounds lately.

"Please, I can tell something is wrong," I said.

"You know what's wrong?" he said, the chair squealing as he leaned back. "You work too much. It's summer, and you're eighteen, and you should be out in the world, sweetie. Doing teenager summer things."

"Dad," I said, smiling at him. "Name one teenage summer thing you'd be okay with me doing."

"Seeing friends."

"I see my friends. They all come here."

"The beach parties every weekend. You never go."

"You're saying you'd let me go to the beach parties?"

"I'm saying I would let you go until ten."

"Dad!" I laughed. "The beach parties don't start until ten."

"Well, that is ridiculous."

Oh, he was just too sweet. I leaned down to hug him. "I want to be here, Dad. With you."

"That's what worries me. Your mother never wanted this diner to be your whole life. She wanted you to leave Calico Cove and go to college and see the world."

I knew that. But this was where all my memories of her were the strongest. Where she was still alive in my memories. If I left, what happened to her? What happened to Dad?

"I can see what you're thinking," my dad said, patting my cheek with his giant hand. "Your mom is gone and staying here doesn't bring her back."

"Okay," I lied. "I will consider going to a party if you tell me what has you in here heavy sighing."

"We need a new dishwasher."

"So, we get a new dishwasher."

"Do you know how expensive they are? Your mom had a small savings account for it but..." He stopped and shook his head. Mom's funeral had eaten up the dishwasher account.

"It's all right," I said, mentally thinking of my tips and how much I could contribute to a new dishwasher fund. "We're going to figure it out."

I LIVED in fear of Jackson returning with his pack of rich wolves to mock and snarl at me. But the gang of perfectly dressed and impeccably rude teenagers he used to spend his summers with seemed to have vanished.

He came in alone—almost every damn day—during that lull between lunch and the mid-afternoon rush of moms coming up from the beach for iced coffees and plates of french fries for their sunburned kids.

He sat in the huge round booth. Alone. Like it was his throne.

I watched him sit there, a single person in a booth big enough for eight, and I fumed.

"I heard his sister was here this summer," Zoe said. It took me a few weeks, but I'd learned not just their names, but also who was whom. Zoe was a tiny bit taller than Chloe and just a little cross-eyed. You had to look for it, but once you saw it, you couldn't unsee it.

Total props to Georgie for figuring that one out.

"Whose sister?" I asked.

"Jackson's."

Vanessa. She rarely came to Calico Cove with the family. I'd always heard the reason was boarding school, but it could have been anything really. Like maybe she spent the summer with her grandparents in some other corner of the world.

Why didn't Jackson spend his summers somewhere else? Why did it always have to be here?

Where I was.

"Damn, he is so freaking hot," Zoe said. She was blatantly staring at him, biting her lower lip like she wanted him on the menu.

So gross.

"Hot?" I asked as if she was delusional. "He's scrawny."

I thought about the collar bone that I'd pressed my forehead to that one morning.

That morning I didn't think about, ever.

Sometimes when he turned on the bench, his shirt went tight against his back, and I could see, like...hints of muscles. Baby muscles.

But mostly I thought he was scrawny.

"He looks like Harry Styles," Zoe said.

"In *what* universe?"

"You want me to take him?" Zoe asked, reaching for the lip-gloss in her apron.

"No," I said, "he's mine."

Which meant that he was in my section. But he was also *mine*.

My nemesis.

If you've never had a nemesis, let me recommend it. All that freedom to actually hate someone when you usually have to be nice all the time. It was freeing.

"I need you to move," I said to him, coming to stand at the edge of his booth.

"Hello to you, too," he said with a smile, stretching his arms wide in both directions over the back of the booth. Yeah, for sure there were muscles hiding there under his shirt.

I glared at him.

He grinned at me. It wasn't a happy to see me smile. Whatever brief moment we may or may not have shared, it was clearly behind us, and now, we were safely back to normal where I hated his breathing guts.

He had a dimple. Did I know that about him?

"There's a two-top free over there." I pointed to the row of two-seater tables closer to the counter. He turned to look. Part of his whole metamorphosis that had happened over the winter occurred in his jaw line and cheekbones. Like... they were there in a very noticeable way. He didn't look like

Harry Styles. He looked like an actor in an old black and white movie. He should have been wearing a fedora and a tie and saying things like "What's the high hat, Harry?"

Not that it was attractive in any way.

"I don't like that seat," he said. "No sunlight."

"Move to the counter. There's loads of sunlight there."

He turned to look at the counter, where the little bit of sun there was, was coming in the window in such an intense way, David who worked for Parks and Rec was wearing sunglasses while he ate his meatloaf sandwich.

"Can't," he sighed. "I forgot my welding visor."

I sighed, unimpressed. "You're taking up a table for eight."

"Lola, give me a break." He glanced around at the quiet restaurant. It was a cool summer day, so those moms ordering iced coffees and fries probably wouldn't be coming. But still.

"It's the principle of it. Only assholes take big tables when they can sit at smaller ones," I pointed out.

"Then this whole thing makes perfect sense, doesn't it?" He smiled again, and I told myself he was not charming.

"You know what I was thinking?" he said.

"That your entire life has been a waste?"

"No," he said with what looked like a genuine smile. "You guys haven't changed the décor in this place since what appears to be the eighties. So by some miracle, it's almost cool again. You should wear kitschy uniforms to go with it. Something pink and short. Tight across the chest. You know...show off your assets."

"*You* should choke on a fishbone."

"Wait," Chloe said, interjecting herself into our conversation. She was clearing plates from the table next to the booth, which was a total ruse, since that, too, was my table, and Chloe was not in the practice of helping me out unless it helped her more. "That's a really good idea, Jackson. Can I call you Jackson?"

"You can call him shit for brains," I muttered.

Part of his statement was true. The place looked like the last renovation had happened in the eighties. Long before my parents took over, back when my grandparents ran the place.

The age was there to see. Brown and mustard yellow tile. All the benches were brown. The tabletops old Formica.

"See?" Jackson said. "Zoe agrees with me."

"I'm Chloe."

"Sorry, darling," he said, and I rolled my eyes so hard I almost blacked out. "I'll get it right one of these days."

Chloe left, undoubtedly to rub her sister's face in that absent-minded *darling*. She, of course, left the plates she'd been pretending to clear.

"You don't like my uniform idea?"

"I just don't like you," I said. "Are you going to order anything?"

"Also, if you aren't married to these crap brown cushions, you could redo everything in blue and white. Nice and clean. Kind of Greek to go with your name."

My father came out from his office to the coffee station behind the counter and reached for a mug to pour himself a cup, but Tiffani with an i was there, and she smiled and poured him a cup and there was something...

Was Tiffani with an i flirting with my father? The way she put her hand on his arm? That hair toss?

"Hello?" Jackson said, waving his hand in front of my face. "You realize you're ignoring a paying customer."

"No one cares," I said, still distracted by the way Tiffani was standing so close to my dad. Like...way too close, right?

"Wow," Jackson said in a low voice. He'd turned and was watching my dad, too. "Looks like someone is moving in on Papa," Jackson said. "That's pretty ballsy."

It was. I hated agreeing with the asshole, but it was ballsy. *If* she was flirting. That would be so...disrespectful. My mom hadn't even been gone a year. My dad wasn't going to, like...buy that? Was he?

"Everyone gets lonely," Jackson said, like he was reading my mind.

"You're disgusting."

"Birds and the bees, Lola. I don't have anything to do with it."

"You just here to be an ass or do you want something to eat?"

"I'm multi-talented," he said. "I think I can do both."

"You know," I said. "You're not as charming as you think you are."

He leaned forward, his face inches from mine, and I forced myself to not jerk away like it bothered me. Because it didn't. He didn't.

"I don't think you're as nice as you pretend to be," he whispered. "All these people looking at you and thinking you're so sweet and innocent. They don't know, do they?"

"Know what?"

"That you're just like your mom."

He hated my mom. I knew that. Knew he hated me, too. So yeah, it probably made sense he thought she was...what?

A bitch.

Tears hot and bright burned in my eyes.

"Fuck you, Jackson."

I walked away without taking his order. Chloe could have him.

THE NEXT DAY during the lull after the lunch crowd, I took my break. I grabbed two slices of that miraculous, part plastic, all delicious American cheese product we served and went out back to sit on the milk crates I'd set up under the pine trees on the other side of the dumpster.

If I turned the milk crates the right way, I could ignore the dumpster and stare out at a view of the pier across the street and the fishing boats bobbing up and down on the water.

That was the awesome thing about Calico Cove. Even though I wasn't on vacation and hadn't been on vacation in, I don't know...ever, just sitting down and looking at the view, pulling in big breaths of salty air, it felt like a vacation.

I sighed, restored and happy again.

"Hey, kitties," I said, and Big Mama, who was starting to show her age, appeared with two smaller kittens. Mom had made a big push years ago to have the feral cats scooped up and spayed. But somehow...somehow there were always kittens.

I tore off pieces of one of the cheese slices and fed them to the cats. The other piece I ate.

"She's not going to start hissing at me again, is she?"

I closed my eyes and swore.

"Hello to you, too, Lola," Jackson said, coming to stand in the patch of pine needles. Blocking my vacation view.

"I'm on a mini-vacation," I said.

"Really?"

"Yes. And I don't want you here."

Yesterday, he all but called me a bitch. Not that I cared about me, but that meant he called my mother a bitch.

"This is my happy place. You going to ruin this for me, too?" I asked.

"Not sure how I can make it worse," he said, looking around. His hair, in this light, was the color of coffee with a tiny bit of cream.

"Just by being here," I said, giving him a mocking smile and blinking my eyelashes at him the way the twins did.

"How is this a vacation?" he asked.

I pointed past his hip at the view I was looking at. There were sailboats amongst the more practical fishing boats. Then there was the pier where tourists were hanging their fishing poles over the sides.

The pink awning of the Big Scoop ice-cream store. The flags from Aimee Piedmont's Book Shop.

People paid to come here. To have this experience.

He turned and looked. I wondered what he saw when he looked at my beautiful town full of good people. What mean awful thing was going through his head.

"Yeah, it's pretty," he said, and I scoffed. "What? You don't think it's pretty?"

"I don't think *you* think it's pretty."

He turned to face me, but also stepped aside so he wasn't blocking my view.

Big Mama hissed at him, and from the open back door of the diner, I could hear my father yelling at the dishwasher.

"Well, it's not going to work if you talk to her like that," Georgie said to my dad.

"The dishwasher is not a her," Dad yelled. "It's a machine."

"She can hear you."

"Something wrong with the dishwasher?" Jackson asked, and then, to my surprise, he crouched. His long, tall body curling in on itself. He wore shorts and a T-shirt, plain gray and black, and it stretched over those nearly non-existent muscles of his back.

Seagulls landed on the ground near him and approached with interest. Maybe they thought he was food. He kind of smelled good actually. With any luck they'd poke his eyes out.

He held out his fingers like he had something in them, and Big Mama, who, despite her crusty distrust of everything and everyone, deeply loved treats, slowly approached.

"You're teasing her," I said. "She's going to go full wombat on you."

"Wombat?"

His lip curled up in a half-smile, and I closed my eyes, unable to watch the carnage that was about to happen. I heard Big Mama hiss and him swear. I grinned.

"Told you."

"That's what I get for trying to be nice," he said, observing the damage the cat had done.

"No, that's what you get for teasing a feral cat with invisible treats."

I turned to glare at him, brought up short by him staring right back at me. He had a bright red scratch down his hand. She'd really gotten him.

If he were anyone else, I'd rush him inside to clean it. But he was Jackson and gangrene was only some of what he deserved.

"You should go home and clean that," I said, and then wanted to kick myself.

"Worried about me?"

"Not even a little. Don't clean it. Let it fester."

There was another thunk from inside. My dad and Georgie both swearing.

"So what is going on with the dishwasher?" he asked.

I put a hand to my head. The bun I'd made this morning too tight, maybe. I had a weird sudden headache.

It's falling apart. We're all falling apart.

Not that I would ever say that. Not out loud. Absolutely not to him. Oh, no.

"Lola?"

"None of your fucking business, Jackson," I snapped. "Okay?"

"There she is. My not-so-sweet-tempered Lola I've come to love."

The sound of my name and the word *love* so close together in his mouth made something awful happen. It was like actual poison, and my whole body went haywire. The nerves in my fingers flashed hot, and my head got cold. I wanted to throw up and run away.

Instead, I glared at him.

He wasn't crouched anymore; he stood tall and straight. Over six feet. The breeze blew that plain gray shirt against his body in a way that I hated noticing.

"Look, Lola—"

"I'm going inside," I said and looked down at Big Mama. "Sic him."

I left him back there, Big Mama hissing at him from the milk crate where I'd been sitting.

I washed my hands and walked into the dining room, in that space behind the counter. Where I could stand and see the whole of my little world. The big booths. The two-tops. The counter full of teenagers, who had just gotten the freedom from their parents to be out on their own. I refilled their Coke glasses, and they thanked me profusely.

The bell rang over the door, and I turned, smiling, to greet a customer, only to see Jackson walking inside the diner. The scratch on his hand was bleeding. Joined by another one.

Good, Big Mamma.

"What happened to you?" Chloe said, pulling napkins from the dispenser and attempting to press them to his hand, which looked like it was becoming infected right in front of me.

"Lola's attack cat got me."

"Attack cat?" Chloe asked, staring at me.

"I'm fine," he said and sat at the counter. Chloe got pulled away by one of her tables asking for more water.

"You've trained that cat to hate me," he accused me.

"No, I think you just bring out the best in her."

"I seem to have that effect on the women around here," he grumbled.

"Yes," I said, looking right at him. "You do. You could try charming Larry."

"Well, I see several problems. One, it's a lobster."

"You're going to let that stop you?" I asked with a casual shrug. "Weak."

"Two, it's dead," Jackson added.

"Well, that just improves your chances for success," I snorted.

"Finally, Larry is a boy. Not that there is anything wrong with that, but it's not the team I'm on."

"Ah-hah! That is where you are wrong," I said haughtily. "Larry is most definitely female. At least according to my grandfather."

He leaned forward. "Seriously? Larry is really a girl? Does the town know this?"

For a second, our eyes locked, it seemed like that smirk on his face wasn't actually a smirk. But more of a smile. His eyes weren't narrowed, they were soft and almost warm. That incredible aqua color I couldn't seem to hate.

"Is there something you wanted, Jackson?" I asked, breaking that strange eye contact.

"Yesterday when I was in here you gave someone the Lola Special," he said. "I'd like that."

I shook my head. "The Lola Special is only for people I like."

He reached into his wallet and put a hundred-dollar bill on the Formica.

A hundred-dollar bill.

`One: it was a stupid amount to pay for a grilled cheese with tomato served with half french fries and half onion rings.

Two: Who walked around with cash?

Three: Who walked around with that much of it?

"It looked good," he said. "Can I get it? To go."

Fuck this guy. I wanted to throw his money in his face but there was the dishwasher to think about, and if he gave that money to Chloe or Zoe, they'd keep it as a tip, and it would get spent down at Star's Style Salon. Nothing against Star or her salon, but we needed that money.

I looked at him and realized...he knew all that.

He'd asked about the dishwasher. Knew it was broken.

This was pity money.

I should be like my mom and tear his dirty Dumont money up and toss it in his stupid face. That would be the best decision. What would have happened if Mom hadn't done that? What position would we be in now if she had just taken the hush money?

Maybe because she had her pride at that moment, I couldn't have mine in this one.

I put my hand on the bill, torn between pride and a

dishwasher.

"Lola," he said. It was the third time he'd said my name today.

I glanced back at him, caught his eyes taking me apart a little. Pulling at the edges of my confidence. Finding something soft and vulnerable, only so he could stick a knife in. I was too worn down to protect myself. I just stood there, ready for him to hurt me.

"Keep the change. Buy yourself something nice. Or maybe..." He waved his hand around his head, his face set in an expression like something smelled bad. "Do something with your hair."

"I hope your hand gets amputated," I shot back and picked up the money and put it in my apron. "You want the Lola Special? Sure, no problem. Give me a few minutes. I'm going to make this myself."

I walked away from the counter and headed into the kitchen.

"You need something, kiddo?" Georgie asked me. He'd apparently abandoned the dishwasher to my dad and was back to running the grill.

"No, I got this."

And no, I wasn't going to do something as gross as spitting in Jackson's food. That was too obvious.

I made a grilled cheese. White American cheese, which I knew he preferred, but instead of the tomato, I substituted slices of pickled beets, and, for fun, a ring of pineapple. There, that was a heck of a Lola Special. Cheese, beet and pineapple. I really hoped he bit into the thing without looking.

I boxed it up with some under-cooked fries and brought it to him in a Styrofoam to-go container.

With a straight face, I said. "Enjoy!"

6

Late August

Lola

Suddenly it was almost over. Our first summer without Mom. The weather changed, and now there was a cool breeze off the ocean. The moms at the tables were talking about back to school and the weekend parties down at the beach were the last of the season.

I, for one, was ready. Glad, even. I loved the tourists, but I wouldn't mind sitting down for a minute. Going back to the beach on Saturday mornings when it was quiet and empty.

All we needed to do was get through the last week of summer, the busiest weekend and then...smooth sailing.

So, of course, that's when everything went to shit.

~

It was the Monday before Labor Day when Simon Turnberry walked into the diner.

Listen, Madame Za had been wrong so many times about people's fortunes it was a joke in town. I'd totally forgotten what she said to me at the very beginning of the season.

Or at least I thought I had.

Then *he* walked in, and it all came rushing back to me. Tall, blonde, extremely handsome.

"Well, look at you, you poor bugger," he said to Larry with...wait for it...a posh British accent.

Chloe and Zoe practically disintegrated on the spot.

"Welcome to Pappas'," I said to him. He smiled at me, and I felt myself blush and sort of giggle. I mean, it was ridiculous. "You can sit anywhere."

"Thank you," he said, with what I can only call intense eye contact.

Chloe, Zoe and I watched him from behind the counter as he made his way through the restaurant. He passed through Chloe's section, and she slumped, defeated. For a second, it looked like he was going to take a window seat in Zoe's section, and she pulled her lip gloss out of her apron pocket in preparation, but then he skipped that seat and took a booth in my section.

It was all I could do not to fist pump.

I could feel them glaring at me as I strolled over. He'd taken out a menu from where we kept them at the table and was studying it like he intended to memorize the thing.

"Can I get you something to drink?" I asked.

"I heard your milkshakes are quite good."

Honestly, that accent. What was a girl to do?

"They are. The strawberries are grown locally. Highly recommend."

He set down the menu and stretched his arm over the back of the booth. "What else do you recommend..." He looked at my name tag pin, which was right above my boob. Which meant he was looking at my boob. "Lola. What a fabulous name. Lola." He pronounced every bit of my name, got his tongue around all the nooks and crannies.

"Well," I said. "If you like a grilled cheese—"

"Love them."

"Then I recommend the Lola Special." The real one with the tomato. Not the ones I'd been making for Jackson.

"Sounds charming. I'll take one and a strawberry milkshake."

I wrote it down, which was ridiculous, most of the time I just remembered the orders and didn't need the pad, but something in me wanted to linger. "Are you here for the last weekend of summer?" I asked.

"Yes, staying with a friend," he said. "I've never been to Maine before."

"What do you think of it?" I asked, glancing up, and then I got caught in his eyes.

"So far—" he grinned "—I quite like it."

It was another one of Calico Cove's rules. Like the Pointe, and Larry, and the cats: Locals didn't get involved with the tourists.

At least not with their hearts. Bodies, yes, and with great frequency.

So, I wondered, what would be wrong with a little flirtation? Something sweet after the awful year I'd had. What if...and stay with me here...I let this handsome blond man, who Madame Za said was practically my destiny, kiss away some of the heartache?

I mean, it sounded like a great idea to me.

Just then the bell over the door rang. There was a rapid

hiss and cat screech. Simon's eyes lifted over my shoulder, and his face split into a wide smile. "Here's my friend now. Jackson."

He lifted his hand and waved Jackson over like the asshole didn't know his way around the place.

But Jackson was caught in the doorway. "This fucking cat," he snapped. "Get. Off." He crouched. Swore. Jumped into the restaurant and shut the door behind him.

He found me and glared. "Your attack cat is a menace."

"Attack cat?" Simon said.

"She's trained a cat to scratch me," Jackson said, stomping across the diner.

"That seems unlikely," Simon said.

"It's actually impossible," I said.

"Not if you're a witch," Jackson said, and it was close enough to the bitch that he basically called me earlier, I stiffened.

"That must explain it then," Simon murmured. "You've cast a spell on me."

Look, flirting is part of the job, and I was good at it. But that top-shelf flirtation took the legs right out from under me.

"Well, I guess you've seen some of the sights," Jackson said, sliding into the booth across from Simon. Together they looked like a cologne ad. For something sexy and masculine and far too rich for me.

"You're disgusting," I said to Jackson, sure he was referring to me being one of the sights.

"I was talking about Larry," he said with false innocence. "How about another Lola Special for me? That last one you made was so interesting."

I smiled with all my teeth. Every time he came to the diner now, he ordered the Lola Special. Which meant I had to get creative. The last special was tuna salad, with hot sauce, topped with strawberry slices on wheat bread.

"Liked that one, did you? I'm thinking today's might come with a side of snails. Fresh from the garden."

"She's hilarious," Jackson said, looking at Simon. But Simon was watching Jackson and me like we were fascinating.

"I've noticed," Simon said.

It was all suddenly way too Lords of the Manor sexually harassing the servant girl for my taste.

"I'll be back with your food."

Chloe and Zoe wanted details when I got to the counter.

"They're friends apparently," was what I told them.

"He must be here for the party," Chloe said.

"Totally here for the party," Zoe said.

"What party?" My dad asked, leaning in the window between the kitchen and the dining room.

"Ordering," I said, and slapped the ticket up on the stainless-steel ledge. Dad took it but was watching Chloe and Zoe.

Today Jackson's Lola Special was going to be a hamburger with mustard, red onion and a slice of water-melon on top covered in blue cheese dressing.

"What party?" he asked again.

"In honor of Jackson's sister being in town, they are having a big bash at their house Sunday. A bonfire on the beach with a DJ from New York and everything," Chloe said.

"Everyone's going to be there," Zoe said.

"It's going to be epic." Chloe finished.

Dad looked over at me, his eyebrows raised.

"No, Dad," I said.

"But everyone is going to be there," he said.

"Not me."

He huffed, then looked at the order I'd just placed. "Does someone actually want this?"

"He was very specific." I smiled.

SIMON CAME in every day after that, at different times during the day. But no matter what time he showed up, Jackson showed up about fifteen minutes later.

"Hey," Simon said on Thursday morning at nine am. He was sweaty from a run, which was both gross and very appealing.

I remembered the smell of Jackson's soaked T-shirt, when I had my face buried into that space between his shoulder and his neck.

Don't think about that. We're never thinking about that moment again.

"You need some water?" I asked him.

"And some serviettes?" he asked.

I came back with a glass of water and a stack of napkins. He wiped his face with the bottom of his shirt, and I tried not to stare at the slice of skin he showed.

"Thank you," he said. "I'd love your eggs benedict," he said.

"Just to really negate that run, huh?"

"It's why I ran here."

"From the Dumont house? That's quite a haul."

"You are familiar with Jackson's family home?"

"It's a small town, Simon."

"In regards to Jackson's family... What does the town know about them?"

That was...strange? Was it strange? Seemed strange. Like he was digging for skeletons. I didn't know how to answer.

"Not much, really," I said. Which felt both true and not true at the same time. "They keep to themselves, mostly."

"I'd imagine," he said, which made me think he understood that they were total asshole snobs. "Listen, there's a party on Sunday—"

"I know," I said stiffly.

"Then you'll be there." He looked, and I'm not exaggerating, like a kid on Christmas.

"I have to work."

"On the last night of summer? Seems a cruel turn."

There was something on his face. Something sharp and different and it made me feel awkward, flattered and maybe a little nervous.

"Can I have your number?' he asked, and I blinked. Startled. Stunned really.

"Why?"

"The usual reasons," he said with a smile that made my stomach tremble.

Holy shit. He was asking me out. He was actually asking for my number.

"Sure," I said, and fumbled with my phone in my apron, pulling it out, typing in my code and handing it over.

The bell over the door rang out. There was the familiar hiss of a cat then Jackson was striding in, shutting the door quickly behind him. He was faster than Big Mama, who it did seem was waiting for him outside that door.

"Hello, Simon," Jackson said, his mouth smiling, but his eyes looking hard. "I thought you were out for a run."

"I was. I ran here."

Yeah, there was something weird happening between these two, and I wanted no part of it. I looked over to ask Simon for my phone back only to find he'd slid it across the table to the edge, where it was about to fall. I grabbed it then slipped it into my apron.

My eyes met Jackson's, and they were not the pretty calm blue of the water inside the breakers. No, they were a storm at sea. They were choppy water and trouble.

"You're staring," Jackson snapped, making me jump.

"Do you want something?" I asked Jackson, and he made a sound in his throat, a kind of growl, or a groan. Something that felt like a rough hand across the back of my neck.

"Your special," he said with a tight voice.

"Coming right up."

"He wants a bowl of cottage cheese covered in chili?" Georgie asked. He wore a bright pink chef jacket and a black bandana tied around his head. "At nine in the morning?"

"Who is to say with these people?" I said with a shrug.

I pushed open the swing door and walked past the kitchen and past Dad's little hidey hole office, empty at the moment because he'd had a meeting at the bank.

Between the office and the walk-in cooler was the store-room where we kept the dried goods, the cat food and all our canned supplies. I stepped in there and shut the door before pulling out my phone to see if Simon had actually put in his number.

Before I could check it, behind me, the door swung open with a bang. I turned, expecting to see Chloe or Zoe only to find Jackson staring at me.

"You can't be back here," I said. "Employees only."

Like that was going to stop Jackson.

"What did Simon say to you?" Jackson asked. "Why does he keep coming here?"

"Oh, my God, that is so none of your business," I gasped.

He crossed the tiny room in three steps crowding me up against the far wall, I put my hand out to stop him, but he just kept coming, and soon, my hand was pressed to his chest. His skin warm under his T-shirt. His heart beating hard against my palm.

I'm touching Jackson Dumont.

"What did he say?" he said with the kind of whisper that made the hair all over my body stand up.

"Why does it matter to you?"

"Because it does."

I wanted to say *fuck you*, but he was so close and so warm, and it was all so...much. I could smell him. Woodsy and clean and *him*. "He...he just told me about the party."

"You can't come. You're not invited."

My mouth fell open. I didn't think this guy had any kind of power left to hurt me but wow. I mean...wow.

"I'm not going to your stupid party."

"Lola—"

His gaze was moving over my face, and his body pushed into my hand. Then he bit his bottom lip, like he was barely holding onto something awful he wanted to say to me, and I wasn't going to stand here and take it.

"I said, I wasn't going, okay? Now, get the hell out of here."

He stood there a second longer, my hand against his chest, both of us breathing hard as if we'd been running as fast as we could.

Why wasn't he leaving? Why was he so...warm?

"Lola," he breathed.

His head dipped tentatively, and I don't know why, but I didn't push him off. I didn't back way. I...looked at him. There was something there, in his eyes, in the way his nostrils flared. A connection that ran so deeply between us.

He dipped his head again and then he was kissing me.

His lips on mine. I opened my mouth to him and I was being crushed up against his chest. How was this happening? Who were these two people? He pushed me back against the wall, and I moaned into his mouth.

I wanted to crawl inside him. I wanted to stay buried there where no one could hurt me. I wanted...

I wanted so much.

His hands were on my ass, then he pushed his hips against me, and I knew what it meant.

He was hard. He *wanted* me.

He broke the kiss. "Fuck...Lola. Fuck, I knew it."

What? What did he know? Because I didn't know anything. One minute Jackson Dumont was my nemesis, and the next minute he was kissing me.

No. *We* were kissing. I was kissing him back. It felt like it was the thing I was supposed to have been doing forever.

"Let's get out of here," he mumbled, even as he was dipping his head to suck on my neck. Gently, teasingly.

Get out of here.

And what? Go for a drive? Let him take my virginity in the back seat of some fancy car? Then make sure not to show my face at the party he clearly didn't want me to go to?

I pushed him away then. Sanity sinking in. This was *Jackson*.

He didn't think I was good enough for a damn party, but a quick lay...sure, that sounded about right.

"No, this was...I don't know what this was. You need to go."

"Lola," he practically growled my name. "We need to talk."

"We don't. This didn't happen. You need to go."

"You can be so damn stubborn," he snapped. "You're just like your mom!"

That's when my vision turned red. "Don't you ever—*ever* —say anything bad about my mom!"

"I wasn't—"

"Go!" I shouted. "Just go!"

He held himself still. His jaw clenching, his hands curled into fists.

"Stay away from Simon," he said, low and mean, like I was going to contaminate his friend with my townie cooties or some nonsense.

Then he was gone.

Lola

Labor Day weekend we were absolutely slammed. Three full days of full tables. At one point during Sunday breakfast, we had a line. A line!

We hadn't been so packed in ages. There were dozens and dozens of college students up from Boston, half of them wearing MIT sweatshirts with their shorts and flip flops.

"MIT," Chloe said, "Isn't that where Jackson goes?"

"I thought it was Harvard," Zoe said.

"Whatever," Chloe said, tucking the hem of her belly shirt under her bra to show more belly. "That table of Lacrosse players is so fucking hot."

"Hey," I snapped and handed her the tray of milkshakes I'd just made. I was covered in chocolate sauce and sweating my ass off trying to help Georgie with the fryer that was— you guessed it—going on the fritz. We'd finally gotten the new dishwasher and a fryer was going to be next. "Take them their shakes."

"Gladly," she said and took the tray with a smirk at her sister.

After that weird morning in the storage room, when the thing that I was in total denial about happened/didn't happen, Simon and Jackson hadn't come back for the rest of the week. Which was a relief, I thought. However, without them as a distraction, I found myself watching Tiffani with an i and my dad.

"Is there something going on with our parents?" I asked Chloe later that afternoon, after the crowds had died down, the tables were ready to be prepped.

Together, we were filling the sugar canisters.

"Like what?" she asked.

"Like *something*?"

It took Chloe a second, but she finally looked up, and I watched as she figured out what I was saying, her face reacting in slow motion.

"Are you joking?" she asked. She could not look more appalled if Larry the Lobster pulled himself off the wall and started dancing the cancan.

"No, I mean…is she flirting with him?"

"My mom? My mom is a MILF, and your dad is…"

"Watch it," I snapped.

"Like, a million years old and he smells like cheese-burgers."

"And is kind and decent and funny. Not to mention charming and if you weren't—"

"Hello, girls," Georgie said, stepping up between us. He threw his arms around us. "Chloe," he said. "Don't you and Zoe have a party to get to?"

"We can go?" Chloe asked, all her offense and disgust vanished. "Early?"

"Please," I said. "Please go early."

Chloe shot me a nasty look but ran off to gather her sister. They would go home, shower the day off their bodies, then go and get drunk on expensive champagne.

Maybe make out with boys.

I'll let you in on a little secret. I haven't made out with a whole lot of boys. Not for lack of trying, maybe just for lack of opportunity. Growing up in a small town I've known most of the boys around here since I was a kid. And it wasn't always easy to get lost in the moment with a guy you remembered throwing up all over the lunch room in 3rd grade.

All that to say...I wanted to make out with someone. I really did.

Strangely, an image of Jackson popped into my head, but I quickly squashed it. Because what happened did not really happen.

I did NOT want to kiss Jackson Dumont.

Again.

In fact, if anything, I needed to kiss someone else as soon as possible, if only to get rid of that last image and feeling altogether. It wasn't right that the most passionate moment of my life was with Jackson Dumont!

"What kind of trouble are you stirring?" Georgie asked.

I told him how it seemed like Tiffani was making a move on my father.

"Do you think I'm nuts?" I asked Georgie.

"No," Georgie said. "I think your dad is lonely. Also, I think he's worried that you are getting sucked into running this place when you should be off being a teenager. Tiffani can help with that."

I looked at Georgie with wide eyes.

"So," he said quietly. "Do your dad a favor, and go be a teenager, would you?"

"I wasn't invited to the party," I said and hated the fact that it still hurt a little.

THAT NIGHT, I locked the door behind the last guest, and I sat down with a big glass of water to cash out.

"How'd you do?" Dad asked, sitting beside me. People didn't carry a whole lot of cash these days. But I still had a pretty good roll of ones and fives in my apron.

"Good." I started to count off half to give him, but he put his hand up.

"No way, you're not giving me those tips."

"The fryer."

"The fryer, the roof, the awning over the door. There will always be something, and it is not your job to solve it," he said and kissed my forehead, and I was awash in the smell of onions and hamburger.

Beneath that, the scent of Old Spice.

Dad smell.

"You should go to that party," he said. "The one the girls were talking about. You work too much."

"Me?!" I cried. "*You* work too much."

"Well," he said. "I am going to go have a drink with a friend tonight."

"What friend?" I asked. "Georgie?"

They weren't really the go out for drinks type.

"No," he said, and I realized he was blushing. At that moment, Tiffani came out from the small closet where we all kept our purses and coats. She had brushed out her hair and put on lipstick. It hit me who his friend was.

Mom hasn't even been gone a year, I wanted to say. *How can you do this?*

"It's just...it's just a drink," he said quickly, reading my mind. "It's not. She's not..."

He was so uncomfortable, and I was so uncomfortable, and I just wanted it all to end.

I smiled at him and said, "Of course, you should go have a good night."

"You'll go to the party?"

"Yes, I will go to the party," I lied, because I couldn't tell him that I'd been told not to go. But he needed me to be a teenager and that's where all the teenagers were.

What the hell was I going to do? Drive around for hours? Sit at the beach?

Dad kissed my forehead again and squeezed himself out of the booth to go talk to Tiffani, who looked at him like he was just the best thing ever. When he walked away, she caught my eye, and I gave her the disapproving glare she so richly deserved. She stiffened and got busy looking through her purse.

That's right, I thought, *you* should *be embarrassed.*

In my apron, my phone binged, and I pulled it out only to find a text from an unknown number.

Unknown: The bonfire is roaring. The party is a rager. But something is missing.

Lola: Who is this?

Unknown: Three guesses.

Lola: Simon?

Unknown: Right in one. Clever girl. So, are you coming?

My skin prickled with a strange apprehension.

I almost said, *Jackson told me to stay away,* but that was outrageously dramatic, and Jackson was not the boss of me. Even though it was his house. Would he even notice me there? The place was going to be packed with people, and if I was just kind of low-key and avoided him...would it be a thing?

Trust me, no one was more surprised than me that I wanted to go. I *wanted* to be at the party.

Lola: I don't know.

Unknown: Please. Save me from this endless boredom.

Lola: I thought you said it was a rager.

Unknown: I lied. Come!

I bit my bottom lip and had to tell myself that what I was feeling wasn't a small amount of guilt. Guilt that I was basically planning a hook up with Jackson's friend, after Jackson and I...did nothing. Because nothing happened.

If anything, it helped me to make up my mind.

Lola: Okay, I'll be there.

Unknown: Be a doll and bring some food, would you? Everything here is garbage.

Lola: Somehow I doubt that.

Unknown: No one really likes oysters, do they? Everyone is just pretending that the cold salty snot is delicious.

Weirdly, that made me feel better. Like I wasn't showing up empty handed. Like, if Jackson caught me there, crashing his party, I could tell him Simon invited me. Simon was hungry. I was bringing food for Simon. That's all this was. Not a hook up.

Lola: I'll be there in a half hour.

"Georgie!" I yelled. "Don't turn off the fryer just yet. I need to put together a sick amount of chicken wings."

∾

IN THE END, I made buffalo wings, onion wings and french fries.

Georgie bagged them up for me with the last of the brownies, while I washed my face and put on a little makeup and slipped on an old dress that I'd left here at the beginning of summer. It was pink and swirled around my knees and dipped between my breasts and tied around my neck.

I thought I looked pretty in it. Of course, the only shoes I had were my beat-up converse but at least I couldn't be accused of trying too hard.

My lip gloss matched my dress, and when I stepped out, Georgie gave me a nod of approval.

"Do I smell like fries?" I asked.

"Undoubtedly," he said, and there wasn't a whole lot I could do about that. "But you look very pretty." He handed me the bags of food.

I crawled into my Toyota hatchback that I couldn't take on the highway or up hills for fear it would disintegrate with the effort of speed or hill-climbing, and I drove along the twisty Harbor Road until it turned into the Beach Road. The line-up of cars down from the Dumont house was almost a half mile long. So I ended up parking in the public beach lot.

It would be faster to cross the beach to get to the house then it would be to walk down the road.

On the other side of the private property sign, I could see on the sand there was, indeed, a roaring fire. The flames were as high as the second floor of the gigantic house. There were people around the fire. Music. The smell of food cooking and drinks spilling.

All at once, the food I was bringing felt a little stupid. Like, what were fifty wings and some onion rings going to mean to this crowd? But I was here. I'd drop off the food in the kitchen, find a beer, drink it quickly on an empty stomach and get into the spirit of things.

I should know people here. People, friends, locals who I grew up with like Jolie and Verity Petit.

Mari, too. Mari was the same year as me and basically my best friend when I had time for best friends. Because there really hadn't been a lot of time since Mom had passed.

Like me, Mari rarely did the party scene. She was always too focused on her art projects. I should have called around. Seen who might actually be coming. But it was just such a last-minute decision.

Still, it sure would be nice to see a familiar face.

A friendly *familiar* face. After all, the twins would also be here.

And Simon.

Halfway across the rocky beach, a shadow moved, and a girl materialized. We both screamed and nearly fell backwards.

"Oh, my God, you scared me," we both said. And then started to laugh.

"I'm sorry," I said, "I was just taking a short cut."

"No problem. I was just..." She looked over at the house. The yellow of the fire gilding her features. She was very pretty. Fine-boned, my mom would say. With long brown hair and light eyes.

Vanessa Dumont.

Jackson's sister. Perfect. "I was hiding."

"Is it that bad in there?" I asked.

"Not for everyone else," she said.

"Vanessa, it's Lola. You probably don't remember me?"

"Oh, my gosh, Lola. From that summer?"

"Yeah."

"My mother wouldn't let us play with you when we were kids. But my brother...he always found a way to sneak out."

I remembered. I remembered every minute of that summer.

"What's in those bags? I can smell it from here."

"Buffalo wings. I didn't want to come empty handed to the party."

She looked at me with her mouth open like I'd said something outrageous. "Every single person in that party came empty-handed. Open handed. People are putting bottles of champagne in their purses."

"That's kind of gross."

She shrugged like it was just the way her world worked.

"You want an onion ring?" I asked, because there was nothing more comforting than fried food when people were stealing your champagne.

Vanessa looked delighted. "Yes. Please."

I pulled out the top to-go container and handed it to her. She fell onto the rings like she hadn't eaten in ages, and maybe, looking at her thin wrists and the press of her collarbone against her skin, the way her dress hugged every single curve she had, she hadn't.

"That's good," she said with a heavy sigh, her mouth full. "Really good."

"I'm glad," I said. Part of loving Pappas' was loving moments like this exact one. This making people happy moment. Feeding hungry people moment. I was suddenly very glad that I'd run into Vanessa out here.

"Have you been in Calico Cove all summer?" I asked her. "I'm surprised we haven't run into each other before now."

"No. Just a few weekends here and there. I had to make up some classes this summer."

"Summer school again?"

"Not really. I mean...sort of. I got kicked out of Foxcroft, and Dad was threatening to send me to Europe, but I promised him I'd do this whole course thing at Madeira. But —" she gave me a conspiratorial look "—the thing about summer programs is the teachers don't want to be there, either."

Across the sand someone shouted, and the music got turned up, and there was dancing. I felt an undeniable craving to be *there*.

"You want to go to the party?" she asked, her eyes reflecting the fire.

"I do," I said. "But I don't want to leave you here."

"Oh, no, I'm going back. I was trying to make a point about something, but clearly neither Jackson nor Simon care about my point." She curled her arm through mine, and I reached back and grabbed the Styrofoam container that she'd been about to leave, and we headed across the sand to the party.

As soon as we reached the throng of people near the patio, Vanessa was called away.

"You all right?" she asked, looking back at me.

"Absolutely." If I wanted to be low-key, going in with Jackson's sister would kind of ruin that.

I wanted to get rid of these bags first because I felt ridiculous carrying them in, but I stopped at the patio door to kick off my shoes, so I could dump out the pounds of sand that had gotten inside.

Avoiding the crowds of people coming in and out of the doors, I moved to the side, set down the big paper bags on a bench on the patio and braced my butt against the cedar siding.

"What the hell are you doing here?"

Crap.

I really should have rubbed Larry before coming here. Of course it was Jackson. And he was furious. And stupidly handsome, his hair rumpled by the wind and his hands.

"I was invited," I said, rather lamely.

"I told you specifically you were not invited. Who told you to come? Because I know you. You wouldn't have come unless someone asked you to be here."

My mouth hung open, my cheeks getting hot with embarrassment. The people who had been ignoring me earlier were now watching me, because of Jackson. They were watching us and staring. I saw Chloe and Zoe just inside the house behind Jackson, their eyes wide with astonishment.

Vanessa, who hadn't gotten far, came back as if to rescue me.

"Jackson," Vanessa said, but he turned on her.

"Vanessa," Jackson said carefully, like she was a fragile piece of glass. "I've got this. Why don't you head back down to the beach near the bonfire?"

"I don't get it. What's the problem? She just wanted to come to the party."

"This was a mistake," I said, feeling my whole body ignite with rage. "I'll just go."

Jackson grabbed me by the arm and all but dragged me down the brick steps to the shadows beside the house. If he thought we were hidden, he was mistaken. People followed, clinging to the edges of the light from the house and the fire on the beach.

This was a nightmare.

"I'm leaving, Jackson," I hissed at him. "You don't have to make this worse."

"What are you wearing?" He looked me up and down, his eyes taking apart my hair, hanging loose over my shoulders. The pink dress I'd thought looked nice. He seemed to have particular disdain for the pink lip gloss that matched.

"It's called a dress, Jackson."

"You're overdressed for a beach party, Lola. Who were you trying to impress?"

"Thanks for the advice. You look nice, too." He wore a white linen shirt, held together with two buttons and a pair of dark shorts. He did look nice. Rich. Like he belonged. No Kmart sale rack for him. "Very uniform for a rich guy."

"You didn't answer my question. Why are you here?"

"Because the whole fucking town is here, Jackson. I thought, jeez, he can't be such an asshole that I'm the only one who can't come? I guess I was wrong. You are just that asshole."

I shoved at his chest and tried to get past him. Over his shoulder, I could see people had their phones out, and, I wanted to die.

Don't do this, Jackson. Please don't do this.

That was the thing about Jackson, he did what he wanted, and clearly what he wanted was to humiliate me.

He grabbed me by the elbow, forcing me to stop. He leaned down, his breath across my face, his voice in my ear. I couldn't stop the chills that ran down my back.

"Who invited you?"

"It doesn't matter."

"It matters to me."

"Why? You going to drag them out, too?"

He leaned even closer, and I could smell the champagne he'd been drinking. I had this stupid, insane thought if I just leaned forward, just a little, I could almost taste it. His eyes widened, as if he read my mind. We were doing it again, the air between us was changing into something else.

Time got weird and so did space, and I wasn't sure if we stood there for a second or ten minutes.

Kiss me. Or let me go.

He did neither, but he did lean back, shattering that terrible moment.

"Who invited you to my house?" he asked.

I didn't see the point in not answering. "Simon," I told him. "Simon texted me and told me to come. Okay?"

"Simon," Jackson repeated.

"Somebody call my name?" It was Simon, strolling up to us, a glass of something in one hand and one of my buffalo wings in the other. He also looked good in his rolled-up khakis and linen shirt.

Jackson whirled on him. "You invited Lola to this party?"

"Simon?" Vanessa said, coming up behind both Simon and Jackson. Apparently, she hadn't taken Jackson's advice and stuck to the bonfire.

Great, I thought. *More people to witness my humiliation.*

Simon smiled at Vanessa. His charming I should be in the royal family smile.

"What? We needed some actual food besides oysters, so I placed a delivery order from the diner girl."

Diner girl.

It was like getting smacked across the face from someone you never expected would hit you. So, it hurt twice as bad.

"She's just here delivering food?" Jackson asked, like he didn't believe Simon. As if to prove it, Simon lifted the wing in his hand. Whatever bullshit was between them, I'd been the stupid serving girl all along.

"Why else would she be here?" Simon asked. "You said she wasn't invited."

Don't cry. Don't cry. Not here. Not in front of these people.

I tried to edge around them. My head down, my hair hiding my blazing red cheeks. The tears in my eyes. I took two steps.

"Lola."

I did not want to turn. Every cell in my body was telling me to move, to keep moving forward. To just leave this moment in the past, but Jackson's voice, the command of it —the stupid fucking authority of it—made me stop.

I turned.

He held out some cash.

"For the food," he said, quietly.

My eyes dropped to the bills in his hand, then I looked up at his face.

We stared at each other, the air between us crackling like the fire roaring on the beach.

He swallowed and looked away first. "Take it, leave it. It doesn't matter to me."

Then he threw the money at my feet. I was strong, but I wasn't that strong. I looked down.

There were hundreds of dollars, lifting and drifting in the breeze off the ocean. *Hundreds*.

It was in that moment I understood my mom. The way she'd turned down that check from Mrs. Dumont that probably would have made our lives easier for a long time. It wasn't about pride. My pride didn't factor into it.

It's that I wouldn't touch that man's disgusting money with a ten-foot pole.

I had just wanted to go to a party, I thought.

Then I turned and walked away.

8

Five Years Later

My Three Favorite Things

Calico Cove
Karaoke Brunch
Two for one sale on cat food

Lola, Age 23

"What is this?" I asked, staring up at the sign and the fence that had gone up around the old radio station building that was on the other side of the pine trees behind Pappas' Diner. The fence surrounded the old brick building, the parking lot and the trees adjacent to our property. The fence almost touched my vacation chair.

"It says it on the sign." Georgie pointed at the sign.

COMING SOON: A SHELLS INCORPORATED OPERATION.

I knew what was on the sign. I could read. When we looked up Shells Incorporated as a business, the first thing that came up was Shells Family Restaurants. It was a chain up and down the East Coast.

"But what does this *mean*?" I shrieked.

I knew what it meant. That a company, apparently specializing in family restaurants, was going to open right next to Pappas' Diner.

But was it a cosmic joke? An existential punishment?

That was the real question.

"Try and calm down, Lola," Georgie said, patting my arm.

"Pappas' is a family restaurant."

"I know."

"We don't need two family restaurants. *Right next to each other*."

The top of my head was lifting off. I couldn't feel my face. The rage was changing me on a cellular level. Or was it fear?

"No," Georgie said. "I can't imagine that would be good for business."

"Who is doing this?" I asked and stepped up to the sign trying to find some fine print. A phone number. A name. Anything. Some place to direct this rage/fear.

But there was nothing. Just a big white sign with blue letters and a cartoon old-fashioned woman holding a coffee pot that might as well have said, LOLA PAPPAS THIS IS THE END OF YOUR WORLD AS YOU KNOW IT.

"Breathe, honey," Georgie said and shifted the patting to my back. I sucked in air and let it out in fits and starts. I was starting to see stars. What was I going to do? How was I going to fix this? The world was going dark.

"Lola!" Georgie said, and led me back around the fence to that little area on our side of the pine trees that I called my vacation spot. I'd upgraded from a milk crate to a deck chair. I had a little table for a cup of coffee and the cat food was now kept in a container outside so the kittens were always around.

Georgie shooed one out of my seat, sat me down and forced my head down between my legs.

"Breathe," he said. "You're no help to me passed out on the sidewalk."

I did what Georgie said until the stars were gone, and I sat back up, sprawled in my vacation chair, unsure how I was going to find the will to go on.

Then I said the one thing to be true above everything else.

"I'm so glad my father isn't here to see this," I whispered to Georgie, who nodded solemnly.

Dad died last year. Heart attack in his sleep. Quick and fast. All the pain was for those he left behind.

Me. Georgie. And his new wife.

"Did you see it?" Tiffani with an i came out the back door.

Speak of the devil.

"It's hard to miss, Tiffani," I said.

She'd been my stepmom for three years, and I couldn't say I hated her, but I did not *like* her. Or enjoy her. I barely tolerated her. And even though she put up a good front, I think it was safe to say the feeling was mutual.

We were like strangers trapped on a desert island who had to smile at each other as we tried to survive a hurricane.

"What do you think it means?" she asked.

"You can go over there and look yourself!" I cried, taking out a tiny bit of my grim feelings on my stepmom. Wasn't that what stepmoms were for?

"Lola," Georgie murmured. Poor Georgie, he was trapped on this island, too, and he was just trying to get us not to kill and eat each other.

"It says a Shells Incorporated Operation. We looked up the company, and apparently, they are a chain of family restaurants," I sighed.

"Like a diner?" she asked.

"That's basically what a family restaurant is, Tiffani."

The competition was moving in directly next door.

"When?" she asked.

"It doesn't say."

"Who is building it? Why are they building it there?"

"Again. It doesn't say."

I stood, pulled down the hem of the uniform we were now wearing at Pappas'. Bright pink with little white collars and cap sleeves that came to a point. They were too short if you asked me. Which Tiffani did, but then ignored me.

Tiffani claimed they were Chloe's idea, and they were so clever and retro and Instagram able—but I knew, and Chloe knew, they were Jackson's idea from years ago. So, I hated them even more.

"What are we going to do?" Tiffani asked, and now it was my turn to take her by the shoulders and lead her to my vacation chair and sit her down. She was not meant to be a restaurant owner.

She didn't ask for it, but when Dad died, he'd left it to her in his will.

Which, let me tell you, had nearly driven me right out of town. Then Georgie had talked me off the ledge.

He wanted you to have a life outside of this place. This was his last chance to try and make it happen.

Dad did not seem to understand that all I wanted was this place.

"Well," I said. "First thing we're going to find out is who is behind Shells Incorporated. We need to talk to a human not a sign."

Tiffani had her arms crossed over her chest and was shaking her head. "No, this is a sign."

Georgie pointed to the sign. "Clearly."

"No, I mean, now is the time. We have to sell the diner before this place gets built."

I sucked in a breath so big it was hard to believe there was oxygen left on the planet. Georgie grabbed my hand.

"Jesus take the wheel," he breathed. He was going through a hard-core Carrie Underwood phase.

"Think about it," Tiffani said, warming up to her idea. "It's win-win. We sell now and avoid going head-to-head with the competition, or maybe we can sell to the competition and let them do what they want with the space."

"We're not selling Pappas'! It's a Calico Cove institution," I said.

"Lola, we've talked about this—"

"No, *you* have talked about this," I said.

She'd started talking about it not a second after we buried my father actually, but that's all it had been for the past year. Just talk.

"The roof is about to go," she said. "One more winter like last winter and the building will fall down."

"We can fix the roof," I said.

"With what? Magic?" Tiffani asked. "There's no money. There hasn't been money for years. Your father lied—"

"He didn't lie," I snapped.

He'd never said we were swimming in money. We'd never pretended to be rich.

We just didn't realize how thin the margin of profit was in this business. When my mom died and we'd hired Tiffani and the girls, they needed to be paid in salary. Whereas my mom had taken none.

Beyond that, we'd learned my dad had taken out a mortgage on the property to cover back taxes he owed, because he'd screwed all that up after mom died.

He could have told me. He could have said he didn't know what he was doing after Mom died. Instead, he'd just smiled and said everything was fine.

The truth was, we were in debt. Not just a dishwasher on the fritz and a leaky roof debt. So much debt, even if we had the best summer ever, the take-home just couldn't cover it.

Tiffani had been looking for a way out since the moment we came to that conclusion.

"We're not selling," I repeated, and Tiffani had the good sense to not comment, and instead, went back inside. "I can fix this," I told Georgie.

I *had* to fix this.

The Next Day

I STOOD JUST outside the front doors of the municipal building and huffed. My mission to find the owners behind the Shells company had failed.

Despite bribing Hector, the town business clerk, with a grilled Reuben, all he could point me to was a corporate address that was just a PO Box in downtown Boston.

It was like there wasn't a human behind the business.

Or if there was, that human didn't want to be known.

The municipal building was directly across from the pier that jutted out into the white tipped waves of the Atlantic. There was a square lined on all sides by tourist shops and ice-cream parlors, although the Big Scoop was, hands down, the best in town. In the past few years, there'd been a change in the businesses around the square—there was a new fancy dress shop with custom bridal gowns and a florist that catered to the wedding business in town.

I started down the steps as Annie, who owned the local bookstore, was coming up.

Annie was one of the Piedmonts who lived out on the small private island past the lighthouse. Well, her parents lived there. She lived above her bookstore. Annie came from summer people but had become a local. It didn't happen often, and it wasn't easy for Annie. Local distrust of summer people was baked in.

But she was one of us now.

"Hey, Lola, I saw the sign and looked them up online," Annie said as soon as she reached me. "You okay?"

"Well, if considering arson is okay, I'm great. How are you?"

Annie smiled and scrunched up her nose to push her glasses back up her face. Annie was kind of adorable. She looked like a sweet mouse.

"If it gets to that point, count me in." She was a sweet mouse with teeth. I loved that about her. "We can't let these chain restaurants eat up our businesses."

"Don't I know it. What are you here for?"

"Gotta see Hector about some permits. You know how it is running a small business. It's all about the permits."

I laughed. "Well, you're in luck. I just made Hector

supremely happy with a free sandwich. He should be in an excellent mood."

"Awesome."

At the bottom of the steps, I turned left to head to the diner, but nearly ran into a woman who wasn't a local but looked really familiar.

Thin and tall with long hair the color of caramel. She wore a cropped pink puffer coat and black leggings with pristine white tennis shoes. Honestly, shoes so white it's like she floated over the ground so they never touched dirt.

"Oh, my God."

I looked up from the white shoes to the woman's face. Slowly she pulled down her mirrored aviator glasses. Oh. Fuck. I immediately looked over her shoulder for her brother, my stomach curdling with remembered humiliation, but she appeared to be alone.

"Lola!" she cried.

"Hello, Vanessa."

To my total surprise—my utter shock, really—she threw her arms around me in a tight hug. She smelled like vanilla and money.

"It's so crazy that I haven't seen you since that night."

That night.

That was one way to put it, I guess. I liked to think of it as The Night of Smoke and Carnage. The Night That Shall Never Be Named.

"How have you been?" I asked, pasting a big fake smile on my face.

"Great," she said, pulling a strand of hair that had gotten stuck to her lip gloss with a finger that looked like a talon. "Totally great. So great."

That was a lot of greats. Made me think maybe things weren't so great.

"What about you?" she asked, wide-eyed like she was on the edge of her seat.

Well, my father died last year. Left my diner to my stepmom. Our roof is caving in, and a chain restaurant is going to put us under. Oh, and now my evil stepmother is threatening to sell the restaurant.

"Great," I said.

"We should totally catch up," she said, and it took everything in me not to laugh. Catch up? On what?

"What are you doing here?" I asked.

"Oh, applying for a wedding license. You haven't heard?" she asked,

"Heard what?"

She lifted one taloned hand to reveal a ring the size of a golf ball. "I'm getting married," she squealed.

"Wow!" I cried. "Who is the lucky guy?"

Approaching us from the parking lot at the side of the building was Simon Turnberry, looking as blonde and handsome and evil as ever.

"Why, Simon of course," she cried, curling her arm around Simon while he looked at me like he'd never seen me before in his life. "Hello, we've only been dating for five years! I finally said Simon, are we getting married or what?"

Five years. They'd been dating for five *years?*

"Hello, Lola, isn't it?" he said with all that cool charm I'd been suckered by before.

"Oh, you can just call me diner girl," I said cheerily. "When and where are you two tying the knot?"

I asked, though I knew. Obviously I knew. They wouldn't apply for a license here in Calico Cove if they were getting married someplace else.

"Here, of course. Labor Day weekend. We've decided to

do it at the house, instead of the hotel, though. It's going to be small and intimate. Right honey?" she asked Simon.

"So, I've been told," he said, like he was being funny.

"Congratulations," I said, without looking at Simon at all. "I hope you're very happy."

I got the fuck out of there.

9

Lola

The next morning, I had the 4:00 AM shift. Which, again, I kind of liked. I wrapped up the bagel sandwiches, made the coffee and talked to the lobstermen.

And watched the world come alive out the windows.

"Morning, Roy," I said to Roy Barnes as he came in for his usual, egg, bacon and cheese bagel and a large coffee. Roy grunted at me. Paid. Then turned to leave.

There were times when I thought, if I could actually have a conversation with Roy, he might be a catch. He was super-hot, owned his boat. He had a kid, although Nora was actually his cousin's baby that had been left to him in a will. A built-in ready-made family.

And Roy was actively looking for a wife. Heck, he had even advertised for one with signs all over town. Except no one really took them seriously. At least not the locals.

The problem with Roy Barnes was any woman with him would be doomed to a life of silence. At least on his part.

He stopped at the door. "This bullshit next door?" he said, pointing in the direction of the Shells sign.

"Yeah?"

"It's bullshit."

Awww. What a sweetheart.

"Thanks, Roy."

He tipped his hat and left.

I went to the back to get more supplies when I heard the bell over the door ring.

"I'll be right there!" I shouted and grabbed a sleeve of to-go cups. The bell rang again, and I arrived out front expecting two customers; instead, there were none.

On the counter, though, there was a thick creamy envelope with black calligraphy on it.

Lola Pappas it read. I ran my finger over the elegant script. There was something about seeing your name written like that. Fancy. Important.

I opened it and pulled out the invitation. Honestly, the paper was so thick there must have been half a tree in it.

You are invited to an evening of romance and mystery celebrating the love of Vanessa Dumont and Simon Turnberry. Dumont Estate. June 30th, 8:00 PM

"Estate," I muttered. "When did it become an estate?" Could anyone just walk around and call their homes estates? If that was the case, I lived in the Pappas' estate behind the public elementary school.

The address was the house at the end of the public beach.

Costumes encouraged, masks mandatory.

No gifts.

Well, la de da, I thought, and flipped it over expecting to see, written in black marker, EVERYONE BUT YOU LOLA. There was nothing written there. There was no extra paper in the envelope. It looked like a regular invitation.

Vanessa might have invited me with sincerity. It had been an awkward but genuine hug in front of the municipal building. But even as I entertained for one millisecond the invitation was real, I was throwing it in the garbage.

Because I knew the truth. It wasn't an invitation…it was a trap.

The question was, who had come into the diner and just left it here for me?

~

LATER THAT DAY, Chloe and Zoe showed up for their shift at the diner all abuzz, their voices at the highest end of the human range.

"What's going on?" I asked, making another pot of decaf while the two of them looked at their phones.

"Everyone in town got invitations delivered last night or this morning to Vanessa's engagement ball."

"It's at the Dumont's house," Zoe said.

"And it's a masquerade. Can you even believe it?"

"Somehow, no," I said. "And also yes."

"And, rumors have been confirmed," Zoe said. "Jackson is back. Apparently, he arrived in the middle of the night."

I felt that hunted feeling along the back of my neck.

Jackson was back. After so long, my tormentor had finally returned.

"In a helicopter." Zoe said, as if he'd flown in on a magic horse. "He's here for the ball, obviously."

I could not care less. I mean, I spent a lot of time not

caring any less about Jackson. I was in negative caring numbers.

"I'm just saying," Chloe said. "The town is going to go crazy about this party so don't like... be sad, or whatever."

"Why would I be sad?"

"Because you're not going to be invited. I mean, even Madame Za got an invitation. They must be really pissed at you for crashing that last party."

"I didn't crash that party," I snapped. "And for your information I got an invitation to this one." I immediately hated myself for giving a shit.

"When did it come?" they asked in unison as if they didn't believe me.

"Someone dropped it off here at the restaurant during the early shift."

"Are you sure it's real?"

I pulled out the plastic garbage can and dug through it until I found the invitation. I waved it in their faces, coffee grinds falling on the floor.

"Wow," Chloe said.

I threw it back into the garbage. "Whatever. I'm not going."

"Because you don't want to get embarrassed like you did last time," Zoe said thoughtfully. "That makes sense. There was, like, video of you getting kicked out all over Instagram."

"Oh yes, thank you for the reminder."

The fall out hadn't been too bad. The summer people were gone practically the next day and some of the dummies in high school passed the video around for the first few weeks of school. But Joey Apeton got pantsed during a basketball practice and the video of that became far more interesting.

By Thanksgiving my humiliation was private once again.

"Besides, you don't have a dress," Chloe added. "Or a mask. You probably wouldn't even know what to do at a fancy party—"

"Chloe!" Georgie yelled from the back. "I need you to clean the bathroom!"

"What?" Chloe shouted. "It's Zoe's turn."

"Nope." Georgie leaned in through the service window from the kitchen. "It's yours."

Chloe sighed dramatically and grabbed the cleaning supplies out of the cabinet and left in a huff.

"Well," Zoe said, like she was trying to make amends. "Chloe is right. It's not really your thing anyway. A fancy party with costumes and champagne and stuff."

"Yeah, gross," I said.

Because, of course, she thought that about me, and of course, she was wrong.

Didn't every girl like parties and champagne?

"Plus, Jackson will be there," Zoe said, "And everyone knows how much you hate him."

"I don't even think about him," I said.

What had he been doing these past few years? Was he different? The same?

Nope. Not thinking about him. At. All.

"We'll have all the fun for you," Zoe said.

I didn't think it was intended to be mean, but it still hurt. Chloe, Zoe and I had not made the transition to stepsisters very well.

The three-bedroom house behind the elementary school I'd called home my whole life was too small for me and all of their beauty supplies. All of their egos and delusions of becoming Kardashian-like influencers.

Sure, the fighting had died down as we'd gotten older,

but the scar tissue of resentment and dislike was going to last forever.

"You do that," I said and walked away.

"EMERGENCY MEETING," Georgie said, later that afternoon, pushing a Cobb Salad through the window from the kitchen.

"When?" I asked.

Emergency meeting sometimes meant we snuck a shot of vodka in the storage room and sometimes meant pooling our money to pay the plumber for some work. Sometimes it meant sitting in my car and scream-singing all the lyrics to Miley Cyrus.

"Ten minutes. Office."

Ten minutes later I pushed the rolly chair under the window ledge so the mechanism wouldn't toss me onto the ground and sat. Georgie followed me in. Something was up with a capital U.

"We're in trouble," he said, his arms crossed over his chest. Mom always said Georgie was built like a spark plug. Even at forty he had muscles on top of muscles in that white T-shirt that said QUEER AF on it.

"*You're* in trouble," I shot back. A lame attempt at our old joke.

"We need a loan so we can buy the business from Tiffani, so she doesn't go selling it to other people. That's what we need."

My first thought was my mom would love that. Me and Georgie keeping the diner alive. It didn't solve the Shells problem but getting Tiffani out of the picture would make life, in general, easier.

"She's not going to sell the diner," I told him. "I mean, I know what she said the other day, but she wouldn't. She couldn't. Tiffani and I are not exactly close, but she has to know what selling this diner would do to me."

Georgie lifted one perfect, manicured eyebrow that sent my stomach into my feet.

"What?" I asked. "What do you know that I don't?"

He threw the *Portland Press* classifieds down on the desk.

"She's already talked to a real estate agent and put an ad in the paper." I grabbed the paper, scanning the listings. "She wants half a million dollars."

There it was. The ad. In black and white. *Established local and beloved diner for sale in up-and-coming busy tourist town. Turnkey. Million-dollar potential.*

"Well, shit just got real, didn't it?" I whispered.

THE SECOND TIFFANI showed up for her shift, I confronted her.

"When were you going to tell me about this?" I asked and put down the paper with the ad on the counter in front of her.

I'd circled the ad in red.

Tiffani sighed and pressed her hand to her forehead. I knew what was coming. She'd claim a migraine or that her nerves just couldn't handle this because it was all too much.

But she didn't do any of that. Tiffani turned and looked me dead in the eye. "I wasn't," she said, and I gasped. "I wasn't until it was sold. Until it was done."

"Why?"

"So you wouldn't do whatever it is you're about to do

right now. Make me feel guilty for getting rid of this chain around our necks."

"It's not your chain!"

"Your father made it my chain! I'm done with it. I thought this was supposed to be a thriving business and all it is...is work. Work and more work. For what? To barely scratch out a living?"

"Fine. Then give it to me. Walk away. Sell the house but let me have this diner."

Was I begging? I was begging. This was my family I was clinging to. My history. My future. She had no right to it.

She looked away from me, her jaw clenched hard. "Your father never wanted that for you. He wanted you to get out of this town. To go to college. When we sell, I'll commit to giving you enough money to do that."

"Don't pretend to care about what my father wanted for me," I nearly spat. Tired of all this bullshit. "You just want the money."

"That's right." She turned on me, eyes blazing, her desperation on full display.

She thought she'd landed some reliable widower with my dad. A successful businessman who maybe couldn't give her everything she ever dreamed of, but could keep her safe. Could keep her girls safe. She'd made a bad bet.

"That's right, I want a half a million dollars, Lola. Because that is what your father owes me. A dollar for every lie he told me."

I rolled my eyes. This was where the twins got their sense of drama, and I wasn't interested in listening to her talk shit about my dad.

"Have you had any offers?" I asked, a terrible shaking in my belly that was part anger and part hopelessness.

"Not offers," she said. "But enquiries."

I moaned, feeling everything I wanted start to slip away. How was this happening?

Dad. How could you not see this happening?

"Would you sell it to me?" I asked.

Tiffani laughed. "How in the world are you going to get half a million dollars?"

"Well, maybe not half a million but surely—"

"No!" Tiffani held up her hand and shook her head. "No. Don't waste your breath. I'm not giving you the diner."

"I'm not asking you to give it to me," I whispered. "I'll pay you. But, Tiffani, come on...half a million? You know this place isn't worth that. The roof needs to be replaced, the kitchen has to be remodeled. If we're even going to try to compete with what's coming next door, then we're going to have to think about redoing the entire decor."

"According to my real estate agent, that's what the comps are for restaurants in this area with an established reputation," Tiffani said, eyes blazing. "It's what I am owed."

I stepped back, because I'd heard all this before. She was only getting more fevered.

"I thought your father was successful." She grabbed my arms so hard it hurt. "I thought he could take care of me. Of my girls. And he couldn't even take care of you," she practically spat.

"When did you ever want for anything?" I demanded.

"This argument is over. If you can get a loan, fine. I'll sell you the diner. But you won't be getting any deals. Not from me."

Story of my life, I thought. I just needed a half million dollars.

∼

"HEY, CAN YOU COVER FOR ME?" I asked Georgie as I popped into the kitchen, leaving Tiffani to stew in her greed in the office she'd retreated to.

"What?" He was flipping pancakes as fast as he could.

"Tiffani said she would sell us the diner, but no special deals. I know Mari's mom got a loan to expand the bakery. I think I should talk to them. They must have had a business plan before going to the bank. If we can follow the same blueprint..."

"Good idea." He nodded. "Go. I'll think of something to tell the wonder twins and the evil stepmother."

I tore off my apron, and in my pink uniform and Converse, I ran down Main Street towards the town square to Bobette and Belle Bakery.

Stephanie had started the bakery when Mari was practically a baby, but it didn't really start to take off until Calico Cove got into the wedding business. Then it grew so fast, they expanded the bakery to accommodate a larger kitchen and a cute dining area. Stephanie started to do really fancy wedding cakes, specialty desserts and high teas. She went from small town to big time with money from somewhere, and I needed that kind of magic.

Walking into Bobette and Belle was like walking into a beautiful cake museum. Stephanie had built a whole wall of display cakes, each more elaborate and beautiful than the last. There was a cake that looked like presents. Another looked like it had been cracked open to reveal gemstones. Another looked like it was covered in beautiful delicate monarch butterflies. Another looked like antique hat boxes.

My favorite cake they'd made, though, was for this fancy wedding of a serious horror fan. We lived in Maine, so the Stephen King groupies were everywhere. The all-black cake looked like it had a million red-eyed spiders crawling out of it.

The secret to their success: the combination of Stephanie's magic in the kitchen and Mari's artistic vision. The year after my mom died and Mari and I had both graduated from high school. Mari had gone to Boston for art school but came back after the first year with a smile on her face I never quite believed.

She didn't go back.

When pushed about what happened, Mari just clammed up, and sometimes I didn't know if being her friend meant pushing harder or letting her have her privacy.

Decorating cakes wasn't her full-time job. Her primary focus was on children's book illustrations, but when she did go all out for her mom, it was magic.

"Hey, Lola!" Stephanie said, coming from the back room wearing a white apron smeared in the palest of pink frosting. "You here to see Mari? Unfortunately she's doing me a favor and delivering a cake."

"No, actually, I wanted to talk to you."

"Really?" she said, her face all smiles. "What's up kiddo?" Then her smile fell. "Is this about that Shells sign? You know we have your back, right?"

"No. I mean, yes. Sort of. I know you got a loan when you expanded the bakery. How did you go about the process?"

"Oh, that was a whole saga. I went to the bank, but they turned me down."

"What?" Banks could do that?

"The bank is notoriously stingy with local businesses. Or they were. It might have changed in the last few years with the wedding boom, but the loan officer at the bank will not be cutting you any favors."

"So, what did you do?"

"Well, Annie over at the bookstore told me about private funding that's available to local businesses."

"From where?"

"There was an application process through the Calico Cove Investment Bureau."

"I've never even heard of that."

"Your dad would have. They started working with small businesses in this area about three years ago. I told him he should take advantage of the money, but you know how he was..."

Proud. Stubborn. She didn't need to finish that sentence.

"I don't really know who is behind it all, probably those summer people looking for tax breaks or something. Anyhoo, my application got accepted, and they gave me the loan. You need a business plan. Do you have one of those?"

"No."

"I'll email you mine. You can copy a lot of the language."

"So this better business thing is still around?" I asked.

It almost sounded too good to be true. I didn't like it when things sounded too good to be true, because I'd already learned at the ripe old age of twenty-three that life, at least for me, was never that easy.

"As far as I know. Let me see what I've got." She went over to the cash register that had what Mari always called the junk drawer to end all junk drawers underneath it. "I saved the card because I was thinking it would be kind of fun to open up a little sidewalk café, but with all this cake business, I don't know where I'd get the time."

She pulled out a pair of scissors, a plastic bird, a giant pair of fuzzy dice, and, finally, a card with a bent down edge.

"Here it is," she said with a whoop. I was reminded suddenly of Stephanie and my mother, who'd been childhood best friends, sitting around our kitchen table telling stories about high school and laughing so hard my mom farted.

Out of the blue I missed my mom so bad.

"Use it in good health," she said, handing it to me. "If there's anything I can do…"

"You've done it, trust me."

"How much do you need?" she asked. "I've got this little nest egg for the sidewalk café—"

"No, Stephanie, I couldn't. Honestly."

"How much?"

"Half a million."

Stephanie's mouth gaped open.

"Yeah," I said, and I took the card. "I know. Tiffani is selling the café, and I'm going to buy it."

"That woman," Stephanie said. When Dad's engagement had been announced, Stephanie stormed into the diner and gave my father an earful. She had not been invited to the wedding.

"I know." I lifted the business card. "Thanks for this."

Calico Cove Investment Bureau is what it said on the card. There was a phone number and an email address. That's it. No names. Not even a logo.

"This couldn't be real," I muttered to myself.

I made my way to the diner and let Georgie know I at least had a place to start. He said Tiffani with an i, had left in a huff not long after our confrontation. Too upset, apparently, to handle her shift.

I sat behind her desk. The advertisement that put my whole past, my whole life up for sale, was still sitting on the desk next to her computer.

No chance I was using that computer to send the email. I didn't want to tip Tiffani off in any way to what I was doing, so I used my personal email on my phone.

To: CCIB@mail.com
From: Lola Pappas
Subject Line: Help.
Hello,

*My name is Lola Pappas, and my family has run the Pappas'
Diner in downtown Calico Cove for three generations. We are a
beloved cornerstone of the town, a tourist destination, and we
need help.*

*I got this email address from Stephanie Smith, who runs
Bobette and Belle, the local bakery. She said you were able to help
with her expansion when the bank couldn't.*

*Before submitting my business plan, I'm sending this email to
determine if this program is still active.*

Thank you in advance for your consideration,
Lola Pappas

HITTING send felt like an absolute act of faith. It was almost
painful how much hope I felt.

*Keep it together. There is a good chance the email won't even
work.*

Georgie barked out that he needed the trash taken out. I
needed a distraction from my phone, so I was happy to
oblige. I picked up the bags where he left them by the door
and pushed out the back exit then tossed them in the
dumpster.

For some reason the Shells sign caught my attention. I
was extremely gratified to see that someone—my guess was
Roy—had taken a can of spray paint and sprayed BULL-
SHIT across the sign in bright blue letters.

Hmmm... I thought with a smile. *Now, that feels like a sign.*

10

Lola

Over the next few weeks, the town started to fill up, not just with tourists, but people who were arriving for that stupid masquerade. It felt like there were double the number of snobs running around town. Not that they ate much at the diner. Our food was never good enough for them.

Every time the bell rang over the door I felt my heart drop, expecting Vanessa. Or Simon.

Or Jackson.

If the rumors were true, he'd been in town for weeks, but I hadn't spotted him once. It wasn't like I was scared of him walking in. I just wasn't relishing the inevitable.

Did he know I was on the guest list for the ball? If he found out, would he uninvite me?

Did he even think of me at all? I mean, who was I to him but the diner girl?

Except sometimes there were those memories of us. As kids. Then not as kids. Buried so deeply in my skull.

I tried never to think about our kiss. I really did.

It was just that every once in a while, when I read a good part in a romance novel— well, I would think about that kiss in the storage room.

Which sadly, was still the most intensely passionate moment of my life.

Note to self: Get a love life!

So, yes, I felt myself living on painful eggshells, waiting for him to walk in.

Day after day, he didn't.

Of course, everyone was talking about their costumes, which didn't help distract me.

Even Georgie.

"I think I'm going with 1970's Hollywood Glamour," he said, and I turned on him, my hands full of creamers.

"You're going to the masquerade?" I asked him, with not a small amount of shock and outrage.

"Don't say that like I'm betraying you."

"But it's the Dumonts. I thought you were going to stand with me in solidarity and *not* go."

He slumped against the fridge. "But...champagne?"

"We have champagne."

"They have the good stuff."

I couldn't argue with that.

"And costumes."

"We do Karaoke Brunch the last Sunday of every month. We wear costumes then, too. Remember my be-dazzled Dolly Parton vest?"

He looked down at his sneakers. "That's not the same. These are the real deal. Come on, honey, it's my chance to wear couture!"

It was my turn to slump. I couldn't deny him the opportunity to go out in full drag and show those yahoos how it was done.

"You know," he said, stepping toward me carefully. "You could still go. You have the invite. We can get you a dress..."

"No. Georgie. No way. Not if I had to."

Georgie shook his head at me, his gold earrings catching the light. "He really did a number on you, didn't he?"

Maybe the smart thing would have been to pretend I didn't know what Georgie was talking about. But we never worked that way, me and Georgie. So, I just put the creamers in the pocket of my apron and headed for the dining room.

CHECKING my phone for email was my new obsession. Not that it helped. I still hadn't heard back from the CCIB, which should have been my sign the program was no longer active.

I'd tried to keep my hopes reasonable, but clearly, I'd lost control of them. It didn't stop us, though. In our down time, which meant very early mornings and sometimes after we closed, Georgie and I pulled together a business plan of which we were proud, and we had an appointment with the bank next month.

We'd gotten lucky that Tiffani's enquiries so far had just been that. No actual offers had been made.

"You good to lock up?" Georgie asked, stifling a yawn. We closed at nine during the week, and Georgie had drawn the short straw and had been here since dawn.

"I got it. You go get some sleep."

He waved goodbye and headed out the door, and I turned off the lights and checked the alarm, not in any hurry to go home to Tiffani, Chloe and Zoe. Their endless talk about the masquerade was enough to drive a person to drink.

There'd been other times since Dad died, when I just choose not to go to the place that had been my home. I slept at the diner instead and woke up early for the lobstermen.

I imagined Mom and Dad in heaven furious with me.

Sometimes I wondered, if heaven was real and they were up there together, how Mom greeted Dad after marrying Tiffani with an i. I smiled thinking of her cussing him out, giving him a whack on the side of his head. Then kissing him like her life depended on it.

Dad and Tiffani never kissed. Not that I ever saw. All her flirtation ended once he married her. Then fighting, mostly over money, started.

I hated that Dad went out like that. My mother's love usurped by Tiffani's anger.

Well, I thought, *I'm not going to let the diner go out the same way. Not on my watch.*

I went to the back to grab my purse, thinking I'd head home for a few hours, maybe sneak in through the garage so I didn't have to talk to Tiffani or the twins. Get some sleep and come right back in the morning.

In front, the bell over the door rang.

"You forget your phone again, Georgie?" I shouted as I made my way to the dining room.

My breath caught.

Standing there, in all his fabulously handsome glory, was Jackson Dumont.

I hated to admit it, but he'd only grown more handsome in the past five years. His dark hair was a little longer, like he wasn't keeping up with his fancy salon visits. His bangs brushed over his eyebrows.

He looked bigger to me. Taller, more filled out in the

chest. When I'd cried in his arms that one time, my chin had been as tall as his shoulder. When he'd pushed me back against the storage room wall to kiss me, he hadn't had to bend down as far as he would now.

Damn.

He wore a simple light-weight blue V-neck sweater. The kind that was perfect for June in Calico Cove once the sun went down and it got a little chilly.

He would know that. He would know what the summer weather was like in Calico Cove because part of it was his home, too. Even if I never wanted to admit that.

Five years he'd been gone. Five years since we'd kissed. Five years since that night at the party...

I didn't even know what I was feeling right now, but somewhere buried under all of that was a sense of relief. Because there might have been a time or two when I'd thought, *what if I never see him again*? And the thought had hurt.

"Lola," he whispered. With this crazy sort of reverence. Like he was seeing a ghost.

My heart was pounding in my chest, and I could feel my palms getting sweaty. Why? Why did I always have this reaction around him? Why did he always make me FEEL?

My skin, my internal organs, my damn eyelashes.

I busied myself with something stupid under the counter so I wouldn't have to look at him.

"Jackson," I said, the word squeezed out of my tight throat. There was no need to be rude, after all. So what if he'd kissed me, then humiliated me, then demeaned my entire existence?

You need to be empathetic.

My mother's words coming back to me.

Did I? Did I really?

"I was just out taking a walk. Getting some air and...my feet led me here."

"You're in town for the big masquerade," I said. Only Vanessa's wedding had been enough to bring him back.

"You're coming, right? I...uh...saw you were on the guest list."

I shook my head, crossing my arms over my stomach, still not directly looking at him. Like he was an eclipse that would burn my eyes. "No, I'm afraid I can't make it that night. I've got to close the restaurant."

Then I thought, *he doesn't know. He doesn't know that my dad married Tiffani, that like my mom, my dad passed too young. That now I was left with no family and a restaurant that wasn't mine.*

It was strange because I wanted to tell him. I wanted to tell him everything. Just blurt it all out and let him carry some of the weight for me.

Then I remembered him tossing the money at my feet the night of the bonfire, and I knew I couldn't.

Because Jackson Dumont wasn't my friend. He wasn't.

"Lola, I was hoping...well, I was hoping maybe we could talk."

I thought of the summer when all we did was talk. Talk and talk and talk. Like we would never run out of things to say to one another. Like everything we said was so freaking important.

"What could you and I possibly have to talk about?"

"You could tell me your three favorite-"

No. No, we wouldn't be doing that.

"We're closed. You need to leave."

He shoved his hands into the pockets of his jeans.

"I wish you would come," he finally said. "To the party."

Was it stupid to believe he was actually being sincere?

All that history was just there sitting in between us.

"I can't."

He nodded. "Okay. Well, maybe I'll see you around town."

"Maybe," I said vaguely.

He looked at me again, stared really, then turned and walked out the door.

I collapsed against the counter and sucked in air.

There. That was done. I'd seen Jackson Dumont again and I hadn't crumbled.

Now, life could go on.

WHEN MY LITTLE pink house belonged to my parents, it was all I'd ever imagined a home could be. It was small, and there wasn't a whole lot of privacy—I'd heard my parents having sex more times then I wanted to count. But it was where I ate my Saturday morning cereal. Where my dad and I watched Patriots games. It was where my mom tried to garden and failed every year.

At the beginning, just after Dad and Tiffani got married, it wasn't too bad. Dad finally redid the attic. While it was small, it was big enough for me. The twins took my old bedroom. The AC never seemed to reach this part of the house, and I had to crouch when I walked in, but I had a door, and I was a little removed from the drama of the twins. Although I could always hear them through the floorboards, constantly bickering. Shouting for Tiffani to do something for them that they were more than capable of doing themselves.

Now, in the tiny attic, I felt how much this place was not

really mine anymore. It was like my memories weren't even here. They were all down at the diner.

The house was someone else's home, and I was the unfortunate ghost in the attic outstaying my welcome.

I had just taken my sneakers off before falling back on my squeaky twin bed.

I had to change into pajamas, wash my face, brush my teeth, all that stuff...but really, I just wanted to lie on this bed and pretend not to think about Jackson.

I wasn't so delusional to think he was sorry for what he'd done. He'd had five years to come back and apologize, but he never had. What was different now?

The phone in the pocket of my uniform dinged.

I took it out and saw the notification of a new email.

"Holy shit!" I said, sitting up. It was from the CCIB.

To: Lola Pappas
    From: CCIB
    Subject line: Delay
    Hello Ms. Pappas,
    Thank you for your interest in our program. Sorry for the delay in getting back to you. We've been tied up with a few other projects. As investors in Calico Cove, we are familiar with your diner. What do you need help with?
    CCIB

IT FELT like being struck by lightning.

I leaned back against the pillow and thought about my words as carefully as I'd thought about anything ever.

·   ·   ·

To: CCIB

From: Lola Pappas

Subject line. Re:Delay

Thank you for getting back to me. I would like to buy the diner from its current owner and make some much-needed repairs and improvements. The amount I'm looking for is $750,000.00.

Lola Pappas

I TOOK A DEEP BREATH, thinking about making it less, but then I'd only need more help. It wasn't just the roof. If I was going to compete with a Shells Family Restaurant, then I was going to need to redo it all.

I hit send and shook out my hands.

My email binged, immediately. Wow, that was fast. It was almost eleven at night. Someone was working late at the CCIB.

To: Lola Pappas

From: CCIB

Subject line: Re: Re: Delay

Lola,

Can I call you Lola if I'm allowed to be so informal? It's an interesting name. I have to wonder if you're named after the song.

Who is the current owner? I thought you owned it. According to your email it had been in your family for generations.

CCIB

⁓

To: CCIB

From: Lola Pappas

Subject line: Re: Re: Re: Delay

Of course you can call me Lola. I'm asking you for a lot of money. You can pretty much call me anything you want! Yes, I'm named after the song. My mom always said, as a name, it was everything she wanted her daughter to be: friendly and unique.

As for the current situation, well, it's a long family drama kind of story. My father died a year ago, and he left everything to his new wife, my stepmother. She's willing to sell it to me. Which is why I'm writing to you. I have a business plan, if you'd like to see it. With projected growth and profit for the next five years.

Never been a show girl,

Lola

≈

To: Lola Pappas

From: CCIB

Subject line: Re: Re: Re: Re: Delay

Lola, I am so sorry to hear about your father. He was a good man. And friendly and unique are great attributes. I imagine your mother was very proud of you.

Our deepest condolences,

CCIB

≈

I BLINKED, stunned and feeling a little... creeped out. I replied back.

To: CCIB

From: Lola Pappas

Subject line: Re: Re: Re: Re: Re: Delay

I'm sorry, maybe I should have asked. But do we know each other? How would you know my father?

Lola

∽

To: Lola Pappas

From: CCIB

Subject line: Re: Re: Re: Re: Re: Re: Delay

Lola,

No, we're not acquainted now. My family spent a few summers there when I was young. I liked the milkshakes your father made. The Investment Bureau is completely anonymous on our end. It keeps things cleaner this way. Please attach your business plan for review. Once we've had a chance to look at it, we'll be in touch.

CCIB

OH. I suppose that made sense. People who were investing in Calico Cove had to have spent time here, and Pappas' was basically a pillar in this town. I smiled sadly because my dad's milkshakes had been legendary.

I attached the business proposal Georgie and I had worked so hard on, then hit send.

Now I was back in the business of keeping my hope under control.

11

Lola

The next morning when I showed up at the diner, the first thing I noticed was the sign next door was gone. The Shells with the Bullshit written across it was just...gone.

"Do you think they changed their minds?" Georgie asked, as we stared, blinking into the gray morning, at the place where the sign used to be.

"Do you think we're that lucky?" I asked him.

"No," he laughed. "I don't."

The day was one of those cool late June days, like summer wasn't ready to commit to Maine quite so fast. I wore a sweater over my uniform and was still cold.

These were my mom's favorite kind of days. She'd tell Dad we'd be late for work, and we'd climb the bluff behind town to Hanolan's Pointe where we could look out at the ocean and the town.

"This is a good place," my mom would say, wrapping me up in her arms, pressing our cheeks together. "But there are lots of good places. You should see all of them."

"This is the best place though, right?" I asked her. Partly because I was a kid, and partly because when I was with her, wherever she was had to be the best place.

"What are you thinking about?" Georgie asked. "You looked so far away for a second."

"Just thinking," I said, feeling strange about my melancholy mood. "Listen. I have to tell you something, but you have to keep your cool."

"I'm now completely losing my cool."

"I'm serious."

"Tell me!" he said. "You're freaking me out."

I filled him in on the CCIB.

"Oh, my God," he breathed.

"Don't." I lifted a finger in warning.

"Lola."

"I'm serious. Stay calm."

"Why didn't you tell me about this?" he cried. "This... this is amazing."

"Or it could be nothing." Now I was being a downer just to squash his hopes. Ugh.

"Right," he said, schooling his face into bored expression. "Well. Keep me posted, will you? Further developments and what not. Not that I care, you understand. Curiosity and whatever."

I gave Georgie a hug. Honestly, what would I do without him? Mom left me with an amazing fairy godfather when she died. "Come on," I said. "Let's go to work."

The Masquerade was coming up at the end of the week and the twins were absolutely full of secrets. I walked into the dining room, behind the counter, and they immediately stopped talking and looked guilty.

"What's going on?" I asked them.

"Nothing." Chloe said.

"Nothing at all," Zoe said.

"Look, just because I'm not going, doesn't mean you can't talk about the party in front of me."

"Oh, my God," Zoe said, cracking first and cracking wide open. "Fiona has the most beautiful Chanel vintage fabric, and I'm going as Cinderella in this poofy—"

"I'm going as Cinderella," Chloe piped up.

"No. You're, like...Sleeping Beauty or something." They kept arguing, but truthfully, my brain short-circuited as soon as she said *Fiona*, the local high-end dressmaker, and *Chanel*.

"I'm sorry," I interrupted their fight, tying a fresh apron around my waist. "You're getting custom dresses made for this party?"

Zoe blinked, her mouth shutting so fast her teeth clicked.

"That's why Mom told us to not tell her," Chloe whispered out of the side of her mouth and then, before I could ask her any more questions, she grabbed the two hamburgers waiting in the service window and went to deliver them.

Tiffani came back behind the counter.

"Ordering," she said and put the ticket on the spindle. Part of me knew there was no point in losing my marbles over the dress thing. Tiffani was going to do what she was going to do, but what was killing me was the why of it all.

"For a woman freaking out about money, you sure are spending a lot of it on dresses for this party," I said. Fiona didn't make a dress that wasn't expensive.

She sighed, looking defeated. "Who told you?"

"Who do you think? The twins aren't capable of secrets. What are you doing, Tiffani?" I asked. "We're up to our ears in debt, and you're spending hundreds of dollars on dresses...."

There was something in her face that made my stomach bottom out. "Thousands?"

"My girls are beautiful. And this is going to be a party filled with summer people. They could meet someone. Someone rich. Someone who could take them out of this stupid town and away from these stupid problems."

"Are you seriously telling me you're trying to marry off your daughters into money? At a ball? Seriously, Tiff, what did I tell you about watching the *Bridgertons* over and over again?"

"No, of course not," she said, her cheeks pink. "You can't deny the reality that it will be a house filled with young, handsome, rich men. I'm just doing what I can to help my girls catch their eyes."

"What about me?"

"What about you?" she asked, blinking like I'd never ever occurred to her.

"What if I wanted a dress for the masquerade? You got enough money for that?"

"Don't be ridiculous. You already said you're not going to the party," Tiffani said dismissively. "Do I have to remind you of the video from five years ago? The one of you literally being kicked out of the place by Jackson Dumont himself? No self-respecting person would even think of going back."

Right. They wouldn't. They wouldn't spend any time talking to Jackson Dumont, either.

"Thanks for the reminder."

"Besides," she said with a smile that was mean. How

could someone have a mean smile? "Someone has to close that night, don't they?"

For the first time since my dad died, I felt tears burning behind my eyes and I didn't know if I could hold them back anymore. I pushed past my stepmother, absolutely not caring what she thought, just knowing I could not give her the satisfaction of crying in front of her.

In the storeroom, I shut the door and pressed my head against it. What was I fighting her for? I wondered. I had a plan. Buy the restaurant. Kick her out. Engaging with her any more was pointless.

As if the universe was backing me up on this reminder, the phone in my apron dinged.

I had an email from CCIB. Great. I thought. The way this day was unfolding, this would be a rejection. A thank you, but no thank you.

To: Lola Pappas
  From: CCIB
  Subject Line: Let's talk.
  Hi Lola,
  I've had a chance to review your plan and just wanted to say you've got some great ideas to bring in new customers. Karaoke Brunch is really unique. I also think Dinner and a Drag Show sounds hilarious. Who doesn't love a Drag show?
  CCIB

"THAT'S WHAT I THOUGHT," I whispered, like CCIB could hear me. I tried to keep my enthusiasm to reasonable levels, but it was hard when this email had touched the very rock bottom of my soul and was bouncing me back into hope.

Someone liked my ideas. They were *great ideas.*
Suddenly my day was looking much brighter.

To: CCIB

From: Lola Pappas

Subject Line: Thank you.

I know this probably isn't very professional of me, but I just wanted to take the time to say thank you for letting me know you appreciated my ideas. Outside of all this pressure and worry, it just meant a lot. To me. So thank you.

Very professional going forward,

Lola

To: Lola Pappas

From: CCIB

Subject Line: Sometimes business is very personal.

Lola,

Don't ever hesitate to reach out. It's been my experience that the most successful small businesses are successful because of the people who work there. What I read in your proposal was love and that tells me how hard you would work to make the diner a success.

Sorry you're going through a difficult time.

CCIB

It was a rare afternoon off, and I decided to take some time for myself. Get out of my head a little and take a walk through town.

The cold gray day hadn't ever cleared, which was always good for the businesses around the square. It drove all the tourists off the beach and into town, buying souvenirs and ice cream, and, judging by the line in front of Madame Za's table, palm readings.

I got a scoop of chocolate ice cream and waited my turn with Madame Za, watching the number of people walking in and out of Fiona's dress shop. All picking up their garment bags filled with gowns for the big day that was right around the corner.

I was happy for her and knew that any success she got, we all got. But when I saw both Zoe and Chloe go marching in there wearing their over large sunglasses despite all the clouds, I could have cheerfully burned the place down.

Someone really needed to tell them they weren't the Kardashians.

"Lola," Madame Za said, pulling me out of my arson daydreams. She waved me over to her scarf-draped card table and I sat down. "They're calling for rain, so we're working fast right now."

Her accent always got a little more Maine when she was talking to the locals.

"Okay." I wasn't even sure why I'd gotten in her line. It's not like I bought her palm readings. It was more about just spending time with a friend. Still, maybe she could just give me a hint if the CCIB was going to give me the money?

"What are you looking for?" she asked. "A fortune? Palm reading? Love potion?"

"I just have a... Love potion?" I shook my head. "You sell love potions?"

"It's just vodka, some rose hips, a couple other odds and

ends...but it does the trick." She started digging through her big bag.

"I don't want a love potion," I said and then felt myself clam up. This really was crazy. I mean, I was desperate for some good news, but of course she was just going to tell me what I wanted to hear.

There was a stirring across the square. On the steps of the courthouse. A couple had emerged from the big wooden doors. A tall blonde man, a thin woman with her hair swept up in an extremely long ponytail.

I recognized both Vanessa and Simon from here.

Someone came jumping out of the bushes beside the steps with a camera.

"That's been happening all week," Madame Za said. "It's the wedding nonsense."

"Hmmm."

"That man she's marrying." Madame Za shook dramatically. "Not good energy off that one."

Yeah, I didn't need an aura reader to tell me that. Simon was a liar, and, I suspected, a cheat. If anything, I felt bad for Vanessa.

"So there is a rumor in town that Jackson Dumont isn't staying at the Dumont House."

"Really? Where's he staying?"

It wasn't that I cared. I didn't. It was more about, oh, what was that saying? Keep your enemies close.

"I don't know," she said. "But remember when he was younger, and he used to run across town in the mornings on the paths behind the shops. Folks have been seeing him run, so they think he might be staying in town."

"Couldn't sleep. Sometimes I like to go for a run."

Yes, I remembered how he liked to run. Like he was outrunning demons.

"Makes sense now that he's a grown man why he wouldn't want to spend too much time at home." Madame Za whistled. "One time, I accidentally bumped into Mr. Dumont, the Senior, right over there," she said, pointing to the fountain. "I swear I almost fainted just getting that close to him. He's cold all the way through."

"Well, his son isn't much different," I said, and then regretted it. I didn't want to gossip about Jackson. Or think about him at all really.

"No," she said. "He gives off entirely too much heat. He's like a volcano, that one."

Jackson and heat. Oh no. Nope. Not going there.

I pulled a five-dollar bill and shoved it in her jar. "Have a good day, Madame Za. I need to—"

"Oh, I know what you need," she said, and before I could pull back, my hand was cradled in hers. Her palm was rough but warm, and her grip, I found out when I tried to shake her loose, was also extremely strong.

"A million dollars," I said, and I meant it as a joke, but it came out kind of serious, and Madame Za didn't even blink at me. I wasn't sure she even heard me, that's how completely involved she was with my hand.

"Love," she said.

Now, that made me laugh.

"I don't need love," I said and maybe it was too loud. I mean, it was loud enough I startled a bird, and a family enjoying their own ice cream on the closest bench all turned to look at me. "I don't need love," I said, in a quieter voice. "I need money."

Madame Za shook her head. "It's unclear," she said and put my hand down. "But I would be careful of frogs."

Oh, my God, frogs.

"Thank you, Madame Za."

"Oh." She grabbed my hand. "Do not go to the masquerade."

I stiffened. "Why? I mean...I'm not. But why? Let me guess..."

"Frogs," we said at the same time.

12

Lola

Later that night while I was in my room, my phone binged, and I rolled over on my squeaky twin mattress and picked it up.

An email from CCIB. I sat up too quickly and banged my head on a rafter.

"Shit," I muttered and opened the email. My heart was pounding, which was crazy but there was something about the exchange with the anonymous CCIB that I was enjoying.

Yes, of course I wanted the money. But the person behind the money seemed...nice. Thoughtful, even.

Yes, I had friends in my life. Mari, Verity and Jolie. And of course, there was Georgie. But this felt new. Exciting. I wondered if, once I got the money, I would get to know who my anonymous benefactor was.

· · ·

To: Lola Pappas

From: CCIB

Subject line: Update

Hi Lola,

I know the tough part is waiting around for the yes or no, but I did want to tell you there is a lot of interest in your restaurant from members of the board. I think I can say this without giving too much away, but a number of them will be present at the ball being hosted by the Dumont's tomorrow. I'm assuming you'll be there as well?

CCIB

To: CCIB

From: Lola Pappas

Subject line: Re: Update.

I'm so glad to hear that. About the interest. I do understand it's a process and I'm trying to be patient. I won't say it's easy, but I'm doing it. As for tomorrow, unfortunately no, I won't be attending.

Patiently,

Lola

~

To: Lola Pappas

From: CCIB

Subject line: Re: Re: Update

If it's a matter of an invitation, I assure you it would be taken care of. You're an important member of this community, Lola. I can't imagine you not being there.

CCIB

To: CCIB
   From: Lola Pappas
   Subject line: Re: Re: Re: Update
   No, I was invited. But I have to work. Someone has to run the diner.
   Loyal,
   Lola

To: Lola Pappas
   From: CCIB
   Subject line: Re: Re: Re: Re: Update
   Your loyalty is admirable. However, it's unlikely you'll have any customers to run the diner for. You should come. Mix and mingle with the people there. Impress them with your business acumen.
   Unless there is another reason for your reluctance? A person you don't wish to see.
   CCIB

WAS THERE a person I didn't wish to see? Or was there a person I *wanted* to see? I shook my head. My run-in with Jackson had just stirred up too many memories. That's all.

None of that was this mystery person at the CCIB's problem.

To: CCIB
   From: Lola Pappas

Subject line: Re: Re: Re: Re: Re: Update

No, no problems with anyone who will be attending. If you think it's important for securing the loan by impressing the right people, then of course, I'll go. But how will I know who to impress?

Will you be there?

Lola

To: Lola Pappas

From: CCIB

Subject line: Re: Re: Re: Re: Re: Re: Update

Just assume anyone you talk to might be part of the board. And yes, I'll be there.

CCIB

∽

THE NEXT MORNING, I stormed into the diner with a purpose. I found Georgie in the office taking a cat nap in the rolly chair, which he often did when he had to work the early shift.

"Georgie!"

He dropped the warm towel that had been pressed against his face into his lap and sat up blinking. "Jesus, what are you yelling for?"

"I have to go to that ball tonight."

"Well, okay. I've been telling you that."

"No, for the restaurant." He blinked at me. "CCIB. They want to meet with me there. Talk to me... there!"

"Well, that makes sense. Everyone with money will be there."

"It doesn't make any sense. At all. This is business and

that's a stupid ball. But I have to go. So..." I held my hands out and stared at him.

"So what?"

"So...fix me."

"Fix you." His face fell. "Lola, you don't need to be fixed."

"You know what I mean," I snapped, uncomfortable. "Fix the way I look."

He stood up and took the warm towel he'd had over his face and put it over his shoulder and then he wrapped me up in his big Georgie arms. The wet towel made a damp spot on my shoulder.

"You're beautiful just as you are," he said. "Let's close at five then go to my place. We're going to show up at that party like two queens."

"Easy for you to say," I said, but hugged him as hard as I could. "I don't have a dress," I said. "I mean, unless you count my prom—"

"I don't. I don't count that monstrosity at all."

"I don't have shoes. Or makeup or a discernible hairstyle."

"I got you." He pulled back and checked his watch. "Come on, lunch rush is about to start."

THERE WAS no lunch rush today. There were trickles of people coming in, talking in excited tones about the party tonight. There were trucks rumbling up the road heading towards the Dumonts' house. The florist's van was back and forth on that road a million times. The fish market truck went up once and didn't seem to return. That was an ominous sign.

"We're going to go," Chloe said. She and Zoe were already out of their uniforms, purses over their wrists and sunglasses on. "We have hair appointments in twenty minutes."

"It's not even three," I said.

"No one is here," Zoe said, and I couldn't argue with her.

"Just go," I said.

Twenty minutes later, Tiffani came out in shorts and a flannel shirt. Her hair in a ponytail. "I'm going, too," she said.

"You're going to the ball?" I asked. It was the first time she'd mentioned it. All the focus had been on Zoe and Chloe, but I suppose it made sense that she would want to be there to see her daughters' triumph if they happened to snag the attention of a summer person.

"Not right now," she said. "I have a...ah...doctor's appointment, though. I'm sure you and Georgie will be fine closing up."

"I'm closing early," I told her, and I wasn't sure why I did it, except that I was tired of the way everyone was treating me, while, at the same time, trying to sell the diner right out from under me.

"Why?" she asked, digging through her purse and not at all paying attention to me.

"I changed my mind. I'm going to the party."

She looked up at me slowly, pushing her sunglasses down her nose. "Is...this a joke?"

"I *was* invited."

"Do you have a dress?"

"Not yet."

"What about your hair?"

"What about it?"

"You can't just put it in a ponytail and...Lola?"

"Oh, my God, what?" I asked, sorry I'd even said anything to her.

"You can't show up there smelling like french fries. Even after you shower, you smell like french fries."

"That's not true!" It was a little true.

Then she stepped forward and grabbed my hand so hard her nails dug into my skin. "You can't ruin Zoe and Chloe's chances at this event." She shook her head. "You can't come."

"What?"

"You can't. You can't arrive at that party in some dress that doesn't fit, smelling like this...place and ruin things for my girls. I forbid it."

"I'm twenty-three years old. You know that, right? You can't forbid anything."

"Who is going to open, then? Tomorrow. You have to open."

"I'm not on the calendar."

"You are now."

"Tiffani," I said, quietly. "Do you hear yourself right now?"

"This is my one chance, and you can't ruin it. So, be here in the morning at 4:30, or you'll never be able to buy your father's diner."

With that she stormed out of the diner, leaving me with my mouth hanging open, torn somewhere between rage and despair.

"Jesus," Georgie whispered, and there was the pop of a champagne bottle. "I thought that woman would never leave." He came around the corner from the kitchen, pouring a flute full of champagne then handing it to me.

"What are we going to do?" I whispered and downed the champagne. "Because she's right. Even after I shower, I smell like this place."

"We're going to show 'em. We're going to show every fucking one of them."

GEORGIE HAD OWNED a bungalow on the north side of town for as long as I've known him. Mom used to take me over there for what she called Drunk Mom Night. I got to play in Georgie's closet or watch movies while he and Mom drank wine and laughed until she called Dad to come get us.

After Mom died, I didn't go over there as much.

His house was across the road from the rocky beach where folklore said a pirate ship broke up and all the drunk pirates swam to the safety of Calico Cove with their cats balanced inside their hats. It probably wasn't true, but we did have a lot of cats in town. Three of them were sleeping in the end of day sun on Georgie's porch.

"Scram," he said, like he didn't feed them cans of tuna every day. The cats just looked at him and licked their paws. I was a little buzzed from the champagne, and when we walked inside, he poured me more.

"Is me being drunk part of the makeover process?"

"I'm hoping it will keep you from arguing with me. And it will help when we get to your eyebrows. Now. Take this." He handed me a plastic cup that said Dollywood in faded letters, filled nearly to the brim with champagne. "Drink it in the shower. Wash everything twice. Use the good stuff in the green bottle."

I did as he told me. When I got out, smelling like eucalyptus and limes, wrapped in a fluffy bathrobe, my hair wrapped up in another towel, he led me to his bedroom off what he called his den. His bedroom was painted a beautiful green and light streamed in through the windows making it sparkle like a jewel.

"I forgot how pretty your house is," I told him, looking at the pictures of all his family on the walls. He had a sister in Boston he went to visit when it was time to cause trouble. But his parents divorced, and his mom died. His father was in the Midwest somewhere and not a fan of Georgie's lifestyle.

Allergic to fabulous, Georgie always said when he talked about him.

"Why don't we ever hang out here more?" I asked.

"Because we're always hanging out at work," he said. He was pulling garment bags from his closet, unzipping them and spreading beautiful gowns across the bed.

"Oh, my God," I said, running my hands across velvets and silks and sequined embroidery. "These are gorgeous."

"Yes, they are, now you need to look at them and try them on. When I get out of the shower you tell me which one speaks to you, and I'll tell you if you're right."

I laughed as Georgie left.

There was a beautiful purple velvet one and the Gucci gold lame that were far too fabulous for me. I pulled a sleeveless black dress with a high neck out of the pile and put it in my maybe pile. As well as an emerald-green vintage dress with a poofy skirt and off the shoulder sleeves. I loved the look of a gold and silver embroidered flapper dress.

He had a beautiful white Marilyn Monroe dress, but white felt like a real risk, and there was another vintage one made of lilac lace with sleeves all the way down to my wrists.

"What did you decide?" he asked, coming in wearing a kimono and gold under eye patches. I showed him my stack.

"No," he said, tossing the black dress aside. "Maybe," he said about the green. "Hard no," he said about the lavender. "Not with your hair, honey."

"Why not the black one?"

"Because it's a party not a funeral. I think the green will do amazing things to your hair and skin. Go try it on."

I took it to the tiny bathroom, dropped both towels from around me, and slipped the dress over my head. It was that heavy kind of satin and looked like something a woman in the 1950s would wear. I loved the retro-ness of it and came out of the bathroom feeling pretty good.

Georgie wrinkled his nose and spun his fingers, indicating I should twirl. I rolled my eyes but did it.

"It's a maybe," he said.

"Why?"

"It's not doing anything for your best features."

"You said my skin and hair would look nice with this color."

"They do, but your best asset is your boobs, and they look a little flat." He turned back to his bed full of dresses. "You know," he finally sighed. "I think you're going to need to wear the big guns."

He lifted the gold lame.

"No way," I said.

It looked like it was held together with dental floss. Shiny bright gold dental floss. Like there wasn't a bra in the world that could work under that dress. Or underwear, for that matter.

"Give it a try, baby. But here..." He opened the top drawer of his dresser and pulled out what looked like pink jelly amoebas.

I flinched away from him.

"What?" he said. "They're bra cutlets."

"Bra what now?"

"You just peel this bit off," he showed me the adhesive. "And use it to push the girls up."

The girls. Right. There was just no way this was going to work. Still, it wasn't like Georgie was giving me a choice.

In the bathroom, the dress slipped over my head like a secret. And it swished across my body like a breeze. It was knee length with a slit up the side that was going to make sitting impossible. I did what I could with the cutlet business, but the bathroom mirror only showed me from the neck up. So, without a clear idea of what I looked like, I stepped out into the bedroom where Georgie, already flawless in a white feather dress, made a sound like a dog barking then clapped his hand over his mouth.

"Are you laughing at me?"

"No," he said. "Just your boobs. Looks like you've got two cats in a fight under there."

"Come on," I cried, clutching my boobs and the stupid bra things. "I don't know what I'm doing."

"I know, honey. Which is why you're going to consent to me feeling you up, and I'm gonna show you what a knockout you are in this dress."

"Georgie, you were just laughing at me. How do I go from being laughed at to a knockout?"

"With my help. Come on. Lay back and think of the queen."

I laughed despite my nerves and my general hating of this moment. After I wiggled out of the bodice of the dress, he unpeeled the amoebas from my boobs then lifted each boob and pressed the amoebae into what I could only assume was a better place, then he stepped back as I wiggled the bodice into place.

"Oh," he said, in an unreadable voice. "Oh."

He took my still damp hair and twisted it up onto the top of my head and leaned back, as if taking in the whole of me. He tugged the dress down a little until I was quite sure a nipple was going to pop out.

"What?" I said, still unable to tell by his face and voice if I looked good, or like I had two fighting cats still going at it under my dress.

He stepped back and clapped his hands. "That's the dress. We're going to need shoes."

He went into his closet and came out with a pair of ruby red velvet heels with peep toes and a tiny ankle strap. They were elegant and bold.

"They've never fit me, obvs," he said. "They're Dior and they were at a garage sale for five dollars. I couldn't let them go to someone who couldn't appreciate them."

He set the shoes down in front of me and I had more than my share of doubts. I had the voices of Tiffani and the twins in my head, telling me that by trying to look beautiful I was only going to look stupid.

Georgie looked up at me with a smile that told me he knew what was going through my head. "You have to trust me, baby," he said. "You're almost there."

I slipped my feet into the shoes, and he took a long time fiddling with one of the little ankle straps. "The prong is missing," He finally said, coming to his feet. "Buckling it without the prong will just have to work."

"Can I look at myself?" I asked.

"No," he said. "Not yet."

He sat me down on the edge of his bed and brought out a blow dryer.

"You're bald. Georgie, why do you have a hair dryer?"

"Because the ice machine in the fridge gets jammed and this is the only way to thaw it out."

He put cream in my hair. And sprayed something in it. He had me bend over then stand up. There was a diffuser. Hot air. Cold air. And then, at the end, swear to God, he pulled it all up into a tight bun on the top of my head.

"All that for a bun?" I asked.

"Hold your horses," he muttered, pulling long strands of hair out and curling them around his finger. The curls tickled my shoulder and the middle of my back. He leaned away and looked me over carefully.

"Jewelry," he said. "Simple but...you know...substantial."

I had no idea what he was talking about but nodded. From his jewelry box he pulled out big gold hoops and handed them to me to put them in my ears.

"Can I look at myself now?" I asked.

"Let's do a little makeup, just to make the reveal that much more shocking."

He pulled a black fishing tackle box out from under his bed. "Wow," I said.

"I know. I went through a whole more is more phase earlier in the year, but now I'm about minimalism."

I wasn't sure if the tackle box was the minimalism or the more is more. Considering I had Chapstick and an expired tube of mascara in my purse, it occurred to me I had no authority with which to speak on the topic.

"Thank God you got your mother's skin," he said, smearing some stuff on my face. "Your father, God bless his soul, never had a pimple he didn't want to torture to death." He put something in my eyebrows and used the same stuff on my eyelashes. There was a little gold eyeshadow, than a bright red lipstick that matched my shoes.

Georgie stepped back and shook his head. "I don't say this enough, but damn. I mean. *Damn*."

He waved me up and opened his closet door to reveal the full-length mirror on the inside. I stepped in front of it and...and I didn't even know who I was looking at. The dress floated and glittered around my body, hugging my boobs but skimming over my hips. My hair was sexy and innocent at the same time and my eyes had never looked so blue.

I leaned forward. "What did you do to my eyebrows?"

"That's what you have to say? All that and you want to talk about your eyebrows?"

"No. No." I laughed. Uncomfortable and giddy all at the same time. "I look amazing."

"You do, Lola, you really do."

"I mean, I look amazing and not at all like myself. I don't even know...like, no one will recognize me."

"Well," he said. "It is a masquerade. It's kind of the point."

"Crap," I turned to him. "Are we supposed to have masks?"

He walked to the kitchen and came back with two masks. The one with peacock feathers he placed on the bed, and the plainer of the two, he put on me, tying the ribbons at the back of my head. I pushed it into position and felt even more like I was looking at a stranger. The mask was black, but it had gold specks in the material, and it kind of looked like butterfly wings and not at all like a mask.

I was sexy and mysterious all at once. I was brand new. Completely different. In a way I never knew I wanted to be.

"Don't cry," Georgie said.

"I'm not crying," I lied. "I'm beautiful, Georgie. You made me beautiful."

I turned and wrapped my arms around him, and he

hugged me back hard, the way my mother would have done. "Honey, you have always been beautiful. I just put you in a dress. You're going to lay them out at that party."

"Thank you, Georgie. I don't know what I would do without you."

"Just don't stand too close to me tonight. *I* want to be the most fabulous queen there. Now let's go get our *business* on!"

13

Lola

The sun set late in Calico Cove in the summer—around eight in the evening. As we approached, the sky was purple like a bruise, but the Dumont mansion was lit up in gold light. I could hear the party from inside the car as we got dropped off.

"First thing," Georgie said, once we crossed the threshold and were inside. "We get champagne. Then we circulate."

"Sure," I said, feeling, all at once, so damn happy I was there. Whether I talked to anyone at the CCIB tonight or not, it was just fun to be dressed up. To drink champagne with my fairy godfather and to look this beautiful.

A waiter walked by with a tray of champagne, and we each grabbed a glass just before we walked through the open doors to the glittering ballroom. I could see a string quartet in the corner and waiters lifting trays of glasses and hors d'oeuvres over the heads of the laughing party people.

"Ready?" Georgie said and clinked the edge of his glass to mine.

"Ready."

We shot back that champagne like it was cheap tequila. The bubbles went right to my head, and I was suddenly having a very good time. We set our glasses down on one of the little cocktail tables, linked arms and walked through the doors into the ballroom.

People watched us as we went past, and I didn't even feel the old urge to curl my shoulders in on themselves, to try and find a spot by the wall where no one would notice me. I threw my shoulders back and lifted my chin and felt amazing.

"Oh, shit," Georgie said. "Incoming."

Tiffani with an i and the twins were coming right at us, and they were trying to smile over their expressions of shock, and, in Tiffani's case, anger.

"Wow," Chloe said. "You two look amaze."

"Thanks," I said. "You look beautiful, too."

Fiona could not make an ugly dress if she tried, and the twins were in gorgeous ball gowns in bright fabulous colors that fit their bodies to perfection. The rest of it, though...the gigantic fake gem necklaces and the hair...and...I looked at Tiffani, then back at them. My God, what had they all done to their lips?

They were gigantic. Like...physically impossible lips. So puffy they looked painful.

"What happened to your mouth?" Georgie asked, without any tact, and I swallowed my laugh. The three of them turned their heads as one and glared daggers at Georgie. He lifted his hands in a don't-shoot gesture then gave me a squeeze. "I'm gonna find more champagne and someone to flirt with. See you around."

Without Georgie there as some kind of protection, the three of them stepped closer, nearly surrounding me.

"Where in the world did you get that dress?" Chloe asked.

"I whistled and some little birds and a couple of mice made it."

"You're not cute," Tiffani said.

"You're right, I'm gorgeous," I said with a false sense of bravado.

The violent menace rolling off my stepmother was astonishing. Was actually kind of scary. I stepped back.

"Anyway, have a good night," I said and turned away. But Tiffani grabbed my elbow so hard I gasped.

"You do anything to ruin this night for my girls—"

"I think who ever made your lips look like that already did that job." I shook my arm free and got away from them as fast as I could.

The doors toward the beach were open, letting in the summer breeze and the smell of the ocean. I grabbed another glass of champagne, and looked at all the beautiful people, searching for a familiar face.

I saw a lot of the summer people. The Dumonts, of course, were greeting the guests. Verity and her husband Josh were talking to Annie from the bookstore. Madame Za was walking about with a glass of champagne in her hand.

Except those were all the people I knew. And I was here to impress the people I didn't know.

Should I just go up to one of the rich summer people and say, *I'm Lola, are you CCIB? I'm Lola, and you said I had great ideas. I'm Lola, give me some money?*

Yeah, that was the winner. I snagged another glass of

champagne. The good stuff went down easy. When I hosted Karaoke brunch, I used mostly orange juice because the cheap stuff tasted like nail polish remover.

"Lola?" a deep voice said, and I turned to come face-to-face with, I swear to God, the last person I expected to be here. Roy Barnes, the grumpy lobsterman.

"Roy? You came to a ball?"

He rolled his eyes behind his simple black mask. "You don't have to say it like that."

"I'm not...it's just... I mean, you look amazing." He did. Tall and lean with those lobsterman shoulders. He filled out that tux like it was a job application. "I just never imagined this was your kind of scene."

"It's not." He shook his head. "You look beautiful."

"Thank you," I said. "You, too. I mean, handsome of course."

He smiled, awkwardly, that rarely seen dimple making an appearance. He opened his mouth to say something, but the band suddenly stopped playing.

"Ladies and gentlemen," a voice said. and the conversations went silent. "It is my pleasure to introduce the couple of the hour. The soon-to-be Mrs. and Mr. Turnberry, Simon Turnberry and Vanessa Dumont."

Simon, wearing a perfect tuxedo with a crisp white shirt and black bow tie, stepped out onto the dance floor, then turned with a flourish while everyone clapped. He held out his hand for Vanessa who wore a short pink dress that made the most of her extremely fabulous legs. She swung out onto the dance floor, her perfect straight shining hair twirling around her. She wore a mask heavily embellished with ribbons and sequins, but there was no hiding who she was.

An absolute princess.

"Wow," I said and turned to Roy, but the space beside me

was empty. I looked onto the stone patio, only to see him striding off into the dark, like he'd seen enough.

The band played an acoustic version of a Taylor Swift song, and Simon and Vanessa started to dance and the light caught in Simon's hair and reflected on his super white teeth. I remembered, with a kind of stab, how he'd called me *diner girl*, and I didn't want to watch those two make love eyes at each other.

I took my glass of champagne and walked out onto the brick patio. Over into the corner where the lights from the party faded into deep dark shadow. Where the air smelled like the lavender they had planted in giant pots.

The moon was behind the clouds and the ocean was dark, but I could hear it crashing against the rocks off the spit in the distance.

"Excuse me?" a voice spoke, and I jumped so high I dropped my champagne glass on the patio where, oddly, it didn't shatter.

"Holy shit." I said with an awkward laugh, my hand against my chest where I could feel my galloping heart. I picked up my empty glass and turned towards the voice. I could see the shadow of a white shirt and the pale skin of a man's cheek. He was sitting on a brick half wall next to one of the big pots of lavender.

"I'm sorry. I didn't mean to startle you," his deep voice said, although it almost sounded like he was whispering. As if he didn't want to be overheard by anyone but me. "I'd offer you another glass of champagne, but I'm out."

"Oh, that's okay," I said, lifting the glass I'd dropped. I stepped away from the guy. "I can get another one inside. Have a good—"

"Actually—" he stopped me "—could I impose on you to go get that tray of champagne from the waiter over there?"

His hand came out of the shadows to point at a waiter just inside the doorway to the ballroom.

"You want me to grab you a glass of champagne?"

"The whole tray actually. I'm stocking up."

I laughed, but he didn't. "You're serious?"

"I am. I will gladly split the champagne with you, if that makes a difference."

"I'm doing all the work. I'll split it with you."

"I agree to those terms. Oh!" His hand came out of the darkness again and brushed my bare arm. Just a slight touch and I blinked, stunned by the contact. "He's on the move. You're losing your window."

Don't ask me why I did it, but I practically ran across the terrace and stopped the waiter. "Excuse me," I said to his blank but smiling face. "Can I?"

"Of course," he said, dipping the tray so I could take a glass.

"I'm actually...I'm going to take the tray. Is that... That can't be all right, can it?"

"It's perfectly fine," he said, probably numb to the odd requests of this crowd. He let me trade him my cracked champagne flute for his full tray of champagne.

I walked back to Mr. Shadows with the tray, feeling a bit victorious.

"I have no idea why I did this for you," I said, handing him the tray.

"Well, the argument could be made you did it for you." He took the tray, and I heard the scrape of it against the brick half-wall as he set it down. "One for you, seven for me," he whispered and handed me a glass from the shadows.

I took it, and I stayed, entertained by Mr. Shadow and maybe...not quite ready to go back there into the light.

"What are you doing out here?" I asked him. "Drinking trays of champagne?"

"Well, I would think it was pretty obvious."

"Are you hiding?" I asked.

"That's one way of putting it."

"How else would you put it?"

There was a pause. "Okay. Hiding. I'm absolutely hiding."

"Why?" I asked. "Is it the dancing?"

"Actually, no. I really like dancing."

"Canapes, then?"

"Very afraid of passed snacks, it's true. Don't get me started on the shrimp."

"Oh." I perked up. "Are there shrimp?" That would explain where Georgie was.

"Betrayed," he sighed.

I glanced over his shoulder as there was a round of applause inside, and the string quartet started another dreamy waltz.

"Do you like dancing?" he asked, his voice still quiet and soft.

"I don't..." I shook my head. "I don't know how, actually. Not like they are dancing inside. Waltzes and stuff."

"It's not hard," he said.

"Easy for you to say."

"Would you like to learn?" A hand reached out of the shadows.

I imagined him wrapping that big hand around my waist. The other holding my hand. I imagined him pulling me up against his body in a way that would be the most touching I'd had in...

Don't think about that. Not about what happened/didn't happen.

I took a step back, and my voice climbed to some ridiculous register only neighboring dogs could hear. "With you? Right now?"

"Not if it's going to freak you out." The hand retreated and I immediately felt stupid.

"I'm not really in the habit of waltzing with men I don't know."

"Probably a good rule."

I took a sip of champagne, feeling rattled and off balance with this man, but somehow really reluctant to leave. It was like I was caught in some electric energy. A little uncomfortable but impossible to walk away from.

"So we've established that I'm hiding from appetizers. Why are you out here tonight, instead of inside enjoying the party?" he asked.

"I'm supposed to meet someone," I said. At least I thought I was. My mystery emailer would probably frown at the fact that I was out here on the patio with Mr. Shadows, instead of inside impressing possible CCIB board members.

"Sounds romantic."

"Hmm? No, I don't do romance. It's a business thing."

"What kind of business?"

"Money," I said.

"Well, there are plenty of those meetings happening in there. On the outside it looks like an engagement party but on the inside it's pure financial planning."

"Sounds like a good time," I said sarcastically, even though I was supposed to be part of that planning.

"Right. So, why aren't you in there talking money?" he asked, again his voice pitched low, and I felt it thrum against the night air. Against my skin. "What are you hiding from?"

Jackson.

I don't know why but the thought immediately came to

mind. I knew he was here, obviously. Did I want to be seen by him? Or not.

If he saw me, would he ask what food I was dropping off for the party?

"Maybe it's a *who* that you are hiding from?"

I went with the easy answer. "My stepmother and step-sisters."

"Oh?"

"You might have seen them. They have mouths that look like balloons."

"Lip fillers gone wrong?"

"So wrong."

"I can only assume it serves them right."

"Thank you, total stranger, for the solidarity."

I reached out my champagne flute, and he lifted his forward until the rims clinked then we both took sips.

"You know, that's not actually the whole truth," I said.

"Lying to me already? I'm wounded."

"There's someone here who...well, have you ever had a nemesis?"

"Like an arch enemy?"

"Yes."

"Are you a superhero?"

"No. I'm just a townie who got sucker punched by a summer person a few years ago. It wouldn't have mattered to him, but it mattered to me."

There was a scrape in the shadows. A glass getting shoved aside. "I'm sorry...that sounds awful."

"He was. I'm assuming he still is, so that's who I'm avoiding."

"What did he do? This summer guy?"

"He made me feel small." I shrugged it off, like it was nothing.

"Are you sure he meant to make you feel that way? Maybe there was…some other motivation for his actions?"

I laughed at that. "You sound like my mom. She would have said that sometimes you can't understand why a person does what he does. That I should have some empathy. Mostly, I think he just hated me."

"Hating you? That doesn't seem possible."

I smiled in his general direction. "Thanks again, stranger."

"My guess is if he saw you tonight, looking the way you do in that dress, he'd regret ever making you feel small."

The compliment went straight to my head, where it joined the champagne and made me do something so reckless, so outrageously out of character. I held out my arms, aware that my dress caught the light and glittered in the darkness.

"And what way do I look in this dress?" I asked.

"Like a dream," he said, without missing a beat. "A very sexy dream."

"Thank you," I said. "Even though I was totally fishing for that compliment, I'll still take it."

"Well, it is a fishing town. Don't be ashamed of what you catch. This guy, this…nemesis of yours. Perhaps he's sorry."

"If he was, he could have said it."

"Would you have believed him?"

"Once maybe. When we were kids. We were friends before he was my nemesis. Or, I thought so at least. I have no idea what he thought."

He hummed in his throat.

"So, how do you know Vanessa and Simon?" I asked, using my *I'm changing the subject* voice.

"We're old friends," he said. Right. A total summer person.

I looked over his shoulder at the glittering ballroom a hundred feet away. "They look like a fairy-tale couple."

"Fairy tale is a stretch. They're more like a business arrangement."

"But...do they love each other?"

He was silent for a moment. Then he asked, "That matters to you?" His voice was even softer now.

"Of course. I mean, they're getting married."

"Is it because you have your eye on Simon?"

"What?" I snorted. "God no. Why in the world would you ask that?"

"I'm told he's a handsome, charming guy who has broken plenty of hearts."

"I don't care at all about Simon. I know Vanessa a little, and she's nice. And we're drinking their champagne and...I don't know, I just want to believe it's real."

"How incredibly..."

"Don't say provincial."

"I wasn't." He was lying, and he was smiling, I could hear both things in his voice.

"Or naive."

"I wasn't going to say that, either. I was going to say sweet. That's very sweet of you. Well, I hate to disappoint the woman who brought me all this champagne," he said. "But if I was going to put money on it, I would say no. I don't think they're in love."

"That's sad."

"It's just...life."

"Because they're rich?" I asked.

"Because they don't know any better."

I blinked at him, slightly stunned by the answer. "What do you mean?"

"Maybe all Simon and Vanessa know are loveless

marriages. Like their parents. Their friends. Marriages that are more like contracts than true partnerships. Simon's new money. The Dumonts have an old name. Maybe they don't know they should expect more."

"Do you believe that?" I asked him.

"No," he said. "I know love exists."

"You're in love?" I asked, leaning back, thinking of this flirtation in another light.

"I've been in love," he said. "Not that it's done me any good. Come to find out I'm not very good at it."

I honestly couldn't see him in the shadows. He was nameless and faceless, but I could feel his attention so keenly. So purely. Like being in a spotlight.

There was a long moment. "Are you in love?" he asked.

I laughed. "No." I'd never been in love, but I had the good sense not to say that to my shadow man. It would reveal, in so many ways, how small my life really was.

"Then what makes you so sure it exists?" he asked.

"My parents. My parents loved each other."

There was a sound beside me, a shift of clothing over a body, someone moving, and I realized he'd sat down again. "That must have been nice," he said.

"It was. It really was." Suddenly, in the shadows of this fancy party, I felt such a longing for my parents. A pinprick in the back of my throat. A burn behind my eyes. Desperate not to cry in front of this stranger, I took another sip of my champagne only to find my glass empty.

"Here," he said, handing me another glass.

"You know," I said, "I wasn't sure about hijacking that tray of champagne, but now I am a convert. Is this what you do at every party?"

"Actually? Yes," he said with a wry laugh. "Perhaps, I'll find you in the shadows again at the next party."

"Oh, no, I won't be at another party."

"That's too bad," he said. "You look like a woman who should go to all the parties."

"It's the dress," I said, uncomfortable and delighted all at the same time. "It's a party dress."

"It's you," he said, his voice rough and slow, imbued with something...familiar. Something that sounded like longing.

I made some awful strange noise in the back of my throat that sounded like I was trying to swallow a frog. I stepped backwards, needing some distance. But I wasn't used to wearing high heels and I tripped over a brick and felt myself falling backwards.

Mr. Shadow stood and grabbed my arm, and it was only then that he was pulled into the light given off by the ballroom. He wore a simple black mask, but it couldn't hide his chiseled jaw line or the size of him. Big and wide and tall.

The mask also couldn't hide the color of his eyes. Which the light hit so perfectly. Blue green. Like the water in the harbor just inside the breakers.

No. No way. No, it couldn't be.

My body went cold and then hot. I flinched inside my skin.

"Lola," he breathed, his mouth inches from mine. His hand on my arm. The sound of my name coming from his lips. With that same reverence he'd used that night at the diner. The first time I'd seen him in years.

"Jackson," I whispered. Oh, my God. This whole time I'd been talking to Jackson! How could I have not known it was him?

His voice. He'd spoken so softly.

"Is this some kind of setup? Some prank?" I whispered through numb lips. It had to be. He'd let me talk to him...about him.

"Lola, no. I said I wanted to talk…"

I wished I could be stronger, fiercer. Throw this champagne in his face the same way he'd thrown that money in my face years ago. Practically in this exact same spot. The memory rolled through me, and all at once, I thought I might be sick.

"What are you going to do to me?" I asked, his hand still on my elbow, and I was so numb I couldn't pull my arm free. Frantic, I looked around, waiting for someone to jump out of the bushes with a camera to capture my humiliation for posterity. I got it together enough to wrench my arm free and step back. The loose shoe giving way even as he reached for me.

"Don't," I said through my teeth.

"Lola…" His stupid lips opened like he was going to say more.

"Stop saying my name!" I hissed.

I turned to run, the shoe slipping off completely. I twisted my ankle, but I didn't stop. I didn't even go back for the shoe. *Sorry Georgie.*

I just ran as far and as fast from Jackson Dumont as I could.

14

My Three Favorite Things

Lola Pappas
Lola Pappas
My sister

Jackson, Age 25

"Hello, Jackson." Vanessa came into our father's study where I was brooding.

It was the one room in the house that wasn't covered in gold glitter and pink balloons. She flopped down on the couch next to me and put her feet up on the table.

She'd changed out of her heels and into fluffy pink slippers. Her hot pink dress was wrinkled, as was my tux. Our masks, long gone.

"Quite a party, sis," I said, and tilted my champagne

glass towards her steaming mug of tea. "Thanks for doing it."

"Did it work?" she asked.

"Not even a little bit." I sighed. This whole night had been a ruse just to get Lola here. That had worked, at least. When she stepped out onto the terrace in that gold dress that looked like it had been poured over her, my heart had nearly stopped. Of course, I recognized her immediately. My body knew hers, even with masks and shadows and fancy clothes.

"You know, there are other women in the world. Dozens of them here tonight, desperate to meet you, desperate to make you happy. Is there some reason you are fixated on the one girl who hates you and smells a little bit like french fries?"

I didn't have an answer. I hadn't had an answer about Lola Pappas when I was eleven years old. When, for one brief summer, she'd been my whole world.

I didn't have an answer for all those summers I'd been so cruel to her because...I'd been a walking time bomb filed with rage, and she'd been my most convenient target.

I didn't have an answer for when I was twenty, purposefully provoking her to take all her rage out on me because I could see the pain inside of her begging for an escape.

I definitely didn't have an answer for why I kissed her. Though I'd really like to know why she kissed me back.

And I didn't have an answer for why I didn't tell her it was me in the shadows tonight, tongue-tied over the sight of her delicate throat and her strong arms and her undeniably sexy body in shiny gold lame.

Her smile. I hadn't seen that smile since we were kids. When she thought I was some other kind of person, the kind that wouldn't hurt her. Who knew how to be kind. Decent.

And I thought she was the sun and the moon.

Until I killed it. Our friendship. The only good thing I had in my life besides Vanessa.

After that, I only ever got her scowls and her anger. Sometimes her pain and her tears.

Once, her passion.

But her smile...those smiles went to my head.

She ruined me. She always had.

Tonight, when I'd had my moment to talk to her, really talk to her and tell her all the things I needed to...I chickened out. Too happy she was smiling at me, flirting even. I didn't want anything to change that smile into a tight-lipped look of pain. That was the worst. The way she flinched and held herself in a defensive clench around me.

"You know," Vanessa said, tilting her head back. "There's no reward when you finally get them."

"Get who?"

"The people who don't seem to want us. The ones who you think are playing hard to get but are actually just...not that into you."

Oh shit. I turned to look at my sister. She was undeniably beautiful. More than that, she was sweet. You'd think it might be the beauty that led her into trouble. But, no. It was always the sweetness.

"What did Simon do?"

"Nothing," she said. "He did nothing." She shrugged, blinking the brightness away from her eyes.

"You can leave him. At any time," I said. "You don't actually have to do this."

"You know that's not going to happen," she said. "Our parents have been expecting this since we were teenagers."

I wanted to argue. I wanted to say, *fuck our parents and fuck Simon's parents,* often enough she would be empowered to say it, too. But that was my style. Not at all my sister's. Expectations and trying to live up to them was a whole thing with her.

"Say the word," I told her. "Say the word, and we will vanish in the night. They'll never find us."

"And go where?" she asked, putting her head on my shoulder. That she was playing along told me how desperate she must be feeling.

"An island," I said.

"Oh, I like a resort."

"It's your fantasy," I said.

"Hmm," she said, her finger tapping her chin. "Five-star, boss pool, excellent spa. Maybe some yoga retreat vibes."

"All the best vibes."

"Top shelf vegan food and no men. Except you."

"Sounds perfect." Sounded like a nightmare. What I wanted was an island with a cranky diner waitress, endless grilled cheese and no one else for miles. Only this wasn't about me.

Vanessa sighed, and I felt the small bit of happiness in the room drain away. It was a sad state of affairs when the only thing that made your life happy was imagining a completely different life.

"I'm just going to say it one more time," I said quietly. "You don't have to do this. People have cancelled weddings a million times."

"The wedding is in two months, Jackson. And...I love him."

I didn't know if I believed that. I didn't know if she believed that. What did we know about love? What I'd said to Lola on the shadowy terrace was true. We'd never learned about it growing up. We didn't know better.

"Why don't you stay at my condo tonight?" I asked her, and she shook her head.

"Simon is here," she said. "But thanks."

It was so sad to see her starting a marriage this way. It was one thing when it was our parents in a marriage void of all emotion except disappointment and anger, but she was young and beautiful and so sweet. She deserved so much more than what she was settling for.

"What are you going to do?" Vanessa asked me, nudging my shoulder. "About Lola?"

What was I going to do about Lola? Such a good question.

"Try again," I said.

It was the only thing I could do.

Lola

So. That happened. I mean...I should have seen it coming. Jackson Dumont lying in wait for me like some kind of snake. I thought about how I'd laughed at Mr. Shadows jokes, and I cringed.

Had he actually offered to teach me to dance?

I'd told him I was avoiding him at the party, and he'd taken my side against himself.

What game was he playing?

"Little dressed up for the morning shift, huh Lola?" Arthur Petit, Jolie and Verity's lobsterman dad, asked as he stepped up to the counter.

I was still wearing the gold dress. Georgie would absolutely kill me if he knew.

"Thought I'd shake things up," I said with a smile for Arthur.

I had an apron on over it and had on my old pair of Converse. My hair, thanks to Georgie's bobby pins and hairspray, wasn't going anywhere without a chisel. I'd washed my face and I looked tired, but at least I looked like myself.

In a gold Gucci dress.

I hadn't been able to go home last night. Couldn't face Tiffani and the twins, so instead, I'd come here and slept, very carefully, in the office rolly chair. Only I hadn't gotten a lot of sleep.

"Well, I don't know if your dad would approve of all that there skin," he said, gesturing in a vague way to my shoulders and bare arms. I had to admit that, if it weren't for the thin gold straps, it looked a little like I was naked under the apron. "But I think you look real nice."

"Thanks, Mr. Petit."

It was pots of coffee and bagel sandwiches wrapped in tin foil as the world woke up around me. If I took deep breaths, closed my eyes and tried to clear my mind, I could almost, almost forget what happened.

My phone buzzed. Expecting an "are you okay and I'm going to be late" text from Georgie, I was surprised to see an email from CCIB.

To: Lola Pappas
    From: CCIB
    Subject line: Last night.
    Hi Lola,
    Obviously, we didn't have the opportunity to talk business

last night. I fear I probably would have been terribly distracted anyway. I don't want you to think you missed your only chance with the funding. It was just a good opportunity for you to mingle. Next time.

    CCIB

OH GOD, in all the drama I'd forgotten why I'd even gone to the stupid ball. I turned and put my butt against the counter. What to say...what to say...

To: *CCIB*

    From: *Lola Pappas*

    Subject line: *Re: Last night.*

    I am sorry to have missed you! I'm afraid I wasn't feeling very well and had to leave early. I know you like to remain anonymous, but is there any way we could arrange to meet formally? I would be happy to drive to your offices if you are not nearby.

    Still desperate,

    Lola

                      ~

"LOLA?"

I looked up at the sound of his voice. A voice I knew now. A voice that was deeper and richer than it had been five years ago. The few words we'd exchanged before the party hadn't been enough to supplant the Jackson voice I knew.

But now...now I knew his voice.

He would never fool me again.

Gone was the tux and the slicked back hair. No wonder I didn't recognize him in the shadows with this man body and man voice. I felt duped all over again, and every barrier against him went back up.

"What do you want, Jackson?" I asked, suddenly exhausted.

Because it was all back. The heart pounding, the sweaty palms. My physical reaction never changed. I was never comfortable in his presence. Never.

I'd been comfortable when we were kids.

I'd been comfortable last night.

Only because I didn't know it was him.

"A chance to apologize," he said, a sheepish expression on his face, then something more serious. "And talk. That's all I want, Lola. To talk to you. It's why I didn't tell you last night who I was, because for once, after so many damn years, we were just talking again. You and me."

"Sorry. I only have bagels and coffee." I refused to give him anything, but it hurt. Even being this close to him was like holding my whole body over a fire.

"I'll take one of each," he said.

I glared at him. He smiled at me. I could write a book about Jackson Dumont's smug smiles, but this one...it looked genuine. It reached his eyes, crinkled the corners. Lightened the aqua blue. He looked...he looked like the boy I once knew.

Ugh.

"Here," I said, and smacked a bagel down and poured him a cup of coffee into a to-go cup.

"Do I get sugar or..."

I poured what had to be a cup of sugar into his coffee.

"Milk?" I asked, with one eyebrow raised.

"No," he said, still smiling. "What do I owe you?"

I remembered the money he threw at me, the time he'd paid a hundred bucks for a really bad grilled cheese sandwich.

I realized the fact that he had money and I needed money had been a tool he'd used to hurt me for a long time.

"Five seventy-five," I said, which was the regular price.

"No bully charge?" he asked, sort of smiling, and there was something about that word and how I'd never thought of him as a bully. As my bully. But really that's what he'd been. Taking such joy in grinding me down. I'd preferred the word *nemesis* because, in my mind, we were equals.

However, there was no world in which the Pappas and Dumonts were equals. Once, he'd been my best friend, but that's what he'd turned into. My bully.

"Lola?" he asked, as I was silent and still.

"Five seventy-five," I said again, my voice froggy. He gave me a ten, and I knew he was about to say, *keep the change*, and I wasn't going to do that—so I gave him the change as fast as I could.

He took his food and sat in the dining room, taking one of the two-tops, not his usual booth. After a sip of coffee he winced. I was a little surprised he didn't slip immediately into a diabetic coma.

The lobstermen had all gone, and it was Sunday, so there wasn't going to be a crowd of office workers grabbing sandwiches to go. We were a long way off from the after-church crowd and the hungover partygoers.

Which meant the restaurant was empty.

I ignored him as long as I could. An hour passed, his bagel long gone, his coffee ice cold. He sat looking at his phone or staring out the window. Looking, generally, like a man who wasn't in a hurry. A super-hot man who wasn't in a hurry. Finally, I couldn't take it anymore.

I stomped over towards him, the gold dress glittering in the sunlight streaming through the windows.

"You're still in your dress," he said, and there was an expression on his face that said he felt some kind of way about that. I didn't have time to decipher his expressions.

"What do you want?" I asked, folding my arms across my chest. And of course, I mean, OF COURSE that would be the moment that the stupid sticky bra thing would decide to just quit. Fall off my boob, roll down my stomach inside the dress and before I could catch it, splat onto the floor between my feet.

Like I'd given birth to a silicone amoeba baby.

We both stared at it.

"What is that?" he asked.

"None of your business," I said and grabbed it, squeezing it as small as I could in my hand, so he couldn't see it.

"Why are you really here?" I snapped.

"Are you all right?" he asked.

"That's not an ans—"

"That's...why I'm here," he said, cutting me off. "To see if you're all right. Last night did not go the way I'd thought it would go."

"Oh, not enough humiliation? Did I run out before you could organize the pig's blood?"

He opened his mouth. Shut it. He pressed a finger against a sesame seed that was on the table, and he did it for a long time, instead of talking. I watched him, simmering with...unrest. This feeling in my stomach. Across my skin, it was pure unrest.

"I am more sorry than I can say that I have led you to believe I would do that."

I opened my mouth to laugh at him. To scoff, to sling my

scorn all over him. But he looked up at me, and even though I didn't trust this guy as far as I could throw him, he looked...contrite. Believably contrite.

I couldn't believe him. I knew that. But...his face.

"I stopped by here the other night hoping to talk, but you didn't seem...open to that," he said, because I'd been silent too long. "Anyway, when I saw you on the terrace, I thought I might have another chance. Yes, I knew you didn't realize it was me. But we were talking, finally talking. You looked so beautiful in your dress, and you were smiling and having a good time... I didn't want that to stop. I'm here, now, because I want to apologize."

There were thirty things I wanted to ask him.

What do you want to apologize for? How long have you wanted to apologize? Can you say that beautiful part again?

I shook my head, squeezed the fake boob in my fist and asked the only question that mattered.

"Why?"

"Why what?"

"Why do you want to apologize?"

His forehead wrinkled. He looked handsome and confused. "Because you said I made you feel small. I should have apologized five years ago, the morning after the bonfire, but I didn't think you would listen then, or understand."

"But you think I'll understand now?"

To my utter surprise, my complete and total shock, he stood up and the way we were standing, if he took a deep breath, his chest and stomach would touch me. If I took a deep breath, my boobs would touch him.

I took a deep breath. Yep. Nipple to chest contact. I felt like I'd been electrocuted. He sucked in a breath, like he was feeling it, too.

I was a deer in headlights. Unable to move. Unable to look away from his terrible beautiful eyes and when he reached up and touched my hair, tucking it behind my ear, his fingertip touching my earlobe... I let it happen.

Worse. I kind of moaned at the touch. I did. I moaned. It's an embarrassment I will take to my grave. It was like the sunshine around us had turned to honey, and we were stuck there, staring at each other. It was the storage room all over again, but without the rage.

I wanted him to kiss me. It felt like he wanted to kiss me.

It's a trap!

Finally, I got it together, and, nipples hard, ear tingling, stepped back. Crossed my arms over my chest for extra protection.

"You're forgiven," I said, just to end this weird pull between us.

"Lola," he said, like he was disappointed in me.

"What?"

"You don't forgive me." How was this man standing here, arms at his side, looking at me like it mattered that I honestly forgave him? What diabolical plan was this?

"You're right. I just don't care. It's over."

He stepped forward again, and I could smell him. Clean and woodsy and rich and awful.

Absolute tremors went through me. Goosebumps rose on my skin. I could stand this guy's bullying. I could stand his mean jokes. But this...this desire?

No, thank you.

I shook my head and took a step back and then another. Until I was all but running for the safety of the counter.

"Wait. Lola, I just..." He looked down at his feet. His face, which I'd been convinced was only capable of revealing his smug superiority, showed something else. The flex in his jaw and the corner of his eyes, there was something that spoke of a more fragile feeling. It left me on unsure footing. "No matter what you believe of me, please know it was not my plan to humiliate you that night. There was a reason I didn't want you to come to my party...but when you got there...because I knew you weren't there for me...I went a little crazy."

"Why would you ever think I would be there for you?"

Because our friendship had long since ended. Because he'd been awful to me for years, every summer. Right here in this very diner. Our kiss aside, there was nothing left of that sweet friendship between us.

He shrugged, then smiled a little sadly. "I don't know. Wishful thinking maybe. Thanks for the bagel and egg sandwich. It's the best thing you've ever served me. The coffee, though, that had all the unique touches of the Lola Special. I'll see you around?"

Shit. I would see him around. Because he was probably here until the wedding.

I didn't say anything. Just stood there in my apron and Gucci dress, squeezing my fake boob in my fist, while I watched him walk out the door.

15

Lola

"The sign is back," Georgie said as he walked in, then he shrieked and fell backwards against the counter. "Tell me I am hallucinating. Tell me that is not my vintage Gucci that you are still wearing. In. A. Diner."

"Georgie," I said, "I'm sorry."

He shook. His hands, his head, his whole body was in seizure. "Go home. Go home right now and change and then bring it back to me for a proper burial."

"I'll take it to the dry cleaner."

"See that you do. The one on Main Street, not the butchers on Beach Road."

"Can you..."

"Cover for you? Yes, you neanderthal, I can. But then we'll be discussing all the ways you owe me."

Because he was Georgie and he was joking, but also a

little not joking, I wrapped my arms around him and kissed his cheek.

"I take it all went well, last night?" he asked, his hands squeezing me around the waist. "I lost you so early, I wasn't sure…"

"I got ambushed by Jackson Dumont."

Georgie leaned back. "What did that little shit do now?"

I blinked a few times, Jackson's words from earlier this morning playing over and over in my head. "He apologized."

"Diabolical," Georgie said with narrowed eyes.

I laughed and shrugged. "Maybe. Or maybe he meant it."

"Oh no, do I sense a weakening in the force?"

"No. He's still my nemesis."

"What about the money people? Did you meet with them?"

"No, but we've been in touch. I better go before the brunch rush." I skedaddled out of there, hopped in my old Toyota that I'd left in the parking lot last night and made my way home.

"Hello?" I said as I entered the house. The wonder twins and Tiffani with an i, looking a little worse for wear and hovering over the coffeepot, all turned and hissed at me.

"Shhhhh…." Tiffani snapped.

I slammed the door shut behind me. "Any of you get engaged to rich men last night?" I asked.

"Why do you have to be so awful?" Chloe asked.

"I could ask you the same question," I said and headed for the stairs and my attic room.

"Lola!" Tiffani yelled, and I paused in the stairwell,

halfway up the stairs, then turned. She stood in the doorway to the kitchen, looking every minute of her age. That was mean of me, and I was okay with that. "I want you to know the real estate agent just called and said we got an offer on the restaurant."

"What?" I asked, my stomach hurling itself into my throat.

"It came in this morning, and apparently, it's serious. Nothing has been signed, but...I just wanted you to be prepared."

"Who?" I asked. I asked the question not even thinking she'd know the name, or if she did, it would be anyone I knew.

Her lips curled up. "Jackson Dumont."

THE FRONT DOORS of the Dumont mansion were huge. The door knobs were, like, in the middle of the doors instead of off to the side, the way doors were supposed to work. I pounded on the wood with my fists and looked through the flowering vine growing up the side of the door for a doorbell. Nothing, of course. I pounded again.

Last night these doors had just stood open, letting the whole world in.

I pounded again.

The door swung open, and I swear to God, a butler stood there. He wasn't in tails or anything, but he wore khaki pants and a red polo shirt that read Dumont Hotels over the chest in gold embroidery. The entry behind him was bustling with staff moving chairs and taking gigantic pots of flowers out of the foyer. The room was framed by big wide spiral staircases that met at a kind of balcony on the second floor. The floor was black and white tile, and the ceiling was gold with a gigantic chandelier. It had all looked fitting for the party last night.

However, in the harsh morning light, it looked like the definition of too much. I felt very small in my jean shorts and flannel shirt.

"May I help you?" the butler said.

"Is Jackson here?" I asked, and I stepped inside. Jeeves very subtly got in my way so I couldn't go storming off to find him on my own.

"May I tell him who is calling?"

"Yeah. The girl he's stabbed in the back, that's who is calling."

"I don't...that's not a name."

"Lola?" Suddenly, on the balcony above, like he was Madonna in that musical about the lady from Argentina, was Jackson. "Is everything all right?"

That he managed to look concerned. That he had the gall to pretend, infuriated me. Lit my hair on fire. That scene this morning at the diner, it must have been about buttering me up. Causing me the most pain possible because he'd put in the offer on the restaurant right afterward.

"No, nothing is all right, you gigantic..." I was suddenly aware of a lot of eyes on me. "Jerk."

"Would you like to talk in private?" he asked, coming down the stairs. He pushed his hand through his hair, sending it standing on end. If I had to guess, I would say he wasn't surprised to see me.

Worried, maybe?

Good.

For what I was planning, it would be better to not have any witnesses. I wondered if Georgie would help me hide the body.

"Fine by me," I said. "Jeeves? You wouldn't happen to have any plastic sheeting and duct tape, would you?"

"Is that...are you joking?" Jeeves asked, looking between me and Jackson as he walked across the foyer to the doorway that led to a whole other part of the house.

"How about bleach?" I asked. "I'm going to need a bunch."

"She's joking, Eric," Jackson said to the doorman.

"Am I?"

"This way," Jackson said.

I followed him through a part of the house that hadn't been open during the party. The dining room then the kitchen, which was bigger than my entire house. Absolutely bustling with people cleaning stuff up.

All the leftover appetizers that I never got a chance to eat were in sealed plastic containers on the massive counter tops.

"Are you hungry?" Jackson asked, as if he noticed me eyeing the leftovers.

Then I remembered his joke about being scared of passed snacks, and I put my chin in the air. "No."

He nodded but grabbed the top container and kept walking through rooms. One with a piano. One with couches and a television. Finally, after what seemed like a mile, we were in a study, with built-in shelves, wooden wainscotting, big leather sofas. A whole bar. The room screamed, *I'm a rich dude.*

I turned towards the desk, fully expecting him to go sit behind it like the lord of the manor, but instead, he went to the leather couch and chairs, set the container on the coffee table. He opened the Tupperware, revealing mini quiches and stuffed mushrooms.

"These would probably be better warm," he said,

contemplating the food. "I can get—"

"You're buying the diner," I said. My hands in fists. My phone was going crazy because Georgie was probably freaking out. Tiffani must have told him about the offer. I'd come right over here from my house once I'd changed.

He closed his eyes and swore under his breath, and I could not get over this version of him. So much like my nemesis but in a totally different package.

"Tiffani told you about the offer?" he asked.

"Yeah. She couldn't fucking wait to tell me about the offer." I felt like my head was going to spin off. I was so angry I hadn't even figured out what I was going to say to this man. I had no speech.

"I'm sorry," he said and stepped forward. "It wasn't supposed to go like that, and I can see how you're interpreting it."

"Go like what? Because from where I'm standing, it goes like it always goes with you. Shitty. For me."

He reached for me. Can you believe that? The asshole reached for me. I smacked his hands, and it felt so good.

"Please, Lola. Calm down—"

I smacked his face.

It was loud and sharp, and my hand hurt, and his head went sideways. In the silence afterwards I could hear my heartbeat.

"I'm so sorry," I said immediately, my voice cracking.

Black eyes, split lips. A broken arm. Those memories of him all came roaring back. This was someone who'd been hurt by people who were supposed to love him.

I'd just joined their ranks.

The tears I wasn't going to cry in front of this guy were welling up in my eyes.

"That's not... That was wrong," I said, stumbling over my

words. "I'm sorry."

I pressed my fingers, still stinging, to my lips and prayed to my parents for control.

Mom, Dad, please, please help me keep it together. I'm trying so hard.

"It's okay. I understand."

"It's not okay," I whispered.

"Lola," he said, and his voice was...sympathetic. Kind. Nothing I could believe from him.

"Don't," I said. "Please, don't be fake nice to me. Just tell me what is going on."

"Listen to me. I handle a lot of real estate. I saw that Pappas' was listed, and it took me by surprise," he said. His cheek was still red from my hand, and this scene all felt so surreal. "I made an enquiry because I couldn't believe you would sell it."

"*I'm* not the one selling it," I insisted.

"I know. I...learned about all of it. Your dad, him leaving the restaurant to your stepmom. Yesterday, someone else heard that it was for sale, so I had to act fast. I put in an offer, and Tiffani accepted it, which means now we're in the attorney review phase, which stops her from taking any other offers."

All I heard was *offer* and *accepted.*

"Why do you hate me so much?" Oh God, I hadn't meant to say it. But it was the source that fed everything else. "What did I ever do to you to deserve this?"

He blinked. "Lola." His voice was scorched. Like he'd dragged it behind him through a fire, and I didn't know this man. He looked like the man who'd hurt me so badly, but now was acting all wrong. "I don't hate you."

Suddenly, it was too much.

"Oh, no? Then why did you bully me all those summers?

You left all those nasty reviews. Do you remember when you destroyed my shells? Oh, and kicking me out of your precious party. Throwing money at me like I was some kind of...?" I wasn't going to say that word. "Why are you buying the diner?"

His jaw flexed so hard it was like he had a rock in there, and he stared out the window for a second. More than a second. I looked out the window, too, wondering what he saw out there, but it was only the shoreline where we'd first met.

"It's all a long story."

"Then skip to the part about buying my diner."

My phone rang. Stopped. Started ringing again.

"Do you need to answer that?" he asked. His eyebrow lifted. Of course he had that kind of eyebrow control. He had all the kinds of control. I swallowed, my neck getting hot.

"Of course I need to answer it, but not until you tell me what's going on."

He licked his lips, which should not have, in any way, been hot. Not a bit. But it was. Because I was wired wrong. I was some kind of messed up. "I'll tell you everything," he said.

"Great."

"Tonight."

"What?"

"Tonight. Once you've had a chance to calm down and I know you can hear what I'm saying. When you're done working. You let me take you to dinner, and I'll tell you what's happening with the restaurant."

I rocked back on my heels. "Like...a date?" As soon as I said the word, I wished I could suck it back into my mouth.

He didn't laugh.

Instead, his lips twitched into a smile. "Like a date."

"Is this a trick?"

"No. It's a date."

"Where?"

"The hotel, if you'd like—"

"No." I shook my head. The Dumont Hotel was his territory. "No, I don't want to go to your shitty steakhouse."

"It's won awards."

"For terrible steak. I'll go anywhere but there."

"Okay." He smiled like he'd won something, and my stomach went cold again. If he was happy, it was probably bad for me. "Leave everything to me."

"I'm done at five," I muttered.

"I can pick you up at your house."

I shook my head. I could not imagine him picking me up at my house, Tiffani and the twins watching with malice through the front window. "No. At the diner is fine."

My phone rang again.

"I need to go," I told him.

"Okay."

I started walking towards the door of the study, out of this dumb mansion, back to my life. Something stopped me though, and I turned back to him.

"You swear it's not a trick?"

He held up his hands, palms up. "How would it be a trick?"

"You let me stand there waiting for you for an hour. You take me somewhere and leave me there, and I have to walk home. You take me somewhere and all your friends are there to laugh—"

"Lola." For a second he looked, there was no other word for it, *pained*. Worse even than when I smacked him. "I'm not that kid anymore. I wouldn't do that."

I stared at him, and he laid his hand across his chest and looked me dead in the eyes.

"Swear to me," I said.

"I swear to you."

"On something you care about." He was silent and my laugh was a harsh bark. "Unless there's nothing you really care about..."

"On my sister," he said quietly. "I swear on Vanessa. It's not a trick. It's a date. Where we're going to talk."

I didn't have a choice, did I? If I wanted the truth, I had to believe him.

∾

Later that Day

Jackson

THIS WAS NOT GOING to be easy. What was that saying...be careful what you wish for?

I had a date with Lola Pappas, when I might have my one and only chance to change her long-cemented opinion of me.

I was standing in the kitchen, probably looking totally hopeless, when Dani, our housekeeper and cook while the family was in residence, breezed in.

"What can I do for you, Jackson?" Dani asked.

She and her husband Eric, who managed the staff, had been with the family for years. Calico Cove locals, they knew that to keep their jobs, they had to work hard and keep their heads down so they didn't see much or hear much.

They certainly knew not to interfere with the family matters.

Still, Dani had always been the one to sneak Vanessa a cookie when Mother was scolding her for eating too many sweets. Or to smuggle me a plate of leftovers whenever I was sent to my room without dinner for talking back.

Talking back was something I did a lot. Even when it hurt.

That summer when my mom and dad were in the city, Dani had been the one to help me get to town. To Lola.

Growing up, I'd always had this vague idea that Vanessa and I had ended up in the wrong family. That the people who called themselves our parents weren't really ours. That we needed to fight them at every turn because they were clearly the enemy.

If my parents were the enemy, then Dani was an ally in our war.

"I need a dinner that will offer a thousand apologies with one bite. Is that something you can make?" I asked her.

She pinched her round chin with her fingers. "This about Lola, huh?"

I lifted an eyebrow.

"Eric told me she showed up at the door blazing mad."

"I tend to have that effect on her."

"Well, when you were kids, she used to like those snickerdoodle cookies I made for you. When you used to sneak out of the house to go play with her. Remember?"

I remembered every minute of that summer.

"You helped me," I said.

"I'd never seen you with a friend before." Dani shrugged. "You two were so sweet."

Well, it all backfired. My parents found out that I'd spent all that time in town with a local girl, and well, tongue lashings and nights without dinner were no longer enough to satisfy my father.

"I think I'm going to need more than snickerdoodles," I said. "I was thinking...maybe a picnic. Does that seem lame?"

"That seems like a fine idea, but to make it special, something Lola would really appreciate, you've got to put it together yourself," she said. "Maybe even make something with your own two hands."

My heart leapt at that idea. My dick did, too. I wanted to feed her. I wanted to sustain her. I wanted her to look at me with gratitude and appreciation. Then I wanted to put my hands in her hair. I wanted to pull her close to me. So I could feel her heartbeat. So I could hear the hitch in her breath and smell her skin.

Last night at the ball, when she tripped, and I had her arms in my hands...my skin still tingled. At the diner this morning, when we'd stood so close, her breasts had touched my chest, and my skin still burned.

Years ago in that storage room, when I'd thought if I didn't kiss her, if I didn't *taste* her in that moment, I would die wanting her, I still thought about it. Ached for it. My head, my body, my heart...every bit of me *ached* for her. To taste her again, touch her again. Because once hadn't been enough.

"Jackson!" My father bellowing my name from some other room in the house changed the temperature in the kitchen. Dani turned away from the noise.

Don't interfere with family matters.

"I'll get started with some homemade bread," she said, her head bowed.

I wanted to protest, but in this house, when Dad called, the easiest thing to do was what he wanted.

I walked through the kitchen to my dad's private office, which was adjacent to the study, where I'd taken Lola. He sat behind his desk, his laptop open in front of him.

"You bellowed?" I asked, adopting the same bored tone I always used with him. Like nothing he said or did mattered.

He was a handsome man, that's what all the write-ups said about Jackson Dumont Senior of the legendary Dumont Hotel family. They called him *stately* and *distinguished*, and since I was his spitting image, I figured I had all that coming my way, too. The silver in the sides of my hair. The straight posture. The cold eyes.

Suddenly, I wondered if he'd ever loved someone. Pined for someone. A childhood crush. A girl who had been forbidden by his wealthy parents. Or maybe he'd been born this way. Empty and cold.

I knew it wasn't right or healthy to hate my father. I knew there were long lasting consequences for it. God knows I'd spent enough time in therapy over the years, working it all out. But it never really changed my gut-level feelings.

I hated this man who called himself my father.

"We lost another property to that Shells Corporation in Philadelphia. Have you found out who is behind them yet?" he asked, not looking at me.

"I told you, there's nothing to learn. It's owned by a private holding company."

"There is always something to learn if you know where to look. What was the point of sending you to Harvard if you can't figure this out," he snapped. "They snatched that old radio station near the diner, now this."

"Why do you even want more property here?" I asked.

According to him, everyone in Calico Cove, particularly the small business owners, were idiots. "You've been calling this a one-pony town my whole life."

"Do you know how much property value has gone up in the last two years?"

Of course, I did. I didn't know he had as well. Dumont Senior was the president of the family-owned company that ran Dumont Hotels, but he'd always served as more of a figurehead. Never really getting his hands into the dirty details until recently.

"The wedding business has changed everything," he grumbled. "I should have been buying property downtown this whole time."

In the last five years, Shells had bought three properties out from under my father's nose. Properties he wanted to develop into steakhouses and hotels. One of them he was going to turn into a parking lot.

It was, for my father, starting to get personal.

"You seem very agitated," I observed. "So what if you missed out on a good deal? It's not like the business is hurting for money."

He looked up at me then, with an expression I don't recall ever seeing on my father's face.

Was that...fear?

Then, as if he realized he'd been caught in a moment of vulnerability, his façade changed to one I was more familiar with.

"You really are useless to me, Jackson." He sneered. "You always have been."

I smiled and shoved my hands in my pockets. "Well, I like to be consistent. If you're done with me, I need to leave. I have a date to prepare for."

Quite possibly the most important date of my life.

16

Lola

The diner was still a buzz of activity at five, but I'd finished my shift and instead of waiting for Jackson out front, I sat in my vacation chair out back. Although now that the Shells sign was back, it wasn't at all relaxing.

"You still have that attack cat?"

I closed my eyes at the sound of his voice. I didn't know how it was possible that a voice could go straight to a woman's nipples, but...whatever. Jackson Dumont was an evil warlock.

"Big Mama died last year," I said, turning to watch him approach. He wore a pair of dark shorts and a T-shirt. When the breeze blew, the T-shirt stuck to his muscles.

I remembered a time when I used to think he was scrawny and that was absolutely _not_ what I would call him now.

"I'm sorry," he said.

"About what?" I'd been distracted by the muscles.

"Big Mama. She was your buddy."

I narrowed my eyes at him. *What is he playing at?* I stood. "Let's get this over with."

"Are you hungry?"

I wanted to say no. I wanted to go wherever he was taking me and sit there and not eat a bite, but I hadn't had anything to eat all day, and truthfully, I was starving.

"I could eat," I said, with a shrug I was proud of.

A smile played at the edges of his mouth, and I was struck for a moment, thinking about how grown up he was. A man. Jackson Dumont was a man now. And I didn't have the slightest clue what he wanted with me.

"Come on then," he said.

He'd parked on the main road, not in the parking lot, so we crossed in front of the Shells sign which had been recently vandalized again. Instead of *bullshit*, this time someone had spray painted a bunch of suggestions:

Go Back to the City! Locals Eat at Pappas'! Down with The Man!

"Someone really doesn't like this sign," he said as he looked at it.

"People think they're going to build a family restaurant here."

He frowned. "Why?"

I shrugged. "Because that's what Shells is. Family restaurants. It only makes sense."

Something came over his face then. A realization. "Now I get it. You all think this competition is coming in next door."

"Obviously?"

He looked at me with a smile on his lips. "So did you spray paint that?"

"Nope. Just some loyal Pappas' eaters."

I would have thought Jackson was a sports car kind of guy. Something sleek and fast with a loud motor, but he drove the same black Jeep he'd always had, that now, years later, had seen better days.

He held open the passenger side door for me, and when I got in, he had to slam the door shut twice before it caught.

He had to do the same on the driver's side.

"You're still driving this Jeep?" I asked.

"Yeah. It's got some quirks, but it's all mine."

"I would think your father would have something to say about you driving around in a car with doors that don't shut."

"Oh, he does," he said and started up the Jeep. "I just don't give a shit anymore." He smiled at me again. I told my nipples to mind their own business. "You okay with the top down? We've got a little drive."

I shrugged like it didn't matter to me, and he put the car in gear, pulled a U-turn and headed south. The sun was warm, and the breeze was cool. It combed through my hair, teasing strands out of my ponytail, and it blew down the collar of my T-shirt.

We went past the main harbor, the cove with the public beach and the Dumont property. Past The Lobster Pot on the edge of town, until we got to the southernmost of Calico Cove's coves on the other side of the inlet from the lighthouse.

Hideaway Beach.

Called that because there were tons of big boulders spread out along the rocky shoreline making it a perfect place for teenagers to come and make out with some semblance of privacy.

Not that I would know.

"I always liked this beach the best," he said, pulling into the overgrown parking area.

"That tracks." I snorted as I climbed out.

"Why?" He stared at me blankly.

"It's a make-out spot."

"Bullshit," he said, and I gaped at him as he grabbed a blanket and a backpack, then a picnic basket. He had a lot of supplies for this dinner.

"Jackson, are you suggesting you and all your rich guy friends who were always visiting didn't come out here and make out with the local girls?"

"That's what I'm saying. It's my favorite because you and I would come out here and jump off those cliffs, remember? Although looking at it now, yeah, I can see how teenagers could put the cover of these boulders to good use."

He stepped onto the sandy trail that cut through the scrubby grass and trees towards the beach. What was he playing at? Self-deprecating was not a word I would use to describe Jackson.

"You coming?" he shouted over his shoulder, and without much choice, I followed him. The trail was short, and soon, we were through the trees and onto the golden beach with perfect end of day sunlight. *My favorite*, I thought. The sunlight so dense it seemed like I should be able to cup it in my hands.

"This is my favorite time of day on the beach," he said, and I looked at him sharply. "My second favorite is early morning and third would be...midnight."

"Don't," I said.

"Don't what."

"Play that game. That game is not for you. Not anymore."

The smile slowly dropped from his face, and he nodded. "Okay."

He set down the basket and the backpack and shook out the blanket. It was a normal sized blanket, but it would still require me to sit too close to him. All of this was too close to him. He sat and opened the backpack.

"I didn't know what you liked to drink, besides champagne," he said. "So I brought some champagne." He pulled out a bottle with moisture trickling down the sides. He must have some kind of cold pack in there. "A bottle of rosé, because my sister says it's the best thing ever. I have some local beer. That blueberry cider that's all over the place this summer and some water."

He laid the beverages all out on the edge of the blanket. A little smorgasbord of cold drinks for my pleasure.

"To eat," he said, and opened the picnic basket. There were plates and forks. Napkins. Little dishes of olives and cheeses. A loaf of sourdough bread wrapped in a napkin. Hummus, smoked trout, fresh ruby-red strawberries. Everything small and delicious and perfect.

"You didn't have to do all this," I said.

"I know." He looked up at me, his aqua eyes squinting against the light.

"Why?" I still wasn't sitting. In fact, I refused to sit. I crossed my arms over my chest. "Just tell me what this is all about?"

"Food. You're hungry." He said it like that made sense. He looked down at all the beautiful things he'd laid out on the blanket. "You don't like this? We can go anywhere or get something else."

Like my issue was with the food.

He got to his feet. "I'm not...I'm not going to pull the blanket out from under you or anything."

"Yeah, well, I don't know if I believe you."

He nodded. "I deserve that. I deserve all your suspicion and the reason why I'm doing this is...I'm sorry. I'm so sorry for the way I treated you when I was a teenager. The way I treated your mom, too. I was beyond an asshole, and I just..." He swallowed. "I was hoping I could make amends."

"With hummus?"

"I made it myself. Actually put the chickpeas in the blender and everything." He said it with a small laugh that indicated he knew both how ridiculous that was and how sweet.

That shouldn't matter, but it did, somehow.

"Listen to me Lola, I know none of my behavior ever made sense to you back then. We were friends once—"

"We were *best* friends," I corrected him. "We spent every day of that summer together and then suddenly you changed."

He nodded. "Yeah, I did. Remember that day your mom found me out on the rocks?"

"Yes. You weren't supposed to be out there. It was dangerous."

"She saw...well, let's just say she saw the truth about how things were with my family. She was kind to me in a way no one was, and more than that, she stood up for me in a way no one did. I didn't know how to handle that. My parents were angry. I was so angry, too. Then I just...made you the bad guy in my story."

"Me?" I whispered. "How could I be the bad guy in *your* story?"

"You had everything I didn't. You had a mom who loved you, who would fight for you. I was so jealous of you. Like, next level jealous. All the locals in town loved you. Georgie loved you. And for that summer, I got to pretend a little. Every time your mom played cards with us. Or when your friends hung out like I was their friend, too. And then my parents would come back and remind me that I didn't belong in your world. That I was an outsider. That all the love wasn't for me. It was for you. Everyone thought I was just a rich punk with an attitude, so I became that. The more everyone liked you, the meaner I was to you. It was that simple for me. Fucked up, yes. But simple."

"Jackson," I breathed out, my brain whirling with this information. All that time he'd been my enemy, but really, I'd been his?

"When I heard about your mom, all I wanted to do was get to where you were. See if you were all right. I know this won't make sense to you. But losing her was like losing an important part of me, too. I needed to...grieve with you. Then I came into the diner, and there you were walking around with your head up, a fake smile plastered on your face. You were trying to make everyone else feel better, you were helping every other person with their grief and all I could see was your pain."

"That's not..." I shook my head, unsure of what I wanted to say. Not true? Because it was. It was painfully, completely true in a way no one else had seen. Not even Georgie.

No one. Except Jackson.

"Your sorrow killed me. While everyone else just saw helpful, smiling, beautiful Lola, I knew what you were feeling. What you were hiding." He put a hand to his chest. "You needed...you needed to let some of that hurt and anger go. All I had to do was push the right buttons."

"You," I said in crazy disbelief. "You *made* me yell at you?"

"It was the only thing I could think of to help you."

I remembered how I screamed at him. How he provoked me. How he stood there and let me sneer and scorn. He gave me someplace to put every ugly emotion I couldn't show anyone else.

Then the next morning, he let me cry it all out on his shoulder.

I sucked in a deep breath, light-headed from the realization.

"Every time you screamed at me. Or gave me a hard time or one of your Lola Specials..." He stopped, his jaw tight again, his eyes on the waves. Then, when he looked back at me, something...shifted. That energy we had sometimes when the hate and animosity between us changed directions and turned to something hot and somehow worse.

It was as if, like me, he found himself—almost against his will—wanting me.

"You had so much fire in you, Lola," he breathed.

The words. The way he said them. That hot, lost look in his eye.

It was my turn to turn away, absolutely eaten by a blush. Destroyed by embarrassment and awful longing.

I couldn't see him, but I could feel him, stepping across that red blanket closer to me. Closer still. Close enough to touch and then...

Ohmygod.

"You still do," he whispered.

He was touching me. His hand on my cheeks, his fingers on my jaw, my hairline. His thumb...oh, my God, his thumb was on my lips. It felt like torture. I could not stop myself from gasping. Being touched by him was one of the most powerful physical things I'd ever experienced. Now it was happening again. Fire and ice all at once.

"Do you believe me?" he whispered.

I looked at him, my body going haywire. I shook my head.

"The party," I said. "That summer."

"Simon was already dating Vanessa," he said. Which, of course in one part of my brain I knew that. But I felt a pang for how easily I'd been suckered. "It wasn't casual, either. In some ways it was...arranged. His parents wanted to be associated with the Dumont name. My parents liked all that new Turnberry money. I saw how he looked at you, Lola. I knew he wanted to fuck you. I couldn't let that happen."

I flinched at his bluntness, which he felt because my face was still in his hands.

"That's not true," I said.

"Of course it is. You were the most fucking desirable person in town, and the second he caught wind that I wanted you, he was going to do everything—"

"Wait," I stopped him. "You wanted me? You just said I was the bad guy in your story."

"*Of course* I wanted you," he said it like I should have known somehow. And that wasn't fair. He'd been nothing but mean, but I should have just figured it out? "When we kissed, and ...it felt so right. Unless you didn't feel that way?"

I'd felt like my soul had been lit on fire but I wasn't telling him that. And I wasn't telling him that it was the hottest thing to ever happen to me.

"I thought you wanted a quick lay with an easy townie."

"I never thought of you that way. There was nothing easy about you and trust me when I say there would have been nothing quick about it."

That was hot. Why was that hot?

"That's why I told you not to come to the party. When you said Simon texted you, and you were all dressed up...I thought, *she's here for him*. Not for me. And I didn't handle it well."

He was so close. So close I could see how his eyes were green at the edges and blue in the middle. His dark hair curled around his ears, fell over his forehead. So close I could press my lips to his neck if I wanted to. I could see the beat of his heart under his skin.

"Do you believe me?" he asked.

I didn't have an answer. What did it matter if I believed him? What did it matter if I didn't?

I just needed him to kiss me.

"Do you believe this?" he whispered, and then to my utter amazement and my total relief, Jackson Dumont, my former best friend and current nemesis, kissed me.

17

Jackson

This wasn't the plan, I thought. It was the dream, for sure. However, I could not have planned this. A good guy would step back, make sure she was okay with this sudden change of events. That this was what she wanted with her head and her body. A good guy would feed her first, talk to her more, make sure she believed him when he said he was sorry.

I think we can all agree that I'm not a good guy.

She gasped, and I, like the asshole I am, took full advantage. I licked into her mouth, tasted her. After all these years, I was tasting Lola Pappas again, and it was just like that first time.

Toothpaste, and, under that, a little coffee, and, under that, the sweetness of her. Of her mouth. Her tongue.

This is how it's supposed to feel.

I groaned in my throat and the hand that had been

cupping her cheek spread into the curly blond perfection of her hair. Some of it caught. Tugged. And she moaned. I wasn't exactly Casanova, but I knew the difference between a moan of "oh, my God, please stop."

And "oh, my God, more."

That was a moan of the more variety.

Her hands were on my shoulders, cat claws grabbing my shirt, and letting go. Grabbing my shirt. Letting go. Oh, sweet fucking Lola was torn. Tortured. Trust me? Don't trust me?

I didn't ever think we'd get to this place. I'd imagined it. Even beat off to the idea in the shower before picking her up. But I'd never thought it would *happen.*

There were other things I needed to say, things I needed to make her understand—important things about that summer and why I'd been such an asshole. I should stop and make sure she understood those things. Except I was *kissing* her. Her mouth was open. Her breasts against my chest. I could drop my hand and palm her lush fucking ass... how could I stop?

Stopping seemed like tearing off my skin.

But I did it.

Because I'd fucked with this girl enough, and this next part I had to navigate carefully.

I leaned back, our lips clinging and then separating. She chased me down—eyes closed, leaning forward, wanting more.

A soft sweet sound of *no* and *come back* and *more* coming out of her throat. Then she realized what she was doing— that I was breaking the kiss, and she was being left vulnerable and wanting.

She dropped her hands. Leaned away from me. I watched her put all that desire away. All that feeling.

Her hair was still in my fist. Her eyes blown out. I could feel the pant of her breathing, the brush of her extremely hard nipples against my chest.

Lola Pappas maybe didn't like me. Didn't trust me. But she wanted me.

I wasn't an idiot. It would take more than a kiss to win her trust. However, I was also an asshole, and I saw my chance.

"Hmmm," I whispered, and her breath shuddered. "This is an interesting turn of events."

"Hardly."

"You don't find me kissing you interesting?"

"I'm practically asleep," she said.

Oh, she was... Well, she was asking for it, wasn't she? Her upturned chin and her blissed out eyes.

I leaned in and kissed her again. I kissed her until she responded with rising on her tip toes, clinging to my shoulders. Until she was kissing me back as hard as I was kissing her. Like the air inside of my mouth was what she needed to breathe. I pulled her up against me, chest to knees, and I knew the second she felt my hard dick pressed up against her stomach. She stilled, and I did, too, like we were on the edge of a knife and one wrong move meant pain.

Shit, I thought in that second of stillness. I pushed her too hard. It was what I did. I pushed and pushed until I broke the thing I was trying to protect. My good intentions never amounted to anything.

Then, Lola arched into me. Her belly against my dick. The sound in her throat a kind of purr. Delicious and *mine*.

I didn't plan this. I planned an apology. Bread and strawberries. An explanation. But this...Lola Pappas grinding against my dick like she needed it. Fuck, I couldn't refuse it. I wasn't superhuman. I'd wanted her for years and here she was acting like she wanted me, too.

My hand against her back slid to her stomach, her ribcage, and I waited every second for her to stop me, but when I finally cupped her full breast in my palm, she moaned again, melting against my chest.

Quickly, I thought about logistics. I wasn't going to fuck her here. Privacy boulders aside, we were not having our first time here on a public beach. God, I could make her feel good, though. An orgasm for every time I hurt her feelings. That would work. Right? I could lay her out on this blanket and beg forgiveness for my sins by turning her into a wet, coming mess of pleasure with my fingers.

Reflexively, my hand on her breast squeezed. She gasped, and I nearly came in my pants right there. I wanted to worship her body. Her fucking ass in these jean shorts. The ridge of her collar bone. The sweet spot between her legs that she was currently grinding against my leg. I pushed against her, she whimpered.

Yeah, this wasn't my plan, but it was perfect.

I wrapped my arm around her waist and lifted her off her feet. She stiffened.

"I got you," I whispered against her lips.

She leaned back. Her lips were so swollen. Her cheeks so flushed. I couldn't stop myself. All the words I'd held back over the years came pouring out of me.

"Fuck me, you're so beautiful, Lola," I whispered.

As soon as the words left my mouth, I knew I'd said too much.

She pushed against my shoulders, and the second I set her down on her feet, she spun away from me. Her shoulders hunched, her face in her hands.

I stood there feeling useless.

~

Lola

GOD. I mean...*God.* My body was a mess. My nipples hurt they were so hard, and between my legs, I throbbed. My lips were hot and swollen, and he did that to me. Jackson Dumont.

He apologized. He made me homemade hummus.

And he kissed me like...*God.*

He'd been so hard against my belly. The hardest dick I'd ever felt. Not that I knew...or had touched a bunch. There was Tommy Warner's sort of limp dick in the limo at prom because he'd been drinking whiskey all night. Needless to say, that night hadn't ended the way I'd planned. However, nothing compared to what had been pressed against my belly on this beach.

That couldn't be a lie, could it? He had to want me. That's what hard dicks meant, right?

"Lola?" His voice was quiet behind me. Pained.

I liked that. I liked it a lot, his strangled voice, the way his heart had pounded so hard I could feel it in his chest. But I didn't know what to do with it. How to take the boy I'd known and the man who'd kissed me, and reconcile them into the same person.

How was I supposed to do that? I knew how to feel about Jackson Dumont.

I had no idea how to feel about the man standing in front of me.

"I didn't want that to happen," he said.

I went cold all the way through. Goosebumps on my skin, the whole of myself flinching away from him.

Oh. Oh, God.

So this was the trick? Kissing me. Making me want him only so he could pull away. All so he could say he didn't want it.

"Me neither," I said, proud of my voice. Proud of my spine and my knees. Proud that I turned and looked him right in the eye.

He stepped forward, and I put my hand up and stepped back.

"That wasn't what I meant," he said, shaking his head. "It came out wrong."

"Sure." I looked down at his blanket all covered in sand and twisted up. "Are we done here?"

"Lola—"

"I think I'm done," I said, wrapping my arms around my stomach. "We should go."

He said nothing for a moment, then finally, "Okay, I'll take you home if that's what you want."

He turned around and shoveled all the stuff back into his picnic basket, the beverages into the backpack that had that cold pack in it and some voice in the back of my head said...

That was a lot of work just to trick me into kissing him.

I walked ahead of him down the path. The sun was setting over the water and the air was getting cool. I tried to fix my hair and ignored the sounds of him behind me.

In the parking lot, he put everything in the back of the Jeep, and I buckled in and crossed my legs and ignored him.

"Where do you want me to drop you?"

"My car is at the diner."

It was a silent awful drive into town. The cold air reinforcing everything I needed to be reminded of. When he came to a stop beside my old Toyota, I reached to the back of the Jeep and pulled out the bottle of champagne, and then, because I was starving and fuck him, I grabbed the cheese, the bread and hummus.

"Do you want the wine, too?"

"Yes."

He took the things out of my hands, put everything in the backpack, then handed it to me.

"I'm not giving this bag back to you," I said.

His lips lifted in the briefest brightest smile, but it never reached his eyes. His eyes were just sad.

I grabbed the backpack, but he didn't let go and tugged it back.

"I didn't want that to happen on a public beach," he said. "That's what I meant. If we didn't stop, I would have—"

"No."

His eyes burned with a truth I couldn't deny. "I would have been making you come for every time I hurt you. I didn't want that to happen when anyone could walk up."

"Because it's embarrassing for you?"

"Because it's private. Because I want you to myself. Every bit of you, Lola."

Heat rolled out from my core.

"Why did you make an offer on the diner?" I asked.

"I found out there were other parties interested. I had to move fast so no one else could make an offer. I am just trying to buy you some time. The attorney review period gives you that."

This time when I pulled on the backpack, he let me go.

"Do you believe me?" he asked.

I wanted to. God, I wanted to. I wanted to believe him about all of it. The diner, the kiss. The apology.

"I don't know," I said honestly.

That dumb motherfucker beamed at me. Just glowed like he'd been given a gift.

"That's not a no. I can work with that," the dummy said.

THAT NIGHT, my belly full of delicious fresh bread and crumbly cheese, and feeling slightly buzzed on my ill-gotten champagne, I wrote and deleted a dozen texts to Georgie.

I made out with Jackson Dumont.

Jackson Dumont kisses like a man who can't survive without kissing.

Jackson says he's sorry.

How can I believe he's sorry?

Should I get a lobotomy?

I was deleting yet another text when my phone buzzed with an email from the CCIB. Which, let me tell you, was a happy and welcome distraction that I dove into headfirst.

To: Lola Pappas

From: CCIB

Subject line: More information

Hi Lola,

You suggested wanting to meet in person. Unfortunately, I wasn't kidding about the importance of anonymity. This way it keeps personal stuff out of the business transactions. For example, if I was your mean fifth-grade teacher from back in the day, you might not want to take our money.

I would still like to learn more about the history of the diner. Why did your father leave the restaurant to his second wife? Why not you? You said it was family drama. I hope there wasn't any foul play involved.

Still interested,
CCIB

"THAT'S FUNNY," I said to the empty room. "My fifth-grade teacher was, in fact, mean."

I took a swig of my champagne straight from the bottle and did not consider that answering these questions while drunk might be ill-advised.

To: CCIB

    From: Lola Pappas
    Subject line: Re: More information.
    Hi back, CCIB. Can I call you CCIB, if I may be so informal? Ha!

    It's funny, or well, maybe not funny ha-ha, but funny. (sad face emoji) My mom and dad never wanted me to stay and run the diner. Well, my mom didn't and Dad kind of did what she wanted. Mom wanted me to see the world and experience stuff so if I came back to the diner, it would be a choice and not because it was the only thing I'd ever known.

    Don't get me wrong, I'd love to see the world, but as for where I'm going to live and the work I want to do—it's Pappas' Diner in Calico Cove. I would be the fourth generation Pappas to run the diner and that means more than I can say. The history, the legacy. A sense of knowing you belong to a special place. Calico Cove isn't perfect. But it's perfect for me. I love it. It's home. All I want to do is make Pappas and Calico Cove the very best they can be.

    Still interested, too,
    Lola

. . .

I SENT IT, took another swig, then watched Harry Styles music videos until my email binged again.

To: Lola Pappas

From: CCIB

Subject line: Re: Re: More information

Lola, you can call me anything you want. It must have hurt when you learned your father gave the diner to your stepmother. I'm so sorry you had to experience that.

CCIB

THAT WASN'T REALLY A QUESTION, but a pretty astute observation from someone I'd never met. It had hurt when we sat in the lawyer's office, and he'd read the will. I knew my dad hadn't intended to betray me. Given what he knew then about the state of the finances, he probably thought he was relieving me of a burden. He didn't understand it was my burden to carry. That I wanted that responsibility.

To: CCIB

From: Lola Pappas

Subject line: Re: Re: Re: More information

It did hurt. All of it hurt. It still hurts. That he didn't trust me to understand myself and what I wanted. That he thought he knew better. Maybe all parents think that. I just thought my dad was different. That he would never try and force me to do something he thought was better for me.

Is this TMI?

Lola, and yes that is TMI.

. . .

I SENT the email and dug in the bag for some chocolate. Honestly, what was a picnic without chocolate? In the very bottom there was a plastic container. I opened the lid and gasped, delighted to find chocolate-covered strawberries.

They were messy and clearly handmade and...wow.

He really had gone to a lot of effort for our picnic.

My email binged.

To: Lola Pappas

From: CCIB

Subject line: Re: Re: Re: Re: More information

Speaking from personal experience, I believe parents do think they always know best. Whether they are right or wrong.

I can sense your pain and anger with your father in the spaces between the words. Take some advice from me. Find a way to make peace with what your father did, or you will have a very expensive therapy bill that will haunt you. Trust me.

It's okay to share, Lola. As I told you before, business can be very personal.

I feel as if in some ways...we're building a friendship?

Your new friend,

CCIB

P.S. We'll have a decision for you soon. Hopefully in ten business days.

WHEN I WOKE up the next morning, I was in bed with a container of chocolate covered strawberries, an empty bottle of champagne and a hangover.

And... some low-level anxiety. What did I do last night besides spite eating and drinking Jackson's picnic?

Then I remembered the email exchange with the CCIB.

Shit!

I'd gotten a little boozy and spilled my soul. Who did that with an investment bureau when they were asking for money?

I needed whoever was on the other side of that email to respect me as a businesswoman. Not some flake with daddy issues.

I read through the exchange again, wincing at my bad jokes. By the time I got to the end, though, I thought...huh.

Was it possible the CCIB was flirting with me?

Ten days. Jackson said there was an attorney review period that would buy me time, but I had no idea how long that was or exactly how much time that bought me.

Shit.

I needed answers and Jackson was the only one who had them.

18

My Three Favorite Things About Lola

Her blond curly hair
Her gigantic heart and sassy mouth
Her brain
Her perfect peach of an ass
I could go on for days...
Yes, I realize that's more than three

Jackson, age 25

I was sitting at one of the booths in the diner—a two-top, because I wasn't *that* guy anymore—waiting for Lola, who, unusually, wasn't here.

"So where is she?" I asked Chloe who was filling my coffee cup and water glass for what had to be the hundredth time. Her lips were still painfully large. So large it was hard to look away from them. So large they were hypnotic. I was curious, if she bit into her lip would it pop? Like a blister?

"Who?" she said.

Right. Why would anyone think I was waiting for Lola? "Lola."

Chloe shrugged. "It's her day off."

That was disappointing.

How was I going to set my evil plan to woo her in motion, if she was off doing chores? That's right, after the amazing kiss, and resulting debacle on the beach, I'd come up with a new plan.

What if I just charmed the hell out of her? What if we put all the past behind us, and…just started fresh? For the first time, we were actually talking to each other. At the ball, she'd been flirting back before she'd known it was me.

We had…chemistry. Connection. We'd had it since we were kids. I'd told her the truth and now I was going to woo her.

"What does she do on her day off?" I asked. No, I wasn't going to stalk her. Just maybe…pass by places she might frequent.

"Usually? She works here. The girl wouldn't know how to get a life if she had to."

Yeah, I thought, *I want to help her with that, too.*

I knew who her friends were. The Petit girls. Mari, the baker's daughter. I'd wander over to the bakery then. Maybe I could woo her through the best friend.

As a rule, I was better with parents, dogs and best friends.

Not so much cats.

Too bad Lola didn't have a dog.

"How are the plans for the wedding?" Chloe asked,

running her cloth over the table for the tenth time. "I heard it's going to be a big wedding."

She was angling for an invite. Everyone in town was angling for an invite.

"Actually, it's going to be very intimate. I don't have much to do with it," I said and fished my phone out of my pocket. She got the hint and wandered off.

I sent a text to Eric, who, as well as managing the estate, also handled our cars and boats. I asked him to call the docks and make sure the Chris Craft Runabout was in working order with a full tank of gas.

This was the thing about wooing someone through a best friend—it helped to have a boat. I imagined Mari, with her long red hair and Lola, in the front of the boat, laughing every time I hit a wave.

My phone rang then. My father was identified as Dumont Senior in my phone. I braced myself and picked up the phone.

"Yes?"

"Did you know Pappas' Diner was up for sale?" he said curtly without any greeting. It wasn't unusual for him.

This was delicate territory. My offer on this place was to be kept private, but Tiffani hadn't wasted any time telling Lola who was behind it. If my father got wind I'd already gone to contract, things might blow up sooner than I was ready for.

"Hmm. Another property available in town? I assume you're interested," I said to deflect the questions.

"Of course I am. We can tear that eyesore down and build something impressive. A real restaurant that serves real food. Not all that fried crap and milkshakes."

I loved Pappas' milkshakes.

"Interesting idea. I'll get some information and then you can decide what you want to offer for the place."

"Finally, you're thinking like a businessman," he said. "I'll show you how to negotiate too. You never take the first offer."

Excellent, my father was going to teach me how to negotiate real estate properties.

The door opened and suddenly Lola was there.

Like I'd wished her into existence.

"I've got to go, Dad. I'll let you know what I find out."

"You better—"

I'd already disconnected the call.

Pink-cheeked and breathless, her hair in a ponytail that bounced as she walked, she looked so...alive. Like she was teaming with ideas and thoughts and plans. Like there wasn't enough time in the day to be her.

Her eyes caught mine and widened. I wasn't sure what to expect after the way we'd left things last night. To my surprise and delight, she stomped over to me.

"I didn't know you would be here," she said, biting her lower lip.

"I came for one of your famous Lola Specials," I said, trying to tease her into smiling.

"It's my day off."

"So I was told," I said.

"Actually, I needed to talk to you anyway. Not about...our stuff."

We had *stuff*. That shouldn't make me as happy as it did.

"Business stuff. I need to understand things about how this whole real estate process works."

Keep cool. Don't jump. She's asking for your help. No big deal. HUGE DEAL! YOU GET TO BE THE HERO NOW!

"Yes, that makes sense," I told her, with my very serious

business tone. "Only, I am late for a meeting, would you mind coming with me? We can talk on the way."

She blinked. "Okay. I guess." Then she laughed. "You're not planning on kidnapping me?"

"No," I lied. Well, was it a lie? A little bit. But these were desperate times, and I was a desperate man. "Drive with me?"

∿

Lola

THE JEEP WAS OPEN, and the wind was blowing. When I tried to ask him my questions, he shook his head and pointed at his ear like he couldn't hear me. So we drove downtown, past the square to the public pier and boat launch. He parked his Jeep in a spot marked "Dumont" and got out. I had no real choice but to follow him.

Jackson walked ahead along the dock, but I stopped to say hi to Matthew first.

Matthew ran the ferry from Calico Cove out to the Piedmont Island, which was half private property owned by the Piedmonts and half state park/nature reserve. He was sitting on a folding chair on the dock beside his small ferry reading his Kindle.

Matthew was Calico Cove through and through. He'd been running that ferry since he was in high school. A job he took over from his dad.

Once, he'd been a track star, the event where you did all the events, whatever that was called. He broke state records and had this fancy scholarship to go to college, but just... never went. He was still, as Mari used to call him, a total looker.

Dark hair, dark eyes, the body of an athlete.

"Heya, Matthew, how is business?" I asked.

"Wicked slow. Waiting on those birds to lay their eggs."

When the birds were laying eggs at the sanctuary, no one could go to the island, except the Piedmonts.

"You love those birds, and you know it. How is Mrs. Piedmont?"

Matthew's eyes followed Jackson as he walked down the pier, stopping in front of a boat slip to talk to a man standing by a classic Chris Craft Motorboat.

"Hanging in there, but it won't be long. The cancer is eating her alive," Matthew said. "Told Annie it was time to call Carrie home."

We hadn't seen Carrie Piedmont in years. Unless you counted the big screen where she was a big deal actress. Once upon a time, there'd been rumors about Carrie and Matthew, since he was basically, like, the Piedmont chauffeur but with boats.

I didn't believe those rumors.

Annie, Carrie's sister who ran the bookstore, was the only Piedmont who was ever very nice to Matthew.

"What are you doing with Jackson Dumont?" Matthew asked in a low voice.

"A business thing," I said.

"A business thing on a boat? I don't trust those Dumonts as far as I can throw them."

"You don't trust any of the summer people," I reminded him.

"True fact. Watch yourself with that guy."

"I will," I said and patted his sun-warmed, extremely muscled shoulder.

Goodness, I thought. Jackson looked up and saw me

touching Matthew, and I mean, it could have been the sun in my eyes, it could have been wishful thinking, but I could have sworn he scowled a little harder.

"You ready?" he shouted at me. He jumped in his fancy motorboat and started to take the lines off the cleats on the dock.

"Where are we going?" I asked, jumping into the back of the boat.

One thing growing up in Calico Cove, you got real comfortable around boats. I undid the last cleat, and Jackson pushed the throttle, and we pulled away from the dock.

"Jackson!" I shouted again.

He either couldn't hear me, or he was ignoring me.

I touched his shoulder to get his attention and that terrible zapping electrical shock ran through my hand, up my arm and settled in my heart. I was nervous. No...maybe not nervous. I was keyed up. Feeling extra everything when I didn't want to feel anything for him.

We made a wide turn around the rocky outcropping of the Southern-most cove, where the Calico Cove Lighthouse stood on the edge.

Malcolm Bettencourt owned the place now. When he'd first come to town nobody really knew him. Nobody except Jolie, who had somehow managed to become his housekeeper.

Last summer something definitely happened between them. And when I say happened, I mean *happened*.

There had been a time when it felt like me and Jolie were the last two twenty-something virgins in town. Then Jolie went and fell for the Beast of Calico Cove.

Except it hadn't ended well that summer. He'd left town, and Jolie had taken off for culinary school. Only Mal came back this past winter, and well, they must have made up.

I'd heard from Jolie's sister Verity that when Jolie was finished her internship, she was coming home.

And for Jolie, home was going to be at the lighthouse with Mal.

I wanted to be happy for her. I was totally happy for her. I was also a little jealous.

She'd gotten her happily ever after.

"Jackson?" I asked, looking around. If we were this far south, I didn't have a sense of where he was taking us. "Where are we going?"

"I think this should do it," he said. Then he turned off the engine, and we eventually slowed until we were bobbing in the water. He opened a small hatch and grabbed an anchor and tossed it over the edge of the boat. I watched it sink.

"Jackson," I said. "What kind of meeting were you going to?"

He held out his hands. "The meeting was a lie."

It dawned on me. "You *are* kidnapping me."

"That seems a bit much."

"No, pretty sure this is what kidnapping looks like."

"Lola—"

"Admit you kidnapped me," I crossed my arms over my chest.

"Fine. Yes. I kidnapped you. For some time alone. You never would have come out here if I didn't lie."

"You don't know that," I said. "You don't know that because you didn't ask. You just jumped right to kidnapping. Who does that?"

"Fine. Would you have come if I asked nicely?"

"Absolutely not."

"Right, so…" He smiled, that crooked smile, pushed his hair back off his head, and I remembered the silk of it between my fingers. "It's a beautiful day on the water, you have questions. Now we can talk privately without worrying about Tiffani or the twins being around."

That was…true. "You don't have to trick me."

"You're right," he said earnestly. That boyish charm gone in a flash. "I'm sorry. I can take you back—"

"No." I held up a hand. "I mean. We're here. It is a really nice day."

"Something fun on your day off."

I narrowed my eyes at him, and he shrugged, that cocky grin back on his face. I didn't want to be happy to be alone out here with him. I didn't want to be secretly pleased that he wanted to be here with me.

"I'm sorry," he said. "I made sure the boat was stocked with food, and there is a cooler filled with drinks."

"Is that what rich people do, just have picnics available at any moment?"

"Not in my experience, but I am trying to woo you."

I sucked in a breath, and he went very still, like he was aware he'd said too much.

"What?" I whispered.

"You had to know I wasn't going to give up that easily, Lola. Not after that kiss."

He stepped forward, then forward again, and I didn't step backwards because one, there was nowhere to go, and two, I didn't want to. I wanted his body to collide with mine. I wanted his sun-warmed skin and his too-long hair.

I wanted him to take his shirt off. I wanted to take off mine.

"Lola, you have to feel it, too. There's something special between us. Admit that. Acknowledge that at least."

I lifted my shoulder in a super tiny acknowledgment. There had always been something between me and Jackson. Whether it was good or bad.

"Maybe you don't trust me to care about you. To care for you. Yet. But I'm just going to keep packing picnics for the snack queen, thinking sooner or later you might understand that I just want to take care of you."

A seagull squawked overhead, and the waves lapped at the glossy wooden sides of the boat. All of this felt real. Everything he said. It had the weight and heft of truth.

He stepped forward. The toes of our shoes touched. As the boat rocked and swayed, my body touched his then his touched mine, and I was suddenly breathless and...strange inside my skin.

Like yesterday, but worse this time. Because I knew how good it could be.

"You had questions," he said. "About real estate."

As if I could remember those.

"Well, now, you're the question," I said.

"What can I do?" he asked, his voice a murmur, low and husky, and my skin was suddenly too tight. "To make it up to you?"

Oh, that was...he was being sexy. He was, like, offering himself up as some kind of pleasure service system. Oh, jeez. I mean, what was a girl supposed to do with that? Talking about the sale of the restaurant was absolutely out of my head. Like, gone. All I could think about were the things I wanted this man to do. For me. To me.

But this was a level of boldness I was not accustomed to. I was not really equipped to handle.

Oh, God, he didn't even know. I was a twenty-three-year-old virgin.

The sneaky devil, it was like he knew that, too. Like he

was so aware of every thought in my head and this rico-cheting desire in my body. He reached up and ran the back of his hand across my breast. Just that, a confident but glancing touch. Teasing that aching nipple. I gasped and practically collapsed at his feet.

"Tell me what you want from me, Lola?" he asked again. "How can I make this right between us? Tell me, how we get to the other side of all our history?"

His cheeks flushed, his eyes dilated. His voice so rough it was like it was pulled up from his guts.

Like it *hurt*.

Like it hurt having me so close and so far away at the same time.

I didn't know how we could do that, get to the other side. I only knew this man wanted to seduce me, and for the first time in my adult life, I wanted exactly that.

"Can you take off your shirt?" I wanted to see him. I wanted to really see the man he'd grown into.

"My shirt?" he asked, his lips lifting on the side, like he liked the idea.

"Off." Where was I finding this boldness? Who the hell knew? But I was deeply into it. I sat on the bench to watch the show.

He did that thing boys do in TV shows that shouldn't be so hot but was. Reaching up behind his head and pulling the T-shirt off from the back. I saw that trail of dark hair that arrowed down his stomach. Then I saw his shoulders.

He dropped the shirt on the chair behind him, and all the muscles in his arms flexed and popped. It was like an anatomy book brought to beautiful sun-splashed life.

"What do you do?" I asked. "To look like that?"

"I still run mostly." He ran his hand down his chest, across his stomach, and I had to squeeze my thighs together.

It was suddenly so warm out here on the water. He wore a pair of loose khaki shorts. With the hem all frayed, that hung off his hips, revealing the waistband of his underwear and the hard ridge of a hip bone. I wanted, with a sudden strange pang, to kiss that ridge of bone, where it pressed against his skin.

"Do it," he said. I looked up, only to find his aqua eyes burning blue green.

"Do what?"

"Whatever you're thinking. Whatever has you looking at me like that and squeezing your thighs together like you need it."

"Need it?"

"Like you need to come."

Oh, my God, Jackson Dumont just said the word *come* in relationship to me and sex. It was very serious and all of a sudden.

"Do you remember—"

"Yes," I cut him off.

"You don't know what I was going to say," he said.

Except I did. I knew what he was going to say. "The storage room?"

"Yes," he hissed.

"It just sort of happened," I said softly. "Like we couldn't help ourselves."

"Swear to God, Lola, I almost took you up against the wall of that damn room. I'm still not sure how I stopped myself."

I looked up at him and swallowed.

"Kiss me like that again, Jackson. Like you can't stop yourself."

It was like I'd fired a gun and said go. He fell to his knees between my legs where I was sitting, wrapped his arms around my hips and pulled me tight up against him. I couldn't swallow my gasp or stop the way I pushed myself against the heavy erection in his pants.

"Yes," he groaned and sank one hand in my hair and kissed me.

Consumed me. Like he'd been waiting for this. For the silence and the sunlight and the permission and me.

I didn't have the strength to worry about how this might hurt me. How this pleasure would turn into pain with one stupid word from his lips, so I didn't give him the chance to say anything. I grabbed onto his face, wrapped my arms around his neck and kissed him the way I'd dreamt of kissing someone my whole life.

His hand slid under my T-shirt in the back and his rough palms over my skin made me shiver and grind against him. He licked into my mouth, sucked on my tongue. Then he lifted the shirt over my head, breaking away to get it off me and that second made me freeze. Nearly naked and trembling in the sunlight, in front of my nemesis.

Quickly, I crossed my arms over my chest.

"No, Lola. I swear to God, you are so fucking beautiful." It wasn't his words so much as the way he said them. Like they were falling out of his mouth without a plan.

"Hot and gorgeous and I've been fucking dreaming of your tits. You're so perfect. Look at all this skin."

His ran his wide calloused hands over my back and my shoulders, down my arms, curling his fingers through mine. Everywhere but my breasts in—thank God—my newest bra.

It was like he was content to look, and I needed him to touch me. I pressed myself against him. Grinding against his erection until I felt that hot sharp spark of pressure on my clit, and I jerked. A kind of full body flinch and I did it again. I grabbed onto his hips, pulling him harder into my body.

"Are you using me to get off?" he asked, and I said nothing, consumed by the need to just be closer to him. To push that hot electric spot on my body against him as hard and as often as I could. "You are," he groaned.

Shut up, I wanted to say. I bit my lip and closed my eyes, and he bent his head, finally cupping my breasts. Finally sucking my painfully hard nipples through the cotton of my bra, and, now, I was crying out his name. It was me saying *fuck*, over and over again. Grinding and whimpering. *So close*, I thought.

"So close," I said.

He slipped his hand inside my bra, his fingers pinching my nipples. He was kissing me again, and it was all too much. His dick between my legs. His hand on my breast, his mouth open and wet and demanding against mine.

I came, gripping his bare shoulders so hard, my nails left marks. I was so far out of my body and out of my head. I was dazed and twitching.

That's never happened, I wanted to say. *Not with another person*. But when I opened my eyes, he was watching me with those eyes of his. I cleared my throat, dropped my hands from his shoulders. Awkward and suddenly extremely cautious.

"No," he said.

"What no?"

"Don't go into your head like that."

I opened my mouth to lie but he kissed me again. Sweetly this time.

"You told me to do what I would have done to you in the storage room," he whispered into my mouth, and I felt like butter that had been left out on the counter. I was all soft, my edges curling. Despite what had happened, the throb between my legs, I was astonished to want more. To...need more. More of him. More of that feeling.

"I think we did that," I whispered, tilting my head back so his lips could make their way down my throat.

"Oh, Lola." He laughed, kissing the trembling top of my breast, now hanging out of my bra that had been pushed aside. "We haven't even started. Lie back," he said.

Sun warmed and drunk on sex, I did what he asked, leaning back against the banquet. He kissed my breasts, licked my nipples, moved down to my belly then he unbuttoned my shorts.

I jerked, thinking I'd close my legs except he was there. Holding me open.

His eyes met mine. "Do you want me to stop?"

"I'm..." My brain was short circuiting. "Wet."

He made this growling laughing sound in his throat and kissed my belly, right where the button was open. "Yeah, honey, I know. Let me taste you," he said. "I'm dying to taste you, Lola."

What was a girl supposed to say to that?

He pulled off my shorts, my damp blue satin underwear going with them, and he sat back on his heels, looking at me. Completely naked to him.

I would have died from embarrassment. I would have curled up into myself, except he kept talking to me. His hands stroking my thighs, telling me constantly that I was so beautiful. So sexy. His fingers slipped into the curls between my legs, and he was holding me open, vulnerable to him, the sunlight and that seagull swooping above us.

Then he was licking me between my legs. Tasting me. Sucking my sensitive clit into his mouth. If I thought rubbing up against him was so hot, this was like being burned in a fire. My arms went wide looking for anything I could hold onto that would keep me on the earth. He pushed deeper between my legs, my knees going wider, and his hand came up and grabbed mine, giving me an anchor to hold.

Yes, him. I would hold onto him, and we'd fly up into the sky together.

Another orgasm was building, curling me up into a tight ball. Every muscle flexed. Then two of his fingers thrust into me. It hurt, a burning stretch, and I gasped, leaning forward, looking down at him.

Ouch.

He looked up at me, our eyes met over my body, and I could see and feel him smile. The burning stretch was gone, and I flopped back down and let him do this thing to me. This intimate, never before done thing.

"Yes," I moaned. "Jackson."

I put my hands in his hair, showing him the pressure and the angle I liked.

Just like that, I came again against his mouth. Jerking and crying out, lost someplace I'd only ever read about.

Geezus, I thought. Sparks at the edge of my vision. My hands numb. My brain blissed out.

"Lola?"

I looked down at him, sitting back on his feet. His face was slick, his hair a mess, and I felt my heart dip. Like, really dip. Like, fall, actually. My heart fell to my stomach, and I realized everything we'd done here, we couldn't undo.

There was the time before I'd let Jackson Dumont go down on me and there was after.

"Are you okay?" he asked, his voice calm and serious. "Did I hurt you?"

"Hurt me?" No. Why? Did I come weird? Ugh. Leave it to me to come weird. "No. That was...that was amazing."

"You're bleeding." He lifted his hand and I saw the blood on his fingers, and he picked up his shirt to wipe at the insides of my thighs, and I realized what this was.

Not my period, which, oh, my God, like, that would have been more than I could take.

Those fingers of his had basically taken my virginity, which, I fully understood and knew, was a social, sexist construct. But a hymen was a hymen, and what it was doing sticking around until now was outrageous. I'd used enough tampons that you'd think the thing would have been dealt with already. But no. Right here. Right now. Not even having full-fledged sex.

"If I hurt you," he breathed, and he looked up at me with such honest and searing regret and pain. "I keep trying to make things better and I—"

"Jackson, no, I'm a virgin. I guess *was* a virgin. I...virgin," I said and felt myself blushing. I leaned forward and pulled my shorts and blue underwear back up my legs and found my shirt.

"It's no big deal."

"No big deal? Lola, I made you bleed."

I shoved my shirt on, inside out as it happened. Fix it? No. Fuck it. I just needed a little distance. I got up and stepped past him, getting as far away from him as I could on a twelve-foot boat.

"How are you...were you still?" he asked, like he was confused by the whole thing.

"My mom died, Jackson. Okay? I had the diner. And then..." I was about to tell him that he came along and ground my confidence into the dirt, but he already looked so stricken. I couldn't put that entirely on him. "I had the diner and then...Dad died. I just, you know, never got around to dealing with it. Why are you freaking out about this?"

"Because, I wouldn't have hurt you! I would have been more careful. I wouldn't have finger-fucked you until you bled!" he shouted. His words echoed around us. I was blushing myself into a pile of ash.

"You want to get louder? I don't think all the fish heard you."

"I'm just saying, I'm sorry."

"Oh, trust me," I said, "me, too."

I turned away from him, blinking back tears.

"Lola," he breathed. He grabbed my hands in a grip so firm I couldn't shake him. "No, we're not doing this. I don't want to fight with you. I don't want to make you cry."

"But you always do," I said, feeling more vulnerable than I had even a few minutes ago with his head between my legs. "We made more sense when we hated each other."

"I never hated you," he said. "Never."

"Well, I hated you enough for both of us."

That was the truth, bitter and hard between us.

"I think you should take me home," I said.

"Lola," he whispered, and I turned away from him, wishing for sunglasses. Wishing for anything that would keep me strong against him. I was sore between my legs. I was sore in my heart. I was sore.

"I just want to go home."

It took him a long second, but he finally pulled up the anchor, started the boat, and turned us towards shore.

19

Jackson

I know what you're thinking. Total disaster, right?

I'd unintentionally hurt her, then embarrassed her. She'd cried. We'd fought.

I piloted us back to the dock, then drove her to the diner in silence. Me thinking about that smear of blood on her thighs, on my hand and wanting to punch myself in the face.

Yes. On paper, total disaster.

Except she'd let me touch her. Kiss her. She told me what she wanted and let me give it to her. Twice. She let me inside of her the way no man ever had before.

I mean...that had to count for something.

Once I'd dropped her off at the diner, she'd taken off so fast I didn't even get a chance to say goodbye, but I still wasn't going to let that shake me.

I'd spent years fucking up with her, and I had to think, at some point, I was going to run out of grace. That one of these times, she'd look at me, cold, and I'd know I was out of chances.

Today was not that day.

I didn't go back to the estate, and instead, I made my way toward a new construction project just at the edge of town. A condo complex, with ten units. None of which were technically ready to be lived in yet, but I'd already claimed my own.

Given that it was my construction project, I was allowed to occupy the place, even though it didn't have countertops yet. The marble delivery was delayed.

Still, it was better than being at home.

The condos were intended to be rustic in design anyway, and the steel beams and brick walls were all original to the building. I had electricity, running water, a couch, a TV, and a bed. I was fine.

I opened the door, then stopped when I saw I wasn't alone.

"Vanessa?" I said, and the lump on the couch moved, a blonde head peaked up at me. God, she was so...soft. Like an overripe peach, just really easily bruised, and I didn't know how to protect her.

"Is it okay that I'm here?"

I tossed my keys on the table I had set up by the door and kicked off my shoes. I stopped in the kitchen that was all along the west wall where the middle of the day sunlight that was coming in through the southern windows was nearly blinding. I pulled a glass out of the box of glasses I'd recently bought and filled it with water and headed over to the big wide deep couch made out of black velvet that my sister told me I needed.

It was a ridiculous couch. I loved it so much.

She flopped sideways. Her arm hitting the floor. "I thought you were nuts for getting a condo in Calico Cove. Now, I am glad you did it."

"Why was that nuts?"

"Like, how often are you ever going to be here?"

I'm moving here, I thought. I wasn't going to tell her my plans because she was an absolute blabbermouth, and we already had a few secrets she was struggling to keep quiet.

"You know staying at the estate for more than a night or two isn't an option for me." I shrugged. "You going to tell me what's happened?"

"I went to a dress fitting with Mom."

I handed her the glass of water, sat and put her feet on my lap. She scooted around so she could take a sip, and I got a good look at her face. Puffy eyes from crying.

"I thought getting married would make everyone happy," she said, holding the glass with two hands.

"I don't think getting married to a guy like Simon is going to make anyone happy."

Simon was going to cheat on her the first minute he could. He might be doing it already, and she knew it, but still she was committed to seeing this shit show through to the end.

"I just want a family. A real family," she said. "A husband and babies and a home. He can give me that."

"Yes, but why does that have to be Simon?"

"You know it's what Dad wants." She sighed.

I did. I also knew she hadn't fought back as hard as I had when it came to my parents.

She took a sip of water, and I watched her, wishing I could change her mind. Wishing I could go back a year and tell her to not get back together with him. Wishing I could go back five years and punch Simon in the face, instead of kicking Lola out.

I wish I could go back ten years ago and never turn to

him in Math class and ask him if he knew where I could buy some weed.

I'd made so many mistakes.

My phone dinged with an incoming email alert.

To: CCIB

From: Lola Pappas

Subject line: Urgent

Hi, it's me again. I hate to ask this, because I know you said you would have an answer in ten days, but someone has made an offer on the restaurant already. I'm afraid if I don't act fast, I might lose my opportunity altogether. Is there any way to reach a decision sooner?

Sincerely desperate,

Lola

"FUCK," I said.

Vanessa, who had been reading the email over my shoulder, sighed then looked at me.

"You should just tell her it's you. You're the CCIB. Then you can explain everything."

"Not...yet," I said, especially after the way things had ended with us on the boat. We needed to build up more trust first.

New things I was coming to understand about Lola.

She didn't like secrets, or tricks, or kidnappings, apparently. She also didn't like being manipulated, and I was doing all of that right now.

Of course, I'm sure she would be thrilled when I told her it was for her own good.

That seemed like the kind of thing she would love.

"What are you waiting for anyway?" Vanessa asked. "Why not just tell her you're going to give her the money?"

It wasn't that simple.

Two years ago, when the manager at the Dumont Hotel started to implement the wedding packages—Vanessa's idea by the way, although she never got credit—Vanessa made the comment that Calico Cove local businesses were going to have to *up their wedding game.*

That's when it struck me. There were a ton of investment opportunities sitting out there in the town just waiting for an influx of cash.

A designer dress studio for wedding gowns and bridesmaids' dresses. A specialty wedding cake bakery. A high-end florist. Photographers, videographers, DJs...all of it could be sourced locally.

Together, Vanessa and I pooled some of our trust-fund money, some of what I'd already made in my real estate company, and some of what she'd made during her brief and disastrous modeling career, and created the CCIB.

We'd invested four million dollars in Calico Cove, completely anonymously, and so far, every one of them had been a success, making us even more money so we could find new businesses looking for cash.

"I've got to do this carefully. It can't look too easy. If she found out who was behind the CCIB, she might not take the money." If Lola Pappas was anything, she was proud.

"Well, that's ridiculous. She needs to save her restaurant!"

"Hmm. You under-estimate how much she hates me."

We made more sense when we hated each other.

Vanessa sat up then. "You really think you can turn her around? What if you can't, and she loses the restaurant?"

"She's not going to lose the restaurant," I said, determined. "Right now, I've got the sale tied up with a pending contract. We just need to stall until the funding comes through."

Seven-hundred and fifty thousand dollars would be the largest cash loan we'd ever provided. That kind of funding took time to liquidate into cash.

"Can I ask a question? How did you know?" Vanessa asked. She was pleating the edge of the blanket and not looking at me.

I didn't have to guess at what she was asking.

"That I loved her?"

She nodded.

"Because the world changed the minute I met her. All I wanted was to be around her. Then I let my shit get in the way. Now I just want to be the man she deserves."

She nodded. "I feel the same way. About Simon," she said, but she was lying.

"Ness," I sighed, and she shook her head. I'd pushed and pushed but I couldn't do this for her. She had to do the hard part and stand on her own two feet.

"You staying here?" I asked.

"Just for a few hours," she said.

"Okay. Where's Simon?"

"Playing golf with Dad."

Right. This was the crux of it, the bitter rotten heart of my sister's decision to marry Simon. Our father liked him, and my sister still thought she could somehow please him. Somehow earn his affection.

If she married Simon, she believed Dad would finally love her the way she deserved to be loved.

It broke my heart. Because I'd already learned there was nothing I could do that would change our father into a different type of man. I could tell her that all day long. Had tried. She was convinced that wasn't what she was doing. That she loved Simon, that she wanted to start a family. But it all came back to our dad.

Daddy issues.

"Hang out as long as you like," I told her.

I stood and went to the sliding glass doors that led out to the stone balcony with views of the ocean and the bike path where I liked to run. I closed the door behind me and texted Lola.

Jackson: Hey. With everything that happened today, I realized you never asked me your question.

Lola: Who is this?

Jackson: The guy who made you come today. Twice.

Lola: Jackson! How did you get this number?

Jackson: Gave Chloe a twenty-dollar tip for it.

Lola: She is SO dead.

I didn't like lying to her. Of course, I'd gotten her number off her loan application. Another lie/secret/manipulation that I had to hope would be forgiven when she trusted me. And yes, I was aware that lying to her to get her trust was probably a bad call, but I didn't have a whole lot of options.

I probably should have waited twenty-four hours before making contact with her.

But a) desperate and b) Vanessa was right. Lola was running out of time.

Lola: I don't even think I'm talking to you. Do you even know what the silent treatment is?

Jackson: Yes, you're rather good at it BTW. But that was personal, and this is business. You have questions, you need answers. Don't let me and what I did to screw things up again get in the way of that.

Jackson: Let's meet. The One-Eyed Gull in two hours. Hopefully by then the silent treatment will have worn off.

One-Eyed Gull was the local dive bar where a Dumont wouldn't be caught dead. It was firmly her ground. She would be surrounded by her people. Completely safe.

Lola: How do I know you're not going to kidnap me again?

Jackson: It's why I picked the Gull. Everyone there is on your side.

Lola: This is messed up. Fine. Two hours. Don't be late.

That was my girl. I grinned and sent her a thumbs up.

∾

Lola

SURE. Yep. Stupid. Totally stupid. Literally hours after jumping off that boat and practically running away from Jackson Dumont, I was sitting at the Gull waiting for him to come in and what? Make me cry again? Make me want to hit him?

I mean, wasn't this what they called insanity?

"What can I get you?" Wendy asked.

Wendy was a few years older than me, but she was lucky enough to have a dad, who had actually given her the bar when he'd decided to retire to Florida a year ago.

Some might think a dive bar for hard-drinking lobstermen was no place for a young woman. But Wendy had grown up with these old guys. There wasn't a single person in town who would think of giving her any grief.

That she was also a competitive Mixed Martial Arts fighter didn't hurt her reputation as being a badass, either.

"Water's fine," I said. The last thing I needed was to actually have a drink with Jackson. I needed total control around him from now on.

"Are you sure? I just put on a pot of coffee." Wendy said, and I managed to keep my face from grimacing. Bar coffee was bad enough. One-Eyed Gull coffee was a special layer of gross.

"I'm fine."

I pulled out my phone to play Wordle and hadn't even gotten to my second guess when Jackson was suddenly beside me. Wearing the clothes he'd worn earlier, smelling like sunshine and the water and...well, me a little bit.

I had a reaction to that between my legs. A primal kind of pleasure.

That's right, world. He's mine.

Only that was stupid, so I took a sip of my water and tried to play it chill. Sure, he'd gone down on me hours ago, but I was cool.

I think?

No, so not cool. I would have to fake coolness.

"Hi," I said as he got onto the stool next to me.

He sat facing me, so I was aware of where his knees were in relationship to my body. If I shifted just a few inches... yep, I'd hit his knee with mine. I scooted back a little, which, of course, only made him move forward.

If I was determined to be distant, he was determined to be charming. Warm. He smiled at me like he was just so happy to see me at a dive bar on a Wednesday night. Like he just couldn't imagine being someplace better.

How was a girl supposed to maintain her chill in the face of that?

"What are you drinking?" he asked, looking at my pint glass full of water.

"Just water."

"Hey, Jackson," Wendy said as she approached him. "The usual?" she asked him, and he nodded.

"You have a usual?" I asked him. "At the Gull?"

"I do. I have a usual at most places I go to more than once."

"Not at Pappas'," I reminded him.

"No, there I always got the Lola Special. I never knew what that was going to be. How did you come up with that stuff anyway?"

I smiled despite my vow to be distant. "I think my favorite was the meatloaf milkshake."

"Ugh," he groaned. "It was the chili and cottage cheese in the same bowl that still gives me nightmares."

"So you've been to the Gull more than once?" I asked him. Of course, that made me take another look at Wendy. She was all lean muscle and no body fat. Long dark wavy hair. Gorgeous if you were into the kind of love interest who could break your arm.

"You say that like it's crazy. It's kind of the only bar in town. I've been here a few times since coming back."

"You know you own the hotel with a bar."

"I like the décor here."

Now, that made me laugh. If Larry the stuffed Lobster was cheesy, then the Gull was a Velveeta factory.

It was fishing nets and fake fish. There was a wooden figure at the door. A fisherman with a blue jacket and a yellow cap that Wendy's dad had commissioned to look like the guy in the fish stick commercials. The drinks were all nautical themed. The food was all from the sea and deep fried.

Basically, it was the last place you'd expect to find a Dumont.

"What's your usual?" I asked him, curious despite myself.

"Guess."

I gave him a cut the shit look, and he laughed. "Just try."

"Scotch or something brown and expensive."

"Booooring," he sang.

"I thought that's what all you Ivy League boys drank?"

"I suppose," he said. Wendy came by with a drink, and I was surprised to see it served in a martini glass. It looked...creamy.

"Thank you," he said and took a sip. "Guess again. You want a sip?"

He pushed the glass over to me, and, caught up in the easy-going charm that Jackson Dumont just oozed, I took a sip.

My mind was blown. "Are you drinking a chocolate martini?"

"I am!" He laughed.

"That's your drink?"

"The first time I came in I told Wendy to surprise me, and this was what she brought me. I think she might have thought I would be embarrassed, but...who can be embarrassed about a chocolate martini? You want one?" he asked.

"No. Thanks."

"If you let me buy you a drink, I will answer all your questions."

"You're going to do that anyway," I said firmly. But that drink had been delicious. "Fine. One drink."

"Wendy, another martini," he called out to her. "Now. Ask me your questions."

I spilled to Jackson about the CCIB and my plans to buy the place from Tiffani and renovate it.

"Why do you need to renovate it so badly?" he asked me.

"Hello? Shells Family Restaurant. If something that shiny and new moves in right next door, we'll go under. I'm sure of it. The locals are loyal, but I need the summer tourists to make ends meet."

He frowned. "I didn't realize..."

"Realize what?" Wendy slipped the drink down in front of me with a wink.

"Well, I don't think you can make assumptions," Jackson said. "It doesn't say Shells Family Restaurant on the sign. It says a Shells Operation. It's unlikely that a chain family restaurant would want to compete with something that's locally loved like Pappas."

"I don't think I can afford to assume that. In any case, you know the diner needs to be updated."

He nodded. "Yeah, it definitely can use some work."

"Anyway, I applied for this loan, but it's going to take another ten days before I hear back from them. You said something about attorney review buying me some time, but I don't know how long that is. You have to back out of the deal in order for me to get the restaurant, but what if someone else steps in before I can make Tiffani an offer?"

"Yeah, that's an issue," he said with a breath. "Don't freak out."

"Oh, my God, now I'm freaking out."

"My dad is interested in buying Pappas."

Jackson Dumont Senior wanted to buy Pappas.

Someone. Kill. Me. Now.

20

Lola

"Are you kidding me? Is this some kind of sick Dumont joke?"

He winced. "Unfortunately, not."

"What on earth would your father want with my diner?"

"He doesn't want the diner. He wants the property. He wants to tear it down and put in some fine dining restaurant."

I slumped. "Of course he does. And the worst part about it, he's not wrong. Fine dining is something the tourists are looking for and Calico Cove doesn't have it."

"Look, normally attorney review is five days—"

"Five days!" I panicked. "That's not enough time."

"Okay, we have options. I can always move forward with the deal," he said.

"No, absolutely not."

"I'll buy the place from Tiffani, and then sell it to you."

I shook my head. "No, Jackson. You buy it, then it's yours and not mine. I'm not taking your charity, which is all this would be, and you, of all people, know that about me."

He sighed. I could see it in his face. He did, at least, know that about me.

"We'll figure it out," he said. "I'll call my attorney, see if we can find some legal mumbo-jumbo that will help us stall the review period. I wish I could tell you I could talk to my father...but there is nothing I could say that would make him listen."

He said *we*. We would figure it out. Why did that make me feel so choked up?

Suddenly, with no warning at all, I was blinking back tears.

"Hey, hey," he said. "Don't do that. I promised myself, for once, I wouldn't make you cry."

I gulped in a breath. "It's not you...this time. I'm just so scared."

"Don't be scared, Lola. I've got you. You're not alone in this."

I turned away, grabbing a cocktail napkin and all but digging it into my tear ducts.

"Sorry," I said. "It's just been a lot, lately."

"It's going to be okay. I promise," he said, with the kind of authority that could only come from having gobs of money. Considering what I needed was gobs of money, it was actually comforting.

We sat then for a bit, sipping our drinks, and I felt something from him that I hadn't felt in a long time. Comfort. It was like when we were kids, he was just there. Jackson had been as reliable as the sun to me. If we were picking shells on the beach, I only ever had to look over my shoulder to know he wasn't far away.

For the first time in a really long time, I allowed myself to just miss him. Or at least acknowledge that was the feeling I had in my chest when it came to him. Instead of always denying it.

Denying Jackson. Missing Jackson. Wanting Jackson.

"Jackson?" I asked in a soft voice. He still heard me.

"Yeah?"

"Where have you been for the last five years?"

"I knew you missed me," he said with a small smile. "Do you want another drink?"

I shook my head. One chocolate martini was enough for anyone.

"Then come for a walk with me. I promise no kidnapping."

I slid off the stool, and as he stood, he offered his hand. I did not take it.

"Embarrassed to be seen holding my hand?"

"No," I insisted. "I'm just not a hand holder."

Was I? There'd never been anyone whose hand I'd wanted to hold besides my mother's.

"Consider this exposure therapy for you. Otherwise known as fake it until you make it."

He took my hand, and suddenly, it was done. We were doing this now. We had officially moved on to hand holding.

Given the activities of this afternoon, it didn't seem like such a stretch.

We left the bar and the fresh sea air hit my lungs, giving me a burst of energy.

"So the last five years. Tell me," I said.

"Well, obviously I finished college, then I went on to get my MBA."

"In Boston?"

"New York City."

"That doesn't explain why you didn't come back here."

He was staring ahead not looking at me when he said it. "I couldn't...I couldn't keep breaking my heart over you, Lola. You hated me, I hated myself. This place became a problem for me. I was an adult with access to my trust fund, so spending time with my parents was now my choice, and I didn't want to be anywhere where they were. I had a business I was starting and that took all my time and attention and..."

He stopped and it felt like I was waiting for the big secret to be revealed. I squeezed his hand.

"And?" I prompted.

He looked at me then. "I needed to figure shit out. Grow up. Find out where all my anger was coming from. I mean, I knew...where it came from. I just needed help dealing with it. With the shit my parents did to me."

"What did they do to you?" I stopped walking. I didn't let go of his hand, though. "That day when my mom found you on the rocks? Was that your dad?"

His jaw tightened, and I could feel the tension seeping from every pore of him. I was about to let him off the hook, tell him he didn't have to talk about it. Only, it seemed if we were ever going to have the chance to talk about our history, it was now.

In this moment.

"Yeah. The night before, I'd said I didn't want to leave, and I told him so. He said what I wanted didn't matter. That I was just a kid. I said, *yeah well, you're an asshole.* And that didn't go over great."

"Oh, Jackson." That he tried to make it a joke broke my heart.

"It wasn't the first time. It was just the worst up until that point. And I think your mom knew that. That day she got one look at my face, and she told me she was going to report my parents. That it had to stop. I told her she couldn't do that. That it wasn't a big deal."

"But it was."

He nodded. "But believing it wasn't, was a coping mechanism. It was how I survived. A careless backhand across my face from my father, an arm squeezed too hard by my mother. All those times I was sent to my room without eating for talking back. There were weeks I never had dinner. I was never what they wanted me to be, and they let me know it. The anger, it just kept building."

"I'm so sorry."

"I was angry at my parents, angry at your mom because I thought she was just going to cause more problems. And I was just a kid who didn't know how to handle any of it. So, I've spent the last five years trying to figure out how to handle it."

"How?" I asked, because I had my own complicated issues to handle.

"Therapy mostly." He laughed. "Anyway, now you know how you became ground zero for all my fucked-up anger. I'm sorry for that. Again," he said, squeezing my hand.

"Now you're back."

"I was always planning on coming back," he said. "Then Vanessa said she was getting married, and she wanted it to be here, and I knew...well, I knew I'd been away too long. It was time to own up to the shitty things I did in this town. Show my face, not just my..."

"Your what?"

He shook his head. "I feel like I've done all the talking."

Yeah, but it had been nice. Walking along the sidewalk, holding his hand. Just talking with him instead of actively hating him.

"Okay," he said, jiggling my hand. "What are your three favorite things now?"

"You're kidding."

"They have to have changed. What did they used to be? The diner, shells, chocolate mint ice cream?"

"Yours was chocolate mint ice cream."

"God, I must have eaten gallons of it that summer."

"What are *your* three favorite things?" I asked, pushing the question onto him because I wasn't ready to be that vulnerable.

"The smell of new construction, running and the Lola Special," he finally said.

I bumped his shoulder with mine. "You did not like the Lola Special."

"I liked how creative you got with it." He laughed softly. "Your turn."

"Okay. Karaoke brunch, a full restaurant and a perfect grilled cheese sandwich. What are your three least favorite things?"

"Hmmm.... Cruelty, mushrooms and anything fake. What about you?"

"Lies. Losing one winter glove at the beginning of the season and cleaning the flat top at the diner."

"Solid list."

"I remember that," I blurted out. "I remember you not liking mushrooms. We were playing on the beach one day, and my mom brought us that pizza."

"Why?" he said, looking up at the now dark sky. "Why in God's name do people insist on ruining something as precious as pizza with something as gross as mushrooms?"

"You kept making that face and picking every single one off. I remember laughing."

He squeezed my hand again. "Yeah. They weren't all bad memories, were they?"

"No. Not all bad."

We were still walking, being quiet with one another when I saw we were at the elementary school.

"Is this where you went to school?" he asked as we stepped on the cracked asphalt playground.

"It is. This is the sight of the epic four square battle that ended with Joey Malone getting a bloody nose and me being crowned the undisputed Queen."

"Four square?"

"Yeah, the game with the ball and the squares." We were standing in the middle of the four square court. He looked at me blankly. "You've never played four square?"

"No," he said. "The boarding schools I went to had really organized recesses. I played a lot of lacrosse and cricket."

"Sounds fancy."

"It was." He said it without much emotion. Or fondness.

In the way of schoolyards, there was a ball that had been left out at some recess and I grabbed it from the scrubby bushes where it was lodged.

"Want to learn?" I asked him.

"Really?" he asked, seeming delighted.

The ball was mostly deflated, and I couldn't completely remember the rules. But I gave him what I could remember. Double bounces. Spikes. Twisters.

"That has to be cheating," he said when I gave him my patented serve, which bounced in the top corner of his square then spiraled all zig zaggy out of bounds.

"My point." I grinned at him.

"Oh, Pappas, it is on."

It was suddenly competitive and a little sweaty, and I was deeply invested in kicking his ass in a playground game, but also laughing the whole time. He seemed to be laughing, too. It was the most fun I'd had in a very long time. Until he spiked the ball so hard in the bottom corner of my square, it bounced up onto the roof of the school.

Like kids, we stared at the roof as if it might do us a solid and throw the ball back.

"Nice shot," I said.

"Does that mean I win?"

"Nope. Sadly. But you gave it a good shot."

"Do we just...leave that ball there?" he asked.

Obviously, wherever he went to school they didn't have Mr. Jenkins who went up to the roof at the beginning of every school year and threw down all the tennis balls, basketballs and frisbees that had been stuck up there.

That seemed like a real lack.

I explained Mr. Jenkins, then we resumed walking.

"Are you friends with anyone you went to school with?" I asked.

"Simon," he said. "He was a grade younger than me. But he stuck around."

"Now he's marrying your sister."

I waited for him to say something, but he was silent. His face carefully blank.

"Were they really an item that summer?" I asked. "Like, was Simon flirting with me while he was with your sister?"

Jackson looked over at me and nodded. "She was crazy about him. He was excited to be dating a Dumont. He liked the doors our name opened for him. The parties he got invited to." One of those helicopter twirly things came down from a tree and he caught it in his hand. "The way he was looking at you..." He shook his head. "I couldn't stand it. I also couldn't stand the way you were looking back at him. I couldn't stand the way my sister wouldn't hear what I was saying about Simon and...well, I fucked it up."

"Are you worried?" I asked

"About Vanessa?"

I nodded.

"Constantly. He doesn't love her now any more than he did then, and she thinks she can love him enough for both of them."

Struck by an urge, I didn't fight it. I dropped his hand and wrapped my arms around his neck, pulling him up tight against me. My head in that place between his neck and shoulder. Where he was warm and smelled like the sea and chocolate.

"What's this for?" he asked, stroking my back.

"Exposure therapy," I said. Because I had a feeling he hadn't been hugged enough in his life.

He paused for a second, every muscle in his body still and poised, and I thought he was going to push me away. Then he wrapped his arms around my back and hauled me up and off my feet.

I kissed him.

Softly. But it didn't stay soft.

Sweetly. But it didn't stay sweet.

His hands came down and grabbed my ass, lifting me right up against him.

"Have I ever told you how much I love your ass?"

"No, Jackson. It's never come up."

"I fucking love it. It's so round." He cupped it in his hands. He squeezed it, and I groaned. "It's so soft and firm at the same time."

"Come on," I said and stepped away, not wanting to get caught making out on the four square court. We ran across the baseball diamond to the street on the other side of the school, and there was my ramshackle house.

"It's pink," he said.

"It was a joke between my parents. My mom said when she was a kid she wanted to live in a pink house, and so when they got married and bought this place, Dad painted it."

"Your dad was a romantic guy."

"He was." I turned to face him. "Do you want to come in? The twins and Tiffani have the late shift, so they won't be home."

He narrowed one eye. "Are you asking me up to your bedroom?"

Crazily, I was. "Do you want to come up to my bedroom?"

"Yes. Lola," he said as if he was reciting a solemn oath. "I would very much like to go up to your bedroom."

21

Lola

W e walked in the door from the garage, and I could feel him wanting to get a look around, but the house was full of the twins and Tiffani. There was no part of me in the main rooms anymore. The pictures of me as a baby had been pushed aside. My mother was completely gone. It was just a place I had to walk through to get to my space.

"Up here," I said and opened the door to the narrow steps leading up to my attic room. The hallway was tight, and he kind of had to duck. I was really aware of my ass, like, in his face as we went up, but he just reached forward and tucked a finger in the pocket of my shorts, and it was such a small thing and a huge thing all at once that I felt giddy.

"Wow," he said, coming to stand in the middle of my room. It was painted turquoise, and I'd put up these wild wall stickers of giant flowers. There were Christmas lights and a reading lamp and a bookshelf stuffed with my books. I kicked some dirty clothes under my bed and pulled the crazy quilt my mother had made me up to cover my sheets.

"This is you," he said, looking at the bulletin board I'd covered with pictures of friends and Georgie and ideas for the diner. I'd written out menu ideas and promotional ideas and my master list of Karaoke brunch themes. "I mean—" he turned towards me "—this is just...totally you."

"I should move out," I said, tucking a Christmas light back over the hook I'd put up for it. "This house isn't mine anymore, and I've had first and last month's rent for an apartment for a while now. But we had to replace the sink in the women's bathroom at the diner and that ate into my savings."

"I have a place," he said.

"In Boston?"

"Here."

"Wait, what? You said you came back for Vanessa's wedding."

He looked at me. His face serious. "I came back for more than that, Lola."

Since that seemed entirely too scary, I diverted.

"Where are you staying?"

"The old newspaper print shop building."

"Where they are building the new condos?"

They were brand new, and as far as I knew, no one was living there yet.

He nodded, and I could only stare at him, blank-faced. He reached up to the curls that had gotten loose during our walk. He tucked a curl behind my ear, his thumb running along my ear lobe in a way that told me a lot about what he'd come back for, but I would deal with all of that later.

"I'm just saying if you need a place to stay."

"With you?"

"You can sleep on the couch," he said as a joke, and I laughed, the tension broken. Foolish, here in my bedroom, surrounded like a shipwreck survivor by all the things I could salvage from my own life, I felt bold and...smitten.

I was smitten with him. By him.

Like he could read my mind, he looped his arms around my back and walked backwards to my bed set up in the dormer of the attic. "So, you brought me up here. What is it you wanted to do with me?"

I toppled backwards onto my bed, bringing him down with me. He caught himself with one arm, and it was so hot and guy-like, and I loved it.

I kissed him, spreading my legs so he kind of just fell in between them. Like a puzzle piece into another puzzle piece.

"We have to talk about what happened on the boat," he said.

"Why?" I kissed his neck. The top of his chest.

"Lola, I was so...rough."

"I liked what we did."

"Be honest," he said.

"I am. I am a virgin, or I am what's left of a virgin after what we did on the boat, and I liked what we did."

"You ran away."

"I was embarrassed because you were making it a thing." I was good at being embarrassed. "A twenty-three-year-old virgin? I mean...that's embarrassing."

"No, it isn't," he said, burying his face in my neck. Tracing the edge of my V-neck T-shirt, his aqua-like eyes burning into mine. "I have to say it, it's actually kind of hot. No one has been inside of you."

He arched forward and that baseball bat was back between his legs, and I couldn't stop the sound I made. The humming laughing groan.

"Has any man made you come before?" he whispered and arched against me again, and I saw sparks.

"No."

"You're killing me." He groaned again. "Just me?"

"Just you."

"So fucking hot." Another push against me, and I lifted my hips again, searching for the right place, the right pressure. "You want to come?" he asked, pushing a curl off my face.

"Isn't that the point?" I asked through clenched teeth. He bent over my breast and sucked me into his mouth. My shirt, my bra. Didn't matter. He used his teeth, and the cotton diffused the sharpness and all I felt was pressure.

"Jackson." I groaned. I was aching, now. All over. One giant bundle of need.

"Are you going to let me fuck you?" he asked, pulling my shirt up and kissing my belly.

"Yes," I said. I wasn't thinking. I was past thinking. I would say yes to everything he wanted to give me at this point.

His hand slipped between my legs, cupping me over my shorts. "I can feel how hot you are," he said.

"Is that weird?"

"No." He laughed. "Lola. It's perfect. You make me feel like a fucking teenager again."

He rubbed me a little through my shorts, and I put my heel up on the bed, spreading my legs wider.

"This is what I wanted to do to you at my party all those years ago," he said, and I looked at him sharply. "That pink dress you were wearing and that fucking lip-gloss?"

He kissed me like he couldn't get enough. Mouth open, lips sucking, tongue everywhere. His curled his hands in my hair and held me still while he ravaged my mouth, and I was drowning in him. In pleasure.

"You wanted to kiss me at that party?" I whispered when he broke the kiss so we could breathe, panting into each other's mouths.

"After that kiss in the storage closet, I wanted to kiss you every time I saw you. I was dying for you, Lola, and I knew I didn't deserve you."

That was...if I was honest, how I felt about him, too. The desire and the frustration were part of the rage. I pushed my hands under his shirt, spreading my palms out wide as I could against his back like I was trying to touch all of his skin. Moaning, he closed his eyes.

"You like this?" I asked him.

"I love it."

I pushed my hands down the back of his shorts, my fingers grazing the top curve of his ass, and he buried his head in my neck. Bold and encouraged by his sudden stillness. By the way he seemed to be waiting for me or soaking in my touch. I shifted, and he, like he knew, lifted his hips so I could get to the button of his shorts. Then the zipper.

His heavy erection his was making itself known against the back of my fingers. I ran my knuckles down him over the thin cotton of his boxer briefs.

I could feel the tremble in all his muscles. "Fuck, yes please. Please."

"Please what?"

"Touch me."

There was so much in those words. Full whole stories about touch in his life. The lack of it, the cruelty of it. He'd had other girlfriends, maybe I'd ask him about that. He'd been touched like this before, I was sure.

But in my attic room, my soul bared as much as I could take it, he was begging me.

He pulled in a deep breath through his nose, and his smile, when it came, was tight. He put his hand over mine. "I'm sorry. I'm pushing you. You don't have to do this," he said.

He was reading my hesitation all wrong.

"I want to. I want to do this, I'm just...warning you."

"About what?"

"I might do it wrong."

He kissed me again. "Everything you do to me is perfect."

"That seems dubious."

"Perfect. Because it's you. I have wanted your hands on my body for as long as I can remember."

Part of me wanted to recoil. Hide somewhere safe, but there was no safe place with him. Or, I realized, maybe every space with him was safe. Could I trust that? Did I care right now?

Later, I decided. I'd worry about that later. Now, I just slipped my hand under the waistband of his underwear and curled my fingers around his heavy dick. Warmer than I expected. Harder even than I'd thought.

"Lola," he groaned.

I pushed him so he rolled over on his back, his arms spread wide against my bed. His coffee-colored hair, flopped up on my pillow. His cheeks pink, his eyes...his eyes on me.

I glanced down at the hard length of him, pink, nearly purple against my hand. The soft head, the creamy liquid oozing from the tip. I gave it no thought. None at all. On some kind of instinct, I bent over him and licked that liquid up with my tongue. My mouth around the tip.

He jerked like I'd brushed him with electricity. His hand flew to the back of my head, cupping my skull. Not pushing, but not not pushing.

"More?" I asked, not really knowing what more was, but I'd read books. I'd seen movies. I could give it a shot.

"Everything." He groaned. "Everything you want to give me, I'll take, Lola. You want to hurt me, hurt me. You want to suck my dick..." He stopped there. Eyes closed, his throat tight. In my hand, his dick leapt and the come was leaking over my fingers.

I squeezed my thighs together. Suddenly more turned on than I'd been on the boat. More turned on then I'd been in my whole life.

I leaned over him, but the angle was wrong. I slipped to the edge of the bed, on my knees in front of him and that made him groan. He grabbed a pillow and handed it to me.

"Don't hurt your knees," he said. Then he took the other pillow and shoved it under his head so he could watch.

Shit. Now I had to do something worth watching.

"You're beautiful," he said, and I let myself soak up the compliment and his belief made me believe it.

"So are you," I said. I yanked down his shorts and under-wear, channeled every romance novel I'd ever read, and went to work on my first blow job. He was salty and warm and somehow hard and soft at the same time. I paid atten-tion to the sounds he made and how he seemed to like it when I cupped his balls in my hand and swirled my tongue around the tip.

"Harder." He groaned once, and I squeezed him in my fist until he flung his head back like he was in pain. He put his hand over mine and showed me how he liked to be touched while I sucked the tip, and I wondered if I should be embarrassed, because I wasn't. It was hot how he showed me what he liked, how he made me touch him the way it felt best.

I fucking loved it.

Between my legs, I was wet through my shorts, and I wanted to touch myself while I was touching him. So I pulled one hand off his dick and put it down the front of my shorts, until my finger was on my clit.

"What are you...?" He lifted his head and saw what I was doing. That was, somehow, the last straw for him. He cupped my head in his hands, fucking his hips up into my mouth without any control.

Oh, God, I loved it so much.

"I'm going to come." He groaned and started to pull me back, and I wasn't sure what the protocol here was, but I was not interested in not seeing this to the end, so I leaned forward, unwilling to move. Which must have been the right decision, because he pulled me closer and exploded in my mouth.

I swallowed, because that seemed the easiest. The most natural thing to do. He took one shuddering breath then bent and picked me up off the floor and all but tossed me on the bed. Then he was on his knees on the floor pillow, spreading my legs wide, looking at the wet spot on my shorts from how turned on I was.

He looked up at the ceiling like he was praying for strength, and I laughed. I laughed because this was fun. It was hot, but also fun.

"What are you laughing at?" he asked, undoing the button and pulling down my shorts and underwear for the second time today.

"Us. This."

"It's funny?"

"It's fun."

He looked at me then.

"It is," he said, then he bent and ate me out like I was a three-course meal. He paid attention, and when I jerked and spasmed with pleasure, he did more of what he was doing. He made me come once, his tongue on my clit, but he didn't stop.

"What...?" I whispered as he carefully slipped one finger inside of me.

"Let me make this right," he said and gently fucked me with that single finger until I begged him for more.

"Jackson!"

He chuckled and slipped another finger inside of me. I was gone. I was air and pleasure. I floated over that bed in a million pieces until collapsing, sweaty and transformed back on the bed.

He leaned up and kissed me, his mouth slick with my juices. It was just one more intimacy, one more thing stripped away between us. We both still wore our shirts. I had on one sock, and I'd never felt more naked.

"You okay?" he asked.

"So good." I sighed, boneless and spent.

He kissed me again, then suddenly, we heard the sound of the garage door opening and the sound of Tiffani and the wonder twins coming home.

Every ounce of good feeling that had happened in this room was suddenly gone.

"Lola?" Tiffani called out from downstairs. "Are you home?"

∼

Jackson

SHE WENT SO STILL in my arms, I looked down to see if she was actually there. Like, somehow, she could will herself to vanish.

"Are you okay?" I asked her, and she gave me an empty smile.

"You have to go."

"Sure. But are you okay?"

She was doing some kind of calculation in her head. I didn't know what it was. Or how to make the calculation come out in my favor. She sat up and started putting on her clothes, and she handed me mine.

"Do you want me to sneak out?" I asked her.

"Yes." She laughed without a lot of humor. "But there's no way to do that. I think we just have to hope they're not in the kitchen when you go down."

"Are you going to get in trouble?"

"No. I mean, I'm an adult. But...they'll just be ugly about it.'

I understood ugly, and I grabbed her hand and pressed a kiss on her knuckles. I would try to figure out how to protect her from the ugly. She crept down the stairs, listening at the door for a second, before waving me down, too.

She opened the door, and we stepped into the small foyer in the kitchen between the garage door and the door to her room. There was no one in the kitchen, and she opened the garage door, which had a painfully loud squeaky hinge. She cringed and tried to hustle through, but there was a pile of shoes by the door. She tripped, and I caught her.

"Lola. Is that you? You are home," Tiffani said and

stepped into the kitchen from another room. Lola went still like a deer, and there was no hiding what we were doing. Sneaking down from her room. Both of us looking freshly fucked.

Tiffani's eyes went wide, and I slipped my arm around Lola's shoulders. Kissed the top of her head. Broadcast in every way I could that I was with this girl, and Tiffani needed to watch what she was going to say.

"Oh, hello, Jackson," Tiffani said with a fake-ass smile on her face. "I didn't expect to see you here."

"Well," I said. "I go where Lola goes."

"Did you have some questions about the diner?" she asked, her eyes wide, but calculating. "Because it's me selling it, not Lola."

"Oh." I waved my hand. "I let my lawyers handle all that."

Tiffani looked like she might combust.

"I was just seeing him out," Lola said. Of course, the twins, who scented drama like bloodhounds, came in, focused on their phones until they saw me. I watched them catch on to what was happening, their eyes going wide, their jaws dropping.

"Come by anytime," Tiffani said. "You're always welcome in our home."

"Thank you," I said and let Lola pull me out through the garage to the sidewalk in front. She was beet red.

"You okay?" I asked.

"You ask me that a lot," she said. I wanted to tell her it was because her being okay was the only thing that mattered to me. I didn't know how to read her, and I'd gotten it so wrong in the past.

"Listen to me, what I said tonight is true. Don't worry

about Tiffani or my dad or anyone else getting their hands on the diner."

"Easier said than done, Jackson."

"I know, but you have help. You're not alone."

She took in a deep breath that shuddered, and I got the sense that I'd unlocked something with those words. I'd done something very, very right.

"Thank you," she whispered and kissed me sweetly on the lips. "You better go. They're watching us from the front window."

I turned and saw them all standing there. Tiffani dropped the curtain like she wasn't staring, but the twins only waved.

"You can come with me," I said.

"Where?"

"My condo. Spend the night with me."

"I don't...that's...I have the early shift."

"That's okay. I'm not scared of your alarm."

I could see she was tempted by my offer but wasn't going to take it. I understood. She'd thought I hated her until, like, three days ago. I was moving fast in her eyes. In my eyes, it had been years of wanting her with me.

"Call me later," I said to her.

"For what?"

"For a weather report." I laughed. "For conversation. To ask me what my favorite television show is."

"What is it?"

"*Love it or List It*," I said, naming my favorite HGTV network show.

She stared at me like I'd blown her mind. Welp. Nothing to do but kiss her again. "What's yours," I asked against her lips.

"*The Great British Baking Show*."

"I've never seen it."

"You're joking."

I wanted her to come over and watch it with me right now, but I took a step back, giving her space.

Space was just as important as being together. She needed to build up those trust levels with me. I knew that. Intellectually.

So why did leaving her behind feel like a mistake?

22

Lola

S o, I knew it was going to be bad, going back into that house. I knew there'd be prying and inappropriate questions. I knew the twins would probably be snide. They'd definitely be jealous.

What I wasn't expecting was Tiffani's rage.

And I really wasn't expecting the slap.

I wasn't in the house two seconds before Tiffani was there absolutely belting me across the face with an open palm.

Startled, I fell backwards against the coat rack, my hand on my face. Holy shit, she really walloped me.

"What do you think you're doing?" Tiffani hissed at me. "You think being a slut is going to make Jackson change his mind about the diner?"

Was she insane?

"No, Tiffani, I'm pretty sure my vagina doesn't have the power to change real estate deals."

She stepped forward again, and I was already crowded against the coat rack. This woman...this woman had pushed me into every single corner of my life, and suddenly, I'd had enough.

I lunged forward, back at her. "Try it," I said to her. With no idea how I'd found that courage. Well, that wasn't true. I could draw a line from this dot back to Jackson pretty easily.

I'd never sounded so badass in my life, and Tiffani's eyes went wide. She stepped back, her face revealing every thought she was having.

Most of which were about kicking me out of my own house. I could see how happy she looked by the idea. Delighted to finally push me out of every single thing that should have been mine.

"Let me stop you," I said, robbing her of her stupid moment. If I couldn't have anything else, at least I could have that. "I'm leaving. You aren't going to kick me out of my house."

"It's not yours anymore," she sneered, and I'd never seen her so ugly. "This house. The diner. It's mine."

"Not for long."

I went up and grabbed some of my stuff, the things I needed for work and a few of the pictures I had of Mom and Dad and me from before. I'd come back for the rest of it.

Downstairs, the twins caught up with me at the door to the garage.

"Are you, like...dating Jackson Dumont?" Zoe asked.

"That's one way of putting it," Chloe said. Like Chloe hadn't been in the back seat of every varsity hockey player's car in high school. I wasn't slut shaming; I was calling out hypocrisy.

"You know he's just using you," Zoe said.

For what? I wondered with the almost desperate urge to laugh.

"Or maybe I'm just using him," I shot back. "Maybe instead of waiting around for some dude to make your life better, you should go out and see what you can do for yourself."

They stared at me blankly, and I realized they would never get it. They wanted Prince Charming and the fairy tale that was never going to happen.

I wanted the work. I wanted something to call my own. I wanted to stand on my own two feet and see that I'd built something.

I tried not to think about what I was leaving behind. The memories. Some of my mom's dishes. I had been fully living in the idea that the only way to keep my mother's memory alive was to keep things the same. To stay the same.

Part of me froze when Mom died, and it was time to warm up.

I drove to Georgie's, thinking I'd crash on his couch for a few days, until I got myself together. After I knocked, he met me at his door wearing his best kimono, a cagey expression and smeared lipstick.

"What are you doing here?" he asked, keeping the door shut behind him.

"What are you doing?" I asked, knowing exactly what he was doing. I'd been doing it myself with Jackson an hour ago. As terribly inconvenient as this was for me, I was delighted for Georgie.

"I...ah...met someone at that Dumont masquerade thing," he said, still guarding that shut door behind him as we talked on his front porch. "He came up from Portland and surprised me."

"Good for you," I said and lifted my backpack. "I'll let you get back to what you were doing." As I turned, he grabbed my hand.

"Did something happen?"

"Not at all," I lied. "Just thought I'd come and hang out with you since I didn't see you all day."

I sold it as best I could. I didn't want my drama to get in the way of Georgie's good time. If I told him what had happened, he'd let Mr. Portland gather dust in his bedroom while listening to my sad story.

I got in my hatchback and drove towards town. It was late. I could try Mari at the bakery, but Stephanie usually went to bed early. Both she and Mari worked long days on their feet, and I didn't want either of them having to get out of bed just to deal with my shit.

I needed to find someone who was already up. Who was maybe at home waiting for a call from me.

Who'd offered me a place to stay.

Was this too soon? Were we moving at, like, rapid speed.

Or was this really the longest build up to a relationship in the history of relationships starting when I was nine years old?

I pulled into the parking lot of the old newspaper building and texted Jackson.

Lola: So, it looks like I might need a place to spend the night after all. Things did not go well with Tiffani. Is your couch still open?

Almost immediately three dots showed up.

Jackson: Shit. I knew I shouldn't have left you with her. Fuck space. Where are you now? I'm coming to get you.

Lola: I'm already at the old newspaper building. Just tell me your unit.

Jackson: Unit 10. The top left corner. Take the stairs in back. The door is unlocked.

I made my way up the second flight of steps and knocked on his door. It opened instantly, almost as if he was on his way to come search for me. He took one look at me then pulled me into his arms. Over his shoulder I saw his big-screen TV was paused.

Paul Hollywood was eating a Bakewell tart.

"You're watching *The Great British Baking Show*?" I whispered.

I'd been smacked in the face, kicked out of my house, and this, this was somehow the thing that was going to move me to tears.

"I am. You didn't say anything about that silver fox dirty talking over all the tarts. Is that why you like it?"

I buried my face in his chest and nodded.

"Are you all right?" he asked.

I am now, I thought.

~

HE GAVE me a tour of the place, including the pretty empty kitchen with no counter tops and the bathroom with the glasses drying on top of the toilet.

Then he showed me the guest room, which was fully furnished with a bed, dresser, full-length mirror and a lot of pink.

"My sister likes to stay over sometimes. She wanted her room done."

We watched a bunch of *The Great British Baking Show* episodes, ordered pizza with absolutely no mushrooms, ate it on his absurdly luxurious couch. I almost didn't want the night to end, but because I had the early shift, I knew I had to get some sleep. It was almost midnight.

Only suddenly, I was uncertain. How did this work?

He'd put my bag in the guest room, so obviously I just needed to say goodnight and head to my room.

Did I kiss him goodnight? I should do that, right?

"Hey," he said, grabbing my hand as I stood, still mid-kiss-or-not-kiss thought.

He tugged me down and down again until I braced one hand on the couch beside his head.

"I'm really glad you're here," he whispered against my mouth, then he took care of the kissing question.

I brushed my teeth, washed my face. Put on my sleep shorts and the tank top I wore to bed then crawled into the pink pillow dream of a bed.

Outside the bedroom, I could hear Jackson turning off the TV. Cleaning up our glasses and the pizza box. Then it was quiet, and I knew he wasn't going to bed, that he was being quiet for me.

It was, somehow, the nicest thing ever.

Because he was being so nice, it made me a little horny. Which, after having all those orgasms today, was utterly ridiculous, but there it was. He was just on the other side of that door.

I pushed the blankets off my legs, got out of bed and opened the door only to find him standing there. His hands braced on the door frame. Muscles in his shoulders and arms popping like he'd been standing there holding himself back for a while.

"Jackson—"

"You belong in my bed," he said, then scooped me up like I was Cinderella and he was Prince Charming, and he took me to his bedroom. Which was dark and quiet and smelled like him.

"You don't have to go to bed now just because I do."

"I'm not," he said, curling up behind me.

Yes, I had an early morning tomorrow, but when Jackson Dumont curls up behind you with a hard dick pressed to your ass, you don't need sleep. Ever.

"Let me just..." he whispered, kissing my neck, his hand squeezing my ass, slipping under the waist band of these ridiculous shorts. "Put you to bed."

I parted my thighs so he could get between my legs, his hand cupping me. The heel of his palm pressing against my clit, his fingers parting the folds between my legs.

"Can I do that for you?" he whispered, and I arched backwards, quickly beyond words. Quickly, so quickly, ready to let him do whatever he wanted to me.

He made me come with his fingers, then, like he couldn't stand it anymore, he got down between my legs, his mouth against me, my hands gripping his hair, and I came again.

He kissed his way up my belly, across my chest, to my throat. My lips. His hair was a mess, and his smile was like a little kid delighted with something he'd made.

God, I thought, *how many orgasms was that in one day?* Too many? Not enough? I was orgasmed into another dimension. Another state.

"I want to have sex with you," I said with all the seduction and subtlety of a puddle of goo.

He shook his head, and I was too blissed out to think that was strange. "Go to sleep," he said.

"But..." I reached for him, thinking someone should make this guy feel as good as he made me feel. I was so into it, but I also seemed to have lost all my bones. Boneless now, I swallowed a yawn. He caught my hand.

"You have to work in the morning," he said and already my eyes were drifting closed. "Go to sleep."

"I owe you."

"It doesn't work like that," he said and kissed my eyes closed. "Not with us."

He turned on his bedside lamp, reached down and adjusted himself, which God, why was that so sexy? Then, if that wasn't enough, he picked up a book on his bedside table and started *reading* it.

"You're not at all who I thought you were," I told him.

He kissed my head. "You're exactly who I thought you were."

23

Lola

The next day the twins had the day off, and I ignored Tiffani.

Which was, I could admit, an absolute delight. So delicious I wondered why I'd taken this long to just stop pretending with her. All those years trying to be nice, trying to find common ground. A waste.

I did my thing, and she did hers while watching me do mine with narrowed eyes. Like I was going to spring something on her at any moment.

Then Mari and her mom came in for breakfast and made a point of snubbing Tiffani, too. I was small enough to really enjoy that. I'd called Mari on my first break this morning and told her what had happened. That and I needed a place to stay.

As much as I'd loved last night—even waking up with

Jackson beside me had been an experience—I couldn't just move in with him. We weren't there. Or I wasn't ready.

Mari lived in the apartment above the bakery while her mom had a split-level ranch around the block from my old house. "You guys are sure this is okay?"

"Absolutely," Mari said. "It will be like we're kids again having sleepovers."

"Your mother would also approve," Stephanie said, once more giving Tiffani the stink eye. They left after giving me a key to the apartment over the bakery and the assurance that I could come and go as I please.

The lunch crowd arrived, and I was happy for the distraction of hungry customers. I stopped when I saw Roy and his little girl sit down in one of my open booths.

"And how is baby Nora today?" I crooned at the sweet little girl who was now just over a year old. We had baby seats that allowed her to sit close to the table while Roy pushed Cheerios at her, one at a time.

"She walks now," he said.

"How exciting!" I said in my best yeah-baby voice.

"What's exciting about walking?" Roy grunted. "She's got legs doesn't she?"

I shook my head. Roy was not a man easily impressed.

"The usual?" I asked, and he nodded.

I was heading to the kitchen to place his order when the door opened and the bell overhead rang.

Jackson walked in, and just like that, he took my breath away.

He wore a white linen shirt, short-sleeved and held closed by three buttons, very faded, loose jeans and flip flops. He looked like an extremely rich guy on vacation. Like a guy in an ad for vacations. His hair was a mess and my fingers itched to smooth it back into place. Unwittingly he sat in Tiffani's section, and when she went to bring him water he stopped her, stood, then looked at me.

I pointed to the corner booth. He walked over to my booth and sat.

All without saying a word. I hadn't told him about what went down between Tiffani and me. I imagined if he knew she'd slapped me, he'd want to have words with her, and I didn't want that.

Tiffani was my problem, not his. All he knew was that I couldn't stand living with her anymore, and that was enough.

"How are you dealing with her all day?" Jackson asked as I stepped up with water and a mug of coffee.

"Ignoring her mostly."

"Look, I have dinner with my parents tonight. But I was thinking, after, if you wanted to come over, we could watch the biscuit-week episode, and I don't know..."

He waggled his very nimble eyebrows at me, and I thought how funny they were as opposed to sexy, which, weirdly, made him even sexier.

"I'm staying at Mari's," I blurted out. "They have an extra room in the apartment above the bakery."

He blinked at me, and maybe I didn't mean to be quite so blunt, but I'd been thinking about how I was going to put up some of the boundaries we'd knocked down last night. Blunt was the only way I knew how to do it.

"Oh. Okay," he said. "You know you're welcome to stay with me."

"Thank you," I said, feeling stupid and formal, so aware that Tiffani was all but glaring at me from behind the counter. "That's nice of you, but I think it's best if I stay at Mari's. If you think about it, you and I are really just getting to know one another."

"I don't know. I think I know you pretty well," he said. If he was flirty and talking about sex, I could laugh. But he wasn't. He was serious.

"I can't just move into your condo. You get that, right?" I said.

Except, I could tell by his face that he didn't agree. In his mind, it made perfect sense for me to move into his unfinished condo. Then suddenly he smiled, and the tension broke and he was charming Jackson again.

"Of course, I get it. Things are moving fast, and that's too fast for you," he said. "But if things change, the door is always open. You always have a place with me, Lola. You get that, right?"

"Yes, Jackson. Now what can I get you to eat?" I asked him.

"How about a Lola Special?" he said, with a wink. "But I'll take it to go."

∾

Jackson

OF COURSE she couldn't move in. I mean, I understood. We'd only just started...whatever it was we were doing. Just because she'd been a fixture in my head for so long didn't mean she thought about me the same way.

But also...she could totally move into my condo. If she wanted to. If she trusted me.

"One Lola Special," she announced as she came back to the table and set the Styrofoam box down in front of me.

I slid out of the booth, with the box in my hand.

"I'll call you later," I said, leaning down to kiss her cheek. "After dinner."

"Sure," she said, blushing the way that I liked. "Good luck with your parents."

I was dreading this dinner. I dreaded every dinner I had with my folks, but now, more then ever, because of what I was giving up.

The Great British Baking Show's biscuit week on the couch with Lola. Watching her blush when Paul Hollywood talked about creamy centers.

God, what I'd give to spend the night with her creamy center.

I left the diner before I begged her to come with me instead.

I took the Styrofoam box out to my Jeep and opened it, wondering what she had in store for me.

This time it looked like a perfectly grilled cheese sandwich with a slice of tomato. I bit into it and groaned at the gooeyness. No tricks this time.

Plus she'd written a note on the napkin beside it. *XO Lola.* I took the small white napkin, folded it and put it in my pocket.

A talisman. For the evening to come.

"THERE YOU ARE," my mother said, when I walked into the dining room later that evening.

She smiled when she said it and walked across the room to air kiss my cheeks.

I grinned and bore the little performance piece of the doting mother.

Over my mom's shoulder I caught Simon's eye, and he lifted his chin.

His standard greeting.

I squashed down the urge to punch him in that chin. It was hard to believe, looking at him, that we were ever friends. How devoid our relationship was of any of the things that really mattered in friendship. There was no chemistry. No respect. No sense of humor. I was old money. He was new money.

He was a social climber.

While I sat at the very top of the mountain.

Gross.

Beside him, my sister looked lovely, as usual. But also like a violin string strung too tight. Her laugh was too loud, her eyes too bright. Like she just wanted so badly for everyone to be happy.

"Hey, Ness," I muttered, and dropped a kiss on top of her head before moving around the table.

"Jackson," my father said, sliding his phone in his pocket. "Good of you to join us."

"Am I late?" I asked my mom with a smile that let everyone know I knew I was late. Just a little.

"Not at all," Mom said, graciously. "Now, sit down. Dani has made a delicious dinner, and we have a lot to discuss."

This was my mother's forte, planning shit. I'd had to go to therapy to understand that her obsessive planning for the future probably had a lot to do with her deep unhappiness of present day.

I sat in the place I'd always sat, in the chair to the right of my father. Close enough for him to reach out and put his hand on my shoulder, if that was the kind of thing he did.

Dani stepped into the room and put down dishes of food. I noticed a couple of my favorites and Vanessa's.

Always taking care of us on the sly. However, I was already sustained by Lola's grilled cheese, and so I only took enough to thwart questions about why I wasn't eating.

"Darling, the wedding is just a few weeks away," Mom said, looking directly at Vanessa, who was scooping her favorite couscous salad with feta cheese and almonds onto her plate.

Vanessa put the spoon back in the bowl and handed it to Simon, who had no idea the dig our mother had just made. Which was ridiculous since Vanessa didn't have an ounce of fat on her. Our mother wouldn't allow it.

"Now, Simon, when will your parents be in town?"

"Mother will be in next week. Father is very busy. We probably won't see him until the day of the ceremony."

"Oh," Mom said. "We'd love to have your mother for dinner when she arrives."

"Yes, she'd quite like that," Simon said, passing the offending couscous salad to my mother, who passed it to me. I took giant heaping spoonfuls of it.

"Really," Mom said, watching me. "Let's remember our manners."

I dropped my napkin in my lap with an arched eyebrow.

"So I heard that you've been spending time with that Pappas girl," Dad said. "Took her out on the boat, did you?"

Vanessa looked at me, her expression guilty, and I knew where he'd gotten his information. There was nothing for her to feel guilty about. I was a man, no longer a child who could be told who I could and could not see.

"Yes, I did."

"Why?" Mom asked, like I'd been spending time with one of the stray cats in town.

Dad clapped his hands together. "Good job, son. Having inside information as we negotiate the purchase of the property is a solid business strategy. A girl like her is bound to be impressed with a boat ride."

"I didn't take her on a boat ride as a strategy, Dad. I did it because I like her, and I wanted to spend time with her."

"Ha! I knew it." Simon laughed, wagging his finger at me. "I knew you had a thing for the diner girl."

"She's nice," Vanessa said.

"Sure," Simon said. "That's one way to put it."

Vanessa glared at Simon, and my mom reached forward and touched my hand. "Are you really dating her, or is this..." She waved her hand in the air, and I realized this was her euphemism for fucking her.

"I'm dating her," I said, like I'd thrown down a challenge. "She'll be my date to the wedding."

"That's taking it a bit far, don't you think?" my dad said like all of this was confusing to him. Probably because he was still stuck on the idea of me wooing the diner out from under Lola. "I understand the property isn't even in her name. It belongs to Tiffani Pappas."

"Hopefully, not for long," Vanessa said, not realizing the significance of her comments to our father. Who still thought he was going to snatch up the property.

"What's that supposed to mean?" he asked.

"Nothing." I sighed. "Vanessa's right. I've looked into it, and it seems that Tiffani might be selling the diner to Lola."

He snorted. "With what money?"

I shrugged.

"I mean, you were tipping her pretty hard back in the day," Simon said, laughing at his own joke.

Only, I didn't think it was very funny. I stood, leaned over the table and grabbed Simon by the front of his shirt, hauling him into his place setting.

"Fuck me, Jackson," Simon said, trying to pull me off.

Mom and Dad were both making exclamations, and someone pounded on the table, and all I could see was the way Simon had been flirting with her five years ago and how I'd messed it all up by not kicking his ass then.

"Jackson," Vanessa breathed. "Please."

Well, that was it. The one person I couldn't ignore. I let him go, and he sagged back in his chair, trying to brush off the bits of herb and feta on his shirt.

"Now, boys, let's behave, shall we? Jackson, I insist you invite this girl to dinner," my mother said.

I laughed. Bring Lola to this crowd of vultures? Not going to happen.

"If she's important to you, you should bring her," Mom said as if issuing her own challenge. "If she's going to be your date to the wedding, you should bring her."

Mom was getting emphatic, and there was only one thing that happened when Mom got emphatic. Dad started twisting the thumb screws to make sure she got her way. Not because he cared so much, as it just made his life easier.

"Last time I checked, you still relied on the money in your trust, Jackson."

And there he was, right on time. *Do what your mother wants, or I cut you off.*

This time I wanted him to say it.

"What do you mean by that, Dad? Do you mean if I don't bring Lola to dinner, to make Mom happy, you'll cut me off from my inheritance? Do I have that clear?"

Dad stared at me, lofty and impervious. I swallowed the urge to grab him by the collar, too, and tell him all the ways I was thwarting him. All the ways I was using his money to undercut his own damn business.

I wanted to tell him the joke, these days, was always on him, and he was the only one who didn't know it.

Except that fucking trust fund was part of it. My own business made money, but the sweet irony of the CCIB was the trust fund money. Without it, I couldn't fund Lola's dream.

"Fine," I said and sat down. "I'll bring her. However, we'll leave the second you guys make her feel bad."

"Honestly, Jackson." Mom laughed and looked over at Simon who was glaring at me. "You're the one making the scene. Not us."

Another thing I'd had to learn in therapy was to recognize the way my mother made my behavior the problem when, after years of abuse, I finally lost my temper.

I looked over at Simon who wasn't meeting my eyes, then Vanessa who was wiping her eyes very carefully with her napkin.

"I'm sorry," I said to her.

"It's all right," she said with a smile she didn't mean.

He's not worth it, I wanted to say. *You're a million times better than him. You deserve so much more.* I'd said that already, though, and I could burn our relationship to the ground if I wasn't careful with her feelings.

I could only be there for her in whatever way was left to me.

It was inevitable that I would have to bring Lola into this world. If I meant to have her in my life, she would have to have at least passing exposure to the people around this table. I could protect her, and I could stand in the way of whatever bullshit might be thrown, but she would have to stand here at some point and face who the Dumont family really was.

"She may not want to come," I said.

"She was gagging to come five years ago," Simon muttered under his breath.

"I'm sorry, Simon, I thought you wanted your face intact for those wedding photos."

"Not over dinner, boys," my mother said. "Come. Let's talk about the wedding."

Mom merrily shifted all the energy through sheer force of will. *No wonder she used to smack us*, I thought. She had to be fucking exhausted all the time.

"I've lost my appetite," I said. "I'll see you all next week."

Before Mom could pretend to give a shit or Dad could order me to sit back down or Vanessa could plead with me with her eyes to not leave her alone there in that bed she made, I walked out of the dining room.

Then I was back in my Jeep, driving way from the estate with the top down, the wind in my hair. Twilight all around me.

There was only one person I wanted. One thing I needed. At the stoplight at the edge of downtown I pulled out my phone.

Jackson: Can you meet me for a few minutes?

Lola: Sure. Where?

I had an anger and a craving and an impossible itch born of anger and frustration. I wanted Lola to scratch it for me.

Jackson: The alley behind the bakery? Somewhere we can be alone.

Lola: You going to rob me?

Jackson: I'm thinking about fucking you.

There was a pause and I wondered if I'd pushed too hard. Again. But finally, the three dots showed up.

Lola: When?

Jackson: Five minutes.

The light turned green, and I threw my phone down on

the passenger seat and I broke the speed limit getting to Lola.

～

Lola

IT WASN'T REALLY a back alley behind the bakery. It was more of a dead end. You could access the brick and cobblestone path by the beach road, but it was a dead end because of the bookshop.

Each of the three businesses, the bakery, the bookshop and the dress shop, had little chairs and tables set up so employees could take breaks. Yes, there were dumpsters, and in August, it smelled bad. But in June…it didn't.

Why that mattered to me, I wasn't sure. If I was about to have sex with Jackson for the first time, and it was going to be in an alleyway, I just didn't want it to be in a smelly alleyway. A girl had her standards, after all.

I was nerves and sweaty hands and a kind of what the fuck incredulity.

When I heard his Jeep stop at the curb and the slam of the door, I walked towards the entrance to the alleyway, eager to see him. To hold him.

Then he was there. Same loose jeans with the tear at the knee and the white linen shirt so casually and perfectly draped over his very excellent chest.

"Are you all right?" I asked when I was in his arms. He was holding me so hard and so close, I was bowed backwards, all my weight in his hands.

"I am now," he said against my neck.

His mouth was open against my skin, and I was

suddenly, unabashedly, turned on. Wild for him. He stepped forward and turned us, so I was pressed up against the brick wall of the bakery, and he leaned forward against me, his arms braced on the wall beside my head, his erection firm against my stomach.

"Ask me inside," he whispered.

"I can't... Mari..."

"Doesn't approve of me?"

"It's a small apartment."

"I need you, Lola," he whispered against my neck, the tops of my breasts. "I need you so bad." He sucked my nipple through my shirt, and I arched into him, sizzling all over. "I need you naked and wet and screaming my name."

"Yes," I said. I needed those things, too. I needed everything. Immediately. That's how he went to my head. One hundred percent.

"I'm two blocks away," he said. "I'll bring you home after."

Fine. Whatever. I grabbed his hand, running towards his Jeep, but he pulled me the other way.

"Faster," he said. "No parking."

He was right. Running kitty-corner, we were at the front door to his building then we were jogging up the stairs to the second floor like we were being chased by monsters.

Except once, he stopped to kiss me in the stairwell. Like he'd gone too long without a taste and needed that extra kiss to finish the journey.

Finally, we were at his unit. He was fumbling with the key. I was pressed against his back, my hand down his jeans stroking his dick through his briefs as he tried to open the door.

"Stop," he said, fumbling with his keys.

"No," I said.

He laughed, finally finding the right key, then we were in his place. That big black velvet couch. In seconds, my shorts were pulled off, his shirt was gone.

He was laying me out on the couch, while he got on his knees. Then he did that thing with his tongue where it just swiveled around my clit. I arched my back, pushing against his mouth. Then his middle finger was inside me, deep, then his other finger. He made this motion with them inside my body that had my eyes rolling back in my head.

"Jackson. Oh, God, oh, God, yes."

He lifted his mouth from my sex. "Say it again. I want to hear you scream my name."

Only I couldn't, because I was coming then, and sound was impossible. I opened my eyes in time to see Jackson stroking himself, hard and fast. Watching his dick shuttle through his palm like that. He picked up his shirt to cover his dick, then head back, the muscles in his neck corded, he came with a grunt.

"Fuck, yes. Fuck," he whispered. Then he tossed the shirt aside, and we collapsed on the couch together. Naked. Sweaty. Sated.

"I want to have sex," I said, when coherent thought was possible again.

"We just did."

"No. *Sex* sex," I said. "The real thing."

He nodded, his eyes on the steel beams of the ceiling.

"I don't have any condoms," he said. I sat up, not because he didn't have any condoms but because it seemed like he was lying.

"What?" he said, smiling into my expression.

"Is that the truth?"

"Why would I lie about condoms?"

"Because you don't want to have sex with me?"

"Lola." He laughed. "You can't possibly think I don't want to have sex with you." He gestured down at our naked bodies.

"If I go look in your bedroom or your bathroom, what will I find?" I asked, not entirely sure why I was pushing this. But I was.

He was silent, and I got to my feet beside the couch and stepped away like I was going to go search those rooms, but he grabbed my hand.

"You're a virgin," he said.

"I knew it! You're still weirded out by me being a virgin!"

"I'm not weirded out, but it feels like your first time, your real first time, should be...special. Not just a fucking frustration bang."

"Is that what this was?" I asked. "A frustration bang?"

I wasn't mad, I was just kind of new to everything.

"Dinner with my parents wasn't great."

So he came to me to feel better. Hmmm. That wasn't *not* nice.

"Are you okay?" I asked.

He grinned up at me, all dimples and sweaty hair. "I am now."

"I don't need special," I said.

His smile faded, and he sat up, hiking his underwear over his dick, then getting dressed. *Well*, I thought, *I guess we aren't having sex*. Somehow this conversation had become about something else, and I wasn't even sure what it was.

He pushed his sweaty flop of hair up off his face, then held himself so still. As if, whatever he was thinking about, required every muscle in his body.

Then with a big breath, he turned to look at me with all the sudden resolve of a guy facing a firing squad.

"Do you even like me?" he asked, his eyes skewering me.

"Not back when we were kids. Now. Today. Do you like me? As a person."

I had to think about it. I thought about the person at the masquerade ball who made me laugh at his jokes. The person on the boat with me who admitted to a minor kidnapping. The man I clearly beat at four square.

Once upon a time, Jackson Dumont had been my everything, until it all turned ugly. Only now I knew why.

Did I like him? Yes. The scary part was that I was beginning to feel so much more than *like*.

"Yes," I said. "I wouldn't be with you, like this, if I didn't like you, Jackson."

"Okay. Do you trust me?"

My hesitation was only a second. Barely even a second and he got to his feet.

"That's why I don't want to have sex," he said softly. Gently. Cupping my face even as he was disappointing me.

"That feels a little like a punishment."

"No, Lola. It's about me earning it."

24

Top Three Things I Want to Do to Lola

Get her to trust me
Tell her the truth
Fuck her

Jackson

There were other reasons I was holding off on sex. Yes, it was about trust. Yes, I was feeling some kind of way about her virginity, and I wanted it to be special or at least not in an alleyway or on my couch because I was pissed at my parents.

But also, I was still—sort of, in an it's-for-her-own-good-way—lying to her.

I honestly didn't feel like I could tell her the truth yet, so I couldn't fuck her yet. Yes, considering where I was putting my mouth and my fingers, I knew I was splitting hairs, but whatever.

A guy had to have some rules.

There was a distance between us that I didn't know how to get past. She didn't even want me to walk her home. As if I was going to let her go alone.

"It's only two blocks," she said.

"Bears," I said.

"There hasn't been a bear downtown for years."

"Mountain lion."

"Jackson..."

"Giant lobster." I made my hands into claws and pretended to snap at her clothes.

"Stop it!"

"I'm walking you home, Lola. Get over it."

She did, and after a slow walk back, we stopped at the old wrought iron fire escape staircase on the outside of the building that led to the apartment above the bakery.

"You know you can always change your mind," I said. "Stay with me. Anytime."

"And miss out on the smell of cinnamon rolls baking fresh each morning? You can't compete with that."

She was saying it to be funny, but it still hurt a little. Because I wanted everything now, and with her, there was still that last wall to climb.

I needed to tell her the truth. About all of it. I just wanted all those pieces to be lined up first. So I could hand her everything she needed on a silver platter, no missteps. Then, she would finally understand where my head was.

"Come to my place tomorrow?"

She blushed, but still she nodded. "Come over to *not* have sex," she said.

"It will happen, when we're ready," I said. "Until then...orgasms."

Her eyes lit up. "I do really like orgasms."

I laughed because, the way she said it, she reminded me of the girl I met on the beach who told me how much she did really like chocolate ice cream.

I tucked a loose curl behind her ear.

This girl. This woman.

And that was how we fell into the best/worst rhythm I'd ever been in, in my life. Every day after whichever shift she had, she came to my place and we made each other come in spectacular ways without ever having sex.

And then she left. Taking my heart with her.

FRIDAY NIGHT, after days of being together, we were engaged in a heated battle.

Now let me tell you, I've had a lot of amazing experiences in my life. I've seen the sunrise over Kilimanjaro and whales off the coast of New Brunswick.

But convincing Lola Pappas to sit on my face while she sucked my dick out-ranked them all.

"This isn't a thing," she said, standing naked beside the bed. Lola Pappas naked was its own kind of miracle. Her curves made my body ache. The curls between her legs were as pale as the curls on her head, and her extremely responsive pink nipples were the most beautiful things I'd ever seen.

"It's a thing," I said, lying on my back, stroking my dick just so I didn't pass out from blood loss in my head.

"It's a porn thing not a real-life thing."

"It's real life, too, I swear."

She put her hands on her hips and glared at me. "How many times have you done this?"

"Enough to know we're both going to like it."

It was funny with Lola. Some girls wanted to hear nothing about your past experiences. But for her, it was like she was looking for *Yelp* reviews. She needed social proof.

I loved it. I loved her, and it was getting harder and harder to keep those words behind my teeth.

"I'm going to suffocate you."

"You won't."

"Your nose will be like in my asshole."

"It won't. You'll be leaning forward. No asshole, unless..." I cocked my head.

"Have you done *that*?" she cried.

I love you so freaking much.

"Fingers, yes. Dick, no."

She eyed my dick, and I squeezed the tip, come leaking out. She loved that, proof that I was so close to coming. Within seconds, she was on my face, my tongue in her pussy, her own mouth around my dick.

As predicted, she loved it.

When I put my finger in her ass, she loved that, too.

But she still didn't trust me.

"Hey," I said. I stood in the doorway between my bathroom and the bedroom. She was putting her clothes on and brushing her hair. Splashing water on her face, like she could hide the fact she had my beard burn all over her neck. I wanted to take her around town, parade her naked body, point to the marks I'd left on her, and the marks she'd left on me. I wanted to scream at everyone that she was mine. We belonged to each other. We always had.

This was what she was making of me.

"Are you busy tomorrow night?"

"No." She shook her head. "I work morning shift. Why?"

"I'd like you to come to dinner at my parent's house. We'd be going. Together. To dinner."

I managed to bungle that because I was more nervous than I thought. Not just about whether or not she'd agree, but also about taking her there. I'd put off asking her all week.

"You okay?" she asked, smiling at me. Looking right past my invitation to the nerves behind it. Who wouldn't be absolutely crazy for this girl?

"Fine. Simon's mother is in town early for the wedding. My mother isn't my mother if she's not entertaining guests. I mentioned I would be bringing you as my date to the wedding, so she wanted to have you over to dinner."

"Your date. To the wedding?" she asked softly. Biting that lower lip. Thinking about what that meant.

For some reason that pissed me off. I mean, this girl had been sitting on my face not an hour ago. Did she think I would bring someone else?

"Yes, Lola," I snapped. "We're seeing each other. We're dating. We're fucking. We're going to my sister's disaster of a wedding. Together. That okay with you?"

She reached out then and touched my face. Her fingers running over the five o'clock shadow that had left those marks all along her skin. It loosened something inside me.

"Okay, Jackson. I'll go with you to the wedding. This dinner at your parent's house is important to you?"

I sighed. "It's important to me they understand you're important to me. But I'm not going to lie or sugar coat it.

They are classist snobs. They might be awful, Lola. I mean, chances are high they will be awful. You can say no."

"What will happen if I say no?"

"Nothing," I said. "I'm not going anywhere. I think you know that. But they are part of my life, and you are part of my life. Eventually those things have to come together."

"I'll go," she said. "For you."

Something deep in my chest and in my back and behind my knees uncoiled, while other tensions took their place. How could I keep her safe? What did I need to do to put bulletproof walls between her and my parents?

"That's probably a mistake," I said. "But I'm happy you're going."

"Everything is going by so fast. I can't believe the wedding is almost here," she said it with a certain amount of wistfulness in her voice I didn't understand.

Then it occurred to me. The reason she thought I came back to Calico Cove was just for Vanessa's wedding. It's basically what I'd told her.

"You think I'm leaving at the end of the summer?" I asked her.

"Aren't you?"

I shook my head and she blinked. "This isn't a summer thing," I told her. "Not for me. Look around. I bought this place. I'm not going anywhere, Lola."

This was the closest I'd gotten to telling her my feelings. My heart pounded. We stared at each other across that tiled room. I willed her to trust me, to believe me fully that *this, us* was the real deal.

"What time?" she asked. "For dinner."

"Seven."

"I need to dress up?"

"Yeah."

"Okay. Pick me up at Georgie's place."

The Next Night

Lola

"Lola," Georgie said as I waited at the door for Jackson to pick me up.

I was wearing a new sundress I'd bought. It was yellow and green and tight around my boobs in a way I knew Jackson would like. Short on my legs, which I also knew he would like.

It also had pockets. Which I liked.

Georgie had done my hair in big "beach curls" as opposed to my normal curls. Which was fascinating to me because he had to straighten my hair out first, only to make it curly again.

Since I'd actually been taking my days off and spending them outside with Jackson—we'd gone on another long boat ride the other day—my cheeks were rosy, and my shoulders were tanned.

I felt...I mean, it was so corny, but I really felt pretty.

"Are you sure you know what you're doing?" Georgie asked.

"I'm going for dinner."

"Yeah, with the Dumonts."

It did sound ridiculous. Like I was going to have dinner with dragons. Like, if you'd told me a month ago I'd be doing this, I would say you were completely nuts. Yet here we were.

Jackson and I were dating.

For how long, I didn't know. He said it wasn't a summer thing, but what else could it be? He said he had a business in Boston. Surely, he had to return to that at some point.

He also bought a condo in Calico Cove. Kitchen counters were coming next week.

"I just...I want you to be careful," Georgie said. "With your heart."

"I am," I said.

Though there was a good chance I was lying. In fact, I was pretty sure I was lying. We still hadn't had actual intercourse. In some ways, I was now glad about that. Like it was this piece of me I was still holding back. As if never having his penis in my vagina was going to somehow save me from heartbreak if Jackson pulled the rug out from under me.

Are you really still waiting for him to do that?

That question I could answer truthfully – no. I didn't think he was going to trick me. Or hurt me on purpose.

"Any updates on the contract for the diner?"

We were still five days away from the CCIB decision. Jackson had worked some legal magic and extended the attorney review period, but only for a few more days. If Mr. Dumont Senior got aggressive with an offer in between that gap...

"Hey, Georgie?" I asked, running my hand down the front of the dress. "What if we don't get the diner?"

"What do you mean?" he asked. We were sitting on his front porch waiting for Jackson. Georgie had one of the cats purring in his lap.

"Like, if we just...don't get it. Our plans don't work. We

don't get the money, or someone else buys the diner. Or what if we get the diner, but in two years, we're out of business because it turns out I'm not good at running a diner? What if I lose it all? Everything my parents have worked for?"

"You won't."

It was strange, but what had sent me into a panic at the beginning of the summer, when I first saw that Shells sign, suddenly didn't seem to matter as much anymore.

If I lost the diner, I lost the diner. Then I would just have to pick myself up and find something else to do.

Where did that sense of peace come from? The idea that even if I lost it all tomorrow, I would still be okay.

It's because you're not alone anymore. Jackson is back.

Jackson's Jeep pulled up on the gravel driveway, and he put it in park and stepped out. He came to the door for me, and my heart leapt at the sight of him.

"Well," Georgie said as Jackson approached. "If he's the devil, he's a good-looking devil."

He wore a light pink shirt and dark blue jacket and pants. Dark brown shoes. No tie, but a pocket square. Pink with purple flowers. His dark hair had product in it, so it didn't fall in his eyes, and he looked like a New Zealand Rugby player, which was a whole vibe.

What if I lost the diner because I was distracted by this guy and the way he made me feel?

The shame of that felt like a cramp in my stomach. Losing my family's diner because every minute of every day, I was thinking about Jackson Dumont? What would my mother say?

"Hey!" he said with a smile and kissed my cheek. He shook Georgie's hand and the cat on Georgie's lap hissed at him.

"What is it with cats in this town?" he cried, eyes wide when he looked at me. "Don't tell me you did it again?"

"Did what again?" Georgie asked.

"She trained a cat to attack me."

"If I remember correctly, you deserved it." Georgie didn't say it like a joke. He said it like a person who loved me and had a front row seat for all the shit Jackson did to me.

"I did," Jackson said, the smile just a ghost on his face. "But I'm trying to change her opinion of me."

"Maybe you should be trying to change the cats' opinion of you, too."

"You're right," he said.

I realized they weren't talking about the cat. They were talking about Georgie.

"Go," Georgie said, stroking the cat like a villain in a story. "Have fun, kids. No breaking anyone's heart, or I'll kill you. Kidding! Not kidding!"

I kissed Georgie's cheek, then walked towards the Jeep only to realize Jackson wasn't with me. He'd turned slightly, his back towards me and was talking to Georgie.

Georgie suddenly laughed and clapped his hand on Jackson's shoulder.

If I felt nothing for Jackson, Georgie's approval wouldn't mean anything. The fact that it did was the sun rising on a cool morning.

"Ready?" Jackson said, his hand on my lower back as he opened the car door for me.

"Sure." The smile he gave me when he shut the door was tight and didn't come anywhere close to his eyes. "Are you okay?" I asked him when he got in the driver's seat.

"There's the expectation that my parents will be on their best behavior because Simon's mother is there, but I've learned the hard way that expectations don't matter." He started the car, and I felt compelled to put my hand over his on the gear shift.

The touch seemed to shock him, and I realized, outside of sex, I very rarely touched him first. Whereas he was always touching me. My shoulder, the small of my back, holding my hand.

For me, though, reaching out to him was always a big deal. Suddenly, that felt wrong of me. He needed comfort and security. Warmth and contact.

The way he smiled at me told me he needed all those things from me.

I curled my fingers through his, and together, we shifted gears and headed up the coast to the Dumont mansion on the other side of town.

25

My Three Favorite Things About Jackson

His honesty
His heart
That thing he does with his tongue

Lola

The house was beautiful tonight. What was I saying? The house was always beautiful. Tonight, though, there were bouquets of June flowers along the front porch. Gerber daises and lilacs. The air smelled delicious.

The butler, who I now knew was named Eric and not Jeeves, was standing at the door when we pulled up, like he was waiting for us.

"Dinner is served outside tonight, Jackson," Eric said, and he reached a hand out towards me.

"Right, I guess we didn't really meet. I'm Lola, and I'm

sorry I called you Jeeves. I was a little pissed off that day." I shook his hand.

Jackson laughed and the butler smiled.

"May I take your purse, Lola?" he said, and I blushed bright red. I handed him the purse, and Jackson curled his fingers through mine.

"That was embarrassing," I muttered as we walked under the big chandelier to the ballroom. Then the patio beyond that.

"It was fantastic," he said. "Eric is already half in love."

At the doorway he paused. "I just..." he said, and I realized he needed a minute. To get himself together.

"Sure."

He took a breath, kissed me, then said, "I apologize in advance for what you are about to experience."

"It's not going to be that bad," I told him.

Was I sure of that? No. But he needed to hear it.

"I'm tough, Jackson," I reminded him. "Tougher than all you Dumonts put together."

That seemed to stiffen his shoulders.

"That's right," he said and led us out onto the terrace.

I recognized everyone standing outside except for an older woman with helmet blonde hair and a very distinct look in her eye. A look that said, *this is it. I've made it.* She held a martini in one hand, and when Jackson and I walked onto the patio, she took a sip and eyed me over the top of it.

"Hello, everyone," Jackson said. "I'd like to introduce Lola Pappas."

Vanessa, who really was a sweetheart, rushed over to hug us. Simon followed, and I braced myself for him to reiterate some joke at the expense of "the diner girl," but he only shook my hand like he didn't even recognize me.

Jackson's mother came over and shook my hand, too.

"It's so nice to see you again, Lola. Of course, I remember you when you were just this high," she said, her hand stretched out, as if she'd been fond of me when I was a child. Which I knew wasn't true, since Jackson had to sneak out of the house to be with me.

Lie number one.

"It certainly has been a while since Jackson brought a girl home to meet his parents."

"I've never brought a girl home to meet my parents," Jackson said, leaning down to kiss his mother's cheek.

"Of course, you did. That Arabella girl, the shipping magnate's daughter. She stayed with us for a week."

"She was *my* friend, Mom," Vanessa said.

If that was an effort to intimidate me, it misfired gloriously. "It's really nice to meet you. Officially."

"Officially?" Mrs. Dumont asked, her perfect silvery blonde hair unmoving in the sea breeze.

"Sure," I said. "I mean, I know who you are, of course. We've just never officially met."

"No," Mrs. Dumont said with a little sniff. "I suppose not."

"Let's talk about that diner in town," Mr. Dumont said, not moving from where he sat on the patio.

"Dad," Jackson said tightly. "We're going to go get a drink. Save the business interrogation until after the salad course, would you?"

Jackson pulled me in through another door into a very elegant bar area. There was seating and a pool table. Background music was playing through a speaker system.

"What would you like to drink?" he asked. "We have everything."

"Absinthe spritzer?"

"You joke, but I'm sure we've got it. I could probably drop one of my mom's Valiums in it."

"It's not that bad," I said.

"Yet."

"White wine is fine. Is there a bathroom..."

"Yes. Just down the hall." He pulled a bottle of white wine I didn't recognize out of a small fridge and took two glasses from a shelf in the bar.

"I'll meet you back out there," I said, and went down the hall to the bathroom because being nervous made me have to pee. I went, washed my hands, then stepped out of the door only to run right into someone.

Simon.

"Whoa, careful there, diner girl," he said.

I stiffened, all the hair on my body went on alert. I tried to step back but there was nowhere to go except into the bathroom. I could smell whatever he was drinking on his breath.

"Well, hats off to you," he said, standing way too close. "You are playing the long game."

"I'm not playing any game," I said.

"Course you are. We both are."

"I'm not playing any game with you," I said, trying to squeeze past him. But he leaned in, and I was caught between his chest and the door. I sucked in my breath, but it didn't do any good. He was still pressed tight against me.

"The game is called Bag the Dumont," he said. "You are the long-shot odds. No one put any money on the fucking diner girl showing up for family dinner."

"Let me pass," I said.

He lifted his hands. "I'm not touching you. But if you want—"

He put his hands on my bare shoulders, and my skin

crawled so hard it hurt. I shoved him back with my hands against his chest.

"Don't touch me," I breathed.

"Lola?"

Simon went pale. Well, paler, and he swallowed audibly. I turned towards where Jackson stood at the end of the hallway. One look at my face and he was walking towards us with violence on his mind.

"What I'm about to do, isn't for you," I said to Simon. "It's for Vanessa."

I rushed to intercept Jackson. Behind me I heard the bathroom door shut as Simon seemed to take the chance to hide.

"What did he do?" Jackson said.

"Nothing I couldn't handle. Calm down."

His eyes went wide, and he tried to get past me, but I stopped him again. Simon wasn't stupid, he would invent a reason to move into that bathroom if Jackson was standing outside of it.

"He's drunk," I said, patting his chest. Stroking it really, like you would an outraged animal. "He's also an asshole and a hundred precent not worth making a hard night harder."

"But you are, do you get that? For you, I would burn this house down."

Oh. Well. I found myself blinking tears. Trying to convince myself that this was a product of a lot of emotions, but I wasn't sure anymore. He twisted me up and got past all my boundaries until I *wanted* to believe what he said.

"Think of your sister," I said finally.

"I always do. I knew he was going to try something," Jackson breathed.

"Guys like him are always going to try something."

It was how they kept evolving. Surviving. The malignant asshole gene just kept mutating forward.

From the kitchen at the end of the hallway a woman came out, holding a platter of steaming grilled shrimp and salmon dotted with fresh herbs.

"Everything all right, Jackson?" she asked.

"Fine," he said. "Lola, this is Dani. Dani, Lola."

"Nice to meet you. Again," Dani said. "I would shake..." She lifted the platter, and Jackson swept in and plucked the platter from her hands. Dani shook my hand with both of hers.

"Thank you, Jackson," Dani said, her face flushed. Her silvery grey hair pulled back in a bun with a headband keeping strands out of her face. "Lola, you are the spitting image of your mother when she was your age."

"You knew her?"

"I did. I was a freshman when your parents were seniors."

"You're Calico Cove?"

"Go Wildcats. Your mother was my idol."

"What?" I asked, my cheeks splitting with the force of my smile.

"She got the dress code changed. Had every girl in the high school sign a petition that said if the administration didn't start policing boys' sexual harassment instead of girls' bodies, we would walk out."

"That is pretty badass."

"Jackson, what in the world is taking so long?" Mrs. Dumont was standing at the end of the hallway, the light from outside cutting across her like a knife. She was ruffled and angry. The evening already clearly slipping out of her control.

"Sorry, Mom, we're coming," he said, and started walking towards the patio and his mother.

"Why are you carrying that tray?" she asked. "For heaven's sake, Jackson, that's Dani's job." She shook her head like she just couldn't understand what was going on in her house.

Dani stepped up to Jackson and tried to take the tray.

"I got it," he said and winked at her. I followed Jackson, but Dani stopped me with her hand on my wrist.

"Don't judge him by his family," she said. "He's better than they are, but family ties are hard to break."

Jackson

THE SECOND I stepped outside with the tray, I knew something had happened. Simon had slithered out of the bathroom and was now talking to my father. Vanessa was staring at them, and as soon as she turned to me, her entire expression said GUILTY.

She'd told Simon something. Obviously. And Simon was now spilling the beans. Because Dad was now standing on the patio, a drink in his hand, looking like a cartoon character with steam coming out of his ears.

I set the platter on the table and wished, as much as I'd ever wished anything, that I hadn't brought Lola here tonight.

I had this sinking feeling shit was about to get real.

"Jackson?" Lola said, coming up next to me, her hand on my wrist, and I turned my palm so I was holding her hand. Gripping it, maybe too hard.

"Come along everyone, and let's sit at the table. Dinner is served," my mother announced dramatically.

Everyone who had been standing around the patio took their seats.

Vanessa wouldn't look at me.

We weren't two seconds into the first course when my father started.

"So Jackson...I hear you're dabbling in real estate now."

I pushed a piece of kale around on my plate trying to think a few steps ahead of him. What, exactly, had Vanessa told Simon? She was awful at keeping secrets. I knew that. I just never expected her to be in a place where she would share anything meaningful with him.

"Lola," my father said carefully. "I'm sure you're aware that my son has made an offer on the diner."

I looked to Lola, who didn't seem fazed.

"Yes, I was aware."

"Maybe you weren't aware that I also had an interest in that property," my father continued.

Lola took a sip of water, probably not understanding the dynamics at play right now. My father was calling me out for what he obviously considered a betrayal.

"Dad, can we please not do this here, in front of company?" I said, gesturing to Simon's mother, who was happily drinking her martini.

"We're all family now," Simon said with a smile, showing off his unnaturally white teeth. I should have re-arranged his face when I had the chance.

"It's okay, Jackson," Lola said. "Yes, Mr. Dumont, Jackson told me you were also interested in the property, but I have to tell you, so am I. It's my family's legacy, and I think it should stay with me."

"Really," my father drawled. "That's very ambitious of

you. Tell me, where would someone *like you* get that kind of money?"

That's it. We were done.

"All right," I said. "Another great evening with all of you. But we're out."

I tugged Lola up and stepped away from the table. Enraged and, beneath that, scared. Scared that what I'd thought was cement was actually sand, and it was vanishing under my feet.

"Jackson, it's fine," she said, tugging back on my hand, trying to hold me in place. She thought she was being brave and strong. She had no idea the lion's den she'd walked into. "I've applied for a loan from the CCIB, which is a group of investors who lend the small businesses of Calico Cove money. I'm sorry, but it's my diner, Mr. Dumont. I'm going to keep it."

Damn it.

"Ah," Dad said, leaning back in his chair. "The CCIB. How quaint. Are you going to tell her, son, or am I?"

That's when Lola looked at me, and for the first time, I could see her uncertainty. "Jackson? Tell me what?"

"Really," my mother said. "Do we have to do this now? I've planned this lovely dinner—"

"Yes," my father barked. "We have to do this now."

"Lola," I said slowly. "I can explain. Everything. Let's just get out of here, now."

"Oh, God." She laughed, her hand covering her mouth. "It's that bad?"

"Lola, you might not be aware of this, but, apparently, my children are responsible for the CCIB," my father said, looking like a villain in a comic book.

She blinked. Blinked again.

"Jackson, what does that mean? Responsible?"

There was no way out. Shit. Why didn't I just tell her? Why didn't I just lay everything out in front of her? All my plans, all my ideas. Everything I'd done for her.

Because she doesn't fully trust you yet.

This wasn't going to help that.

"He's right. I am the CCIB. Vanessa and I pooled our money together, and we've been the ones investing in Calico Cove."

"You. You've been the one... The bakery and Annie's bookshop..." she said, her words trailing off.

She looked at me, then Vanessa, then back at me. My sister and I nodded.

Then all the pennies started to drop. She went from being confused to angry.

"I've been emailing *you*," she said. "This whole time."

I nodded. "Yes."

Lola sucked in a deep breath. I knew she was thinking back to all our exchanges. How she'd talked about her father. How I'd talked about mine.

Daddy issues. They weren't going to get any better after tonight.

"Is this the trick?" Lola looked at me, then at Vanessa who was mouthing the words *I'm sorry* to me.

"It's not." I reached for her, and she stepped back, and it was the night of the masquerade all over again. She tripped over the uneven cobblestones, and I caught her in my arms. She held herself so stiffly. So distant, even though I was touching her. Even though she was in my arms, she might as well have been miles away.

"I'd like to leave now," she said, not looking at my face.

"We're going," I told her.

"That's not all of it, though, is it?" my father said.

I tried to ignore him and lead Lola away from this disastrous dinner. My dad stood up from the table, throwing down his napkin like a gauntlet, and stepped in front of us. We were a few feet from the steps that would take us down to the path that led to the beach.

A few seconds from escape.

"You betrayed me," Dad snapped. "You betrayed the family name. How could you? All those properties you've been stealing out from underneath me. Did you think this was some joke?"

That had me seeing red. "How could I? Is that what you're really asking me? Yes, *Dad,* I did buy those properties out from under you. Any chance I got to beat you at your own game I took, and you know damn well why."

"Shells Family Restaurants?" My dad sneered. "Was that supposed to mean something?"

I heard Lola gasp.

I closed my eyes, defeated. Behind me, it was like a blast of cold air. Then she was walking around both of us, toward those steps and her escape.

"Lola," I cried and went after her, but my dad grabbed my arm.

"You owe me an explanation," he said, his fingers digging into my skin, down to the muscle and bone where I carried all the pain he and my mother caused me over the years. I shook him loose, then I did what I'd never done before, I shoved him. I shoved the old man out of my way to go after what I wanted.

Which was Lola.

26

Lola

So, for those keeping score at home, it was currently Jackson Dumont 3. Lola Pappas 0.

Jackson currently had an offer in for the diner. He was the CCIB. He, apparently, was also behind the Shells Corporation.

Oh, yeah, and he was also fucking me.

I was being fucked. From every direction.

I was so furious I practically levitated over the sand. I was halfway across the public beach before he caught up to me.

"Lola," he said, sounding winded.

"No."

"Lola."

"No."

"Please let me explain."

"Explain what?" I asked.

"It's not...none of that..." He sprinted past me and turned around. I attempted to walk around him, but he got in my way.

"Are you serious right now?" I breathed, so angry and so...hurt, I felt like I was on fire.

"I've never been so serious in my life."

I stared at him, and he only stared back at me, practically oozing apology. "Fine," I snapped. "Try to explain this, Jackson. You're taking my family diner away from me. Is that what you wanted? Was it like a game to you, to see how many ways you could set me up only to take it all away in the end? Exactly how humiliated did you want me to feel? What did I ever do to you to make you want to hurt me this bad?"

"This was never ever a plan to humiliate you. Or hurt you. Or trick you. I promise on everything that matters to me, I only wanted to keep the thing you loved the most safe."

Was that real? What was true?

"Why didn't you tell me you were behind CCIB?"

He looked up at the sky, his shirt rippling over his body in the breeze.

"When?" he asked. "When would have been the right time? If you knew at the beginning, you never would have even emailed me. If I told you after you applied, you'd have yanked your application. I knew you were never going to take money from me. I had no choice but to..."

"Lie," I said. "*Lie* is the word you're looking for. All those email exchanges where I spilled my guts to some stranger who I thought was a little old man in a lonely office in Boston with an incontinent cat?"

"Because I... an incontinent cat?"

"*A few more days, Lola. We need more time, Lola,*" I quoted from those emails as I stumbled along the sand, my shoes making traction impossible. "If you were trying to help, why were you making me wait so long for the money?"

"Lola, you asked for almost a million dollars! Vanessa and I had to move things around to make that happen. As for those emails...you're right. You're totally right. I guess...I don't have a good answer. Other than you were talking to me. We were talking, and I...liked it."

He stepped closer to me, but I stepped back. I couldn't let him do that. I couldn't let him make me believe he was telling the truth.

He'd lied...about everything. He'd lied, and he'd tricked me.

Even if he was telling the truth about the money, he was going to give me something he knew I couldn't take from him. Knew I would never. Not from a Dumont.

"Lola..."

"No," I said. "We're done. I don't trust you."

His face changed then. Suddenly he was no longer looking regretful or earnest. Now he seemed...pissed.

He nodded and slowly clapped his hands. "That's it. Isn't it? You don't trust me. I'm the guy who broke up your shell garden all those years ago, and no matter what, I can't be trusted."

"Jackson..."

"No, no," he said angrily. "I get it, Lola. You have your excuse now to run."

My jaw dropped. "My excuse?"

"Yes, to go home and hide away and not be in this fucking relationship. Because it is a relationship, Lola. It has been since I was twelve years old. I left this place to work on becoming a better man for *you*. I came back to this place for *you*. I've donated money to businesses and people in this town because you love this place and I want to help it flourish – with you. For you. I've given you everything I can, every piece of me, and you just keep pulling away. Holding yourself back. That's on *you*."

His anger shook something loose inside me. He wasn't wrong. I was always holding something back from him, even before tonight. Was I looking for a way out?

Or was I just so scared that this was real?

"I bought the property next to Pappas because I knew my dad would have, and he wouldn't have given a fuck what that did to your business. You emailed the CCIB first, and I didn't tell who I was because I knew you wouldn't have taken the money, and you need to take the money in order to save your restaurant, Lola. So yes, I did that. Ask yourself, Lola. Why did I do all that?"

It was too scary. What he was saying. And I couldn't make myself walk away from him.

"I love you, Lola!" he shouted to the beach, to the water, to the night sky. To me. "I have loved you for years. I loved you even when I was so jealous and so mad and I know, I know that makes me an asshole. I know...I was always the asshole." He sighed, his anger now spent. "Have you ever seen a Shells Family Restaurant? Pictures of the décor?"

I shook my head.

He fished his phone out of his pocket. "When I bought the first property, I was completely unprepared. I had no idea what to do with it once I had it. The whole goal was just to beat my father at his own game. I hired this local consultant, and he did all this market research and focus group stuff. He said the neighborhood would be best served by a family restaurant. A diner. So I made a version of my favorite diner."

He handed me his phone, and there was a picture of the inside of a Shells Family Restaurant.

It was an almost exact replica of Pappas. The counter with the stools. The big middle booth in a semi-circle. The two-tops by the window. The tiles on the floor and on the walls were the same design, but except yellow and brown they were blue and white.

Like the flag of Greece. Everything was new and sparkling. It was what I dreamed of Pappas looking like. I made a sound, half-gasp, half-strangled.

"This is the menu," he said, and he reached over and swiped to the next picture.

It was a smaller menu than Pappas, but all the same types of food.

Under sandwiches was the Lola Special with the description: Changes Daily.

I was breathing hard, and tears were burning in my eyes.

"I never would have built a Shells Family Restaurant next to the original," he whispered. "I'm sorry you thought that's what that sign meant. I put it up...just to piss my father off that he'd been beaten again."

"Why did you call the company Shells?" I whispered, still not looking at him.

"Why do you think, Lola?" His voice was nearly pleading, and I knew what he was asking me. All the years between us. Everything we'd been too young to understand or too proud to reveal.

"Because of my shell garden?" I asked, and I felt more than saw him nod.

"Because I love you and it was how I kept you with me."

The sob came tearing out of me. I clapped my hand over

my mouth and nearly dropped the phone, but he grabbed it. Then he grabbed me, carefully at first, but then his arms were around me so hard like there was no way he'd ever let me go.

"I've loved you for so long," he whispered. "I know I messed up so bad. This was the only way I could think of to keep you safe, to protect what you loved until I convinced you to trust me. I was trying not to be an asshole and still somehow managed to be one."

I hiccupped, a half laugh, half sob. My arms were hard around his neck, and I was crying against his skin, which smelled like expensive cologne and sea air and him.

It was my favorite smell.

I kissed him, and he was my favorite flavor.

I loved him, and he was my favorite feeling.

"I'm sorry for back then," I whispered into his ear. "For not seeing how much pain you were in. For not sticking by you and trying to help."

"No, Lola, I...that's too much."

He squeezed me tighter.

"I'm sorry for now," I said into his other ear. "I have been holding back. I didn't want to believe you could be real. But you are, aren't you?"

"For you, Lola, I'm as real as it gets. I love you."

"I want to go home with you," I said.

He blinked. "Okay."

"I want to have sex."

He smiled. "Okay."

"You inside me sex."

He groaned, and for an answer he kissed me.

We had to go back up to the house to get his Jeep. Thankfully, Eric had driven it down to the edge of the driveway, so we were able to avoid any more interaction with his family.

Then Jackson drove us to his place.

Once inside, he led me to the bedroom and drew the shades, so the room was cool and dark. When the bedroom door closed behind us, I felt alone *with* him in a way I hadn't before. There were no more secrets. Nothing to be hidden. I didn't have to pretend not to feel what I felt.

He crouched at my feet and undid the tiny little buckles on my sandals. He slipped my feet free, while I rested my hand on top of his head. A reverse Cinderella situation that put a lump in my throat. All this time, he'd been walking around with different glass slippers waiting for the chance to save me. While I'd been refusing to see that he was Prince Charming all along.

He pushed the edge of my dress up. "Hold this," he said, handing me the hem, and I did. He wrapped his arms around my butt and pressed his face to my underwear. His breath hot against me through the satin.

"Jackson," I whispered. I loved it, I did. Only I was ready for what was next. I needed what was next.

"Just let me," he whispered against me. Since I was a pushover, I let him.

I was amazed at how he knew my body in a way I didn't. He had an experience of it, completely removed of my own, and when I was with him, I felt different. I *was* different.

Holding my skirt with one hand, and the back of his head with the other, while his tongue did wicked things to my insides, I felt myself grow. My edges expand. I was suddenly capable of things I hadn't been capable of before. I was fuller and brighter and more complete with his hands on me. His mouth on me.

"Jackson," I gasped, folding over him, my legs sagging,

the orgasm rolling over and through me. He held me up and got to his feet. I dropped my skirt reaching for him, hard beneath his pants.

"Oh, no," he said and grabbed my hand. "You want me inside you sex, then we're not messing around."

"Then what was that?" I asked, gesturing around his mouth, which was all juicy from me.

"Necessary," he said with his devastating grin, and all but tossed me onto his bed with the rumpled covers and gazillion thread count sheets.

Standing next to the bed, he shrugged out of his jacket, yanked off his shirt. Toed off his fancy shoes.

"Come on, baby. Get naked for me," he said as I just watched him. He dropped his pants and the movement of his pants over his erection made him hiss and flinch.

"Are you okay?" I asked. I sat up to pull my dress over my head. I wasn't wearing a bra, and he groaned as my hair fell down around my shoulders. The beachy waves grazing my nipples. He looked up at the ceiling and wrapped his hand around his dick.

"You need some help?" I asked, crawling across the bed towards him. I put my hand against his stomach, and it was like I'd hit some kind of game over button.

The next thing I knew I was on my back and my underwear was lost to the ages, and he was between my legs, his lips on my neck.

I could feel him, hard and big, between my legs, and I arched into him. He slipped between my folds, the soft sweet head of his dick hitting my clit. I spread my legs wider.

He groaned, his arms around me so tight like he couldn't bear to let me go.

"Condom," he muttered.

"You have some now?" I whispered. There was something so tender about him this close to the edge. Something hot, yes, but vulnerable, and I wondered if this was part of the reason why he wouldn't fuck me before. Because he couldn't bear to show himself this way while I was holding myself back.

"Tell me where the condoms are, Jackson," I whispered, stroking his hair.

"Bedside table," he said, and I reached out an arm and managed to pull the knob on the drawer and fish out the box.

"A little faster please," he said.

"Lean up, babe," I said, and he pushed himself up on his knees between my legs. He was wet, not just with me, but also with the come leaking out of his tip. I tore open the package. I didn't really know how to put one of these things on a guy, but it seemed pretty self-explanatory. I reached for him, the condom in my hand, and he shook his head.

"No way," he said. "Next time. You touch me now, this is over."

I watched, breathless as he rolled on the condom. Why was that sexy? I wondered. Then I realized everything about him was sexy. Watching him grocery shop was going to be sexy. Watching him do dishes. Flossing his teeth. Well, maybe not that one, but I wasn't going to count anything out.

"Come on, baby," he said, crawling over me. "This is going to be a very short, very intense ride."

He braced himself over me, one hand guiding himself between my legs.

"You okay?" he asked, and I nodded.

Suddenly there he was. Pushing his way inside of me. I remembered the strange sting and burn of his fingers when we were on the boat. This was that times a thousand.

"Jackson?"

"Are you okay?" he asked, his face suddenly stricken. He held himself so still I could feel the tremble of the effort in his arms.

"Yeah," I said. "You're just *inside* me."

"That's the idea. Am I hurting you?"

"No," I lied. Because I didn't want him to stop.

"Do you like it?"

"Yes," I said truthfully. Because he was inside me.

"Can we... Do you still want to talk about it or...?"

I laughed, cracked wide open by him. Not just physically, but every way a person could be cracked open by another. I was flooded with love. Absolutely flooded.

"Please just fuck me, Jackson."

He growled and thrust hard inside me. I gasped, and his gaze flew to mine, always making sure I was okay and that was so sweet but not what I wanted. I didn't know how to say that yet. But Jackson was right there with me. He shoved my body around. Shifted my legs wider, lifted my hips. He pulled back, thrust again, and I felt it all. Everything. All at once.

All I could do was hold on tight. The orgasm, when it hit, came from deep inside my body, and it was almost scary. The very top of the rollercoaster before you hurtled downhill. But Jackson was with me, and I didn't have to be scared. I didn't have to be scared of anything if Jackson was with me. Things were only better with him.

"Lola." He groaned, and I could feel him losing it.

"Yes," I urged. "Come on."

He thrust so hard my head hit the headboard, and his hand on my hip would leave me with a bruise tomorrow, but I didn't care. It was all so worth it. Everything that brought me to this place. Every bit of pain. I wouldn't trade it. Not for anything.

"I love you," I whispered, when he was sagged, hot and sweaty, against me. A boneless lump, breathing hard. At my words, he stopped breathing and lifted his head.

"What did you say?" he asked.

"I love you," I said, pushing back that swoop of hair, looking deep in his eyes.

"Is that the amazing orgasm I just gave you talking or do—"

"I love you, Jackson."

He exhaled. His face lost for a moment before filling with hope.

This poor man, raised by those people. I knew hope was not the easiest thing for him. He was almost scared of it. It was why he tried to save me three ways, because he had to make it concrete. Hope wasn't something he could count on. I thought of his job, how he turned the abstract into the concrete, and I realized how that was him, down to his bones. Even the CCIB, the way they helped people turn wishes into plans.

"I see you," I said, stroking his face. Maybe it was a weird thing to say. It was just so clear. He was so clear. Because I saw him with my heart.

"I see you, too," he said. "I've seen you since I was just a kid."

It was a lot—what we felt for each other, what we'd been to each other. It was a lot a lot. I loved him, and he loved me, and this was far from the beginning of us, but this moment felt like a new chapter.

"What a story, huh?" I whispered against his mouth as he kissed me.

"What story?"

"Us. We're just a really amazing story."

He laughed against me, and I felt him slip from my body, and I immediately missed him. Immediately wanted more.

"So, how many of those condoms do you have?" I asked against his smiling lips.

27

Lola

The next morning, we took coffee over to Georgie's house and filled him in on everything.

"Wait," he said, putting down his cappuccino. Never a good sign. Georgie liked his cappuccino so hot it burned the top of his mouth. "You're Shells Corporation Coming Soon?"

"I am," Jackson admitted. "Only I'm not building a family restaurant there."

"Then what are you building?"

Jackson shrugged. "I don't know. What do you think we should build?"

"We?" Georgie asked.

"Yeah." Jackson looked over at me, then back at Georgie. "We. I mean, I have some ideas, but I figured you two have lived your whole lives here. It would be crazy not to bring you into this on a professional level."

Georgie looked over at me with his eyebrows raised. *You sure about this?*, those eyebrows asked.

I nodded and drank my latte, and after a second, he sipped his cappuccino, and it seemed like Jackson, or at least his position as the property owner next door, got Georgie's seal of approval.

We tossed around ideas.

"You know the one idea I really liked when we were emailing?" Jackson said, stretched out in the sun. One of the cats, Rascal—or was it Jezebel, hard to tell those two apart—was sniffing his shoes. Georgie and I smiled at each other.

The cat pounced up on Jackson's lap and started purring and digging its claws into his stomach.

"Ouch," he muttered, arms out wide as he glared down at the cat who did not care about his glaring. "Do I just—"

"Let it happen?" Georgie said. "Yes."

"Which idea?" I asked Jackson, rubbing his arm as the cat finally curled up into a ball in his lap.

"What about another bar?" he said. "Somewhere fun, but a little upscale. Good music. Good drinks. Excellent patio. Better food than the Gull but a place for the tourists to go, letting the locals have their own place. We could have dancing on the weekends...and maybe a Drag Show on Sundays? I mean, who doesn't love a Drag Show?"

Georgie heaved a big sigh and ran a finger across one of his eyebrows. "I cannot believe I'm going to end up liking you after all the shit you pulled."

"I know," I said to Georgie. My two guys were going to be friends. I couldn't be happier.

We tabled the conversation about what to do about the lot next to Pappas and moved onto what to do about Tiffani.

"Well," Georgie said. "I know what I want to do..."

"You know, maybe it's love hormones, or that I don't have

to be so worried about the future, but I'm not as mad at her as I was."

"Fine. I'm mad enough for the both of us," Georgie said.

"Me, too," seconded Jackson, and the two of them cheered with their paper cups.

"She's alone. She's in over her head. She's scared," I said.

"She kicked you out of your home," Jackson said. "I think we should go over there and kick her out."

I shook my head. "I'm not kicking her out. We should go talk to her and let her know that she's going to get paid no matter what, and that she doesn't need to be scared anymore. I think that's the right thing to do."

"I suppose," Jackson said and leaned over and kissed me. The cat protested with a full-throated meow. "What the heck? What am I supposed to do with this cat? Do I just..." He made a gesture as if to move it, and both Georgie and I shook our heads.

"I'll make us some breakfast," Georgie said, standing up and retying his kimono. "You can leave when the cat decides to move."

"This is no way to live," Jackson said.

"Welcome to Calico Cove," I said and turned my face up to the sun, happier than I could have ever imagined.

Jackson

GEORGIE MADE us eggs with bacon, and the cat finally got off my lap, allowing us to leave. We shook hands, and the cat meowed after me.

"That means come back and visit in cat," Georgie yelled

at us, and I lifted my hand up in a wave and caught Georgie's
eye. He'd managed, with incredible care and deftness, to be
a friend and a parent-figure to Lola, and I was grateful to the
guy. I imagined we would, over time, get to be pretty good
friends. Should we decide to make the property next to
Pappas a bar, I could not imagine anyone better to help
figure it out.

"What are you thinking?" Lola asked me.

I reached over and brushed the hair off her shoulders,
my fingers grazing the warmth of her neck. "That I'm going
to have to pay Georgie a ton of money to get him to leave
Pappas and run my bar next door."

"You wouldn't!" She gasped.

"I think you know how ruthless I am, Lola." I lifted an
eyebrow like a Disney villain.

"Actually, it's probably smart. His feet are killing him at
the end of the day. My dad was in so much pain working
behind that grill for thirty years. I don't want that to happen
to Georgie."

"You both could use some time off your feet." I thought
of all the ways I could get Lola off her feet and wondered
how to get her back to my place.

"You know who else we need to talk to?" Lola said as we
got into the Jeep. "Your sister."

I was still annoyed with her for telling Simon anything
about my business or the CCIB. Sure, Simon was supposed
to be her fiancé, but it just didn't seem real to me.

"I think she's made her bed," I said.

"Jackson," Lola sighed, like I was disappointing her. I
never wanted to disappoint her. "Simon was hitting on me,
and she wasn't a hundred feet away. He's never going to be
faithful to her."

"She knows that," I said and put the Jeep in gear.

"And she doesn't care?"

"I'm sure she does," I said. "Beneath not wanting to disappoint our parents. Beneath the lies she's told herself about loving him. Beneath all her fear. She has to know it."

"She can't marry him," Lola said.

"Other than kidnapping her, which you know I'm not opposed to, I don't know what else we can do."

She read my frustration loud and clear and reached over to pet my shoulder. She was touching me all the time now. I liked that.

I liked the petting.

We pulled into Pappas' parking lot about twenty minutes before Lola's shift started.

"Hey," I said. "I can come in or stay in the car if you want to handle this on your own." Lola was an amazing woman, and she'd been handling more than any person should have to on her own, so it wasn't that I didn't believe she could take care of Tiffani, but I just wanted to help shoulder the load.

"No," she said. I was relieved. "Come with me."

"My pleasure," I said, kissing her quickly before we got out of the car.

We walked in hand in hand, and I liked how everyone greeted Lola. It was so obvious that she was loved here, and all that jealousy I once felt was gone. Evaporated into smoke because now, now I got to share in that love.

This was her real home. She was different inside the walls of this diner; she was more fully herself. Her smile was brighter. Her back straighter. Her eyes sharper. I could see her mind calculating things that were done, that weren't done, that could be done.

"Where's your mom?" she asked Zoe and Chloe, who were standing behind the counter on their phones, their heads pressed together.

"In the back," they said in unison, and I looked closer because it looked like...

"Did you braid your hair together?" I asked.

"It started that way, but now it's tangled."

Lola laughed. "Go in the back, sort it out, put your hair in ponytails, or I swear to God, I'll cut it myself. And tell your mom to come out here."

That, I thought, *is my girl*.

The twins shuffled off, wincing, and telling each other to stop pulling. I sat at the counter, and Lola went around to the other side, putting her apron on.

"You want a water, or something?" she asked.

"No, I'm stuffed," I said.

"That's what she said," Lola joked, her eyes sparkling as she looked at me under her lashes.

"No, that's what *you* said," I told her. "Last night."

She pursed her lips. "Hmm. I think I've forgotten." She shrugged. "I'm going to need a reminder."

Oh, my God, this girl. Was this how it was going to be for the rest of my life? Walking around full from good food and needing a nap from fucking her all night, but also horny because I wanted to fuck her all night again?

I couldn't wait.

Actually, I didn't have to, I realized. It was happening. It was now. It was me and Lola and all of those things for the rest of our lives. Being happy always felt like something I had to earn. Like I had to stockpile my good deeds so I could trade it in for happiness in the future. It was never a now thing, it was always a future thing.

But it was now, and I was gut punched that I'd managed to get here. To Lola. The place I wanted to be for so long.

Tiffani stepped around the doorway and sighed. "You're not in uniform," she said. And I realized Lola wasn't wearing that pink dress she hated so much. She was in khaki shorts and an old Pappas' Diner T-shirt.

"You're right," Lola said. "Those uniforms are uncomfortable and make us look like characters instead of real people."

"No one else is complaining," Tiffani said.

"I don't want to fight about the uniforms, Tiffani. I want to talk about the future of Pappas."

"Before you do that," Tiffani said, stepping closer, but Lola didn't seem too worried. "I want to apologize."

Lola looked as stunned as I felt.

"I never should have done what I did to you." She shook her head and twisted her hands in front of her. "Kicking you out of your home like that. Your father..." The breath Tiffani pulled in shuddered.

I looked to Lola to make sure she was all right. She stood there, stalwart.

"I never knew what to do with you," Tiffani said with a sound that tried to be a laugh but sounded like a sob. "You were more mature than any girl your age. You didn't need a mother, and I'd ruined any chance we might have had to be friends, and so I..." A tear fell. "I just kept my distance, and you kept yours. I was selfish. On behalf of my own daughters, I was just...very selfish. I'm so sorry."

"Okay," Lola said slowly, maybe a little stunned by the direction of the conversation. "I want to talk about the future, Tiffani. Not the past."

"Are you able to secure the money?" Tiffani asked.

"I am," she said confidently. The funds we needed were transferred that morning.

"Then it's yours. Free and clear. Not a penny more than what it was valued at. I wish I was in a different position to just give you the diner but the girls..."

Lola lifted her hand. "I know. I understand. When my dad gave you the diner, you got stuck in a very long and very old power struggle between me and my parents, and it's not your fault."

"You're being more generous than you need to be," Tiffani said. "It's a deal. No more offers. I'm selling you the restaurant."

Lola turned to me and blew out a breath. "Wow," she said. "It's...done?"

I got to my feet. "Can I come back there?" I asked.

"Behind the counter? Yes, Jackson. Let's face it, you basically own the place."

"No," I said and walked around the counter. "No way. Pappas is yours. It's always been yours. It always will be. The money has no strings."

I kissed her, then she swatted me away. "Now, go," she said. "I've got to work."

"Okay, but first, what are your three favorite things?"

"In no particular order?" she asked.

"Sure."

"My town," she said and kissed me. "My diner," she said and kissed me. "And you. What are yours?"

"You, you and you," I told her.

We were standing there, kissing, when Madame Za walked in.

"Hello, Lola you look—" She stopped when she saw us.

"Hi, Madame Za," Lola said. "Take any table you want. I'll be with you in a second."

"Are you two lovely kids an item now?"

I wanted to protest being called a kid, but Lola nodded, her arm squeezing me around my waist. "We are."

"Well, don't say I didn't predict it," she said, flinging one glittery scarf over her shoulder.

"Predict me and Jackson?" Lola asked.

She pointed at me. Lola and I both looked down at my T-shirt. An old favorite my sister had given me displaying a fat green frog on a skateboard.

"Didn't I say something about frogs?"

EPILOGUE

Vanessa

My brother and Lola were too much. They were...well, they were distracting. Sex just seemed to be oozing off them. Sex and happiness. The way they couldn't keep their hands off each other. Not in a gross way, but in a loving way. In a brushing hair off shoulders and picking lint off ties and...whatever. It was gross. Love and happiness and sex, gross.

After all, it was my wedding day.

We were standing together in the study. The crafted altar was set up in the ballroom, along with the guest chairs lined up in neat rows, now filled with people.

We were just waiting for my father to come get me, so we could get the show started. Lola and Jackson were supposed to be helping me with my nerves, but all they were really doing was making me want to rip their eyes out.

That's how jealous of their love I was.

"The car is right outside," Jackson said quietly.

He thought he was being helpful. He thought... I don't know what he thought.

That I would change my mind? Did he not know me even a little bit? I didn't change my mind. I went down with every ship.

I was the girl who got caught at the sorority party for underage drinking. Everyone else had run when the cops showed up, but I stayed in the bathroom with puking Maggie because it felt really mean to run away and leave her to be arrested.

I was the girl who, even when Janice's nose got infected from being pierced at the same grody tattoo parlor on Market Street in Boston, went and got hers done there, too, because I'd promised her I would.

Dad practically had to buy me a whole new nose.

I was the girl who broke up with Roy Barnes that one summer because my father told me I had to.

I walked away then, didn't I? Even though my heart was, like, destroyed.

I was also the girl marrying Simon because my father told me I had to.

Of course, I knew Simon was a dirt bag. Any affection for him I'd once had was *looooooong* gone. Sometimes I even questioned if I had ever actually loved him.

But Daddy told me that he needed this marriage to work. That Simon's parents were bailing him out of some financial trouble. The fact that my father would even admit that to me, meant it was serious.

I couldn't tell Jackson that. Jackson's whole life was about destroying our father's business. If he found out I was trying to save it? I was lucky he was still speaking to me after the whole CCIB fiasco. Why had I trusted Simon with any of it?

I'd just been...showing off. Trying to prove to him I wasn't some worthless ex-model.

"Ness?" Jackson asked. "Did you hear me?"

"Yes!" I snapped. It was hard to breathe in this dress, and I was getting super light-headed. "I heard you. I heard you the first twenty million times you said it."

Jackson blinked at me, and I almost apologized.

But it was my goddamn wedding day. Yes, I knew the marriage was shit, but couldn't I have this day? Didn't I at least get to enjoy this fabulous Vera Wang dress and my perfect Grace Kelly hair?

Lola, of course, was right there, hand on Jackson's arm.

GAWD. Could they just not...for a second, rub their love in every one's faces?

"I just want you to be happy."

"Then go out there and make sure Simon isn't throwing up at the altar."

I told Simon not to have his bachelor party the night before the wedding, but he told me not to worry. He told me not to worry all the time. It was his rich dude way of saying, *I don't care about what you're saying to me.*

Oh, God, why was it so hard to breathe in this dress? I'd lost the 2.8 pounds needed to make it look perfect.

"We'll go," Lola said, pushing Jackson out the study door. "But if you need us—"

"I know." I sighed, closing my eyes. I loved them. I did. But I was losing my shit. Then they were gone, and it was just me and my, yes, very perfect reflection in the mirror.

Honestly, I should have been a bridal dress model.

Like, what had I been thinking going for high fashion? I didn't look like some kind of fierce half-French, half-forest creature warrior goddess. I looked like a bride. A cow being led, wide-eyed, long-lashed and docile, to its death.

A beautiful death.

There was a knock on the door, and I whirled, ready to take Jackson's whole head off.

"Oh. Hi, Daddy."

My father was handsome, tall and slim in his tux. He exuded benevolent father of the bride vibes.

"Look at you honey," he whispered.

I swear I didn't imagine it. I'd been working very hard with my therapist not to imagine things in my father's voice or face that weren't actually there...like respect. Or affection.

However, right now, in this moment, I didn't think I was making it up. My father sounded...emotional.

"You're beautiful," he said. "My little girl. All grown up."

Maybe it was the boning in the dress, but I couldn't actually feel those words penetrate me. Like, they bounced off me. Instead of crying and wrapping my arms around him, I wanted to shout, *Is this really necessary?*

He walked over to me, took my hands in his and bent down to kiss my knuckles.

Well...that was sweet.

"You are so precious to me. So loyal to this family. Unlike your brother—"

"Daddy." I stopped him. I didn't need another lecture on how Jackson had failed him.

"I can't thank you enough for this," he said.

Damnit. Damnit. I didn't know how to resist that. When I was a little girl, literally begging him for a scrap of any of the affection a dad would give his daughter, those were the words I would have wanted to hear.

Instead, I heard them only because I was saving his company by marrying a complete and total scumbag.

"Shall we?" he said. "Everyone is waiting for you."

I couldn't move forward. I couldn't do it. He actually had to tug on my hand. Had to pull.

"Vanessa, we need to do this. Now."

There was my real father. Cold. A little mean. The kind of man who'd pinch you on a golf course when you missed a shot during a father-daughter charity match. The kind of man who'd ask his daughter to give up her whole soul for his company.

However, since I was the girl who got pinched on that golf course, during family pictures and once, memorably, when we met a former president, I stiffened and said, "Yes, Daddy."

My therapist wanted to talk about the "abuse," but I always told her it wasn't abuse and refused.

So therapy was going great.

"Then let's get this over with."

I pushed down really deep inside of myself. That was the only way to do this. My number-one trick I learned at a young age. I grabbed my bouquet—white roses wrapped in bright red ribbon—tucked my hand in my father's elbow and we left the study.

The wedding was at my parents' beach house in Calico Cove. I had very little attachment to this house. But for some reason, when my mom asked me where I wanted to get married, this was the place I picked.

The aisle ran through the ballroom, paved with a red carpet strewn with white rose petals.

Simon stood under the constructed archway, covered in flowers, looking like he was being held up by his best man. His hair was a mess, and his tie was crooked.

The pictures were going to be terrible.

The front door to our house was open as Eric greeted

the guests. I caught Eric's eye, and he tipped his head in acknowledgement. Except he looked sad.

Sad on my wedding day.

Dad lifted his hand, and the stringed quartet we brought in from Boston started playing "Canon in D."

The song every Dumont bride had walked down the aisle to for hundreds of years.

Everyone rose to their feet and turned to look at me.

Dad's hand tightened on mine, and I accidentally dropped the bouquet.

"Whoops," I said, and Dad shot me an annoyed look, but bent down to pick it up.

And that's when I ran.

WANT to read more Lola and Jackson? Click here and sign up for my newsletter and get a BONUS epilogue Lola and Jackson Epilogue

WANT to find out what happens to Vanessa next...read her story in The Grump, The Bride & The Baby. DOWNLOAD NOW!

THE GRUMP, THE BRIDE & THE BABY

The Masquerade Ball
June
Vanessa

What's that saying about the bed and making it? The one that basically means – it doesn't matter how awful this thing is you're doing, how much you hate it, or wish you could make it stop – it was your choice, so you had to suck it up.

This is my bed so I have to make it?

Something like that.

There was a whole masquerade engagement party happening in this house right now. In rooms decorated in pink and gold (my signature colors) with servers passing around canapés (keto and paleo) to celebrate my engagement to Simon.

My father was telling everyone who'd listen how proud he was of me. That he loved Simon like a son. I'm sure my brother, Jackson loved that. Jackson was not a big fan of Simon's.

Meanwhile, I was hiding in this dark study, drinking

expensive champagne that tasted like dirt, because hours earlier my fiancé had been fucking a girl I knew from boarding school.

I *hated* this bed.

I'd caught them coming out of one of the guest bedrooms. Disheveled, touching, laughing at their little dirty secret.

Thankfully, they hadn't seen me, so I'd been spared any lying explanations.

Still. Today? He couldn't keep it in his pants, *today*?

This engagement, this whole marriage between Simon and I was really a business arrangement between my family and his. I knew it. My family got something monetarily out of it, I was sure. And Simon's family got our Dumont connections.

I tried for a really long time to convince myself I could love Simon. And if I couldn't love him I could be...content with him. I could put together some kind of fairy tale to tell the world. As long as I believed in that fairy tale, everything would be okay.

Tonight, I looked the part of the fairy princess in my Reformation Barbiecore Veria silk dress. My legs were ten miles long. My hair was a golden sheet so straight and shiny you could see your reflection in it. I was thin enough to please even my mother, who was never pleased.

Still Simon cheated on me.

Tonight, of all nights.

He'd probably screw one of my bridesmaids on my wedding day, too.

"This fairy tale sucks," I muttered.

I traded out the empty champagne glass and filled a glass with dad's good bourbon and settled back into the leather couch that was all but swallowing me whole.

Which wouldn't be the worst thing that happened to me tonight.

It wasn't always like this. When we first met, Simon had been charming. Sweet. Sexy in his backwards hat, gym body way.

He'd wooed me. Flowers, flirting, little gifts. He'd made me feel special for the first time in my life.

I was in love. Or I thought I was. Was there a difference? Maybe that was the bourbon talking, but right now it seemed like love was something you had to convince yourself you actually felt.

Except I knew the difference. Deep down. I'd had the real thing once and I'd given it up.

For Simon. For my family. Because my father had asked me to.

Years ago, the first time I'd caught Simon cheating, it was with a waitress from the yacht club. I'd called him out and he'd said it was a slip up and it would never happen again.

The second time, I'd broken up with him. I wasn't such a push over. I'd left him. Made a scene at brunch. I hadn't returned his calls for like...four days.

Except he'd begged and pleaded and I had the backbone of a jellyfish.

I am only guessing they don't have backbones, I don't actually know.

Back then he'd made me feel like the cheating was my fault. If only I'd liked sex more, or was better at it – he wouldn't have had to cheat.

Which, I guess was fair. I didn't *love* sex, the way everyone else on the planet seemed to love it. Simon made it clear I was bad at it. So, could I blame him?

The third time he'd cheated, he thought I didn't know. Because I hadn't even bothered to call him out for it. That summer I left Simon in Boston and came up to Calico Cove.

That was the summer I'd met Roy.

The summer that had changed everything and weirdly, had changed nothing at all.

Because eventually Dad had found me in Calico Cove and said he'd needed my help. That only I could save the family. *Me.*

Sure, yes, I had to get back together with Simon, but that was nothing compared to the shining light of my father's sudden love for me.

How was I supposed to resist that? My daddy needed me.

So I'd fallen for it. I was still falling for it.

The door to the den clicked open and a slice of light was cut out of the darkness I was drowning in. Mom, probably. The announcement was to be made soon and Simon and I had this whole choreographed dance to perform. How I supposed to do that without throwing up, I didn't know. I only knew I had to make it happen.

This was my bed and I was lying in it.

That's it! That's how the saying went.

"Hey, Messy Nessy."

I gasped at the sound of his voice. At that ridiculous nickname.

"Roy," I whispered.

Was this a dream? It had to be a dream. I'd passed out from the bourbon. Or I'd hit my head or was having some kind of breakdown. Because after what I'd done to him two years ago there was no way he'd ever talk to me again. Even if I ran into him on the street, he would ignore me like he never knew me.

He had every right, too.

The door closed and darkness swept around us. I heard him step further into the study. My father's inner sanctum. Roy always was brave. He didn't care this was my father's private space.

I felt him watching me in the darkness only broken by strips of moonlight shining through the curtains. The urge to turn and look at him was so intense, but equally intense was the urge to throw myself out the window to get away from him.

This guy I'd liked so much. This guy I'd hurt so bad.

Be brave, Vanessa. For once in your stupid life.

I turned my head and found him in the shadows. He was in a rented tux that fit him like it was custom. Filling it out with muscles built from hard work. Seeing him, made me want to smile. Made me want to throw myself at him. Made me want to cry.

"Hi," I said, like dummy.

"Hi," he said back.

"I'm...surprised you're here."

"That makes two of us."

"If you're here to yell-"

"I don't want to yell, Ness."

He pulled at his tie as if it was choking him.

"You need help with that tie?"

"The fucker," he said, and then just tugged on one end until it lost its knot. He undid the button at the neck and suddenly he looked like a man in an expensive watch commercial.

"You look good," I told him. Understatement.

"I look like an ass in this penguin suit," he said.

Roy would feel that way about a tuxedo. Uncomfortable. Out of place. But he still looked better than any man out there.

"Why did you come?" I asked him, my voice barely a whisper while I waited for an answer I wasn't sure I wanted. Or an answer I desperately needed:

Because I love you, I've always loved you. That summer meant everything to me and I can't watch you lie in this stupid bed even though you made it.

He was frowning. He was always frowning. He had resting frown face. Except when I got him to laugh. Which I'd gotten pretty good at that summer.

Those had been my favorite times. The best times of my whole life really.

Why hadn't I been strong enough to hold onto to him? To us?

"You know how when you have a toothache and you can't stop poking at it with your tongue?" he asked.

I think I am the toothache in this situation.

"I do," I said quietly.

"You gonna marry him?"

"That's a ridiculous question, Roy."

There were hundreds of people in this house all here to celebrate my upcoming nuptials. Who would ask me, the bride to be, a question like that?

Roy Barnes. That's who. He'd come to see it for himself. To poke that toothache one last time. And maybe, because it was a thing he did, to save me. One last time. Save me from this marriage. From myself.

From this stupid bed.

"I don't think it is," he said.

Should I tell him the truth? That I didn't want to marry Simon. I never wanted to marry Simon. That I'd left Roy that summer because I'd picked my family over him. My father over him, not Simon. Would it matter?

He'd save me, again and then what? He'd be stuck with

me. A spoiled princess with daddy and *sex* issues. No. It wasn't fair.

Roy Barnes deserved better than Messy Nessy.

"I don't...I can't...Yes," I finally said. I shook my head, trying to find some bravery. Like a captain going doing down with a ship. "Yes, I'm going to marry him."

He nodded and shoved his hands in his pockets, ruining the lines of the suit.

"You love him then" he said like it was fact he was trying to convince himself of.

"It's not... it's not about love."

"Geezus, please don't tell me it's about money," his harsh laugh was a knife that sliced at me. "You're as bad as your father. Whatever, Ness. Good luck."

I wanted to tell him not to go. Tell him I could never love Simon because my heart would always be Roy's. But what would be the point?

He took my silence for an answer and turned for the door.

"Wait," I said, getting up from the couch and following him. I sounded desperate. I was desperate. For just one more second, one more...touch. "Your tie."

He stopped but didn't turn around. I could feel him wanting to storm out. Or to turn and tell me off. I deserved all of it. It was stupid to ask him for anything else.

"Let me fix it."

I held my breath until he turned and bent down so I could reach his neck.

Our faces were close, our breaths mingled. I could feel the warmth of his neck. His skin.

I could always smell the sea on Roy. A scent he could never shake. I could see the stubble on his cheeks and chin, even though he'd probably shaved just hours ago. He kept his caramel brown eyes locked on some fixed place over my head.

Look at me, please. One more time. Just look at me.

Like he heard me, his eyes met mine and instantly I couldn't breathe. A pang of longing hit my chest so furiously, I had to look away.

"You're good at this," he said.

"We...we go to a lot of black-tie events."

I tied Simon's tie every time but he never ducked down to make it easier for me. He always made me stretch up on my tiptoes. It was a little thing that felt so big right now.

"Makes sense."

"There," I said when I was done and couldn't stretch it out any longer. I patted his impossibly broad chest, remembering how thick his muscles were beneath his chest hair.

"Ness," he said, and brushed a finger against my cheek.

He was going to say something. Something like I didn't have to go through with this terrible marriage if I didn't want to. How I could make my own decisions for my life.

He was so obviously wrong.

None of this was in my control. Because I gave all that up the summer I met and left Roy. And instead said yes, to what my father needed me to do.

Thankfully, he didn't say any of that. He just dropped his hand and walked out the door, shutting it quietly behind him.

I don't know how long I stared at that closed door but it seemed like some deep metaphor for my life.

Until it opened again, and my mother poked her head inside.

"There you are!" she exclaimed. "I've been looking everywhere for you. Come, come. They're about to make the introductions."

I plastered a fake smile on my face, because that's what I was expected to do and followed my mother out into the small foyer outside the ballroom.

Where my bastard, cheating fiancé was waiting for me with a huge smile on his face too.

Run.

Where?

Roy.

"Ladies and gentleman," the DJ announced after getting everyone's attention. "It is my pleasure to introduce the couple of the hour. The soon to be Mr. and Mrs. Turnberry. Simon Turnberry and Vanessa Dumont."

I slipped on my mask.

That was my cue.

The Wedding Day
September
Vanessa

I looked down at the glob of lobster mac & cheese that had fallen on the bodice of my wedding dress and tried not to cry.

I did not succeed.

I mean, in the grand scheme of everything that happened today, this smear of cream, butter and cheese, leaving a grease stain on my twenty-thousand-dollar, hand-beaded Swarovski crystal Vera Wang dress, shouldn't have even registered.

"Are you...I'm sorry, but are you okay?" A woman asked me.

She was leaving with a few items in her hand that she'd

just bought at the register of the store, but it was hard to walk by a devastated non-bride without checking in. She seemed nice. She wore unflattering capri pants and her concern was a maybe little judgey, but it was nice that she asked.

No one except for Jackson, had asked me if I was okay in years.

I tried to push my veil off my face, but there was just so much of it, so I yanked it off sending a small waterfall of bobby pins onto the floor.

"I'm great. Thank you for asking," I said. "Could you..." I pointed at the drinks fridge against the wall. I couldn't get to it, surrounded as I was by the ten foot long, Irish-lace train attached to my dress that I'd had to wedge into the small booth with me.

"A drink?" she asked.

"Yes. That would be so nice of you. Like just really nice."

Nice Lady opened the drink fridge and reached for a diet coke.

"No!" I barked.

Then she reached for the regular full sugar Coke on the top shelf and waited for me to nod.

"Yes. That would be so nice," I said.

She even popped the top on it and set it down in front of me. I guzzled down that can of Coke in three seconds.

"Honey, are you sure you're okay?"

"I was just so hungry," I said with a laugh. With renewed vigor, I dove back into what was actually my second helping of lobster mac & cheese. I'd finished the first one so fast, I'd made Verity who was working at The Lobster Pot today, give me another. "Mom wanted me to be a size four for the wedding."

"Well, the dress looks beautiful."

"Thanks. It's ruined. I mean it's all ruined. The dress. The day. The wedding. Everything's ruined. I ruined it."

Me. Messy Nessy. Maybe everyone should have seen that coming.

"I'm so sorry to hear that," Nice Lady said, although it was obvious now she was looking for an escape.

"Have you had this lobster mac & cheese?" I asked, pointing my plastic fork at what was left in bowl.

"I have."

"It's the best thing I've ever eaten."

I hadn't eaten in years. Not like I'd wanted to. Not like my body needed me to. No, I ate what other people told me to eat.

My mother. My agent. Photographers. Other models.

When all that time I was so hungry.

Now, I was eating forbidden noodles covered in cheese sauce with big chunks of lobster and it was changing my life.

One of the crystals fell off the bodice of my dress and rolled off the table, onto the floor. Nice Lady casually picked it up and set it back down on the edge of my booth. She gingerly patted my shoulder as she walked past me and out the door.

The wedding was definitely off now.

I grimaced thinking about the house full of guests, all probably still in a state of shock having watched the bride take off at a full sprint out the front door.

I had one job today. Marry Simon, save my family, make my father happy and in the end ...I couldn't do it. I didn't love Simon. I didn't even like him. Actually... I think I hated him.

I know I hated myself with him.

Jackson, to his wonderful credit, had kissed my cheek

and told me his Jeep was right out front. Like he'd known all along I might bolt at the last moment. He'd always given me more credit than I gave myself.

I left the family mansion to the sound of the string quartet coming to a violent stop, while my father shouted my name and the guests gasped and swiveled in their chairs.

I'd jumped in the Jeep, lowered the sun visor and the car keys had fallen into the creamy white folds of my dress. I took off as fast as the old Jeep would go even as people came out of the front door behind me.

I didn't bother checking the rear-view mirror to see if Simon was one of those people.

The key to a life on the run was to be inconspicuous. Which wasn't the easiest thing to do in a silk wedding dress with a ten foot train. Everyone in Calico Cove would recognize Jackson's Jeep. So I'd left the Jeep at the diner and was suddenly starving. Faint and dizzy and famished.

Pappas was too obvious a choice.

No, the better option for food oblivion was The Lobster Pot on the other side of town. I had no problem navigating the walk in my three-inch heels. Having once had to walk down a catwalk draped in twenty pounds of designer couture on five-inch stilettos, these three inch Jimmy Choo's felt like sneakers.

I'd made the right choice by coming here.

Lobster mac & cheese....'nuff said.

Verity left the kitchen to bring me some extra napkins and pointed to the grease stain on my dress.

"I can maybe get some hot water to try..." She didn't finish her sentence.

"It's not like I'm going to be wearing it again," I told her.

"Vanessa, it's Vanessa right?"

I nodded. People in this town didn't know me like they

knew Jackson. I hadn't spent most of my summers here like he had. Summers weren't play time for me. They were a time for improvement and catching up.

I always needed to improve on something.

"Tell me who to call, honey," Verity said gently.

I shook my head. There was no one. I could head over to Jackson's new condo, but my father was sure to show up there. I had no idea what Simon might do. I doubted he actually cared, but he would be embarrassed and that was never a good look on him.

I needed to plan. I needed a place I could lay low. Now that the immediate need for comfort food had been filled, it was time think.

Only I wasn't the best thinker.

It's why I needed the special tutors, the summer school programs, all that catching up.

I was only good for being pretty and for making other things look pretty.

In my life, I'd never done anything so disobedient as running away from my own wedding. I had no idea what to do next.

My stomach cramped.

"Oh my God. What was I thinking?" I groaned, putting my hand over my stomach.

"Oh honey, do you want to go back to the wedding?" Verity asked me. "I'm sure you can. Lots of brides get last minute jitters. Well, not me, but that's because I was marrying Josh..."

"No, I don't want to go back to the wedding. I meant what was I thinking ordering two servings of mac & cheese. My stomach hates me."

"Oh. Okay. Well, let me get you some water."

I could call an Uber...

No phone.

I could use Verity's phone to call a taxi...

No money to pay the taxi.

No money to pay Verity for the lobster mac & cheese either.

Here I was stuffed with pasta and Coke with no money, a stained wedding dress and designer shoes.

Verity came back with a plastic cup of water.

"What size shoe do you wear?" I asked her. She looked at me like I was crazy, which was fair. I was considering selling her my shoes for enough money to get out of Calico Cove. Then I glanced over at the community bulletin board on the wall. It was covered with flyers and advertisements for babysitting and pet-sitting services.

Then I saw the yellowed paper with large bold letters that read:

WANTED:WIFE

Now that was a job I was perfect for. I was just about to commit myself for life to a man I didn't love. How hard could it be to do that with someone else?

I already came with the dress.

Hysterical laughter bubbled out of my chest.

Shoving my train out of the way, I got up from the booth and walked over to the board. I pulled out the pin holding up the notice.

"Oh, don't pay attention to that. That's just Roy's idea of a joke," Verity said cleaning up the dishes behind me. "I think."

"Roy," I repeated softly. "Roy Barnes?"

"His cousin died a year ago and left him with a baby, she's oh, gosh, sixteen, maybe seventeen months now? Anyway he freaked out and put that sign up last summer.

Thought he needed a wife to manage. But they're doing just fine."

"A baby?"

Roy hadn't said anything about a baby the night of the masquerade ball.

Roy Barnes wanted a wife. So much he was willing to advertise for one.

If he put this notice up on a bulletin board in town, he hadn't done it as a joke.

Roy wasn't known for his sense of humor.

I bit my bottom lip and ran my thumb over the phone number on the paper. It was Roy's old number. It had been seared into my memory.

Was this smart?

Maybe not. But my father was about to tear apart this town looking for me.

I needed a place to stay. I didn't have a phone. A car or any money to get out of town. Every penny of my personal funds had gone toward the Calico Cove Investment Bureau which currently was invested heavily in Pappas Diner. No surprise there, given Lola was Jackson's girlfriend.

I knew Dad would cut off my access to the family account the first chance he got. Same with the credit cards. He'd probably already done it.

No family money, no personal money. Jackson of course would try and help me out, but we were both cash poor after pulling together the funds needed for Lola to buy and restore the diner.

Not to mention the upscale bar Jackson was building in the lot behind Pappas.

It's not even like I could stay with Jackson now that he and Lola were officially living together. Like who wanted to be a third wheel on the bicycle of new love?

Then there was the little matter of Simon.

My father would still want me to marry him. He'd see my escape as nothing more than a setback to his plans. Simon obviously had his reasons for agreeing to an arranged marriage with a woman he cared so little for, he would screw another woman on the same day of his engagement party.

There really was nothing stopping my father from using all his financial strings, guilt strings and flat out mean strings to bring me back home.

Unless of course I was married to someone else.

I couldn't. *Could I?*

No way Roy would say yes to this.

I had no talents, no skills. To date my greatest accomplishment had been a year modeling in Europe, walking in really high shoes. However, after designers and photographers determined my face wasn't interesting enough, the jobs dried up.

After that, I'd been nothing more than Simon's arm piece for parties.

Sure, I had been helping Jackson with the CCIB. But all I really did was tell him which businesses I thought would make the best return on his money. Which let me tell you was not a highly scientific process on my part. I mostly went with my gut. It was kind of like the work I'd been doing with Lola, helping her with the remodel of Pappas.

It wasn't skill, it was just guessing with some good taste thrown in.

Roy was a private fisherman, with a house to run and now a baby. Those were serious things. He probably needed serious help.

Not some runaway bride, who was running harder from her daddy than her fiancé.

Oh, and don't forget Roy hated me for what I did to him. The idea was preposterous. Even I knew that.

He saved you once. He showed up at the engagement party. Maybe...

Whelp, the absolute worst thing he could say was...no.

∽

Roy

"I said no, Nora and I meant it. I won't crack. Not this time."

I picked up my screwdriver from my tool box and glared at her. She curled her little hands over the top of the play pen and screamed bloody murder.

She was crying for no damn reason, which sometimes she just liked to do to get under my skin. She was fed, changed, well rested and her teeth were all in now, but every once and a while she got stubborn about something and let me know it.

Today it was because she wanted out of her pen. That wasn't happening. I had the little play pen set up on deck, filled with all of her favorite toys, including the Elmo doll that didn't shut up, while I did some repair work to the rear winch.

Apparently, that wasn't good enough for Nora. Nope.

Life had been a whole lot easier when the bugger couldn't walk. I could carry her in a backpack contraption while I captained the boat. Or she'd sleep in her pen in the cabin below deck.

Now she wanted to be mobile all the time, and that just wasn't safe on a fishing boat.

Those lunatics who put their kids on leashes, maybe it wasn't such a bad idea.

"I gotta fix this," I told her. I'd replaced the bearings in the winch and shit just needed to be tightened so I only needed about five more minutes. Except Nora didn't understand time. Or patience. These days she only understood freedom.

As fast as I could, I tightened the screws and ran the lines through the self-guiding system when suddenly Nora stopped crying.

I turned, positive she'd climbed out of the pen, just like in my nightmares, and was either playing with knives or was about to fall into the water.

No, she was fixated on someone walking down line of slips towards my boat, *The Surly Bird.*

Clearly, I was officially cracked in the head. It was the only explanation for what looked like Vanessa Dumont in a full bridal gown navigating the docks as she made her way toward us.

"Are you seeing that?" I asked Nora.

Vanessa was careful where to step in her fancy shoes. When she finally reached me, she stopped and held out the advertisement I'd posted on the board in The Lobster Pot last summer.

"I want to apply," she said. "For the, you know...Wife. Job-thingy."

This had to be my poker crew having a laugh. For which there would be fists in faces.

"Look," she laughed a little hysterically. "I'm even dressed for the part!"

She held up the glittery, lace dress in her arms, revealing the garter just above her knee. The hem was covered in mud and her hair was coming down from whatever style she'd had it in.

Messy Nessy. Once upon a time, I'd given her that name

for a reason.

"What are you doing here, Ness?"

"I told you," she shook the paper in her hand. "I want to be your wife."

It wasn't hard to guess what happened. I knew the wedding was today. Of course, I knew. Everyone in town knew. It's why I'd avoided everyone by spending the day out on the water alone with Nora. Not even fishing, I just took the boat out and was...away.

The wedding should have been over by now. The Best Man should be giving his speech. People should be eating fancy food and drinking champagne. Instead, she was in her dress standing in front of my boat.

She must have had a panic attack in the last minute and bolted.

Not. My. Fucking. Problem.

"Go home, Ness." She'd made her choice a long time ago and it wasn't me.

"I can't do that. I can't go back." She tried to shake some of the hair out of her face. "I *won't* go back."

Well, we both knew that wasn't true.

"You're embarrassing yourself, Ness," I told her.

Just like I'd embarrassed myself when I showed up at her stupid engagement party in that monkey suit. Just to hear the words out of her mouth that she was going to marry that asshole.

"Of course I am! You think I don't know that? This must be hilarious for you. I mean, you must be cracking up on the inside."

I wasn't. I didn't know what I was doing on the inside, but it was not cracking up.

"But here's the thing, Roy," she continued. "I know you. You live to save helpless little creatures. You always want to be everyone's hero."

"That's ridiculous."

Nora shrieked.

"Hi baby, girl," Vanessa crooned to Nora. "I see you. Did he save you too?"

"You don't know what the fuck you're talking about," I snapped.

"I know you probably shouldn't say *fuck* around a baby who is just starting to absorb language skills."

Fuck. I'd been working on it, hadn't I? Making sure not every word out of my mouth was a curse.

Vanessa spread out her arms. "In the history of the universe no one needs saving more than me, Roy. I have no money, no fiancé, my father...I don't know what he'll do, but it's never a good thing when he's desperate. You put the notice on that bulletin board. You need help with that little girl. Here I am. Ready to help."

I stepped up onto the rail of the boat and hopped down onto the dock with enough force to make the boards rattle under her feet. That dress she was wearing probably cost more than I made in a season.

"I don't like liars."

"I didn't...," she stopped herself, most likely knowing it was only going to make matters worse. We'd been over this ground a few times. "I'm sorry, Roy. I'm so sorry about all of it."

I didn't like to think of myself as vindictive or vengeful. But Vanessa Dumont was the one fucking person on planet Earth I couldn't forgive.

Because she did something I didn't think anyone was capable of.

She made me happy.

Then she took it all away.

"Well," I said. "My hero days are over. Go back to Daddy. Go back to Simon. Those are *your* people. Remember?"

She looked crestfallen, but it didn't stir me. Not even a little bit.

Which should be some comfort.

Vanessa Dumont no longer had any hold over me.

I glared her down and finally she nodded.

"Okay, okay" she whispered, but it sounded like she was talking to herself. "It's fine. I'll be fine."

She turned and started her trek back up the dock.

I tore my eyes from her slumped back only to find Nora watching me. Her eyes narrowed.

We needed help. I thought we needed help last summer when I posted that sign, but things were much, much worse now that Nora was mobile.

"Not her," I told the kid. "Anyone else. Just not her."

Except no one else had answered that stupid ad.

Vanessa

I stopped at the end of the docks. There was a bench there situated next to a garbage can. A person could sit and watch the boats go out and come back in. Have a cup of coffee, then toss the cup away when they were done.

Maybe I could take this bench, I thought. Take the bench and sit here for the rest of my days. Like a twisted Calico Cove version of Dicken's Miss Havisham.

Who's that old lady sitting on the bench at the end of the docks in that yellow dress that's practically dissolving around her?

Oh her? She's the runaway bride who didn't have a plan and no one wanted to save.

Couldn't she save herself?

No. She didn't know how.

I would become a Calico Cove legend. Like the story about the pirates who saved the cats in their pirate hats. Or Larry the Lobster at Pappas Diner.

I would be the *Runaway Bride of Calico Cove.*

It sort of had a nice ring to it, actually. I could charge people to take pictures with me.

I thought about going back to the diner to pick up Jackson's Jeep. I could drive as far as the gas he had in the tank would take me, then call him to see if he could send me some money. What little cash he had. It would have to be enough.

I looked down at the now stained and ruined dress. I needed to get out of these clothes. If I headed back to the diner, Lola might have some spare T-shirts and shorts in her office. It wasn't much, but at least it was a start.

There was the screech of tires around a corner and I froze as the black Escalade come to a sudden stop. The driver's side door popped open and my father, still wearing his tuxedo, came rushing toward me. His face redder then I'd ever seen it.

Dangerously red.

"Do you know what you've done!" he shouted. "Do you have any idea the havoc you've caused. You...you...stupid girl!"

"Daddy, I..."

"Don't talk! Don't say a goddamn word. You're going to get in that car. I'm taking you back to Simon. You'll apologize. You'll beg if you have to, and tomorrow I'll have a judge marry you."

I shook my head, my hands in fists, clinging to my courage.

"I won't go back," I said, my voice shaking, but firm. Sort of firm. Mostly shaking. "I'm not going to marry Simon."

He took a deep breath and I could see him trying to push the rage off his face. To perform for me the act of a loving father and it made me so sad. So sad and so angry that I'd fallen for it before. Also that he thought I'd fall for it again.

"I need you, honey. Remember?" he said, his voice softening. "You're the only person who can save this family. Don't we mean anything to you?"

"I won't marry him, Daddy," I whispered.

The loving father act quickly vanished. He grabbed my arm so hard it hurt, his red face inches from mine. I could feel his rage like heat rolling off of him. "Your mother is telling anyone who will listen about your mental health issues. Simon looks like the long-suffering fiancé who loves you in spite of your unfortunate condition. Everyone is playing their parts. Except for you. So, you've had your tantrum, now it's time for you to remember who you are!"

I tried to pull away from him, but his fingers dug into my skin. "You're hurting me," I told him.

"I don't care! Get in the fucking car!"

"No!" I shouted in his face. "No! I won't get in the car! No! I won't marry Simon! You can't make me!"

His open palm blazed across my face, snapping my head back so hard my neck hurt. My cheek burned, my eyes filled with tears. There was a buzzing in my head.

Did he just hit me? *My Dad?*

I'd pushed my father a step too far. Defied him in a way he hadn't expected from me. From Jackson, it happened all the time. But not from me. I'd always tried to be so good.

This is what being good gets you in my family.

He had his arm around my waist and was practically carrying me towards the car.

"No!" I whispered. Was that blood? That copper taste in my mouth?

"Get in the car!"

"Let her go."

He was like a lobsterman super hero in his faded jeans and a flannel shirt over a white T. The wind ruffling his dark hair. His eyes narrowed to slits. Not even the baby in the purple stroller, sucking on the leg of a stuffed bunny could diminish how scary Roy Barnes was.

He never scared me though.

Relief made me dizzy. I knew he would rescue me.

"This isn't your concern. It's family business," my father said.

Roy pushed the stroller to the side and then used his foot to put on the wheel lock, so it didn't roll away. "Where I come from, family doesn't smack the shit out of their daughters."

"Oh for heaven's sake," my father shouted. "I was just trying to slap some sense into her. She's got mental health issues."

"Nah," Roy said, his arms crossed over his wide chest. "She's got daddy issues. Known that for years. Remove your hand or I'll do it for you."

"Touch me and I'll have you arrested."

"You could try, but when Bobby, he's the town sheriff by the way, shows up and takes one look at Ness's face, he's going to know who to arrest. Now you let her go, and I'll let you get back in your car and drive off. You don't let her go, then I have permission to beat the fucking shit out of you. You ever get hit, Mr. Dumont? Ever had your cheek broke?

Your nose re-arranged? I'm guessing no. I'm here to tell you, it's not going to feel good. Let. Her. Go."

Whether it was shock or fear, dad's hand loosened around my waist. I'd been pulling away so hard, I fell to the ground. At least I was free. I crab-walked backwards. Away from my father and towards Roy.

The little girl, who had been silent in her purple stroller, giggled hysterically.

Who could blame her? I had to look ridiculous.

"So help me, Vanessa, you don't get in this car right now you are forever disowned," my father barked at me, even as he stepped backwards away from Roy. "The only thing you're taking with you is the dress on your back. Do you understand me?"

I got to my feet and looked at my hands which were scraped raw. My cheek throbbed.

So, this was it. Twenty-five years of trying to make this man happy, proud, pleased with me, when the reality was, I was never going to be enough.

"I'm not getting in that car. I'm not marrying Simon. If that costs me my family...so be it."

I said it like a vow.

"You're a bigger disappointment to me than your brother," he hissed.

"Yeah, well you're sort of a big disappointment to me too, *Dad!*"

The car door slammed. The engine which had been running this whole time revved as he sped off, screeching around the corner until he was gone. Out of my life.

Maybe not forever. I doubted I was that lucky.

But certainly, for now.

I turned back to Roy and offered him a weak smile. "Thank you, Roy. You didn't have to-"

He snarled. "He fucking hit you, Ness!"

"Don't say the f-word in front of the baby. I'm fine."

"You're not fine," he snapped. "Your cheek is swollen. Come with me."

"Where?"

"To get ice."

"Okay." I didn't have any fight left in me anyway. I would basically go in whatever direction the wind was blowing. The adrenaline was gone and I felt like a limp rag. I wanted to pull the blankets over my head and sleep for a million years.

But I didn't even have blankets.

I walked alongside him as he navigated the stroller over the wooden dock.

"This doesn't mean I'm saving you," he said.

"Nope."

"We're absolutely not getting married."

"Of course not."

"You're getting an ice bag and a trip to the bus stop if you want."

"Sure," I said. I didn't have any money for a bus ticket, but now that there was no point hiding from my father, I could head back to the diner and wait for Jackson and Lola.

Roy stopped walking and instinctively, I stopped too.

"Has he done that before? Hit you like that?"

I shook my head and the words I never said aloud tumbled out. "Pinches. My dad liked to pinch me, to let me know when I was failing him. He saved the hitting for Jackson."

All my therapist had ever wanted to talk about was my abusive father and I wouldn't let her. Like if I could pretend he wasn't who I *knew* him to be, he might someday be the man I *wanted* him to be.

Except it was never going happen. He was the kind of man who hit his children. That's who he was.

"You cryin'?"

Roy hated tears. I could only imagine his life with a baby in it.

I lifted my head and sniffed. "No, I'm not crying. Where are we going?"

"My house. But just for-"

"The ice bag. I know, Roy. Trust me, I get it."

I was Messy Nessy. No one wanted me.

We didn't talk the rest of the way until we reached the parking lot. Roy drove a rusted out pickup truck that was stacked with lobster pots in need of repair.

"Nora has to go in the baby seat, so you need to get in the back of the truck."

The truck only had the one bench seat up front and the baby seat looked secure. Still.

"Don't car seats always have to be in a back seat?"

"Working on buying a new car, okay?" he growled.

Okay. Touchy subject. While he situated Nora in her car seat and handed her a stuffed toy to play with, I climbed into the back of the truck with the lobster pots. It was covered in mud, smelled like dead fish, and this wedding dress was never going to recover, but I was free.

DOWNLOAD NOW!

ALSO BY HAILEY SHORE

Happily Ever Maybe?

Printed in Great Britain
by Amazon

26199539R00203